OFF TO SEE THE WIZARD

"What's going on?" Ross asked harshly.

It was the technician who gave a sharp order. "Get in that seat! Strap down! If it's what I think, fella—" He shoved Ross back into the nearest chair.

"We're through time, aren't we?" Travis still watched that wonderful peaceful patch of blue sky in the alien ship's viewscreen.

"Sure—we're through. Only how long we're going to stay here . . ." The technician stumbled to the third chair, that in which they had discovered the dead alien pilot days earlier. He sat down with a suddenness close to collapse.

"What do you mean?" Ross's eyes narrowed. His dangerous look was coming back.

"Dragging us through time by the energy of the grid did something to the engines here. Don't you feel that vibration, man? I'd say this ship was preparing for a take-off!"

"We can't!" Travis began and then shivered, knowing the futility of that protest even as he shaped it.

"Anything you can do?" Ross asked, his control once more complete.

The technician laughed, choked, and then waved his hand at the array on the strange ship's control board. "Just what?" he asked grimly. "I know the use of exactly three little buttons here. We never dared experiment with the rest without dismantling all the installations and tracing them through. I can't stop or start anything. So we're off to the moon and points up, whether we like it or not."

BAEN BOOKS by ANDRE NORTON

Dark Companion
Darkness and Dawn
Gods and Androids
Janus
Masks of the Outcasts
Moonsinger
Star Soldiers
Time Traders
Time Traders II
Warlock

TIME TRADERS

ANDRE NORTON

BAEN

TIME TRADERS

A Baen Books Original

Baen Publishing Enterprises
P.O. Box 1403
Riverdale, NY 10471
www.baen.com

ISBN: 0-671-31829-2
ISBN 13: 978-0-671-31829-1

Cover art by Stephen Hickman

First paperback printing, August 2001
Second paperback printing, July 2006

Distributed by Simon & Schuster
1230 Avenue of the Americas
New York, NY 10020

Production by Windhaven® Press, Auburn, NH
Printed in the United States of America.

Contents

The Time Traders
- 1 -

Galactic Derelict
- 221 -

TIME
TRADERS

The Time
Traders

1

Ross Murdock wouldn't have seemed formidable to any one glancing casually at him as he sat within the detention cell. He was a little above average height, but not enough to make him noticeable. His brown hair was cropped conservatively and there was nothing remarkable about his unlined boy's face—unless one noted those light-gray eyes and caught the chilling, measuring expression that showed now and then for an instant in their depths.

He was neatly and inconspicuously dressed. In this first quarter of the twenty-first century his like was to be found on any street of the city ten floors below—to all outward appearances. But under the protective coloration Ross so assiduously cultivated was another person who could touch heights of encased and controlled fury which Ross himself did not understand. He was only just learning to use it as a weapon against a world he had always found hostile.

Ross was aware, though he gave no sign of it, that a guard was watching him. The cop on duty was an old hand—he probably expected some reaction other

3

than passive acceptance from the prisoner, but he was not going to get it.

The law had Ross sewed up tight this time. Why didn't they get about the business of shipping him off? Why had he had that afternoon session with the psychologist? Ross had been on the defensive then, and he hadn't liked it. He had given to the other's questions all the attention his shrewd mind could muster, but a faint, very faint, apprehension still clung to the memory of that meeting.

The door of the detention room opened. Ross did not turn his head, but the guard cleared his throat as if their hour of mutual silence had dried his vocal cords. "On your feet, Murdock! The judge wants to see you."

Ross rose smoothly, with every muscle under fluid control. It never paid to talk back, to allow any sign of defiance to show. He would go through the motions as if he were a bad little boy who had realized his errors. The meek-and-mild act had paid off fine in Ross's checkered past. So he faced the man seated behind the desk in the other room with an uncertain, diffident smile, standing with boyish awkwardness, respectfully waiting for the other to speak first. Judge Ord Rawle. It was his rotten luck to pull old Eagle Beak on his case. Well, he would simply have to take it when the old boy dished it out. Not that he had to remain stuck with it later . . .

"You have a bad record, young man."

Ross allowed his smile to fade; his shoulders slumped. But under concealing lids his eyes showed an instant of cold defiance.

"Yes, sir," he agreed in a voice carefully cultivated to shake convincingly about the edges. Then suddenly all Ross's pleasure in the skill of his act was wiped away. Judge Rawle was not alone; that blasted skull thumper was sitting there, watching the prisoner with the same keenness he had shown the other day.

"A very bad record for the few years you have had to make it." Eagle Beak was staring at him, too, but without the same look of penetration, luckily for Ross. "By rights, you should be turned over to the new Rehabilitation Service . . ."

Ross froze inside. That was the "treatment," icy rumors of which had spread throughout his particular world. For the second time since he had entered the room his self-confidence was jarred. Then he clung with a degree of hope to the phrasing of that last sentence.

"Instead, I have been directed to offer you a choice, Murdock. One which I shall state—and on record—I do not in the least approve."

Ross's twinge of fear faded. If the judge didn't like it, there must be something in it to the advantage of Ross Murdock. He'd grab it for sure!

"There is a government project in need of volunteers. It seems that you have tested out as possible material for this assignment. If you sign for it, the law will consider the time spent on it as part of your sentence. Thus you may aid the country which you have heretofore disgraced—"

"And if I refuse, I go to this rehabilitation. Is that right, sir?"

"I certainly consider you a fit candidate for rehabilitation. Your record—" He shuffled through the papers on his desk.

"I choose to volunteer for the project, sir."

The judge snorted and pushed all the papers into a folder. He spoke to a third man who'd been waiting in the shadows. "Here then is your volunteer, Major."

Ross bottled in his relief. He was over the first

hump. And since his luck had held so far, he might be about to win all the way...

The man Judge Rawle called "Major" moved into the light. At first glance Ross, to his hidden annoyance, found himself uneasy. To face up to Eagle Beak was all part of the game. But somehow he sensed one did not play such games with this man.

"Thank you, your honor. We will be on our way at once, before the weather socks us in completely."

Before he realized what was happening, Ross found himself walking meekly to the door. He considered trying to give the major the slip when they left the building, losing himself in a storm-darkened city, but they did not take the elevator downstairs. Instead, they climbed two or three flights up the emergency stairs. And to his humiliation Ross found himself panting and slowing, while the other man, who must have been a good dozen years his senior, showed no signs of discomfort.

They came out into the wind and snow on the roof, and the major flashed a torch toward a dark shadow waiting for them with rotating blades. A helicopter! For the first time Ross began to doubt the wisdom of his choice.

"Keep away from the tail rotors, Murdock!" The voice was impersonal enough, but that very impersonality got under one's skin.

Bundled into the machine between the silent major and an equally quiet pilot in uniform, Ross was lifted over the city, whose ways he knew as well as he knew the lines on his own palm, into the unknown he was already beginning to regard dubiously. The lighted streets and buildings, their outlines softened by the soft wet snow, fell out of sight. Now they could mark the outer highways. Ross refused to ask any questions. He could take this silent treatment, he *had* taken a lot of tougher things in the past.

The patches of light disappeared, and the country opened out. The plane banked. Ross, with all the familiar landmarks of his world gone, could not have said if they were headed north or south. But moments later not even the thick curtain of snowflakes could blot out the pattern of red lights on the ground, and the helicopter settled down.

"Come on!"

For the second time Ross obeyed. He stood shivering, engulfed in a miniature blizzard. His clothing, protection enough in the city, did little good against the push of the wind. A hand gripped his upper arm, and he was drawn forward to a low building. A door banged and Ross and his companion came into a region of light and very welcome heat.

"Sit down—over there!"

Too bewildered to resent orders, Ross sat. There were other men in the room. One, wearing an odd suit of padded clothing, a bulbous helmet hooked over his arm, was reading a paper. The major crossed to speak to him and after they conferred for a moment, the major beckoned Ross with a crooked finger. Ross trailed the officer into an inner room lined with lockers.

From one of the lockers the major pulled a suit like the pilot's, and began to measure it against Ross. "All right," he snapped. "Climb into this! We haven't all night."

Ross climbed into the suit. As soon as he fastened the last zipper his companion jammed one of the domed helmets on his head. The pilot looked in the door. "We'd better scramble, Kelgarries, or we may be grounded for the duration."

They hurried back to the flying field. If the

helicopter had been a surprising mode of travel, this new machine was something straight out of the future—a needle-slim ship poised on fins, its sharp nose lifting vertically into the heavens. There was a scaffolding along one side, which the pilot scaled to enter the ship.

Unwillingly, Ross climbed the same ladder and found that he must wedge himself in on his back, his knees hunched up almost under his chin. To make it worse, cramped as those quarters were, he had to share them with the major. A transparent hood snapped down and clicked secure, sealing them in.

During his short lifetime Ross had often been afraid, bitterly afraid. He had fought to toughen his mind and body against such fears. But what he experienced now was no ordinary fear; it was panic so strong that it made him feel sick. To be shut in this small place with the knowledge that he had no control over his immediate future brought him face to face with every terror he had ever known, all of them combined into one horrible whole.

How long does a nightmare last? A moment? An hour? Ross could not time his. But at last the weight of a giant hand clamped down on his chest, and he fought for breath until the world exploded about him.

He came back to consciousness slowly. For a second he thought he was blind. Then he began to sort out one shade of grayish light from another. Finally, Ross became aware that he no longer rested on his back, but was slumped in a seat. The world about him was wrung with a vibration that beat in turn through his body.

Ross Murdock had remained at liberty as long as he had because he was able to analyze a situation quickly. Seldom in the past five years had he been at a loss to deal with any challenging person or action.

Now he was aware that he was on the defensive and was being kept there. He stared into the dark and thought hard and furiously. He was convinced that everything that was happening to him this day was designed with only one end in view—to shake his self-confidence and make him pliable. Why?

Ross had an enduring belief in his own abilities and he also possessed a kind of shrewd understanding seldom granted to one so young. He knew that while Murdock was important to Murdock, he was none too important in the scheme of things as a whole. He had a record—a record so bad that Rawle might easily have thrown the book at him. But it differed in one important way from that of many of his fellows; until now he had been able to beat most of the raps. Ross believed this was largely because he had always worked alone and taken pains to plan a job in advance.

Why now had Ross Murdock become so important to someone that they would do all this to shake him? He was a volunteer—for what? To be a guinea pig for some bug they wanted to learn how to kill cheaply and easily? They'd been in a big hurry to push him off base. Using the silent treatment, this rushing around in planes, they were really working to keep him groggy. So, all right, he'd give them a groggy boy all set up for their job, whatever it was. Only, was his act good enough to fool the major? Ross had a hunch that it might not be, and that really hurt.

It was deep night now. Either they had flown out of the path of the storm or were above it. There were stars shining through the cover of the cockpit, but no moon.

Ross's formal education was sketchy, but in his own fashion he had acquired a range of knowledge which would have surprised many of the authorities who had

had to deal with him. All the wealth of a big city library had been his to explore, and he had spent much time there, soaking up facts in many odd branches of learning. Facts were very useful things. On at least three occasions assorted scraps of knowledge had preserved Ross's freedom, once, perhaps his life.

Now he tried to fit together the scattered facts he knew about his present situation into some proper pattern. He was inside some new type of aircraft, a machine so advanced in design that it would not have been used for anything that was not an important mission. Which meant that Ross Murdock had become necessary to someone, somewhere. Knowing that fact should give him a slight edge in the future, and he might well need such an edge. He'd just have to wait, play dumb, and use his eyes and ears.

At the rate they were shooting along they ought to be out of the country in a couple of hours. Didn't the Government have bases over half the world to keep the "cold peace"? Well, there was nothing for it. To be planted abroad someplace might interfere with plans for escape, but he'd handle that detail when he was forced to face it.

Then suddenly Ross was on his back once more, the giant hand digging into his chest and middle. This time there were no lights on the ground to guide them in. Ross had no intimation that they had reached their destination until they set down with a jar which snapped his teeth together.

The major wriggled out, and Ross was able to stretch his cramped body. But the other's hand was already on his shoulder, urging him along. Ross crawled free and clung dizzily to a ladderlike disembarking structure.

Below there were no lights, only an expanse of open snow. Men were moving across that blank area, gathering at the foot of the ladder. Ross was hungry and very tired. If the major wanted to play games, he hoped that he'd wait until the next morning.

In the meantime he must learn where "here" was. If he had a chance to run, he wanted to know the surrounding territory. But that hand was on his arm, drawing him along toward a hillock of snow. Either the storm or men had done a very good cover-up job and when a door in the side of the snow opened, Ross knew the camouflage was intentional.

That was Ross's introduction to the base, and after his arrival his view of the installation was extremely limited. One day was spent in undergoing the most searching physical he had ever experienced. And after the doctors had poked and pried he was faced by a series of other tests no one bothered to explain. Thereafter he was introduced to solitary, that is, confined to his own company in a cell-like room with a bunk that was more comfortable than it looked and an announcer in a corner of the ceiling. So far he had been told exactly nothing. And so far he had asked no questions, stubbornly keeping up his end of what he believed to be a tug of wills. At the moment, safely alone and lying flat on his bunk he eyed the announcer, a very dangerous young man and one who refused to yield an inch.

"Now hear this . . ." The voice transmitted through that grill was metallic, but its rasp held overtones of Kelgarries' voice. Ross's lips tightened. He had explored every inch of the walls and knew that there was no trace of the door which had admitted him. With only his bare hands to work with he could not break out, and his only clothes were the shirt, sturdy slacks, and a pair of soft-soled moccasins that they had given him.

" . . . to identify . . ." droned the voice. Ross realized

that he must have missed something, not that it mattered. He was almost determined not to play along any more.

There was a click, signifying that Kelgarries was through braying. But the customary silence did not close in again. Instead, Ross heard a clear, sweet trilling which he vaguely associated with a bird. His acquaintance with all feathered life was limited to city sparrows and plump park pigeons, neither of which raised their voices in song, but surely those sounds were bird notes. Ross glanced from the speaker in the ceiling to the opposite wall. What he saw there made him sit up, the instant response of an alerted fighter.

The wall was no longer there! Instead, a sharp slope of ground cut down from peaks where the dark green of fir trees ran close to the snow line. Patches of snow clung to the earth in sheltered places, and the scent of those trees was in Ross's nostrils, real as the wind touching him with its chill.

He shivered as a loud, echoing howl sounded, the age-old warning of a wolf pack, hungry and a-hunt. Ross had never heard that call before, but his human heritage subconsciously recognized it for what it was—death on four feet. Similarly, he was able to identify the gray shadows slinking about the nearest trees, and his hands balled into fists as he looked wildly about for some weapon.

The bunk was under him and three of the four walls of the room enclosed him like a cave. But one of those gray skulkers had raised its head and was looking directly at him, its reddish eyes alight. Ross ripped the top blanket off the bunk with a half-formed idea of snapping it at the animal when it sprang.

Stiff-legged, the beast advanced, a guttural growl sounding deep in its throat. To Ross the animal, larger

than any dog he had ever seen and twice as vicious,
was a monster. He had the blanket ready before he
realized that the wolf was not watching him after all:
its attention was focused on a point out of his line
of vision.

The wolf's muzzle wrinkled in a snarl, revealing
long yellow-white teeth. There was a singing twang.
The animal leaped into the air, fell back, and rolled
on the ground, biting despairingly at a shaft protruding from just behind its ribs. It howled again, and
blood broke from its mouth.

Ross was beyond surprise now. He pulled himself
together and got up, to walk steadily toward the dying
wolf. And he wasn't in the least amazed when his
outstretched hands flattened against an unseen barrier. Slowly, he swept his hands right and left, sure
that he was touching the wall of his cell. Yet his eyes
told him he was on a mountain side, and every sight,
sound, and smell was making it real to him.

Puzzled, he thought a moment and then, finding
an explanation that satisfied him, he nodded once and
went back to sit at ease on his bunk. This must be
some superior form of TV that included odors, the
illusion of wind, and other fancy touches to make it
more vivid. The total effect was so convincing that
Ross had to keep reminding himself that it was all
just a picture.

The wolf was dead. Its pack mates had fled into
the brush, but since the picture remained, Ross
decided that the show was not yet over. He could still
hear a click of sound, and he waited for the next bit
of action. But the reason for his viewing it still eluded
him.

A man came into view, crossing before Ross. He
stooped to examine the dead wolf, catching it by the
tail and hoisting its hindquarters off the ground.

Comparing the beast's size with the hunter's, Ross saw that he had not been wrong in his estimation of the animal's unusually large dimensions. The man shouted over his shoulder, his words distinct enough, but unintelligible to Ross.

The stranger was oddly dressed—too lightly dressed if one judged the climate by the frequent snow patches and the biting cold. A strip of coarse cloth, extending from his armpit to about four inches above the knee, was wound about his body and pulled in at the waist by a belt. The belt, far more ornate than the cumbersome wrapping, was made of many small chains linking metal plates. It supported a long dagger which hung straight in front. The man's round blue cloak, now swept back on his shoulders to free his bare arms, was fastened by a large pin under his chin. His footgear, which extended above his calves, was made of animal hide, still bearing shaggy hair. He was beardless, though a shadowy line along his chin suggested that he had not shaved that particular day. A fur cap concealed most of his dark-brown hair.

Was he an Indian? No, for although his skin was tanned, it was as fair as Ross's under that weathering. And his clothing did not resemble any Indian apparel Ross had ever seen.

In spite of his primitive trappings, the man had an aura of authority, of self-confidence, and competence, it was clear he was top dog in his own section of the world.

Another man, dressed much like the first, but with a rust-brown cloak, came along, pulling behind him two very reluctant donkeys. Their eyes rolled fearfully at sight of the dead wolf. Both animals wore packs lashed on their backs by ropes of twisted hide. A third man followed with another brace of donkeys. Finally, a fourth man, wearing skins for covering and with a mat of beard on his cheeks and chin, appeared. His uncovered head, a bush of uncombed flaxen hair, shone whitish. He knelt beside the dead beast, a knife with a dull-gray blade in his hand, and set skillfully to work skinning the wolf. Three more pairs of donkeys, all heavily laden, were led past the scene before he finished his task. Finally, he rolled the bloody skin into a bundle and gave the flayed body a kick before he ran lightly after the disappearing train of pack animals.

2

Ross, absorbed in the scene before him, wasn't prepared for the sudden and complete darkness which blotted out not only the action but the light in his own room as well.

"What—?" His startled voice rang loudly, too loudly, for all sound had been wiped out with the light. The faint swish of the ventilating system, which he hadn't noticed until it had disappeared, was also missing. A trace of the same panic he had known in the cockpit of the aircraft tingled along his nerves. But this time he could meet the unknown with action.

Ross slowly moved through the dark, his hands outstretched before him to avoid the wall. He was determined that he would discover the hidden door, escape from this dark cell . . .

There! His palm struck flat against a smooth surface. He swept out his hand—and suddenly it passed over emptiness. Ross explored by touch. There *was* a door and now it was open. For a moment he hesitated, nagged by fear that if he stepped through he would be out on the hillside with the wolves.

"That's stupid!" Again he spoke aloud. And, just because he did feel uneasy, he moved. All the frustrations of the past hours built up in him a raging desire to do something—anything—just so long as it was what *he* wanted to do and not at another's orders.

Nevertheless, Ross continued to move slowly, for the space beyond that open door was as deep and dark as the room he left. To squeeze along one wall, using an outstretched arm as a guide, was the best procedure, he decided.

A few feet farther on, his shoulder slipped from the surface and he half tumbled into another open door. But there was the wall again, and he clung to it thankfully. Another door . . . Ross paused, trying to catch some faint sound, the slightest hint that he was not alone in this blindman's maze. But without even air currents to stir it, the blackness itself took on a solidity which encased him as a congealing jelly.

The wall ended. Ross kept his left hand on it, flailed out with his right, and felt his nails scrape across another surface. The space separating the two surfaces was wider than any doorway. Was it a cross-corridor? As he was about to make a wider arm sweep, he heard a sound. He was not alone.

Ross went back to the wall. Flattening himself against the wall, Ross tried to control the volume of his own breathing in order to catch the slightest whisper of the other noise. He discovered that lack of sight confuses the ear. He could not identify those clicks, that wisp of fluttering sound that might be air displaced by the opening of another door.

Finally, he detected something moving at floor level. Someone or something must be creeping, not walking, toward him. Ross pushed back around the corner. It never occurred to him to challenge the crawler. An encounter in the dark could be dangerous. Who was his fellow explorer?

The sound of crawling was not steady. Long pauses convinced Ross that each rest was punctuated by heavy breathing as if the crawler was finding progress an exhausting effort. He fought the picture that persisted in his imagination—that of a wolf snuffling down the blacked-out hall. Caution suggested a quick retreat, but Ross's urge to rebellion held him where he was, crouching, straining to see what crept toward him.

Suddenly, blinding light blazed forth. Ross covered his dazzled eyes. And he heard a cry of despair from near floor level. The light that normally filled hall and room was steady again. Ross found himself standing at the juncture of two corridors—he was absurdly pleased to have deduced that correctly—and the crawler—?

A man—at least the figure was a two-legged, two-armed manlike form—was lying several yards away. But the body was so wrapped in bandages and the head so totally muffled, that it lacked all identity.

One of the mittened hands stirred, raising the body slightly so it could squirm forward an inch or so. Before Ross could move, a man ran into the corridor from the far end. It was Major Kelgarries. Ross licked his lips as the major went down on his knees beside the creature on the floor.

"Hardy! Hardy!" That voice, which carried the snap of command whenever it addressed Ross, was now warmly human. "Hardy, man!" The major's hands were on the bandaged body, lifting it, easing the head and shoulders back against his arm. "It's all right, Hardy. You're back—safe. This is the base, Hardy." He spoke slowly, soothingly, as if comforting a frightened child.

Those mittened paws which had beat feebly in the

air fell onto the bandage-wreathed chest. "Back—
safe—" The voice croaked rustily behind the face
mask.

"Back, safe," the major assured him.

"Dark—dark all around again—" protested the
croak.

"Just a power failure, man. Everything's all right
now. We'll get you into bed."

The mitten pawed again until it touched Kelgarries'
arm. It flexed a little as if the hand under it was trying
to grip.

"Safe—?"

"You bet you are!" The major's tone carried reassurance. Kelgarries looked up at Ross as if he knew
the other had been there all the time.

"Murdock, get down to the end room. Call Dr.
Farrell!"

"Yes, sir!" The "sir" came so automatically that Ross
had already reached the end room before he realized he had used it.

Nobody explained matters to Ross Murdock. The
bandaged Hardy was carried away by the doctor and
two attendants. The major walked beside the stretcher,
still holding one of the mittened hands in his. Ross
hesitated, sure he wasn't supposed to follow, but not
prepared to explore farther or return to his own room.
The sight of Hardy, whoever he might be, had radically
changed Ross's perception of the project he had too
speedily volunteered to join.

That what they did here was important, Ross had
never doubted. That it was dangerous, he had already
suspected. But his awareness had been abstract until
Hardy came crawling through the dark. From the
first, Ross had nursed vague plans for escape; now
he knew he must get out of this place lest he end
up a twin for Hardy.

"Murdock?"

Startled by the soundless approach, Ross whirled around, ready to use his fists if need be. But he did not face the major or any of the other taciturn officers that he recognized.

The newcomer's sun-browned skin and dark hair stood out sharply against the pale wall and contrasted with the vivid blue of his eyes.

Expressionless, the dark stranger stood quietly, his arms hanging loosely by his sides. He studied Ross, as if the younger man was some problem he had been assigned to solve. When he spoke, his voice was a flat monotone devoid of feeling.

"I am Ashe." He introduced himself baldly; he might have been saying "This is a table and that is a chair."

Ross's quick temper took spark from the other's indifference. "All right—so you're Ashe!" He strove to make a challenge of it. "And what is that supposed to mean?"

But the other did not rise to the bait. He shrugged. "For the time being we have been partnered—"

"Partnered for what?" demanded Ross, controlling his temper.

"We work in pairs here. The machine sorts us . . ." he answered and consulted his wrist watch. "Mess call soon."

Ashe had already turned away, and Ross could not stand the other's lack of interest. Although Murdock refused to ask questions of the major or any others on that side of the fence, surely he could get some information from a fellow "volunteer."

"What is this place, anyway?" he asked.

The other glanced back over his shoulder. "Operation Retrograde."

Ross swallowed his anger. "Okay, but what do they

do here? Listen, I just saw a fellow who'd been banged up as if he'd been in a concrete mixer, creeping along this hall. What sort of work do they do here? And what do we have to do?"

To his amazement Ashe smiled, at least his lips quirked faintly. "Hardy got under your skin, eh? Well, we do have our failures. They are as few as it's humanly possible to make, and they give us every advantage that can be worked out for us—"

"Failures at what?"

"Operation Retrograde."

Somewhere down the hall a buzzer whirred softly.

"That's mess call. And I'm hungry, even if you're not." Ashe walked away as if Ross Murdock had ceased to exist.

But Ross Murdock did exist. As he trailed along behind Ashe he determined that he was going to continue to exist, in one piece and unharmed, Operation Retrograde or no Operation Retrograde. And he was going to pry a few enlightening answers out of somebody very soon.

To his surprise he found Ashe waiting for him at the door of a room from which came the sound of voices and a subdued clatter of trays and tableware.

"Not many in tonight," Ashe commented in a take-it-or-leave-it tone. "It's been a busy week."

The room was sparsely occupied. Five tables were empty, while the men gathered at the remaining two. Ross counted ten men, either already eating or coming back from a serving hatch with well-filled trays. All of them were dressed in slacks, shirt, and moccasins like himself—the outfit seemed to be a sort of undress uniform—and six of them were ordinary looking. The other four differed so radically that Ross could barely conceal his amazement.

Since their fellows accepted them without comment,

Ross stole glances at them as he waited behind Ashe for a tray. One pair were clearly Oriental; they were small, lean men with thin brackets of long black mustaches on either side of their mobile mouths. Yet they spoke his own language with the facility of the native born. In addition to the mustaches, each wore a blue tattoo mark on the forehead and on the backs of their hands.

The second duo were even more fantastic. The huge rugged men wore their flaxen hair in braids long enough to swing across their powerful shoulders, a fashion unlike any Ross had ever seen

"Gordon!" One of the braided giants swung half-way around from the table to halt Ashe as he came down the aisle with his tray. "When did you get back? And where is Sanford?"

One of the Orientals laid down the spoon with which he had been vigorously stirring his coffee and asked with real concern, "Another loss?"

Ashe shook his head. "Just reassignment. Sandy's holding down Outpost Gog and doing well." He grinned and his face came to life with an expression of impish humor Ross would not have believed possible. "He'll end up with a million or two if he doesn't watch out. He takes to trade as if he were born with a beaker in his fist."

The Oriental laughed and then glanced at Ross. "Your new partner, Ashe?"

Some of the animation disappeared from Ashe's brown face; he was noncommittal again. "Temporary assignment. This is Murdock." The introduction was flat enough to daunt Ross. "Hodaki, Feng," he introduced the two Easterners with a nod as he put down his tray. "Jansen, Van Wyke." That accounted for the blonds.

"Ashe!" A man arose at the other table and came

to stand beside theirs. Thin, with a dark, narrow face and restless eyes, he was much younger than the others, younger and not so well controlled. He might answer questions if there was something in it for him, Ross decided, and pushed the thought away.

"Well, Kurt?" Ashe's recognition was as dampening as it could be, and Ross's estimation of the younger man went up a fraction when the snub appeared to have no effect upon him.

"Did you hear about Hardy?"

Feng looked as if he were about to speak, and Van Wyke frowned. Ashe made a deliberate process of chewing and swallowing before he replied. "Naturally." His tone reduced whatever had happened to Hardy to a matter-of-fact proceeding far removed from Kurt's implied melodrama.

"He's smashed up . . . kaput . . ." Kurt's accent, slight in the beginning, was thickening. "Tortured . . ."

Ashe regarded him levelly. "You aren't on Hardy's run, are you?"

Still Kurt refused to be quashed. "Of course, I'm not! You know the run I am in training for. But that is not saying that such can not happen as well on my run, or yours, or yours!" He pointed a stabbing finger at Feng and then at the blond men.

"You can fall out of bed and break your neck, too, if your number comes up that way," observed Jansen. "Go cry on Millaird's shoulder if it hurts you that much. You were told the score at your briefing. You know why you were picked, and what might happen . . ."

Ross caught a faint glance aimed at him by Ashe. He was still totally in the dark, but he would not try to pry any information from this crowd. Maybe part of their training was this hush-hush business. He would wait and see, until he could get Kurt aside and do a little pumping. Meanwhile he ate stolidly and tried to cover up his interest in the conversation.

"Then you are going to keep on saying 'Yes, sir,' 'No, sir,' to every order here—?"

Hodaki slammed his tattooed hand on the table. "Why this foolishness, Kurt? You well know how and why we are picked for runs. Hardy had the deck stacked against him through no fault of the project. That has happened before; it will happen again—"

"Which is what I have been saying! Do you wish it to happen to you? Pretty games those tribesmen on your run play with their prisoners, do they not?"

"Oh, shut up!" Jansen got to his feet. Since he loomed at least five inches above Kurt and probably could have broken him in two over one massive knee, his order commanded attention. "If you have any complaints, go make them to Millaird. And, little man"—he poked a massive forefinger into Kurt's chest—"wait until you make that first run of yours before you sound off so loudly. No one is sent out without every advance, and Hardy was unlucky. That's that. We got him back, and that was lucky for him. He'd be the first to tell you so." He stretched. "I'm for a game—Ashe? Hodaki?"

"Always so energetic," murmured Ashe, but he nodded as did the small Oriental.

Feng smiled at Ross. "Always these three try to beat each other, and so far all the contests are draws. But we hope . . . yes, we have hopes . . ."

So Ross had no chance to speak to Kurt. Instead, he was drawn into the knot of men who, having finished their meal, entered a small arena with a half circle of spectator seats at one side and a space for contestants at the other. What followed absorbed Ross as completely as the earlier scene of the wolf killing. This too was a fight, but not a physical struggle.

All three contenders were not only unlike in body, but as Ross speedily came to understand, they were also unlike in their mental approach to any problem.

They seated themselves crosslegged at the three points of a triangle. Then Ashe looked from the tall blond to the small Oriental. "Territory?" he asked crisply.

"Inland plains!" That came almost in chorus, and each man, looking at his opponent, began to laugh.

Ashe himself chuckled. "Trying to be smart tonight, boys?" he inquired. "All right, plains it is."

He brought his hand down on the floor before him, and to Ross's astonishment the area around the players darkened and the floor became a stretch of miniature countryside. Grassy plains rippled under the wind of a fair day.

"Red!"

"Blue!"

"Yellow!"

The choices came quickly from the dusk masking the players. And upon those orders points of the designated color came into being as small lights.

"Red—caravan!" Ross recognized Jansen's boom.

"Blue—raiders!" Hodaki's choice was only an instant behind.

"Yellow—unknown factor."

Ross was sure that sigh came from Jansen. "Is the unknown factor a natural phenomenon?"

"No—tribe on the march."

"Ah!" Hodaki was considering that. Ross could picture his shrug.

The game began. Ross knew of computer games and had heard of chess, of war games played with miniature armies or ships, and of board games which demanded a quick wit and a trained memory. This game, however, was all those combined, and more.

As his imagination came to life, the moving points of light were transformed into perfect simulations of the raiders, the merchants' caravan, the tribe on the march. There was ingenious deployment, a battle, a retreat, a small victory here, to be followed by a bigger defeat there. The game might have gone on for hours. The men about him muttered, taking sides and arguing heatedly in voices low enough not to drown out the moves called by the players. Ross was thrilled when the red traders avoided a very cleverly laid ambush, and indignant when the tribe was forced to withdraw or the caravan lost points. It was the most fascinating game he had ever seen, and he realized that the three men ordering these moves were all masters of strategy. Their respective skills checkmated each other so equally that an outright win was far away.

Then Jansen laughed, and the red line of the caravan gathered in a tight knot. "Camped at a spring," he announced, "but with plenty of sentries out." Red sparks showed briefly beyond that center core. "And they'll have to stay there for all of me. We could keep this up till doomsday, and nobody would crack."

"No"—Hodaki contradicted him—"someday one of you will make a little mistake and then—"

"And then whatever bully boys you're running will clobber us?" asked Jansen. "That'll be the day! Anyway, truce for now."

"Granted!"

The lights of the arena went on and the plains vanished into a dark, tiled floor. "Any time you want a return engagement it'll be fine with me," said Ashe, getting up.

Jansen grinned. "Put that off for a month or so, Gordon. We push into time tomorrow. Take care of yourselves, you two. I don't want to have to break in another set of players when I come back."

Ross, finding it difficult to shake off the illusion which had held him entranced, felt a slight touch on his shoulder and glanced up. Kurt stood behind him, apparently intent upon Jansen and Hodaki as they argued over some point of the game.

"See you tonight." The boy's lips hardly moved, a trick Ross knew from his own past. Yes, he *would* see Kurt tonight, or whenever he could. He was going to learn what it was this odd company seemed determined to keep as their own private secret.

3

Ross stood cautiously against the wall of his darkened room, his head turned toward the slightly open door. A slight shuffling sound had awakened him, and he was now poised like a cat before her spring. But he did not hurl himself at the figure now easing the door farther open. He waited until the visitor was approaching the bunk before he slid along the wall, closing the door and putting his shoulders against it.

"What's the pitch?" Ross demanded in a whisper.

There was a ragged breath, maybe two, then a little laugh out of the dark. "You are ready?" The visitor's accent left no doubt as to his identity. Kurt was paying him the promised visit.

"Did you think that I wouldn't be?"

"No." The dim figure sat without invitation on the edge of the bunk. "I would not be here otherwise, Murdock. You are plenty . . . have plenty on the ball. You see, I have heard things about you. Like me, you were tricked into this game. Tell me, is it not true that you saw Hardy tonight?"

"You hear a lot, don't you?" Ross was noncommittal.

"I hear, I see, I learn more than these big mouths, like the major with his do's and don'ts. That I can tell you! You see Hardy. Do *you* want to be a Hardy?"

"Is there any danger of that?"

"Danger!" Kurt snorted. "Danger—you have not yet known the meaning of danger, little man. Not until now. I ask you again, do you want to end like Hardy? They have not yet looped you in with all their big talk. That is why I came here tonight. If you know what is good for you, Murdock, you will make a break before they tape you—"

"Tape me?"

Kurt's laugh was full of anger, not amusement. "Oh, yes. They have many tricks here. They are big brains, eggheads, all of them with their favorite gadgets. They put you through a machine to get you registered on tape. Then, my boy, you cannot get outside the base without ringing all the alarms! Neat, eh? So if you want to make a break, you must try it before they tape you."

Ross did not trust Kurt, but he was listening to him attentively. The other's argument sounded convincing to one whose general ignorance of science led him to believe that all kinds of weird inventions were entirely possible and probable—usually in some dim future, but perhaps today.

"They must have you taped," Ross pointed out.

Kurt laughed again, but this time he was amused. "They believe that they have. Only they are not as smart as they believe, the major and the rest, including Millaird! No, I have a fighting chance to get out of this place, only I cannot do it alone. That is why I have been waiting for them to bring in a new guy I could get to before they had him pinned down for good. You are tough, Murdock. I saw your record, and I'm betting that you did not come here with the intention of staying. So—here is your chance to go along with one who knows the ropes. You will not have such a good one again."

The longer Kurt talked, the more convincing he was. Ross lost a few of his suspicions. It was true that he had come prepared to run at the first possible opportunity, and if Kurt had everything planned, so much the better. Of course, it was possible that Kurt was a stool pigeon, leading him on as a test. But that was a chance Ross would have to take.

"Look here, Murdock, maybe you think it's easy to break out of here. Do you know where we are, boy? We're near enough to the North Pole as makes no difference! Are you going to leg it back some hundreds of miles through thick ice and snow? A nice jaunt if you make it. I do not think that you can—not without plans and a partner who knows what he is about."

"And how *do* we go? Steal one of those planes? I'm not a pilot—are you?"

"They have other things besides planes here. This place is strictly hush-hush. Even the aircraft do not set down too often for fear they will be tracked. Where have you been, boy? Don't you know the Russians are circling around up here? These fellows watch for Russian activity, and the Russians watch them. They play it under the table on both sides. We get our supplies overland by cats—"

"Cats?"

"Snow sleds, like tractors," the other answered impatiently. "Our stuff is dumped miles to the south, and the cats go down once a month to bring it back. There's no trick to driving a cat, and they tear off the miles—"

"How many miles to the south?" asked Ross

skeptically. Granted Kurt was speaking the truth, travel over an arctic wilderness in a stolen machine was risky, to say the least. Ross had only a very vague idea of the polar regions, but he was sure that they could easily swallow up the unwary forever.

"Maybe only a hundred or so, boy. But I have more than one plan, and I'm willing to risk *my* neck. Do you think I intend to start out blind?"

There was that, of course. Ross had early sized up his visitor as one who was first of all interested in his own welfare. He wouldn't risk his neck without a definite plan in mind.

"Well, what do you say, Murdock? Are you with me or not?"

"I'll take some time to chew it over—"

"Time is what you do not have, boy. Tomorrow they will tape you. Then—no over the wall for you."

"Suppose you tell me your trick for fooling the tape," Ross countered.

"That I cannot do, seeing as how it lies in the way my brain is put together. Do you think I can break open my skull and hand you a piece of what is inside? No, you jump with me tonight or else I must wait to grab the next one who lands here."

Kurt stood up. His last words were spoken matter-of-factly, and Ross believed he meant exactly what he said. But Ross hesitated. He wanted to try for freedom, a desire fed by his suspicions of what was going on here. He neither liked nor trusted Kurt. But he thought he understood him—better than he understood Ashe or the others. Also, with Kurt he was sure he could hold his own; it would be the kind of struggle he had experienced before.

"Tonight . . ." he repeated slowly.

"Yes, tonight!" There was new eagerness in Kurt's voice, for he sensed that the other was wavering. "I have been preparing for a long time, but there must be two of us. We have to take turns driving the cat. There can be no rest until we are far to the south. I tell you it will be easy. There are food caches arranged along the route for emergencies. I have a map marked to show where they are. Are you coming?"

When Ross did not answer at once the other moved closer to him.

"Remember Hardy? He was not the first, and he will not be the last. They use us up fast here. That is why they brought you so quickly. I tell you, it is better to take your chance with me than on a run."

"And what is a run?"

"So they have not briefed you? Well, a run is a little jaunt back into history—not nice comfortable history such as you learned out of a book when you were a little kid. No, you are dropped back into some savage time before history—"

"That's impossible!"

"Yes? You saw those two big blond boys tonight, did you not? Why do you suppose they sport those braids? Because they are taking a little trip into the time when he-men wore braids, and carried axes big enough to crack a man open! And Hodaki and his partner . . . Ever hear of the Tartars? Maybe you have not, but once they nearly overran most of Europe."

Ross swallowed. He now knew where he had seen braids pictured on warriors—the Vikings! And Tartars, yes, that movie about someone named Khan, Genghis Khan! But to return into the past was impossible.

Yet, he remembered the images he had watched today with the wolf slayer and the shaggy-haired man who wore skins. Neither of these was of his own world! Could Kurt be telling the truth? Ross's vivid

memory of the scene he had witnessed made Kurt's
story more convincing.

"Suppose you get sent back to a time where they
do not like strangers," Kurt continued. "Then you are
in for it. That is what happened to Hardy. And it is
not good—not good at all!"

"But why?"

Kurt snorted. "*That* they do not tell you until just
before you take your first run. I do not want to know why.
But I do know that I am not going to be sent into any
wilderness where a savage may run a spear through me
just to prove something or other for Major John Kelgarries, or for Millaird either. I will try my plan first."

The urgency in Kurt's protest carried Ross past the
wavering point. He, too, would try the cat. He was
only familiar with this time and world; he had no
desire to be sent into another one.

Once Ross had made his decision, Kurt hurried him
into action. Kurt's knowledge of the secret procedures
at the base proved excellent. Twice they were halted
by locked doors, but only momentarily, for Kurt had
a tiny gadget, concealed in the palm of his hand, which
had only to be held over a latch to open it.

There was enough light in the corridors to give
them easy passage, but the rooms were dark, and twice
Kurt had to lead Ross by the hand, avoiding furniture or installations with the sureness of one who had
practiced that same route often. Murdock's opinion
of his companion's ability notched upward during that
tour. He began to believe that he was really in luck
to have found such a partner.

In the last room, Ross willingly followed Kurt's
orders to put on the fur clothing Kurt passed to him.
The fit was not exact, but he assumed that Kurt had
chosen as well as possible. A final door opened, and
they stepped out into the polar night of winter. Kurt's

mittened hand grasped Ross's, pulling him along.
Together, they pushed back the door of a hangar shed
to get at their escape vehicle.

The cat was new to him, but Ross was given no
time to study it. Kurt shoved him into the cockpit and
tossed him a pair of night vision goggles.

A plastic hatch locked down over them and the
engine came to life under Kurt's urging. The cat
must be traveling at its best pace, Ross thought. Yet
the moonlit crawl which took them away from the
mounded snow covering the base seemed hardly
better than the pace of a man afoot.

For a short time Kurt headed straight away from
the starting point, but Ross soon heard him counting slowly to himself as if he were timing something.
At the count of twenty the cat swung to the right and
made a wide half circle which was copied at the next
count of twenty by a similar sweep in the opposite
direction. After this pattern had been repeated for six
turns, Ross found it difficult to guess whether they
had ever returned to their first course. When Kurt
stopped counting he asked, "Why the dance pattern?"

"Would you rather be scattered in little pieces all
over the landscape?" the other snapped. "The base
doesn't need fences two miles high to keep us in, or
others out; they take other precautions. You should
thank fortune we got through that first mine field
without blowing up."

Ross swallowed, but he refused to let Kurt know
that he was rattled. "So it isn't as easy to get away
as you said?"

"Shut up!" Kurt began counting again, and Ross
had some cold apprehensive moments in which to re-
flect upon the folly of quick decisions. He wondered
bleakly why he had not thought things through before he leaped.

Again they sketched a weaving pattern in the snow, but this time the arcs formed acute angles. Ross glanced now and then at the intent man at the wheel. How had Kurt managed to memorize this route? His urge to escape the base must certainly be a strong one.

Back and forth they crawled, gaining only a few yards in each of those angled strikes to right or left.

"Good thing cats carry extra fuel," Kurt commented during one of the intervals between mine fields. "We'd run out otherwise."

Ross fought down the impulse to shiver. Luckily, Kurt was now back to a straight track, with no more weaving.

"We are out!" Kurt said with exultation. But he added no more reassurance.

The cat crawled on. To Ross's eyes there was no trail to follow, no guideposts in the darkness, yet Kurt steered ahead with confidence. A little later he pulled to a stop and said to Ross, "We have to drive turn and turn about—your turn."

Ross was dubious. "Well, I can drive a car—but this—"

"Is foolproof." Kurt caught him up. "The worst was getting through the mine fields, and we are out of that now. See here—" his hand made a shadow on the lighted instrument panel, "this will keep you straight. If you can steer a car, you can steer this. Watch!" He started up again and once more he swung the cat to the left.

A light on the panel began to blink at a rate which increased rapidly as they veered farther away from their original course.

"See? You keep that light steady, and you are on course. If it begins to blink, you cast about until it steadies again. Simple enough for a baby. Take over and see."

It was hard to change places in the sealed cabin of the cat, but they succeeded, and Ross took the wheel gingerly. Following Kurt's directions, he started ahead, his eyes focused on the light rather than the dark expanse before him. And after a few minutes of strain he caught the hang of it. As Kurt had promised, it was very simple. After watching him for a while, his instructor gave a grunt of satisfaction and settled down for a nap.

Once the first excitement of driving the cat wore off, the operation tended to become monotonous. Ross caught himself yawning, but he kept at his post with dogged stubbornness. This had been Kurt's game all the way through—so far—and he was certainly not going to resign his first chance to show that he could be of use also. If there had only been some break in the eternal snow, some passing light or goal to be seen ahead, it would not have been so bad. Finally, every now and then, Ross had to jiggle off course just enough so that the warning blink of light would alert him and keep him from falling asleep. He was unaware that Kurt had awakened during one of those maneuvers until the other spoke. "Your own private alarm clock, Murdock? Okay, I do not quarrel with anyone who uses his head. But you had better get some shut-eye, or we will not keep rolling."

Ross was too tired to protest. They changed places, and he curled up as best he could on his small share of the seat. Only now that he was free to sleep, he realized he no longer wanted to. Kurt must have thought Ross had fallen asleep, for after perhaps two miles of steady grinding along, he moved cautiously behind the wheel. Ross saw by the trace of light from the instrument panel that his companion was digging into the breast of his parka to bring out a small

object which he held against the wheel of the cat with
one hand, while with the other he tapped out an irregular rhythm.

To Ross the action made no sense. But he did not
miss the other's sigh of relief as he restored his treasure to hiding once more, as if some difficult task was
now behind him. Shortly afterward the cat ground to
a stop, and Ross sat up, rubbing his eyes. "What's the
matter? Engine trouble?"

Kurt had folded his arms across the wheel. "No.
It is just that we are to wait here—"

"Wait? For what? Kelgarries to come along and pick
us up?"

Kurt laughed. "The major? How I wish that he
would arrive presently. What a surprise he would
receive! Not two little mice to be put back into their
cages, but the tiger cat, all claws and fangs!"

Ross sat up straighter. This now had the bad smell
of a frame, a frame with himself planted right in the
middle. He figured out the possibilities and came up
with an answer which would smear Ross Murdock all
over any map. If Kurt were waiting to meet friends
out here, they could only be one kind.

For most of his short life Ross had been engaged
in a private war against the restrictions imposed upon
him by laws to which something within him would not
conform. And he had, during those same years filled
with attacks, retreats, and strategic maneuvering, form-
ulated a code by which to play his dangerous game.
He had not murdered, and he would never follow the
path Kurt took. To one who was supremely impatient
of restraint, the methods and aims of Kurt's employ-
ers were not only impossibly fantastic and illogical—
they were to be opposed to the last ounce of any man's
energy.

"Your friends late?" He tried to sound casual.

"Not yet, and if you now plan to play the hero, Murdock, think better of it!" Kurt's tone held the crack of an order—that note Ross had so much disliked in the major's voice. "This is an operation which has been most carefully planned and upon which a great deal depends. No one shall spoil it for us now—"

"The Russians planted you on the project, eh?" Ross wanted to keep the other talking to give himself a chance to think. And this was one time he had to think, clearly and fast.

"There is no need for me to tell you the sad tale of my life, Murdock. And you would doubtless find much of it boring. If you wish to continue to live— for a while, at least—you will remain quiet and do as you are told."

Kurt must be armed, for he would not be so confident unless he had a weapon he could now turn on Ross. On the other hand, if what Ross guessed were true, this *was* the time to play the hero—when there was only Kurt to handle. Better to be a dead hero than a live captive in the hands of Kurt's dear friends across the pole.

Without warning, Ross threw his body to the left, striving to pin Kurt against the driver's side of the cabin. His hands clawed at the fur ruff bordering the other's hood, trying for a throat hold. Perhaps Kurt's over-confidence betrayed him and left him open to a surprise attack. He struggled hard to bring up his arm, but both his weight and Ross's held him tight. Ross caught at his wrist, noticing a gleam of metal.

They threshed about, hampered by the bulkiness of the fur clothing. Ross wondered fleetingly why the other had not made sure of him earlier. As it was he fought with all his might to keep Kurt immobile, to try and knock him out with a lucky blow.

In the end Kurt aided his own defeat. When Ross

relaxed somewhat, the other pushed against him, only to have Ross flinch to one side. Kurt could not stop himself, and his head cracked against the wheel of the cat. He went limp.

Ross made the most of the next few moments. He brought his belt from under his parka, twisting it around Kurt's wrists with no gentleness. Then he wriggled about, changing places with the unconscious man.

He had no idea of where to go, but he was sure he was going to get away—at the cat's top speed—from that point. And with that in mind and only a limited knowledge of how to manage the machine, Ross started up and turned in a wide circle until he was sure the cat was headed in the opposite direction.

The light which had guided them was still on. Would reversing its process take him back to the base? Lost in the immensity of the frozen wilderness, he made the only choice possible and gunned the cat again.

4

Once again Ross sat waiting for others to decide his future. He was as outwardly composed as he had been in Judge Rawle's chambers, but inwardly he was far more apprehensive. Out in the wilderness of the polar night he had had no chance for escape. Heading away from Kurt's rendezvous, Ross had run straight into the search party from the base. He had seen in action that mechanical hound that Kurt had said they would put on the fugitive's trail—the thing which would have gone on hunting them until its metal rusted away. Kurt's boasted immunity to that tracker had not been as good as he had believed, though it had won them a start.

Ross did not know just how much it might count in his favor that he had been on his way back, with Kurt a prisoner in the cat. As his waiting hours wore on he began to think it might mean very little indeed. This time there was no show on the wall of his cell, nothing but time to think—too much of that—and no pleasant things to think about.

But he had learned one valuable lesson on that cold expedition. Kelgarries and the others at the base were the most formidable opponents he had ever met, and all the balance of luck and equipment lay on their side of the scales. Ross was now convinced that there could be no escape from this base. He had been impressed by Kurt's preparations, knowing that some of them were far beyond anything he himself could have devised. He did not doubt that Kurt had come here fully prepared with every ingenious device the Russians could supply.

At least Kurt's friends had had a rude welcome when they did arrive at the meeting place. Kelgarries had heard Ross out and then had sent ahead a team. Before Ross's party had reached the base there had been a blast which split the arctic night wide open. And Kurt, conscious by then, had shown his only sign of emotion when he realized what it meant.

The door to Ross's cell room clicked, and he swung his feet to the floor, sitting up on his bunk to face his future. This time he made no attempt to put on an act. He was not in the least sorry he had tried to get away. Had Kurt been on the level, it would have been a bright play. That Kurt was not, was just plain bad luck.

Kelgarries and Ashe entered, and at the sight of Ashe the taut feeling in Ross's middle loosened a bit. The major might come by himself to pass sentence, but he would not bring Ashe along if the sentence was a really harsh one.

"You got off to a bad start here, Murdock." The major sat down on the edge of the wall shelf which doubled as a table. "You're going to have a second chance, so consider yourself lucky. We know you aren't another plant of our enemies, a fact that saves your neck. Do you have anything to add to your story?"

"No, sir." He was not adding that "sir" to curry any favor; it came naturally when one answered Kelgarries.

"But you have some questions?"

Ross met that with the truth. "A lot of them."

"Why don't you ask them?"

Ross smiled thinly, an expression far removed and years older than his bashful boy's grin when playing shy. "A wise guy doesn't spill his ignorance. He uses his eyes and ears and keeps his trap shut—"

"And goes off half cocked as a result . . ." the major added. "I don't think you would have enjoyed the company of Kurt's paymaster."

"I didn't know about him then—not when I left here."

"Yes, and when you discovered the truth, you took steps. Why?" For the first time there was a trace of feeling in the major's voice.

"Because I don't like the set-up on his side of the fence."

"That single fact has saved your neck this time, Murdock. Step out of line once more, and nothing will help you. But just so we won't have to worry about that, suppose you ask a few of those questions."

"How much of what Kurt fed me is the truth?" Ross blurted out. "I mean all the stuff about shooting back in time."

"All of it." The major said it so quietly that it carried complete conviction.

"But why—how—?"

"You have us on the spot, Murdock. Because of your little expedition, we have to tell you more now than we tell any of our men before the final briefing. Listen, and forget all of it except what applies to the job at hand.

"Once Greater Russia emerged from the wreckage of the old Soviet Union and started gobbling up its neighbors, joint space ventures were out of the question. But they didn't start a new space race either. Not that we've sent men to the moon ourselves—" the major's voice tightened "—in more years than I care to count. So why weren't they interested in taking the high ground?"

Ross stared back blankly. Did "high ground" mean space?

"Any discovery in science comes about by steps. It can be traced through those steps by another scientist. But suppose you were confronted by a result which apparently had been produced without any preliminaries. What would you guess had happened?"

Ross stared at the major. Although he didn't see what all this had to do with time-jumping, he sensed that Kelgarries was waiting for a serious answer, that somehow Ross would be judged by his reply.

"Either that the steps were kept strictly secret," he said slowly, "or that the result didn't rightfully belong to the man who said he discovered it."

For the first time the major regarded him with approval. "Suppose this discovery was vital to your life—what would you do?"

"Try to find the source!"

"There you have it! Within the past five years our friends across the way have come up with three such discoveries. One we were able to trace, duplicate, and use, with a few refinements of our own. The other two remain rootless; yet they are linked with the first. We are now attempting to solve that problem, and the time grows late. For some reason, though the Russians now have their super, super gadgets, they are not yet ready to use them. Sometimes the things work, and sometimes they fail. Everything points to the fact that the Russians are now experimenting with discoveries which are not actually their own—"

"Where did they get them? From another world?" Ross's imagination came to life. Had a successful space voyage been kept secret? Had contact been made with another intelligent race?

"In a way it's another world, but the world of time—not space. Seven years ago we got a man out of Moscow. He was almost dead, but he lived long enough to tape some amazing data, so wild it was almost dismissed as the ravings of delirium. But we didn't dare disregard any hints from the other side. So the recording was turned over to our scientists, who proved it had a core of truth.

"Time travel has been written about in fiction; it has been discussed otherwise as an impossibility. Then we discover that the Russians have it working—"

"You mean, they go into the future and bring back machines to use now."

The major shook his head. "Not the future, the past."

Was this an elaborate joke? Somewhat heatedly Ross snapped out the answer to that. "Look, here, I know I haven't your education, but I do know that the farther back you go into history the simpler things are. We ride in cars; only a hundred years ago men drove horses. We have guns; go back a little and you'll find them waving swords and shooting guys with bows and arrows—those that don't wear tin plate on them to stop being punctured—"

"Only they were, after all," commented Ashe. "Look at Agincourt, m'lad, and remember what arrows did to the French knights in armor."

Ross disregarded the interruption. "Anyway," he stuck doggedly to his point—"the farther back you go, the simpler things are. How are the Russians going to find anything in history we can't beat today?"

"That is a point which has baffled us for several

years now," the major returned. "Only it is not *how* they are going to find it, but *where*. Because somewhere in the past of this world they have contacted a civilization able to produce weapons and ideas so advanced as to baffle our experts. We have to find that source and either mine it ourselves or close it off. As yet we're still trying to find it."

Ross shook his head. "It must be a long way back. Those guys who discover tombs and dig up old cities— couldn't they give you some hints? Wouldn't a civilization like that have left something we could find today?"

"It depends," Ashe remarked, "upon the type of civilization. The Egyptians built in stone, grandly. They used tools and weapons of copper, bronze, and stone, and they were considerate enough to operate in a dry climate which preserved relics well. The cities of the Fertile Crescent built in mudbrick and used stone, copper, and bronze tools. They also chose a portion of the world where climate was a factor in keeping their memory green.

"The Greeks built in stone, wrote their books, kept their history to bequeath it to their successors, and so did the Romans. And on this side of the ocean the Incas, the Mayas, the unknown races before them, and the Aztecs of Mexico all built in stone and worked in metal. And stone and metal survive. But what if there had been an early people who used plastics and brittle alloys, who had no desire to build permanent buildings, whose tools and artifacts were meant to wear out quickly, perhaps for economic reasons? What would they leave us—considering, perhaps, that an ice age had intervened between their time and ours, with glaciers to grind into dust what little they did possess?

"There is evidence that the poles of our world have

changed and that this northern region was once close to being tropical. Any catastrophe violent enough to bring about a switch in the poles of this planet might well have wiped out all traces of a civilization, no matter how superior. We have good reason to believe that such a people must have existed, but we must find them."

"And Ashe is a convert from the skeptics—" the major slipped down from his perch on the wall shelf— "he is an archaeologist, one of your tomb discoverers, and knows what he is talking about. We must do our hunting in time earlier than the first pyramid, earlier than the first group of farmers who settled by the Tigris River. But we have to let the enemy guide us to it. That's where you come in."

"Why me?"

"That is a question which our psychologists are still trying to answer, my young friend. It seems that the majority of the people of several nations linked together in this project have become too civilized. The reactions of most men to given sets of circumstances have become set in such regular patterns that they cannot break that conditioning, or if personal danger forces them to change those patterns, they are afterward so adrift they cannot function at their highest potential. Teach a man to kill, as in war, and then you have to recondition him later.

"But during these same wars we also develop another type. He is the born commando, the secret agent, the expendable man who lives on action. There are not many of this kind, and they are potent weapons. In peacetime that particular collection of emotions, nerve, and skills becomes a menace to the very society he has fought to preserve during a war. In a peaceful environment he becomes a criminal or a misfit.

"The men we send out from here to explore the past are not only given the best training we can possibly supply for them, but they are all of the type once heralded as the frontiersman. History is sentimental about that type—when he is safely dead—but the present finds him difficult to live with. Our time agents are misfits in the modern world because their inherited abilities are born out of season now. They must be young enough and possess a certain brand of intelligence to take the stiff training and to adapt, and they must pass our tests. Do you understand?"

Ross nodded. "You want crooks because they are crooks?"

"No, not because they are crooks, but because they are misfits in their time and place. Don't, I beg of you, Murdock, think that we are operating a penal institution here. You would never have been recruited if you hadn't tested out to suit us. But the man who may be labeled murderer in his own period might rank as a hero in another, an extreme example, but true. When we train a man he not only can survive in the period to which he is sent, but he can also pass as a native born in that era—"

"What about Hardy?"

The major gazed into space. "No operation is foolproof. We have never said that we don't run into trouble or that there is no danger. We have to deal with both natives of different times and, if we are lucky and hit a hot run, with the Russians. They suspect that we are casting about, hunting their trail. They managed to plant Kurt Vogel on us. He had an almost perfect cover and conditioning. Now you have it straight, Murdock. You satisfy our tests, and you'll be given a chance to say yes or no before your first run. If you say no and refuse duty, it means you must become an exile and stay here. No man who has gone

through our training can return to normal life; there
is too much chance of his being picked up and
sweated by the opposition."

"Never?"

The major shrugged. "This may be a long-term
operation. We hope not, but there is no way of telling now. You will be in exile until we either find what
we want or fail entirely. That is the last card I have
to lay on the table." He stretched. "You're slated for
training tomorrow. Think it over. Then let us know
your answer when the time comes. Meanwhile, you
are to be teamed with Ashe, who will see to putting
you through the course."

It was a big hunk to swallow, but once down, Ross
found it digestible. The training opened up a whole
new world to him. Judo and wrestling were easy
enough to absorb, and he thoroughly enjoyed the
workouts. But the patient hours of archery practice,
the strict instruction in the use of a long-bladed bronze
dagger were more demanding. Mastering one new
language and then another, intensive drill in unfamiliar social customs, memorizing of strict taboos and
ethics was difficult. Ross learned to keep records in
knots on hide thongs and was inducted into the art
of primitive bargaining and trade. He came to understand the worth of a cross-shaped tin ingot compared
to a string of amber beads and some well-cured white
furs. He now understood why he had been shown a
traders' caravan during that first encounter with the
purpose behind Operation Retrograde.

During the training days his feeling toward Ashe
changed. A man could not work so closely with
another and continue to resent his attitude; either
he blew up entirely, or he learned to adjust. His awe
at Ashe's vast amount of practical knowledge, freely
offered to serve his own blundering ignorance, created

a respect which might have become friendship, had Ashe ever relaxed his own shield of impersonal efficiency. Ross did not try to breach the barrier between them mainly because he was sure that the reason for it was the fact that he was a "volunteer." It gave him an odd new feeling that he avoided analyzing. He had always had a kind of pride in his record; now he had begun to wish sometimes that it was a record of a different type.

Men came and went. Hodaki and his partner disappeared, as did Jansen and his. One lost track of time within that underground warren which was the base. Ross gradually discovered that the whole establishment covered a large island under an external crust of ice and snow. There were laboratories, a well-appointed hospital, armories which stocked weapons usually seen only in museums, but which here were free of any signs of age, and ready for use. There were libraries with mile upon mile of tape recordings as well as films. Ross could not understand everything he heard and saw, but he soaked up all he could so that once or twice, when drifting off to sleep at night, he thought of himself as a sponge which had nearly reached its total limit of absorption.

He learned to wear naturally the clumsy kilt-tunic he had seen on the wolf slayer, to shave with practiced assurance, using a leaf-shaped bronze razor, to eat strange food until he relished the taste. Making lesson time serve a double duty, he lay under sunlamps while listening to tape recordings, until his skin darkened to a weathered hue approaching Ashe's. There was always talk to listen to, important talk which he was afraid to miss.

"Bronze." Ashe weighed a dagger in his hand one day. Its hilt, made of dark horn studded with an intricate pattern of tiny golden nail heads, had a gleam not unlike that of the blade. "Do you know, Murdock, that bronze can be tougher than steel? If it wasn't that iron is so much more plentiful and easier to work, we might never have come out of the Bronze Age? Iron is cheaper and easier found, and when the first smith learned to work it, an end came to one way of life, a beginning to another.

"Yes, bronze is important to us here, and so are the men who worked it. Smiths were sacred in the old days. We know that they made a secret of their trade which overrode the bounds of district, tribe, and race. A smith was welcome in any village, his person safe on the road. In fact, the roads themselves were under the protection of the gods; there was peace on them for all wayfarers. The land was wide then, and it was empty. The tribes were few and small, and there was plenty of room for the hunter, the farmer, the trader. Life was not such a scramble of man against man, but rather of man against nature—"

"No wars?" asked Ross. "Then why the bow-and-dagger drill?"

"Wars were small affairs, disputes between family clans or tribes. As for the bow, there were formidable things in the forests—giant animals, wolves, wild boars—"

"Cave bears?"

Ashe sighed with weary patience. "Get it through your head, Murdock, that history is much longer than you seem to think. Cave bears and the use of bronze weapons do not overlap. No, you will have to go back maybe several thousand years earlier and then hunt your bear with a flint-tipped spear in your hand if you are fool enough to try it."

"Or take a rifle with you." Ross made a suggestion he had longed to voice for some time.

Ashe rounded on him swiftly, and Ross knew him well enough to realize that he was seriously displeased.

"That is just what you don't do, Murdock, not from this base, as you well know by now. You take no weapon from here which is not designed for the period in which your run lies. Just as you do not become embroiled while on that run in any action which might influence the course of history."

Ross went on polishing the blade he held. "What would happen if somebody did break that rule?"

Ashe put down the dagger he had been playing with. "We don't know—we just don't know. So far we have operated in the fringe territory, keeping away from any district with a history which we can trace accurately. Maybe some day—" his eyes were on a wall of weapon racks he plainly did not see— "maybe some day we can stand and watch the rise of the pyramids, witness the march of Alexander's armies . . . But not yet. We stay away from history, and we are sure that the Russians are doing the same. It has become the old problem once presented by nuclear bombs. Nobody wants to upset the balance and take the consequences. Let us find their outpost and we'll withdraw our men from all the other runs at once."

"What makes everyone so sure that they have an outpost somewhere? Couldn't they be working right at the main source, sir?"

"They could, but for some reason they are not. As for how we know that much, it's information received." Ashe smiled thinly. "No, the source is much farther back in time than their halfway post. But if we find that, then we can trail them. So we plant men in suitable eras and hope for the best. That's a good weapon you have there, Murdock. Are you willing to wear it in earnest?"

The inflection in that question caught Ross's full attention. His gray eyes met those blue ones. This was it—at long last.

"Right away?"

Ashe picked up a belt of bronze plates strung together with chains, a twin to that Ross had seen worn by the wolf slayer. He held it out to the younger man. "You take your trial run any time—tomorrow."

Ross drew a deeper breath. "Where—to when?"

"An island which will later be Britain. When? About two thousand B.C. Beaker traders were beginning to open their stations there. This is your graduation exercise, Murdock."

Ross fitted the blade he had been polishing into the wooden sheath on the belt. "If you say I can do it, I'm willing to try."

He caught that glance Ashe shot at him, but he could not read its meaning. Annoyance? Impatience? He was still puzzling over it when the other turned abruptly and left him alone.

5

Ross might have said yes, but that didn't mean that he was to be shipped off at once to early Britain. Ashe's "tomorrow" proved to be several days later. The cover was that of a Beaker trader, and Ross's impersonation was checked again and again by experts, making sure that the last detail was correct and that no suspicion of a tribesman, no mistake on Ross's part would betray him.

The Beaker people were an excellent choice for infiltration. They were not a closely knit clan; suspicious of strangers and alert to any deviation from the norm, as more race-conscious tribes might be. For they lived by trade, leaving to Ross's own time the mark of their far-flung influence in the beakers found in graves scattered in clusters from the Rhineland to Spain, and from the Balkans to Britain.

They did not depend only upon the taboo of the trade road for their safety, for the Beakermen were master bowmen. A roving people, they pushed into new territory to establish posts, living amicably among peoples with far different customs—the Downs farmers, horse herders, shore-side fisherfolk.

With Ashe, Ross passed a last inspection. Their hair had not grown long enough to require braiding, but they did have enough to hold it back from their faces with hide headbands. The kilt-tunics of coarse material, duplicating samples brought from the past, were harsh to the skin and poorly fitting. But the workmanship of their link-and-plate bronze belts, the sleek bow guards strapped to their wrists, and the bows themselves approached fine art. Ashe's round cloak was the blue of a master trader, and he wore wealth in a necklace of polished wolf's teeth alternating with amber beads. Ross's more modest position in the tribe was indicated not only by his red-brown cloak, but by the fact that his personal jewelry consisted only of a copper bracelet and a cloak pin with a jet head.

He had no idea how the time transition was to be made, nor how one might step from the polar regions of the Western Hemisphere to the island of Britain lying off the Eastern. And it was a complicated business as he discovered.

The transition itself was a fairly simple, though disturbing, process. One walked a short corridor and stood for an instant on a plate while the light centered there curled about in a solid core, shutting one off from floor and wall. Ross gasped for breath as the air was sucked out of his lungs. He experienced a moment of deathly nausea with a sense of being lost in nothingness. Then he breathed again and looked through the dying wall of light to where Ashe waited.

Quick and easy as the trip through time had been, the journey to Britain was something else. There could be only one transfer point if the secret was to be preserved. But men from that point must be moved swiftly and secretly to their appointed stations. Ross, knowing the strict rules concerning the transportation of objects from one time to another, wondered how that travel could be effected. After all, they could not spend months, or even years, getting across continents and seas.

The answer was ingenious. Three days after they had stepped through the barrier of time at the outpost, Ross and Ashe balanced on the rounded back of a whale. It was a whale which would deceive anyone who did not test its hide with a harpoon, and whalers with harpoons large enough to trouble such a monster were yet well in the future.

Ashe slid a dugout into the water, and Ross climbed into that unsteady craft, holding it against the side of the disguised sub until his partner joined him. The day, misty and drizzling, made the shore they aimed for a half-seen line across the water. With a shiver born of more than cold, Ross dipped his paddle and helped Ashe send their crude boat toward that half-hidden strip of land.

There was no real dawn; the sky lightened somewhat, but the drizzle continued. Green patches showed among the winter-denuded trees back from the beach, but the countryside facing them gave an impression of untamed wilderness. Ross knew from his briefing that the whole of Britain was as yet only sparsely settled. The first wave of hunter-fishers to establish villages had been joined by other invaders who built massive tombs and practiced an elaborate religion. Small village-forts had been linked from hill to hill by trackways. These were "factories," which turned out in bulk such fine flint weapons and tools that a thriving industry was in full operation, not yet superseded by the metal the Beaker merchants imported. Bronze was still so rare and costly that only the head man of a village could hope to own one of the long daggers.

Even the arrowheads in Ross's quiver were chipped
of flint.

They drew the dugout well up onto the shore and
ran it into a shallow depression in the bank, heaping
stones and brush about for its concealment. Then Ashe
intently surveyed the surrounding country, seeking a
landmark.

"Inland from here . . ." Ashe used the language of
the Beakermen, and Ross knew that from now on he
must not only live as a trader, but also think as one.
All other memories must be buried under the false
one he had learned; he must be interested in the
present rate of exchange and the chance for profit.
The two men were on their way to Outpost Gog,
where Ashe's first partner, the redoubtable Sanford,
was playing his role so well.

The rain squished in their hide boots, made sodden burdens of their cloaks, plastered their woven caps
to their thickly matted hair. Yet Ashe bore steadily on
across the land with the certainty of one following a
marked trail. His self-confidence was rewarded within
the first half mile when they came out upon one of
the link trackways, its beaten surface testifying to
constant use.

Here Ashe turned eastward, stepping up the pace
to a ground-covering trot. The peace of the road held—
at least by day. By night only the most hardened and
desperate outlaws would brave the harmful spirits who
roved in the dark.

All the lore that had been pounded into him at the
base began to make sense to Ross as he followed his
guide, sniffing strange wet smells from the brush, the
trees, and the damp earth; piecing together in his
mind what he had been taught and what he now saw
for himself, until it made a tight pattern.

The track they were following sloped slightly upward,

and a change in the wind brought to them a sour odor, blanking out all normal scents. Ashe halted so suddenly that Ross almost plowed into him. But he was alerted by the older man's attitude.

Something had been burned! Ross drew in a deep lungful of the smell and then wished that he had not. It was wood—burned wood—and something else. Since this was not possibly normal, he was prepared for the way Ashe melted into cover in the brush.

They worked their way, sometimes crawling on their bellies, through the wet stands of dead grass, taking full advantage of all cover. They crouched at the top of the hill while Ashe parted the prickly branches of an evergreen bush to make a window.

The black patch left by the fire, which had come from a ruin above, had spread downhill on the opposite side of the valley. Charred posts still stood like lone teeth in a skull to mark what must have once been one of the stockade walls of a post. But all they now guarded was a desolation from which came that overpowering stench.

"Our post?" Ross asked in a whisper.

Ashe nodded. He was studying the scene with an intent absorption which, Ross knew, would impress every important detail upon his mind. That the place had been burned was clear from the first. But why and by whom was a problem vital to the two lurking in the brush.

It took them almost an hour to cross the valley— an hour of hiding, casting about, searching. They had made a complete circle of the destroyed post and Ashe stood in the shadow of a copse, rubbing clots of mud from his hands and frowning up at the charred posts.

"They weren't rushed. Or, if they were, the attacker covered their trail afterward—" Ross ventured.

The older man shook his head. "Tribesmen would

not have muddled a trail if they had won. No, this was no regular attack. There have been no signs of a war party coming or leaving."

"Then what?" demanded Ross.

"Lightning for one thing—and we'd better hope it was that. Or—" Ashe's blue eyes were as cold and bleak as the countryside about them.

"Or—?" Ross dared to prompt him.

"Or we have made contact with the Russians in the wrong way!"

Ross's hand instinctively went to the dagger at his belt. Little help a dagger would be in an unequal struggle like this! They were only two in the thin web of men strung out through centuries of time with orders to seek out that which did not fit properly into the pattern of the past: to locate the enemy wherever in history or prehistory he had gone to earth. Had the Russians been searching, too, and was this first disaster their victory?

The time traders had their evidence when they at last ventured into what had been the heart of Outpost Gog. Ross, inexperienced as he was in such matters, could not mistake the signs of the explosion. There was a crater on the crown of the hill, and Ashe stood apart from it, eyeing the fragments about them—scorched wood, blackened stone.

"The Russians?"

"It must have been. This damage was done by explosives."

It was clear why Outpost Gog could not report the disaster. The attack had destroyed their one link with the post on this time level; the concealed communicator had gone up with the blast.

"Eleven—" Ashe's finger tapped on the ornate buckle of his wide belt. "We have about ten days to stick it out," he added, "and it seems we may be able to use them to better advantage than just letting you learn how it feels to walk about some four thousand years before you were born. We have to find out— if we can—what happened here and why!"

Ross gazed at the mess. "Dig?" he asked.

"Some digging is indicated."

So they dug. Finally, black with charcoal smudges and sick with the evidence of death they had chanced upon, they collapsed on the cleanest spot they could find.

"They must have hit at night," Ashe said slowly. "Only at that time would they find everyone here. Men don't trust a night filled with ghosts, and our agents conform to local custom as usual. All of the post people could be erased with one bomb at night."

All except two of them had been true Beaker traders, including women and children. No Beaker trading post was large, and this one was unusually small. The attacker had wiped out some twenty people, eighteen of them innocent victims.

"How long ago?" Ross wanted to know.

"Maybe two days. And this attack came without any warning, or Sandy would have sent a message. He had no suspicions at all; his last reports were all routine, which means that if they were on to him—and they must have been, judging by the results—he was not even aware of it."

"What do we do now?"

Ashe looked at him. "We wash—no—" he corrected himself— "we don't! We go to Nodren's village. We are frightened, grief-stricken. We have found our kinsmen dead under strange circumstances. We ask questions of one to whom I am known as an inhabitant of this post."

So, covered with dirt, they walked along the

trackway toward the neighboring village with a weariness they did not have to counterfeit.

The dog sighted or perhaps scented them first. It was a rough-coated beast, showing its fangs with a wolflike ferocity. But it was smaller than a wolf, and it barked between its warning snarls. Ashe brought his bow from beneath the shelter of his cloak and held it ready.

"Ho, one comes to speak with Nodren—Nodren of the Hill!"

Only the dog snapped and snarled. Ashe rubbed his forearm across his face, the gesture of a weary and heartsick man, smearing the ash and grime into an awesome mask.

"Who speaks to Nodren—?" There was a different twist to the pronunciation of some words, but Ross was able to understand.

"One who has hunted with him and feasted with him. The one who gave into his hand the friendship of the ever-sharp knife. It is Assha of the traders."

"Go far from us, man of ill luck. You who are hunted by the evil spirits." The last was a shrill cry.

Ashe remained where he was, facing into the bushes which hid the tribesman.

"Who speaks for Nodren yet not with the voice of Nodren?" he demanded. "This is Assha who asks. We have drunk blood together and faced the white wolf and the wild boar in their fury. Nodren lets not others speak for him, for Nodren is a man and a chief!"

"And you are cursed!" A stone flew through the air, striking a rain pool and spattering mud on Ashe's boots. "Go and take your evil with you!"

"Is it from the hand of Nodren or Nodren's young men that doom came upon those of my blood? Have war arrows passed between the place of the traders and the town of Nodren? Is that why you hide in the shadows so that I, Assha, cannot look upon the face of one who speaks boldly and throws stones?"

"No war arrows between us, traders. *We* do not provoke the spirits of the hills. No fire comes from the sky at night to eat us up with a noise of many thunders. Lurgha speaks in such thunders; Lurgha's hand smites with such fire. You have the wrath of Lurgha upon you, trader! Keep away from us lest Lurgha's wrath fall upon us also."

Lurgha was the local storm god, Ross recalled. The sound of thunder and fire coming out of the sky at night—the bomb! Perhaps the very method of attack on the post would defeat Ashe's attempt to learn anything from these neighbors. The superstitions of the people would lead them to shun both the site of the post and Ashe himself as cursed and taboo.

"If the Wrath of Lurgha had struck at Assha, would Assha still live to walk upon this road?" Ashe prodded the ground with the tip of his bowstave. "Yet Assha walks, as you see him; Assha talks, as you hear him. It is ridiculous to answer him with the nonsense of little children—"

"Spirits so walk and talk to unlucky men," retorted the man in hiding. "It may be the spirit of Assha who does so now—"

Ashe made a sudden leap. After a flurry of action behind the bush screen, he reappeared, dragging into the gray light of the rainy day a wriggling captive, whom he dumped without ceremony onto the beaten earth of the road.

The man was bearded, wearing his thick mop of black hair in a round topknot secured by a hide loop. His skin tunic, now in considerable disarray, was held in place with a woven, tasseled belt.

"Ho, so it is Lal of the Quick Tongue who speaks so loudly of spirits and the Wrath of Lurgha!" Ashe

studied his captive. "Now, Lal, since you speak for
Nodren—which I believe will greatly surprise him—
you will continue to tell me of this Wrath of Lurgha
from the night skies and what has happened to Sanfra,
who was my brother, and those others of my kin. I
am Assha, and you know of the wrath of Assha and
how it ate up Twist-tooth, the outlaw, when he came
in with his evil men. The Wrath of Lurgha is hot, but
so too is the wrath of Assha." Ashe contorted his face
in such a way that Lal squirmed and looked away.
When the tribesman spoke, all his former bluster had
gone.

"Assha knows that I am his dog. Let him not turn
upon me his swift-cutting big knife, nor the arrows
from his lightning bow. It was the Wrath of Lurgha
which smote the place on the hill, first the thunder
of his fist meeting the earth, and then the fire which
he breathed upon those whom he would slay—"

"And this you saw with your own eyes, Lal?"

The shaggy head shook an emphatic negative.
"Assha knows that Lal is no chief who can stand
and look upon the wonders of Lurgha's might and
keep his eyes in his head. Nodren himself saw this
wonder—"

"And if Lurgha came in the night, when all men
keep to their homes and leave the outer world to the
restless spirits, how did Nodren see his coming?"

Lal crouched lower to the ground, his eyes darting to the bushes and the freedom they promised, then
back to Ashe's firmly planted boots.

"I am not a chief, Assha. How could I know in what
way or for what reason Nodren saw the coming of
Lurgha—?"

"Fool!" A second voice, that of a woman, spat the
word from the brush which fringed the roadway.
"Speak to Assha with a straight tongue. If he is a spirit,

he will know that you do not tell him the truth. And if he has been spared by Lurgha . . ." She showed her wonderment with a hiss of indrawn breath.

So urged, Lal mumbled sullenly, "It is said that there came a message for one to witness the Wrath of Lurgha in its descent upon the outlanders so that Nodren and the men of Nodren would truly know that the traders were cursed, and should be put to the spear should they come here again—"

"This message—how was it brought? Did the voice of Lurgha sound in Nodren's ear alone, or came it by the tongue of some man?"

"Ahee!" Lal lay flat on the ground, his hands over his ears.

"Lal is a fool and fears his own shadow as it skips before him on a sunny day!" Out of the bushes stepped a young woman, obviously of some importance in her own group. Walking with a proud stride, her eyes boldly met Ashe's. A shining disk hung about her neck on a thong, and another decorated the woven belt of her cloth tunic. Her hair was bound in a thread net fastened with jet pins.

"I greet Cassca, who is the First Sower." There was a formal note in Ashe's voice. "But why should Cassca hide from Assha?"

"There has been death on your hill, Assha—" she sniffed— "you smell of it now—Lurgha's death. Those who come from that hill may well be some who no longer walk in their bodies." Cassca placed her fingers momentarily on Ashe's outstretched palm before she nodded. "No spirit are you, Assha, for all know that a spirit is solid to the eye, but not to the touch. So it would seem that you were not burned up by Lurgha, after all."

"This matter of a message from Lurgha—" he prompted.

"It came out of the empty air in the hearing not only of Nodren, but also of Hangor, Effar, and myself, Cassca. For we stood at that time near the Old Place . . ." She made a curious gesture with the fingers of her right hand. "It will soon be the time of sowing, and though Lurgha brings sun and rain to feed the grain, yet it is in the Great Mother that the seed lies. Upon her business only women may go into the Inner Circle." She gestured again. "But as we met to make the first sacrifice there came music out of the air such as we have never heard, voices singing like birds in a strange tongue." Her face assumed an awed expression. "Afterward a voice said that Lurgha was angered with the hill of the men-from-afar and that in the night he would send his Wrath against them, and that Nodren must witness this thing so that he could see what Lurgha did to those he would punish. So it was done by Nodren. And there was a sound in the air—"

"What kind of a sound?" Ashe asked quietly.

"Nodren said it was a hum and there was the dark shadow of Lurgha's bird between him and the stars. Then came the smiting of the hill with thunder and lightning, and Nodren fled, for the Wrath of Lurgha is a fearsome thing. Now do the people go to the Great Mother's Place with many fine offerings that she may stand between them and that Wrath."

"Assha thanks Cassca, who is the handmaiden of the Great Mother. May the sowing prosper and the reaping be good this year!" Ashe said finally, ignoring Lal, who still groveled on the road.

"You go from this place, Assha?" she asked. "For though I stand under the protecting hand of the Mother and so do not fear, yet there are others who will raise their spears against you for the honor of Lurgha."

"We go, and again thanks be to you, Cassca."

He turned back the way they had come, and Ross fell in beside him as the woman watched them out of sight.

6

"That bird of Lurgha's—" said Ross, once they were out of sight of Cassca and Lal, "could it have been a plane?"

"Sounds like it," snapped his companion. "If the Russians have done their work efficiently—and there's no reason to suppose otherwise—then there is no use in contacting either Dorhta's town or Munga's. The same announcement concerning the Wrath of Lurgha was probably made there—to their good purpose, not ours."

"Cassca didn't seem to be overly impressed with Lurgha's curse, not as much as the man was."

"She is the closest thing to a priestess that this tribe knows, and she serves a goddess older and more powerful than Lurgha—the Mother Earth, the Great Mother, goddess of fertility and growth. Nodren's people believe that unless Cassca performs her mysteries and sows part of the first field in the spring there won't be any harvest. Consequently, she is secure in her office and doesn't fear the Wrath of Lurgha

too much. These people are now changing from one
type of worship to another, but some of Cassca's beliefs
will persist clear down to our day, taking on the
coating of 'magic' and a lot of other enameling along
the way."

Ashe had been talking the way a man talks to
cover furious thinking. Now he paused again and
turned toward the sea. "We have to stick it out
somewhere until the sub comes to pick us up. We'll
need shelter."

"Will the tribesmen come after us?"

"They may well. Let the right men get to talking
up a holy extermination of those upon whom the
Wrath of Lurgha has fallen and we could be in for
plenty of trouble. Some of those men are trained
hunters and trackers, and the Russians may have
planted an agent to report the return of anyone to
our post. Just now we're about the most important
time travelers out, for we know the Russians have
appeared on this line. They must have a large post
here, too, or they couldn't have sent a plane on that
raid. You can't build a time transport large enough to
take through a considerable amount of material.
Everything used by us in this age has to be assembled
on this side, and the use of all machines is limited
to where they can not be seen by any natives. Luckily large sections of this world are mostly wilderness
and unpopulated in the areas where we operate the
base posts. So if the Russians have a plane, it was put
together here, and that means a big post somewhere."
Again Ashe was thinking aloud as he pushed ahead
of Ross into the fringes of a wood. "Sandy and I
scouted this territory pretty well last spring. There is
a cave about half a mile to the west; it will shelter
us for tonight."

Ashe's plans would probably have been easily

accomplished if the cave had been unoccupied. Without incident they came down into a hollow through which trickled a small stream, thinly edged with ice along its banks. Under Ashe's direction Ross collected an armload of firewood. He was no woodsman and his prolonged exposure to the chilling drizzle made him eager for even the very rough shelter of a cave, so eager that he plunged forward carelessly. His foot came down on a slippery patch of mud, sending him sprawling on his face. There was a growl, and a white bulk rushed him. The cloak, rucked up about his throat and shoulders, then saved his life, for only stout cloth was caught between those fangs.

With a startled cry, Ross rolled as he might have to escape a man's attack, struggling to unsheathe his dagger. A white-hot flash of pain scored his upper arm. The breath was driven out of him as a fight raged over his prone body. He heard grunts, snarls, and was severely pummeled. Then he was free as the bodies broke away. Shaken, he got to his knees. A short distance away the fight was still in progress. He saw Ashe straddle the body of a huge white wolf, his legs clamped about the animal's haunches, his hooked arm under the beast's head, forcing it up and back while his dagger rose and sank twice in the underparts of the heaving body.

Ross held his own weapon ready. He leaped from a half crouch, and his dagger sank cleanly home behind the short ribs. One of their blows must have reached the animal's heart. With an almost human cry the wolf stiffened convulsively. Then it was still. Ashe squatted near it, methodically driving his dagger into the moist soil to clean the blade.

A red rivulet trickled down his thigh where the lower edge of his kilt-tunic had been ripped up to the link belt. Although breathing hard, he remained as

composed as always. "These sometimes hunt in pairs
at this season," he observed. "Be ready with your
bow—"

Ross strung his with the cord he had been keeping
dry within the breast folds of his tunic. He fitted
an arrow to the string, grateful to be a passable
marksman. The slash on his arm smarted in protest
as he moved, and he noted that Ashe did not try
to get up.

"A bad one?" Ross indicated the blood now thickening into a stream along Ashe's thigh.

Ashe pulled away the torn tunic and exposed a nasty
looking gash on the outside of his hip. He pressed
his palm against the gaping wound and motioned Ross
to scout ahead. "See if the cave is clear. We can't do
anything until we know that."

Reluctantly Ross followed the stream until he found
the cave, a snug-looking place with an overhang to
keep it dry. The reek of a lair hung about its mouth.
He chose a stone from the stream, chucked it into
the dark opening, and waited. The stone rattled as it
struck an inner wall, but there was no other sound.
A second stone from a different angle followed the
first, with the same results. Ross was now certain that
the cave was unoccupied. Once they were inside with
a fire going at the entrance, they could hope to keep
intruders out. A little heartened, he cast about a bit
upstream and then turned back to where he had left
Ashe.

"No male?" the other greeted him. "This is a
female, and she was close to whelping—" He nudged
the white wolf with his toe. His hands held a pad
of rags against his hip, and his face was shaded with
pain.

"Nothing in the cave anyway. Let's see about
this . . ." Ross laid aside the bow and kneeled to

examine Ashe's thigh wound. His own slash was more of a smarting graze, but this tear was deep and ugly.

"Second plate—belt—" Ashe got the words out between set teeth, and Ross clicked open the hidden recess in the other's bronze belt to bring out a small packet. Ashe made a wry face as he swallowed three of the pills within. Ross mashed another pill onto the bandage he prepared, and when the last cumbersome fold was secured Ashe relaxed.

"Let us hope that works," he commented a little bleakly. "Now come here where I can get my hands on you and let me see your scratch. Animal bites can be a nasty business."

Bandaged in turn, with the bitterness of an antibiotic pill on his tongue, Ross helped Ashe limp upstream to the cave. He left the older man outside while he cleaned up the floor of the cave and then made his companion as comfortable as he could on a bed of bracken. The fire Ross had longed for was built. They stripped off their sodden clothing and hung it to dry. Ross wrapped a bird he had shot in clay and tucked it under the hot coals to be roasted.

They'd had their share of bad luck, he thought, but they were now undercover, had a fire, and food. His arm ached, sharp pain shooting from fingers to elbow when he moved it. Though Ashe made no complaint, Ross gauged that the older man's discomfort was far worse than his own, and he carefully hid all signs of his own twinges.

They ate the bird with their fingers. Ross savored each greasy bit, licking his hands clean afterward while Ashe lay back on the improvised bed, his face gaunt in the half light of the fire.

"We are about five miles from the sea here. There is no way of raising our base now that Sandy's installation is gone. I'll have to lay up, since I can't risk any more loss of blood. And you're not too good in the woods—"

Ross accepted that valuation with a new humbleness. He was only too well aware that if it had not been for Ashe, he and not the white wolf would have died down in the valley. Yet a strange shyness kept him from trying to put his thanks into words. The only kind of amends he could make for the other's hurt was to provide hands, feet, and strength for the man who did know what to do and how to do it.

"We'll have to hunt—" he ventured.

"Deer," Ashe caught him up. "But the marsh at the mouth of this stream provides a better hunting ground than inland. If the wolf laired here very long, she has already frightened away any game. It isn't the matter of food which bothers me—"

"It is being tied up here," Ross filled in for him with some daring. "But look here, I'll take orders. This is your territory, and I'm green at the game. You tell me what to do, and I'll do it the best that I can." He glanced up to find Ashe surveying him intently, but as usual there was no readable expression on the other's brown face.

"The first thing to do is get the wolf's hide," Ashe said briskly. "Then bury the carcass. You'd better drag it up here to work on it. If her mate is hanging around, he might try to jump you."

Why Ashe should think it necessary to acquire the wolf skin puzzled Ross, but he asked no questions. The skinning took four times as long and was far from being the neat job the shock-haired man of the record tape had accomplished. Ross had to wash himself off in the stream before piling stones over the corpse in temporary burial. When he pulled his bloody burden back to the cave, Ashe lay with his eyes closed. Ross thankfully sat on his own pile of bracken and tried not to notice the throbbing ache in his arm.

He must have fallen asleep, for when he roused it was to see Ashe crawl over to mend the dying fire from their store of wood. Ross, angry at himself, beat the other to the task.

"Get back," he said roughly. "This is my job. I didn't mean to fail."

Surprisingly, Ashe settled back without a word, leaving Ross to sit by the fire, a fire he was very glad to have a moment or so later when a wailing howl sounded down-wind. If this was not the white wolf's mate, then it was another of her kin who prowled the upper reaches of the small valley.

The next day, having provided Ashe with a supply of firewood, Ross went to try his luck in the marsh. The thick drizzle which had hung over the land the day before was gone, and he faced a clear, bright morning, though the breeze had an icy snap. But it was a good morning to be alive and out in the open, and Ross's spirits rose.

He tried to put to use all the woodlore he had learned at the base. But the classroom was one thing, the field quite another. He was uncomfortably certain that Ashe would not have found his showing very good.

The marsh was a series of pools between rank growths of leafless willows and coarse tufts of grass, with hillocks of firmer soil rising like islands. Ross, approaching with caution, was glad of it, for from one of those hillocks arose a trail of white smoke, and he saw a black blot which was probably a rude hut. Why one should choose to live in the midst of such country he could not guess, though it might be merely the temporary camp of some hunter.

Ross also saw thousands of birds feeding greedily on the dried seed of the marsh grasses, paddling in the pools, and setting up a clamor to drive a man mad. They did not seem in the least disturbed by that distant camper.

Ross had reason to be proud of his marksmanship that morning. He had in his quiver perhaps half a dozen of the lighter shafts made for shooting birds. In place of the finely chipped and wickedly barbed flint points used for heavier game, these were tipped with needle-sharp, light bone heads. He had a string of four birds looped together by their feet within almost as many minutes. For the flocks rose in their first alarm only to settle again to feast.

Then he knocked over a hare—a fat giant of its race—that stared at him brazenly from a tussock. The hare kicked back into a pool in its death struggle, however, and Ross was forced to leave cover to retrieve its body. But he was alert and he stood up, dagger out and ready, to greet the man who parted the bushes to watch him.

For a long minute gray eyes stared into brown ones, and then Ross noted the other's bedraggled and tattered dress. The kilt-tunic smudged with mud, scorched and charred along one edge, was styled like his own. The fellow wore his hair fastened back with a band, unlike the topknot of the local tribesman.

Ross, his dagger still ready, broke the silence first. "I am a believer in the fire and the fashioned metal, the climbing sun, and the moving water." He repeated the recognition speech of the Beakermen.

"The fire warms by the grace of Tulden, the metal is fashioned by the mystery of the smith, the sun climbs without our aid, and who can stop the water from running?" The stranger's voice was hoarse. Now that Ross had time to examine him more closely he saw the dark bruise on his exposed shoulder, the raw red mark of a burn running across the man's broad chest. He dared to test his surmise concerning the other.

"I am the kin of Assha. We returned to the hill—"

"Ashe!"

Not "Assha" but "Ashe!" Ross, though sure of that pronunciation, was still cautious. "You are from the hill place, where Lurgha smote with thunder and fire?"

The man slid his long legs across the log which had been his shelter. The burn across his chest was not his only brand, for Ross noticed another red stripe, puffed and fiery looking, which swelled the calf of one leg. The man studied Ross closely, and then his fingers moved in a sign which to the uninitiated native might have been one for the warding off of evil, but which to Ross was the "thumbs up" of his own age.

"Sanford?"

At that name the man shook his head. "McNeil," he named himself. "Where is Ashe?"

He might really be what he seemed, but on the other hand, he could be a Russian spy. Ross had not forgotten Kurt. "What happened?" he parried one question with another.

"Bomb. The Russians must have spotted us, and we didn't have a chance. We weren't expecting any trouble. I'd been down to see about a missing pack donkey and was about halfway back up the hill when she hit. When I came to I was all the way down the hill with part of the fort on top of me. The rest . . . Well, you saw the place, didn't you?"

Ross nodded. "What are you doing here?"

McNeil spread his hands in a tired little gesture. "I tried to talk to Nodren, but they stoned me away. I knew that Ashe was coming through and hoped to reach him when he hit the beach, but I was too late. Then I figured he would pass here to make contact with the sub, so I was waiting it out until I saw you. Where is Ashe?"

It all sounded logical enough. Still, with Ashe injured, Ross was taking no chances. He pushed his dagger back into its sheath and picked up the hare. "Stay here," he told McNeil, "I'll be back—"

"But—wait! Where's Ashe, you young fool? We have to get together."

Ross went on. He was sure that the stranger was in no shape to race after him, and he would lay a muddled trail before he returned to the cave valley. If this man was a Russian plant, he would have to reckon with one who had already met Kurt Vogel.

The laying of that muddled trail took time. It was past midday when Ross came back to Ashe, who was sitting up by the mouth of the cave at the fire, using his dagger to fashion a crutch out of a length of sapling. He surveyed Ross's burden with approval, but lost interest in the promise of food as soon as the other reported his meeting in the marsh.

"McNeil—chap with brown hair, light brown eyes, a right eyebrow which quirks up toward his hairline when he smiles?"

"Brown hair and eyes, okay—and he didn't smile any."

"Chip broken off a front tooth—upper right?"

Ross shut his eyes to visualize the stranger. Yes, there had been a small break on a front tooth. He nodded.

"That's McNeil. Not that you didn't do right not to bring him here without being sure. What made you so watchful? Kurt?"

Again Ross nodded. "And what you said about the Russians' planting someone here to wait for us."

Ashe scratched the bristles on his chin. "Never underrate them—we don't dare do that. But the man you met is McNeil, and we'd better get him here. Can you bring him?"

"I think he's able to get about, in spite of that leg. From his story he's been stirring around."

Ashe bit absent-mindedly into a piece of hare and swore mildly when he burned his tongue. "Odd that Cassca didn't tell us about him. Unless she thought there was no use causing trouble by admitting they had driven him away. You going now?"

Ross moved around the fire. "Might as well. He didn't look too comfortable. And I'll bet he's hungry."

He took the direct route back to the marsh, but this time no thread of smoke spiraled into the air. Ross hesitated. That shelter on the small island was surely the place where McNeil had holed up. Should he try to work his way out to it now? Or had something happened to the man while he was gone?

Again that sixth sense of impending disaster, which is perhaps bred into some men, alerted Ross. Why he turned suddenly and backed against a bushy willow, he could not have explained. However, because he did so the loop of hide rope meant for his throat hit his shoulder harmlessly. It fell to the ground, and he stamped one boot down on it. Then it was the work of seconds to grasp it and give it a quick jerk. The surprised man who held the other end was brought sprawling into the open.

Ross had seen that round face before. "Lal of the town of Nodren." He found words to greet the ropeman even as his knee came up against the fellow's jaw, jarring Lal so that he dropped a flint knife. Ross kicked it into the willows. "What do you hunt here, Lal?"

"Traders!" The voice was weak, but it held anger.

The tribesman did not try to struggle against Ross's hold, and Ross, gripping him by the nape of the neck, moved through a screen of brush to a hollow. Luckily there was no water cupped there, for McNeil lay in the bottom of that dip, his arms tied tightly behind him and his ankles lashed together with no thought for the pain of his burned leg.

7

Ross whirled the rope which had been meant to bring him down around Lal. He lashed the tribesman's arms tight to his body before he knelt to cut loose his fellow time traveler. Lal now huddled against the far wall of the hollow, fear in every line of his small body. So apparent was this fear that, far from feeling satisfaction, Ross felt increasingly uneasy.

"What is this all about?" he asked McNeil as he stripped off his bonds and helped him up.

McNeil massaged his wrists, took a step or two, and grimaced with pain. "Our friend seeks to be an obedient servant of Lurgha."

Ross picked up his bow. "The tribe is out to hunt us?"

"Lurgha has ordered—out of thin air again—that any traders who escaped are to be brought in and introduced to him personally at the sacrifice for the enrichments of the fields!"

The old, old gift of blood and life at the spring

sowing. Ross recalled grisly details from his cram lessons. Any wandering stranger or enemy tribesman taken in a raid before that day would meet such a fate. On unlucky years when people were not available a deer or wolf might serve. But the best sacrifice of all was a man. So Lurgha had decreed—from the air—that traders were his meat? What of Ashe? Let any hunter from the village track him down.

"We have to move fast," Ross told McNeil as he took up the rope which made a leading cord for Lal. Ashe would want to question the tribesman about this second order from Lurgha.

Impatient as Ross was, he had to mend his pace to accommodate McNeil. The man from the hill post was close to the end of his strength. He had started off bravely enough, but now he wavered. Ross sent Lal ahead with a sharp push, ordering him to stay there, while he went to McNeil's aid. It was well into the afternoon before they came up the stream and saw the fire before the cave.

"Macna!" Ashe hailed Ross's companion with the native version of his name. "And Lal. But what do you here, Lal of Nodren's town?"

"Mischief." Ross helped McNeil within the cave and to the pile of brush which was his own bed. "He was hunting traders as a present for Lurgha."

"So—" Ashe turned upon the tribesman— "and by whose word did you go hunting my kinsman, Lal? Was it Nodren's? Has he forgotten the blood bond between us? For it was in the name of Lurgha himself that that bond was made—"

"Aaaah—" The tribesman squatted down against the wall where Ross had shoved him. Unable to hide his head in his arms, he brought his face down upon his knees so that only his shaggy topknot of hair was exposed. Ross realized, with stupefaction, that the little man was crying like a child, his hunched shoulders rising and falling with the force of his sobs.

"Aaaah—" he wailed.

"Be quiet!" Ashe shook him, but not too harshly. "Have you yet felt the bite of my sharp knife? Has an arrow holed your skin? You are alive, and you could be dead. Show that you are glad you live and continue to breathe by telling us what you know, Lal."

The woman Cassca had displayed a measure of intelligence and ease at their meeting upon the road. But it was very plain that Lal was of different stuff, a simple man in whose head few ideas could find house room at one time. And to him the present was all terror. Little by little they dragged the story out of him.

Lal was poor, so poor that he had never dared dream of owning for himself some of the precious things the hill traders displayed to the wealthy of Nodren's town. But he was also a follower of the Great Mother, rather than one who made sacrifices to Lurgha. Lurgha was the god for warriors and great men; he was too high to concern himself with such as Lal.

So when Nodren reported the end of the hill post under the storm fist of Lurgha, Lal had been impressed only to a point. He was still convinced it was none of his concern, and instead he began thinking of the treasures which might lie hidden in the destroyed buildings. It occurred to him that Lurgha's Wrath had been laid upon the men who had owned them, but perhaps it would not stretch to the fine things themselves. So he had gone secretly to the hill to explore.

What he had seen there had utterly converted him to a belief in the fury of Lurgha and he had been frightened out of his simple wits, fleeing without making the search he had intended. But Lurgha had seen him there, had read his impious thoughts . . .

At that point Ashe interrupted the stream of Lal's story. How had Lurgha seen Lal?

Because—Lal shuddered, began to cry again, and spoke the next few sentences haltingly—that very morning when he had gone out to hunt wild fowl in the marshes Lurgha had spoken to *him*, to Lal, who was less than a flea creeping upon a worn out fur rug.

And how had Lurgha spoken? Ashe's voice was softer, gentle.

Out of the air, even as he had spoken to Nodren, who was a chief. He said that he had seen Lal in the hill post, and so Lal was his meat. But not yet would he eat him, not if Lal served him in other ways. And he, Lal, had lain flat on the ground before the bodiless voice of Lurgha and had sworn that he would serve Lurgha to the end of his life.

Then Lurgha had told him to hunt down one of the evil traders who was hiding in the marshes, and bind him with ropes. Then he was to call the men of the village and together they would carry the prisoner to the hill where Lurgha had loosed his wrath and leave him there. Later they might return and take what they found there and use it to bless the fields at sowing time, and all would be well with Nodren's village. And Lal had sworn that he would do as Lurgha bade, but now he could not. So Lurgha would eat him up—he was a man without hope.

"Yet," Ashe said even more gently, "have you not served the Great Mother all these years, giving to her a portion of the first fruits even when the yield of your one field was small?"

Lal stared at him, his woebegone face still smeared with tears. It took a second or two for the question to penetrate his fear-clouded mind. Then he nodded timidly.

"Has she not dealt with you well in return, Lal? You are a poor man, that is true, but you are not gaunt of belly, even though this is the thin season when men fast before coming of the new harvest. The Great Mother watches over her own. And it is she who has brought you to us now. For this I say to you, Lal, and I, Assha of the traders, speak with a straight tongue. The Lurgha who struck our post, who spoke to you from the air, means you no good—"

"Aaaah!" wailed Lal. "So do I know, Assha. He is of the night and the wandering spirits of the dark!"

"Just so. Thus he is no kin to the Mother, for she is of the light and of good things, of the new grain, and the newborn lambs for your flocks, of the maids who wed with men and bring forth sons to lift their fathers' spears, daughters to spin by the hearth and sow the yellow grain in the furrows. Lurgha's quarrel lies with us, Lal, not with Nodren nor with you. And we take upon us that quarrel." He limped into the outer air where the shadows of evening were beginning to creep across the ground.

"Hear me, Lurgha," he called into the coming night, "I am Assha of the traders, and upon myself I take your hate. Not upon Lal, nor upon Nodren, nor upon the people who live in Nodren's town, shall your wrath lie. Thus do I say it!"

Ross, noticing that Ashe concealed from Lal a wave of his hand, was prepared for some display meant to impress the tribesman. It came in a spectacular burst of green fire beyond the stream. Lal wailed again, but when that fire was followed by no other manifestation he ventured to raise his head once more.

"You have seen how Lurgha answered me, Lal. Toward me only will his wrath be turned. Now—"

Ashe limped back and dragged out the white wolf skin, dropping it before Lal— "this you will give to Cassca that she may make a curtain for the Mother's home. See, it is white and so rare that the Mother will be pleased with such a fine gift. And you will tell her all that has chanced and how you believe in her powers over the powers of Lurgha, and the Mother will be well pleased with you. But you shall say nothing to the men of the village, for this quarrel is between Lurgha and Assha now and not for the meddling of others."

He unfastened the rope which bound Lal's arms. Lal reached out a hand to the wolf skin, his eyes filled with wonderment. "This is a fine thing you give me, Assha, and the Mother will be pleased, for in many years she has not had such a curtain for her secret place. Also, I am but a little man; the quarrels of great ones are not for me. Since Lurgha has accepted your words, this is none of my affair. Yet I will not go back to the village for a while—with your permission, Assha. For I am a man of loose and wagging tongue and oftentimes I speak what I do not really wish to say. So if I am asked questions, I answer. If I am not there to be asked such questions, I cannot answer."

McNeil laughed and Ashe smiled. "Well enough, Lal. Perhaps you are a wiser man than you think. But also I do not believe you should stay here."

The tribesman was already nodding. "That do I say, too, Assha. You are now facing the Wrath of Lurgha, and with that I wish no part. So I shall go into the marsh for a while. There are birds and hares to hunt, and I shall work upon this fine skin so that when I take it to the Mother it shall indeed be a gift worth her smiles. Now, Assha, if it pleases you, I would go before the night comes."

"Go with good fortune, Lal." Ashe stood apart while

the tribesman ducked his head in a shy, awkward farewell to the others and pattered out into the valley.

"What if they pick him up?" McNeil asked
wearily.

"I don't think they can," Ashe returned. "And what
would you do—keep him here? If we tried that, he'd
scheme to escape and try to turn the tables on us.
Now he'll keep away from Nodren's village and out
of sight for the time being. Lal's not too bright in some
ways, but he's a good hunter. If he has reason for
hiding out, it'll take a better hunter to track him. At
least we know now that the Russians are afraid they
did not make a clean sweep here. What happened,
McNeil?"

While he was telling his story in more detail both
Ashe and Ross worked on his burns, making him
comfortable. Then Ashe sat back as Ross prepared
food.

"How did they spot the post?" McNeil rubbed his
chin and frowned at the fire.

"Only way I can guess is that they picked up our
post signal and pinpointed the source. That means they
must have been hunting us for some time."

"No strangers about lately?"

McNeil shook his head. "Our cover wasn't broken
that way. Sanford was a wonder. If I hadn't known
better, I would have sworn he was born one of the
Beaker folk. He had a network of informants running
all the way from here into Brittany. Amazing how he
was able to work without arousing any suspicions. I
suppose his being a member of the smiths' guild was
a big help. He could pick up a lot of news from any
village where there was one at work. And I tell you,"
McNeil propped himself up on his elbow to exclaim
more vehemently— "there wasn't a whisper of trouble
from here clear across the channel and pretty far to

the north. We were already sure the south was clean before we ever took cover as Beakers, especially since their clans are thick in Spain."

Ashe chewed a broiled wing reflectively. "The permanent Russian base with the transport *has* to be somewhere within the bounds of the territory they hold in our own time."

"They could plant it in Siberia and laugh at us," McNeil exploded. "No hope of getting in there—"

"No." Ashe threw the stripped bone into the fire and licked grease from his fingers. "Then they would be faced with the old problem of distance. If what they are exploiting lay within their modern boundaries, we would never have tumbled to the thing in the first place. What the Russians want must lie outside their twenty-first century holdings, a slender point in our favor. Therefore they will plant their shift point as close to it as they can. Our transportation problem is more difficult than theirs will ever be.

"You know why we chose the arctic for our base; it lies in a section of the world never populated by other than roving hunters. But I'll wager anything you want to name that their point is somewhere in Europe where they have people to contend with. If they are using a plane, they can't risk its being seen—"

"I don't see why not," Ross broke in. "These people couldn't possibly know what it was—Lurgha's bird—magic—"

Ashe shook his head. "They must have the inter-ference-with-history worry as much as we have. Any-thing of our own time has to be hidden or disguised in such a way that the native who may stumble upon it will never know it is manmade. Our sub is a whale to all appearances. Possibly their plane is a bird, but neither can bear too close an examination. We don't know what could result from a leak of real knowledge in this or any primitive time . . . how it might change history—"

"But," Ross advanced what he believed to be the best argument against that reasoning, "suppose I handed Lal a gun and taught him to use it. He couldn't duplicate the weapon—the technology required lies so far beyond his age. These people couldn't reproduce such a thing."

"True enough. On the other hand, don't belittle the ingenuity of the smiths or the native intelligence of men in any era. These tribesmen might not be able to reproduce your gun, but it would set them thinking along new lines. We might find that they would think our time right out of being. No, we dare not play tricks with the past. That is the same situation we faced immediately after the discovery of the atom bomb. Everybody raced to produce that new weapon and then sat around and shivered for fear we'd be crazy enough to use it on each other.

"The Russians have made new discoveries which we have to match, or we will go under. But back in time we have to be careful, both of us, or perhaps destroy the world we *do* live in."

"What do we do now?" McNeil wanted to know.

"Murdock and I came here only for a trial run. It's his test. The sub is to call for us about nine days from now."

"So if we sit tight—if we *can* sit tight—" McNeil lay down again— "they will take us out. Meanwhile we have nine days."

They spent three more days in the cave. McNeil was on his feet and impatient to leave before Ashe was able to hobble well enough to travel. Though Ross and McNeil took turns at hunting and guard duty, they saw no signs that the tribesmen were tracking them. Apparently Lal had done as he promised, withdrawing to the marsh and hiding there apart from his people.

In the gray of pre-dawn on the fourth day Ashe wakened Ross. Their fire had been buried with earth, and already the cave seemed bleak. They ate venison roasted the night before and went out into the chill of a fog. A little way down the valley McNeil joined them out of the mist from his guard post. Keeping their pace to one which favored Ashe's healing wound, they made their way inland in the direction of the track linking the villages.

Crossing that road they continued northward, the land beginning to rise under them. Far away they heard the blatting of sheep, the bark of a dog. In the fog, Ross stumbled in a shallow ditch beyond which lay a stubbled field. Ashe paused to look about him, his nostrils expanding as if he were a hound smelling out their trail.

The three went on, crossing a whole series of small, irregular fields. Ross was sure that the yield from any of these cleared strips must be scanty. The fog was thickening. Ashe pressed the pace, using his hand-made crutch carefully. He gave an audible sigh of relief when they were faced at last by two stone monoliths rising like pillars. A third stone lay across them, forming a rude arch through which they saw a narrow valley running back into the hills.

Through the fog Ross could sense the eerie strangeness of the valley beyond that massive gate. He would have denied that he was superstitious. He had merely studied these tribal beliefs as lessons; he had not accepted them. Yet now, if he had been alone, he would have avoided that place and turned aside from the valley. That which waited within was not for him. To his secret relief Ashe paused by the arch to wait.

The older man gestured the other two into cover.

Ross obeyed willingly, though the dank drops of condensing fog dripped on his cloak and wet his face as he brushed against prickly-leafed shrubs. Here were walls of evergreen plants and dwarf pines almost as if this tunnel of year-round greenery had been planted with some purpose in mind. Once his companions had concealed themselves, Ashe called, shrill but sweetly, with a bird's rising notes. Three times he made that sound before a figure moved in the fog, the rough gray-white of its long cloak melting in the wisps of mist.

Down that green tunnel, out of the heart of the valley, the other came, a loop of cloak concealing the entire figure. It halted right in back of the arch and Ashe, making a gesture to the others to stay where they were, faced the muffled stranger.

"Hands and feet of the Mother, she who sows what may be reaped—"

"Outland stranger who is under the Wrath of Lurgha," the other mocked him in the voice of Cassca. "What do you want, outlander, that you dare to come here where no man may enter?"

"That which you know. For on the night when Lurgha came you also saw—"

Ross heard the hiss of a sharply drawn breath. "How knew you that, outlander?"

"Because you serve the Mother and you are jealous for her and her service. If Lurgha is a mighty god, you wanted to see his acts with your own eyes."

When she finally answered, there was anger as well as frustration in her voice. "And you know of my shame then, Assha. For Lurgha came—on a bird he came, and he did even as he said he would. So now the village will make offerings to Lurgha and beg his favor, and the Mother will no more have those to harken to her words and offer her the first fruits of—"

"But from whence came this bird which was Lurgha, can you tell me that, she who waits upon the Mother?"

"What difference does it make from what direction Lurgha came? That does not add nor take from his power." Cassca moved beneath the arch. "Or does it in some strange way, Assha?"

"Perhaps it does. Only tell me."

She turned slowly and pointed over her right shoulder. "From that way he came, Assha. Well did I watch, knowing that I was the Mother's and that even Lurgha's thunderbolts could not eat me up. Does knowing that make Lurgha smaller in your eyes, Assha? When he has eaten up all that is yours and your kin with it?"

"Perhaps," Assha repeated. "I do not think Lurgha will come so again."

She shrugged, and the heavy cloak flapped. "That shall be as it shall be, Assha. Now go, for it is not good that any man come hither."

Cassca paced back into the heart of the green tunnel, and Ross and McNeil came out of concealment. McNeil faced in the direction she had pointed. "Northeast—" he commented thoughtfully, "the Baltic lies in that quarter."

8

". . . And that is about all." Ten days later Ashe, a dressing on his leg and a few of the pain lines smoothed from his face, sat on a bunk in the arctic time post nursing a mug of coffee in his hands and smiling, a little crookedly, at Nelson Millaird.

Millaird, Kelgarries, Dr. Webb, all the top brass of the project had not only come through the transfer point to meet the three from Britain but were now crammed into the room, nearly pushing Ross and McNeil through the wall. Because this was it! What they had hunted for months—years—now lay almost within their grasp.

Only Millaird, the director, did not seem so confident. A big man with a bushy thatch of coarse graying hair and a heavy, fleshy face, he did not look like a brain. Yet Ross had been on the roster long enough to know that it was Millaird's thick and hairy hands that gathered all the loose threads of Operation Retrograde and deftly wove them into a workable pattern. Now the director leaned back in a chair

which was too small for his bulk, chewing thoughtfully on a toothpick.

"So we have the first whiff of a trail," he commented without elation.

"A pretty strong lead!" Kelgarries broke in. Too
excited to sit still, the major stood with his back against
the door, as alert as if he were about to turn and face
the enemy. "The Russians wouldn't have moved against
Gog if they did not consider it a menace to them.
Their big base must be in this time sector!"

"A big base," Millaird corrected. "The one we are
after, no. And right now they may be switching times.
Do you think they will sit here and wait for us to show
up in force?" But Millaird's tone, intended to deflate,
had no effect on the major.

"And just how long would it take them to dismantle
a big base?" that officer countered. "At least a month.
If we shoot a team in there in a hurry—"

Millaird folded his huge hands over his barrel-
shaped body and laughed, without a trace of humor.
"Just where do we send that team, Kelgarries? Northeast of a coastal point in Britain is a rather vague
direction, to say the least. Not," he spoke to Ashe now,
"that you didn't do all you could, Ashe. And you,
McNeil, nothing to add?"

"No, sir. They jumped us out of the blue when
Sandy thought he had every possible line tapped,
every safeguard working. I don't know how they
caught on to us, unless they located our beam to this
post. If so, they must have been deliberately hunting us for some time, because we only used the
beam as scheduled—"

"The Russians have patience and brains and probably some more of their surprise gadgets to help them.
We have the patience and the brains, but not the
gadgets. And time is against us. Get anything out of

this, Webb?" Millaird asked the hitherto silent third member of his ruling committee.

The quiet man adjusted his glasses on the bridge of his nose, a flattish nose which did not support them very well. "Just another point to add to our surmises. I would say that they are located somewhere near the Baltic Sea. There are old trade routes there, and in our own time it is a territory closed to us. Their installation may be close to the Finnish border. They could disguise their modern station under half a dozen covers; that is a strange country."

Millaird's hands unfolded and he produced a notebook and pen from a shirt pocket. "Won't hurt to stir up some of our present-day intelligence agents. They might just come up with a useful hint. So you'd say the Baltic. But that's a big slice of country."

Webb nodded. "We have one advantage—the old trade routes. In the Beaker period they are pretty well marked. The major one into that section was established for the amber trade. The country is forested, but not so heavily as it was in an earlier period. The native tribes are mostly roving hunters, and fishermen along the coast. But they have had contact with traders." He shoved his glasses back into place with a nervous gesture. "The Russians may run into trouble themselves there at this time—"

"How?" Kelgarries demanded.

"Invasion of the ax people. If they have not yet arrived, they are due very soon. They formed one of the big waves of migratory people, who flooded the country, settled there. Eventually they became the Norse or Celtic stock. We don't know whether they stamped out the native tribes they found there or assimilated them."

"That might be a nice point to have settled more definitely," McNeil commented. "It could mean the difference between getting your skull split and continuing to breathe."

"I don't think they would tangle with the traders. Evidence found today suggests that the Beaker folk simply went on about their business in spite of a change in customers," Webb returned.

"Unless they were pushed into violence." Ashe handed his empty mug to Ross. "Don't forget Lurgha's Wrath. From now on our enemies might take a very dim view of any Beaker trade posts near their property."

Webb shook his head slowly. "A wholesale attack on Beaker establishments would constitute a shift in history. The Russians won't dare that, not just on general suspicion. Remember, they are not any more eager to tinker with history than we are. No, they will watch for us. We will have to stop communication by radio—"

"We can't!" snapped Millaird vehemently. "We can cut it down, but I won't send the boys out without some means of quick communication. You lab boys see what you can turn out in the way of talk boxes that they can't snoop. Time!" He drummed on his knee with his thick fingers. "It all comes back to a question of time."

"Which we do not have," Ashe observed in his usual quiet voice. "If the Russians are afraid they have been spotted, they must be dismantling their post right now, working around the clock. We'll never again have such a good chance to nail them. We must move now."

Millaird's lids drooped almost shut; he might have been napping. Kelgarries stirred restlessly by the door, and Webb's round face had settled into what looked like permanent lines of disapproval.

"Doc," Millaird spoke over his shoulder to the fourth man of his following, "what is your report?"

"Ashe **must** be under treatment for at least five days. McNeil's burns aren't too bad, and Murdock's slash is almost healed."

"Five days—" Millaird droned, and then flashed a glance at the major. "Personnel. We're tied down without any useful personnel. Who in processing could be switched without tangling them up entirely?"

"No one. I can recall Jansen and Van Wyke. These ax people might be a good cover for them." The momentary light in Kelgarries' eyes faded. "No, we have no proper briefing and can't get it until the tribe does appear on the map. I won't send any men in cold. Their blunders would not only endanger them but might menace the whole project."

"So that leaves us with you three," Millaird said. "We'll recall what men we can and brief them again as fast as possible. But you know how long that will take. In the meantime—"

Ashe spoke directly to Webb. "You can't pinpoint the region closer than just the Baltic?"

"We can do this much," the other answered him slowly, and with obvious reluctance. "We can send the sub cruising offshore there for the next five days. If there is any radio activity—any communication—we should be able to trace the beams. It all depends upon whether the Russians have any parties operating from their post. Flimsy—"

"But something!" Kelgarries seized upon it with the relief of one who needed action.

"And they will be waiting for just such a move on our part," Webb continued deliberately.

"All right, so they'll be watching!" the major said, about to lose his temper, "but it is about the only move we can make to back up the boys when they do go in."

He whipped around the door and was gone. Webb

got up slowly. "I will work over the maps again," he told Ashe. "We haven't scouted that area lately, and we don't dare send a reconnaissance plane over it now. Any trip in will be a stab in the dark."

"When you have only one road, you take it," Ashe replied. "I'll be glad to see anything you can show me, Miles."

If Ross had believed that his pre-trial-run cramming had been a rigorous business, he was soon to laugh at that estimation. Since the burden of the next jump would rest on only three of them—Ashe, McNeil, and himself—they were plunged into a whirlwind of instruction, until Ross, dazed and too tired to sleep on the third night, believed that he was more completely bewildered than indoctrinated. He said as much sourly to McNeil.

"Base has pulled back three other teams," McNeil replied. "But the men have to go to school again, and they won't be ready to come on for maybe three, four weeks. To change runs means unlearning stuff as well as learning it—"

"What about new men?"

"Don't think Kelgarries isn't out now beating the bushes for some! Only, we have to be fitted to the physical type we are supposed to represent. For instance, set a small, dark-headed pugnose among your Norse sea rovers, and he's going to be noticed— maybe remembered too well. We can't afford to take that chance. So Kelgarries had to discover men who not only look the part but are also temperamentally fitted for this job. You can't plant a fellow who thinks as a seaman—not a seaman, you understand, but one whose mind works in that pattern—among a wandering tribe of cattle herders. The protection for the man and the project lies in his being fitted into the right spot at the right time."

Ross had never really thought of that point before. Now he realized that he and Ashe and McNeil were of a common mold. All about the same height, they shared brown hair and light eyes—Ashe's blue, his own gray and McNeil's hazel—and they were of similar build, small-boned, lean, and quick-moving. He had not seen any of the true Beakermen except on the films. But now, recalling those, he could see that the three time traders were of the same general physical type as the far-roving people they used as a cover.

It was on the morning of the fifth day while the three were studying a map Webb had produced that Kelgarries, followed at his own weighty pace by Millaird, burst in upon them.

"We have it! This time *we* have the luck! The Russians slipped. Oh, how they slipped!"

Webb watched the major, a thin little smile pulling at his pursed mouth. "Miracles sometimes do happen," he remarked. "I suppose the sub has a fix for us."

Kelgarries passed over the flimsy strip of paper he had been waving as a banner of triumph. Webb read the notation on it and bent over the map, making a mark with one of those needle-sharp pencils which seemed to grow in his breast pocket, ready for use. Then he made a second mark.

"Well, it narrows it a bit," he conceded. Ashe looked in turn and laughed.

"I would like to hear your definition of 'narrow' sometime, Miles. Remember we have to cover this on foot, and a difference of twenty miles can mean a lot."

"That mark is quite a bit in from the sea." McNeil offered his own protest when he saw the marking. "We don't know that country—"

Webb shoved his glasses back for the hundredth time that morning. "I suppose we could consider this critical, condition red," he said in such a dubious tone that he might have been begging someone to protest his statement. But no one did. Millaird was busy with the map.

"I think we do, Miles!" He looked to Ashe. "You'll parachute in. The packs with which you will be equipped are special stuff. Once you have them off, sprinkle them with a powder Miles will provide and in ten minutes there won't be enough of them left for anyone to identify. We haven't but a dozen of these, and we can't throw them away except in a crisis. Find the base and rig up the detector. Your fix in this time will be easy—but it is the other end of the line we must have. Until you locate that, stick to the job. Don't communicate with us until you have it!"

"There is the possibility," Ashe pointed out, "the Russians may have more than one intermediate post. They probably have played it smart and set up a series of them to spoil a direct trace, as each would lead only to another farther back in time—"

"All right. If that proves true, just get us the next one back," Millaird returned. "From that we can trace them along if we must send in some of the boys wearing dinosaur skins later. We *have* to find their primary base, and if that hunt goes the hard way, well, we do it the hard way."

"How did you get the fix?" McNeil asked.

"One of their field parties ran into trouble and yelled for help."

"Did they get it?"

The major grinned. "What do you think? You know the rules—and the ones the Russians play by are twice as tough on their own men."

"What kind of trouble?" Ashe wanted to know.

"Some kind of a local religious dispute. We do our best with their code, but we're not a hundred percent perfect in reading it, I gather they were playing with a local god and got their fingers burned."

"Lurgha again, eh?" Ashe smiled.

"Foolish," Webb said impatiently. "That is a silly thing to do. You were almost over the edge of prudence yourself, Gordon, with that Lurgha business. Using the Great Mother was a ticklish thing to try and you were lucky to get out of it so easily."

"Once was enough," Ashe agreed. "Though using it may have saved our lives. But I assure you I am not starting a holy war or setting up as a prophet."

Ross had been taught something of map reading, but mentally he could not make what he saw on paper resemble the countryside. A few landmarks, if there were any outstanding ones, were all he could hope to impress upon his memory until he was actually on the ground.

Landing there according to Millaird's instruction was another experience he would not have chosen of his own accord. To jump was a matter of timing, and in the dark with a measure of rain thrown in, the action was anything but pleasant. Leaving the plane in a blind, follow-the-leader fashion, Ross found the descent into darkness one of the worst trials he had yet faced. But he did not make too bad a landing in the small parklike expanse they had chosen for their target.

Ross pulled loose his harness and chute, dragging them to what he judged to be the center of the clearing. Hearing a plaintive bray from the air, he dodged as one of the two pack donkeys sent to join them landed and began to kick at its trappings. The animals they had chosen were the most docile available and they had been given sedation before the jump so that now, feeling Ross's hands, the donkey stood quietly while Ross stripped it of its hanging straps.

"Rossa—" The sound of his Beaker name called through the dark brought Ross facing in the other direction.

"Here, and I have one of the donkeys."

"And I the other!" That was McNeil.

Their eyes adjusted to a gloom which was not as thick as it would be in the forest and they worked fast. Then they dragged the parachutes together in a heap. The rain would, Webb had assured them, add to the rapid destruction wrought by the chemical he had provided. Ashe shook it over the pile, and there was a faint greenish glow. Then they moved away to the woodland and made camp for the balance of the night.

So much of their whole exploit depended upon luck, and this small part had been successful. Unless some agent had been stationed to watch for their arrival, Ross believed they could not be spotted.

The rest of their plan was elastic. Posing as traders who had come to open a new station, they were to stay near a river which drained a lake and then angled southward to the distant sea. They knew this section was only sparsely settled by small tribes, hardly larger than family clans. These people were generations behind the developmental level of the villages of Britain—roving hunters who followed the sweep of game north or south with the seasons.

Along the seashore the fishermen had established more permanent holdings which were slowly becoming towns. There were perhaps a few hardy pioneer farmers on the southern fringes of the district, but the principal reason traders came to this region was to get amber and furs. The Beaker people dealt in both.

Now as the three sheltered under the wide

branches of a towering pine Ashe fumbled with a
pack and brought out the "beaker" which was the
identifying mark of his adopted people. He measured
into it a portion of the sour, stimulating drink which
the traders introduced wherever they went. The cup
passed from hand to hand, its taste unpleasant on
the tongue, but comfortingly warm to one's middle.

They took turns keeping the watch until the gray
of false dawn became the clearer light of morning.
After breakfasting on flat cakes of meal, they packed
the donkeys, using the same knots and cross lashing which were the mark of real Beaker traders.
Their bows protected from dampness under their
cloaks, they set out to find the river and their path
southward.

Ashe led, Ross towed the donkeys, and McNeil
brought up the rear. In the absence of a path they
had to set a ragged course, keeping to the edge of
the clearing until they saw the end of the lake.

"Woodsmoke," Ashe commented when they had
completed two thirds of their journey. Ross sniffed and
was able to smell it too. Nodding to Ashe, McNeil
oozed into nothingness between the trees with an ease
Murdock envied. As they waited for him to return,
Ross became conscious of another life about them, one
busy with its own concerns, which were in no way
those of human beings, except that food and shelter
were to be reckoned among them.

In Britain, Ross had known there were others of
his kind about, but this was different. Here, he could
have easily believed that he was the first man to walk
this way.

A squirrel ran out on a tree limb and surveyed the
two men with curious beady eyes, then clung head
down on the tree trunk to see them better. One of
the donkeys tossed its head, and the squirrel was gone

with a flit of its tail. Although it was quiet, there was a hum underneath the surface which Ross tried to analyze, to identify the many small sounds which went into its making.

Perhaps because he was trying so hard, he noted the faint noise. His hand touched Ashe's arm and a slight movement of his head indicated the direction of the sound. Then, as fluidly as he had melted into the woods, McNeil returned. "Company," he said in a soft voice.

"What kind?"

"Tribesmen, but wilder than any I've seen, even on the tapes. We are certainly out on the fringes now. These people look about cave level. I don't think they've ever heard of traders."

"How many?"

"Three, maybe four families. Most of the males must be out hunting, but there're about ten children and six or seven women. I don't think they've had good luck lately by the look of them."

"Maybe their luck and ours are going to run together," Ashe said, motioning Ross forward with the donkeys. "We will circle about them to the river and then try bartering later. But I do want to establish contact."

9

"Not to be too hopeful but—" McNeil rubbed his arm across his hot face— "so far, so good."

After kicking from his path some of the branches Ross had lopped from the trees they had been felling, he went to help his companion roll another small log up to a shelter which was no longer temporary. If there had been any eyes other than the woodland hunters' to spy upon them, they would have seen only the usual procedure of the Beaker traders, busily constructing one of their posts.

That they were being watched by the hunters, all three were certain. That there might be other spies in the forest, they had to assume for their own safety. They might prowl at night, but in the daytime all of the time agents kept within the bounds of the roles they were acting.

Barter with the head men of the hunting clan had brought those shy people into the camp of the strangers who had such wonders to exchange for tanned deer hides and better furs. The news of the traders' arrival spread quickly during the short time they had been here, so that two other clans had sent men to watch the proceedings.

With the trade came news which the agents sifted and studied. Each of them had a list of questions to insert into their conversations with the tribesmen if and when that was possible. Although they did not share a common speech with the forest men, signs were informative and certain nouns could be quickly learned. In the meantime Ashe became friendly with the nearest and first of the clan groups they discovered, going hunting with the men as an excuse to penetrate the unknown section they must quarter in their search for the Russian base.

Ross drank river water and mopped his own hot face. "If the Russians aren't traders," he mused aloud, "what *is* their cover?"

McNeil shrugged. "A hunting tribe—fishermen—"

"Where would they get the women and children?"

"The same way they get their men—recruit them in our own time. Or in the way lots of tribes grew during periods of stress."

Ross set down the water jug. "You mean, kill off the men, take over their families?" This was a cold-bloodedness he found sickening. Although he had always prided himself on his toughness, several times during his training at the project he had been confronted by things which shook his belief in his own strong stomach and nerve.

"It has been done," McNeil remarked bleakly, "hundreds of times by invaders. In this setup—small family clans, widely scattered—that move would be very easy."

"They would have to pose as farmers, not hunters," Ross pointed out. "They couldn't move a base around with them."

"All right, so they set up a farming village. Oh, I see what you mean—there isn't any village around here. Yet they are here, maybe underground."

How right their guesses were they learned that night when Ashe returned, a deer's haunch on his shoulder. Ross knew him well enough by now to sense his preoccupation. "You found something?"

"A new set of ghosts," Ashe replied with a strange little smile.

"Ghosts!" McNeil pounced upon that. "The Russians like to play the supernatural angle, don't they? First the voice of Lurgha and now ghosts. What do these ghosts do?"

"They inhabit a bit of hilly territory southeast of here, a stretch taboo for all hunters. We were following a bison track until the beast headed for the ghost country. Then Ulffa called us off in a hurry. It seems that the hunter who goes in there after his quarry never reappears, or if he does, it's in a damaged condition, blown upon by ghosts and burned to death! That's one point."

He sat down by the fire and stretched his arms wearily. "The second is a little more disturbing for us. A Beaker camp about twenty miles south of here, as far as I can judge, was exterminated just a week ago. The message was passed to me because I was thought to be a kinsman of the slain—"

McNeil sat up. "Done because they were hunting us?"

"Might well be. On the other hand, the affair may have been just one of general precaution."

"The ghosts did it?" Ross wanted to know.

"I asked that. No, it seems that strange tribesmen overran it at night."

"At night?" McNeil whistled.

"Just so." Ashe's tone was dry. "The tribes do not

fight that way. Either someone slipped up in his briefing, or the Russians are overconfident and don't care about the rules. But it was the work of tribesmen, or their counterfeits. There is also a nasty rumor speeding about that the ghosts do not relish traders and that they might protest intrusions of such with penalties all around—"

"Like the Wrath of Lurgha," supplied Ross.

"There is a certain repetition in this which rouses the suspicious mind," Ashe agreed.

"I'd say no more hunting expeditions for the present," McNeil said. "It is too easy to mistake a friend for a deer and weep over his grave afterward."

"That is a thought which entered my mind several times this afternoon," Ashe agreed. "These people are deceptively simple on the surface, but their minds do not work along the same patterns as ours. We try to outwit them, but it takes only one slip to make it fatal. In the meantime, I think we'd better make this place a little more snug, and it might be well to post sentries as unobtrusively as possible."

"How about faking some signs of a ruined camp and heading into the blue ourselves?" McNeil asked. "We could strike for the ghost mountains, traveling by night, and Ulffa's crowd would think we were finished off."

"An idea to keep in mind. The point against it would be the missing bodies. It seems that the tribesmen who raided the Beaker camp left some very distasteful evidence of what happened to the camp's personnel. And those we can't produce to cover our trail."

McNeil was not yet convinced. "We might be able to fake something along that line, too—"

"We may not have to fake anything," Ross cut in

softly. He was standing close to the edge of the clearing where they were building their hut, his hand on one of the saplings in the palisade they had set up so laboriously that day. Ashe was beside him in an instant.

"What is it?"

Ross's hours of listening to the sounds of the wilderness were his measuring gauge now. "That bird has never called from inland before. It is the blue one we've seen fishing for frogs along the river."

Ashe, not even glancing at the forest, went for the water jug. "Get your trail supplies," he ordered.

Their leather pouches which held enough rations to keep them going were always at hand. McNeil gathered them from behind the fur curtain fronting their half-finished cabin. Again the bird called, its cry piercing and covering a long distance. Ross could understand why a careless man would select it for the signal. He crossed the clearing to the donkeys' shelter, slashing through their nose halters. Probably the patient little beasts would swiftly fall victims to some forest prowlers, but at least they would have their chance to escape.

McNeil, his cloak slung about him to conceal the ration bags, picked up the leather bucket as if he were merely going down to the river for water, and came to join Ross. They believed that they were carrying it off well, that the camp must appear normal to any lurkers in the woods. But either they had made some slip or the enemy was impatient. An arrow sped out of the night to flash across the fire, and Ashe escaped death only because he had leaned forward to feed the flames. His arm swung out and sent the water in the jar hissing onto the blaze as he himself rolled in the other direction.

Ross plunged for the brush with McNeil. Lying flat

on the half-frozen ground, they started to work their
way to the river bank where the open area would
make surprise less possible.

"Ashe?" he whispered and felt McNeil's warm
breath on his cheek as he replied:

"He'll make it the other way! He's the best we have
for this sort of job."

They made a worm's progress, twice lying still,
with dagger in hand, while they listened to a faint
rustle which betrayed the passing of one of the
attackers. Both times Ross was tempted to rise and
try to cut off the stranger, but he fought down the
impulse. He had learned self-control that would have
been impossible a few months earlier.

The glimmer of the river was pale through the
clumps of bushes which sometimes grew into the
flood. In this country winter still clung tenaciously in
shadowy places with cups of leftover snow, and there
was a bite in the wind and water. Ross rose to his
knees with an involuntary gasp as a scream cut through
the night. He jerked around toward the camp, only
to feel McNeil's hand clamp on his forearm.

"That was a donkey," whispered McNeil urgently.
"Come on, let's go down to that ford we discovered!"

They turned south, daring now to trot, half bent
to the ground. The river was swollen with spring floods
which were only now beginning to subside, but two
days earlier they had noticed a sandbar at one spot.
By crossing that shelf across the bed, they might hope
to put water between them and the unknown enemy
tonight. It would give them a breathing space, even
though Ross privately shrank from the thought of
plowing into the stream. He had seen good-sized trees
swirling along in the current only yesterday. And to
make such a dash in the dark . . .

From McNeil's throat burst a startling sound which

Ross had last heard in Britain—the questing howl of a hunting wolf. The cry was answered seconds later from downstream.

"Ashe!"

They worked their way along the edge of the water with continued care, until they came upon Ashe at last, so much a part of his background that Ross started when the lump he had taken for a bush hunched forward to join them. Together they made the river crossing and turned south again to head for the mountains.

It was then that disaster struck.

Ross heard no birdcall warning this time. Though he was on guard, he never sensed the approach of the man who struck him down from behind. One moment he had been trailing McNeil and Ashe; the next moment was black nothingness.

He was aware of a throb of pain which carried throughout his body and then localized in his head. Forcing open his eyes, the dazzle of light was like a spear point striking directly into his head, intensifying his pain to agony. He brought his hand up to his face and felt stickiness there.

"Assha—" He believed he called that aloud, but he did not even hear his own voice. They were in a valley; a wolf had attacked him out of the bushes. Wolf? No, the wolf was dead, but then it came alive again to howl on a river bank.

Ross forced his eyes open once more, enduring the pain of beams he recognized as sunshine. He turned his head to avoid the glare. It was hard to focus, but he fought to steady himself. There was some reason why it was necessary to move, to get away. But away from what and where? When Ross tried to think he could only see muddled pictures which had no connection.

Then a moving object crossed his very narrow field of vision, passing between him and a thing he knew was a tree trunk. A four-footed creature with a red tongue hanging from its jaws. It came toward him stiff-legged, growling low in its throat, and sniffed at his body before barking in short excited bursts of sound.

The noise hurt his head so much that Ross closed his eyes. Then a shock of icy liquid thrown into his face aroused him to make a feeble protest and he saw, hanging over him in a strange upside-down way, a bearded face which he knew came from the past.

Hands were laid on him. The roughness with which he was moved sent Ross spiraling back into the dark once more. When he aroused for the second time it was night and the pain in his head was dulled. He put out his hands and discovered that he lay on a pile of fur robes, and was covered by one.

"Assha—" Again he tried that name. But it was not Assha who came in answer to his feeble call. The woman who knelt beside him with a horn cup in her hand had neatly braided hair in which gray strands showed silver by firelight. Ross knew he had seen her before, but again where and when eluded him. She slipped a sturdy arm under his head and raised him while the world whirled about. The edge of the horn cup was pressed to his lips, and he drank bitter stuff which burned in his throat and lit a fire in his insides. Then he was left to himself once again and in spite of his pain and bewilderment he slept.

How many days he lay in the camp of Ulffa, tended by the chief's head wife, Ross found it hard to reckon. It was Frigga who had argued the tribe into caring for a man they believed almost dead when they found him, and who nursed Ross back to life with knowledge acquired through half a hundred exchanges between those wise women who were the doctors and priestesses of these roaming peoples.

Why Frigga had bothered with the injured stranger at all Ross learned when he was able to sit up and marshal his bewildered thoughts into some sort of order. The matriarch of the tribe thirsted for knowledge. That same urge which had led her to certain experiments with herbs, had made her consider Ross a challenge to her healing skill. When she knew that he would live she determined to learn from him all he had to give.

Ulffa and the men of the tribe might have eyed the metal weapons of the traders with awe and avid desire, but Frigga wanted more than trade goods. She wanted the secret of the making of such cloth as the strangers wore, everything she could learn of their lives and the lands through which they had come. She plied Ross with endless questions which he answered as best he could, for he lay in an odd dream state where only the present had any reality. The past was dim and far away, and while he was now and then dimly aware that he had something to do, he forgot it easily.

The chief and his men prowled the half-built station after the attackers had withdrawn, bringing back with them a handful of loot—a bronze razor, two skinning knives, some fishhooks, a length of cloth which Frigga appropriated. Ross eyed this spoil indifferently, making no claim upon it. His interest in everything about him was often blanked out by headaches which kept him limp on his bed, uncaring and stupid for hours or even full days.

He gathered that the tribe had been living in fear of an attack from the same raiders who had wiped out the trading post. But at last their scouts returned with the information that the enemy had gone south. There was one change of which Ross was not aware but which might have startled both Ashe and McNeil. Ross Murdock had indeed died under that blow which had left him unconscious beside the river. The young man whom Frigga had drawn back to sense and a slow recovery was Rossa of the Beaker people. The same Rossa nursed a hot desire for vengeance against those who had struck him down and captured his kinsmen, a feeling which the family tribe who had rescued him could well understand.

There was the same old urgency pushing him to try his strength now, to keep to his feet even when they were unsteady. His bow was gone, but Ross spent hours fashioning another, and he traded his copper bracelet for the best dozen arrows in Ulffa's camp. The jet pin from his cloak he presented to Frigga with all his gratitude.

Now that his strength was coming back he could not rest easy in the camp. He was ready to leave, even though the gashes on his head were still tender to the touch. Ulffa indulgently planned a hunt southward, and Rossa took the trail with the tribesmen.

He broke with the clan hunters when they turned aside at the beginning of the taboo land. Ross, his own mind submerged and taken over by his Beaker cover, hesitated too. Yet he could not give up, and the others left him there, his eyes on the forbidden heights, unhappy and tormented by more than the headaches which still came and went with painful regularity. In the mountains lay what he sought—a hidden something within his brain told him that over and over—but the mountains were taboo, and he should not venture into them.

How long he might have hesitated there if he had not come upon the trail, Ross did not know. But on the day after the hunters of Ulffa's clan left, a glint of sunlight striking between two trees pointed out a woodsman's blaze on a third tree trunk. The two halves of Ross's memory clicked together for an instant as he examined that cut. He knew that it marked a trace and he pushed on, hunting a second cut and then a third. Convinced that these would lead him into the unknown territory, Ross's desire to explore overcame the grafted superstitions of his briefing.

There were other signs that this was an often-traveled route: a spring cleared of leaves and walled with stone, a couple of steps cut in the turf on a steep slope. Ross moved warily, alert to any sound. He might not be an expert woodsman, but he was learning fast, perhaps the faster because his false memories now supplanted the real ones.

That night he built no fire, crawling instead into the heart of a rotted log to sleep, awakening once to the call of a wolf and another time at the distant crash of a dead tree yielding to the wind.

In the morning he was about to climb back to the trail he had prudently left the night before when he saw five bearded, fur-clad men resembling Ulffa's people. Ross hugged the earth and watched them pass out of sight before he followed.

All that day he wove up-and-down a trail behind the small band, sometimes catching sight of them as they topped a rise well ahead or stopped to eat. It was late afternoon when he crept cautiously to the top of a ridge and gazed down into a valley.

There was a town in that valley, sturdy houses of logs behind a stockade. He had seen towns vaguely like it before, yet it had a dreamlike quality as if it were not as real as it appeared.

Ross rested his chin on his arms and watched that town and the people moving in it. Some were fur-clad hunters, but others dressed quite differently. He started up with a little cry at the sight of one of the men who had walked so swiftly from one house to the next; surely he was a Beaker trader!

His unease grew stronger with every moment he watched, but it was the oddness he sensed in that town which bothered him and not any warning that he, himself, was in danger. He had gotten to his knees to see better when out of nowhere a rope sang through the air, settling about his chest with a vicious jerk which not only drove the air from his lungs but pinioned his arms tight to his body.

10

Having been cuffed and battered into submission more quickly than would have been possible three weeks earlier, Murdock now stood sullenly surveying the man, who, though he dressed like a Beaker trader, persisted in using a language Ross did not know.

"We do not play as children here." At last the man spoke words Ross could understand. "You will answer me or else others shall ask the questions, and less gently. I say to you now—who are you and from where do you come?"

For a moment Ross glowered across the table at him, his inbred antagonism to authority aroused by that contemptuous demand, but then common sense cautioned. His initial introduction to this village had left him bruised and with one of his headaches. There was no reason to let them beat him until he was in no shape to make a break for freedom when and if there was an opportunity.

"I am Rossa of the traders," he returned, eyeing the man with a carefully measured stare. "I came into this land in search of my kinsman who were taken by raiders in the night."

The man, who sat on a stool by the table, smiled slowly. Again he spoke in the strange tongue, and Ross merely stared stolidly back. His words were short and explosive sounding, and the man's smile faded; his annoyance grew as he continued to speak.

One of Ross's two guards ventured to interrupt, using the Beaker language. "From where did you come?" He was a quiet-faced, slender man, not like his brutish companion, who had roped Murdock from behind and had been able to subdue Ross in short order.

"I came to this land from the south," Ross answered, "after the manner of my people. This is a new land with furs and the golden tears of the sun to be gathered and bartered. The traders move in peace, and their hands are raised against no man. Yet in the darkness there came those who would slay without profit, for what reason I know not."

The quiet man continued the questioning and Ross answered fully with details of the past of one Rossa, a Beaker merchant. Yes, he was from the south. His father was Gurdi, who had a trading post in the warm lands along the big river. This was Rossa's first trip to open new territory. He had come with his father's blood brother, Assha, who was a noted far voyager, and it was an honor to be chosen as donkey-leader for such a one as Assha. With Assha had been Macna, one who was also a far trader, though not as noted as Assha.

Of a certainty, Assha was of his own race! Ross blinked at that question. One need only to look upon him to know that he was of trader blood and no uncivilized woodsrunner. How long had he known Assha? Ross shrugged. Assha had come to his father's post the winter before and had stayed with them through the cold season. Gurdi and Assha had mingled blood after he pulled Gurdi free from the river in flood. Assha had lost his boat and trade goods in that rescue, so Gurdi had made good his loss this year. Detail by detail he gave the story. In spite of the fact that he provided these details glibly, sure that they were true, Ross continued to be haunted by an odd feeling that he was indeed reciting a tale of some adventure which had happened long ago and to someone else. Perhaps that pain in his head made him think of these events as very colorless and far away.

"It would seem"—the quiet man turned to the one behind the table— "that this is indeed one Rossa, a Beaker trader."

But the man looked impatient, angry. He made a sign to the other guard, who turned Ross around roughly and shoved him toward the door. Once again the leader gave an order in his own language, adding a few words more with a stinging snap that might have been a threat or a warning.

Ross was thrust into a small room with a hard floor and not even a skin rug to serve as a bed. Since the quiet man had ordered the removal of the ropes from Ross's arms, he leaned against the wall, rubbing the pain of returning circulation away from his wrists and trying to understand what had happened to him and where he was. Having spied upon it from the heights, he knew it wasn't an ordinary trading station, and he wanted to know what they did here. Also, somewhere in this village he hoped to find Assha and Macna.

At the end of the day his captors opened the door only long enough to push inside a bowl and a small jug. He felt for those in the dusk, dipping his fingers into a lukewarm mush of meal and drinking the water from the jug avidly. His headache dulled, and from experience Ross knew that this bout was almost over. If he slept, he would waken with a clearer mind and no pain. Knowing he was very tired, he took the precaution of curling up directly in front of the door so that no one could enter without arousing him.

It was still dark when he awoke with a curious urgency remaining from a dream he could not remember. Ross sat up, flexing his arms and shoulders to combat the stiffness which had come with his cramped sleep. He could not rid himself of a feeling that there was something to be done and that time was his enemy.

Assha! Gratefully he seized on that. He must find Assha and Macna. Surely the three of them could find a way to get out of this village. That was what was so important!

He had been handled none too gently, and they were holding him a prisoner. But Ross believed that this was not the worst which could happen to him here, and he must be free before the worst did come. The question was, How could he escape? His bow and dagger were gone, and he did not even have his long cloak pin for a weapon, since he had given that to Frigga.

Running his hands over his body, Ross inventoried what remained of his clothing and possessions. He unfastened the bronze chain-belt still buckled in his kilt tunic, swinging the length speculatively in one hand. A masterpiece of craftsmanship, it consisted of patterned plates linked together with a series of five finely wrought chains and a front buckle in the form of a lion's head, its protruding tongue serving as a hook to support a dagger sheath. Its weight made it a weapon of sorts, which if added to the element of surprise might free him.

By rights they would be expecting him to produce

some opposition, however. It was well known that only
the best fighters, the shrewdest minds, followed the
traders' roads. It was a proud thing to be a trader in
the wilderness, a thought that warmed Ross now as
he waited in the dark for what luck Ba-Bal of the
Bright Horns would send. Were he ever to return to
Gurdi's post, Ba-Bal, whose boat rode across the sky
from dawn to dusk, would have a fine ox, jars of the
first brewing, and sweet-smelling amber laid upon his
altar.

Ross had patience which he had learned from the
mixed heritage of his two parts, the real and the false
graft. He could wait as he had waited many times
before—quietly with outward ease—for the right
moment to come. It came now with sharply ringing
footsteps that halted before his cell door.

Silently as a hunting cat, Ross flung himself from
behind the door to a wall, where he would be hidden from the newcomer for that necessary instant or
two. If his attack was to be successful, it must occur
inside the room. He heard the sound of a bar being
slid out of its brackets, and he poised himself, the belt
rippling from his right hand.

The door was opening inward, and a man stood
silhouetted against the outer light. He muttered, looking toward the corner where Ross had thrown his
single garment in a roll to suggest a man curled in
slumber. The man in the doorway took the bait,
coming forward far enough for Ross to send the door
slamming shut as he himself sprang with the belt
aimed for the other's head.

There was a startled cry, cut off in the middle as
the belt plates met flesh and bone. Luck was with
him! Ross caught up his kilt and belted it around
him after a hurried examination of the body now
lying at his feet. He didn't think the man was dead,

but at any rate he was unconscious. Ross stripped off the man's cloak, located his dagger, freed it from the belt hook and snapped it on his own.

Then inch by inch Ross edged open the door, peering through the crack. As far as he could see, the hall was empty, so he jerked the portal open. Dagger in hand he sprang out, ready for attack. He closed the door, slipping the bar back into its brackets. If the man inside revived and pounded for attention, his own friends might think it was Ross and delay investigating.

But the escape from the cell was the easiest part of what he planned to do, as Ross well knew. To find Assha and Macna in this maze of rooms occupied by the enemy would be far more difficult. Although he had no idea in which of the village buildings they might be confined, this one was the largest and seemed to be the headquarters of the chief men, so it might also serve as a prison.

Light came from a torch in a bracket halfway down the hall. The wood burned smokily, giving off a resinous odor, and the glow gave Ross enough light. He slipped along as close to the wall as he could, ready to freeze at the slightest sound. But this portion of the building seemed deserted, for he saw or heard no one. He tried the only two doors opening out of the hall, but they were secured on the other side. Then he came to a bend in the corridor, and stopped short, hearing a murmur of low voices.

If he had used a hunter's tricks of silent tread and watchfulness before, Ross was doubly on guard now as he wriggled to a point which enabled him to see beyond that turn. Mere luck prevented him from giving himself away a moment later.

Assha! Assha, alive, well, apparently under no restraint, was just turning away from the same quiet man who had had a part in Ross's interrogation. That was surely Assha's brown hair, his familiar tilt of the head convinced Ross, though he could not see the man's face. The quiet man went down the hall, leaving Assha before a door. As he passed through it Ross sped forward and followed him inside.

Assha had crossed the bare room and was standing on a glowing plate in the floor. Ross, aroused to desperate action by some fear he did not understand, leaped after him. His left hand fell upon Assha's shoulder, turning the man half around as Ross, too, stepped upon the patch of luminescence.

Murdock had only an instant to realize that he was staring into the face of an astonished stranger. His hands flashed up in an edgewise blow which caught the other on the side of the throat, and then the world came apart about them. There was a churning, whirling nausea which gripped and bent Ross almost double across the crumpled body of his victim. He held his head lest it be torn from his shoulders by the spinning thing which seemed based behind his eyes.

The sickness lasted only a moment, and some buried part of Ross's mind accepted it as a phenomenon he had experienced before. He came out of it gasping, to focus his attention once more on the man at his feet.

The stranger was still breathing. Ross stooped to drag him from the plate and began binding and gagging him with lengths torn from his kilt. Only when his captive was secure did he begin looking about him curiously.

The room was bare of any furnishings and now, as he glanced at the floor, Ross saw that the plate had lost its glow. The Beaker trader Rossa rubbed sweating palms on his kilt and thought fleetingly of forest ghosts and other mysteries. Not that the traders bowed to those ghosts which were the plague of lesser men and tribes, but anything which suddenly appeared and disappeared without any logical explanation needed thinking on. Murdock pulled the prisoner, who was now reviving, to the far end of the room and then went back to the plate with the persistence of a man who refused to treat with ghosts and wanted something to explain the unexplainable. Though he rubbed his hands across the smooth surface of the plate, it did not light up again.

His captive having writhed himself half out of the corner of the room, Ross debated the wisdom of another silencing—say a tap on the skull with the heavy hilt of his dagger. Deciding against it because he might need a guide, he freed the victim's ankle bonds and pulled him to his feet, holding the dagger ready where the man could see it. Were there any more surprises to be encountered in this place, Assha's double would test them first.

The door did not lead to the same corridor, or even the same kind of corridor Ross had passed through moments earlier. Instead they entered a short passage with walls of some smooth stuff. It had almost the sheen of polished metal and was sleek and cold to the touch. In fact, the whole place was chill, chill as river water in the spring.

Still herding the prisoner before him, Ross came to the nearest door and looked within, to be faced by incomprehensible frames of metal rods and boxes. Rossa of the traders marveled and stared, but again, he realized that what he saw was not altogether strange. Part of one wall was a board on which small lights flashed and died, to flash again in winks of bright color. A mysterious object made of wire and disks hung across the back of a nearby chair.

The bound man lurched for the chair and fell,

rolling toward the wall. Ross pushed him on until he was hidden behind one of the metal boxes. Then he made the rounds of the room, touching nothing, but studying what he could not understand. Puffs of warm air came in through grills near the floor, but the room was as chilly as the hall outside.

Meanwhile the lights on the board had become more active, flashing on and off in complex patterns. Ross now heard a buzzing, as if a swarm of angry insects were gathered for an attack. Crouching beside his captive, Ross watched the lights, trying to discover the source of the sound.

The buzz grew shriller, almost demanding. Ross heard the tramp of heavy footgear in the corridor, and a man entered the room, crossing purposefully to the chair. He sat down and drew the wire-and-disk frame over his head. His hands moved under the lights, but Ross could not guess what he was doing.

The captive at Murdock's side tried to stir, but Ross's hand pinned him quiet. The shrill noise which had originally summoned the man at the lights was interrupted by a sharp pattern of long-and-short sounds, and his hands flew even more quickly while Ross took in every detail of the other's clothing and equipment. He was neither a shaggy tribesman nor a trader. He wore a dull-green outer garment cut in one piece to cover his arms and legs as well as his body, and his hair was so short that his round skull might have been shaved. Ross rubbed the back of his wrist across his eyes, experiencing again that dim other memory. Odd as this man looked, Murdock had seen his like before somewhere, yet the background had not been Gurdi's post on the southern river. Where and when had he, Rossa, ever been with such strange beings? And why could he not remember it all more clearly?

Boots sounded once more in the hall, and another figure strode in. This one wore furs, but he, too, was no woods hunter, Ross realized as he studied the newcomer in detail. The loose overshirt of thick fur with its hood thrown back, the high boots, and all the rest were not of any primitive fashioning. And the man had four eyes! One pair were placed normally on either side of his nose, and the other two, black-rimmed and murky, were set above on his forehead.

The fur-clad man tapped the one seated at the board. He freed his head partially from the wire cage so that they could talk together in a strange language while lights continued to flash and the buzzing died away. Ross's captive wriggled with renewed vigor and at last thrashed free a foot to kick at one of the metal installations. The resulting clang brought both men around. The one at the board tore his head cage off as he jumped to his feet, while the other brought out a gun.

Gun? One little fraction of Ross's mind wondered at his recognition of that black thing and of the danger it promised, even as he prepared for battle. He pushed his captive across the path of the man in fur and threw himself in the other direction. There was a blast to make a torment in his head as he hurled toward the door.

So intent was Ross upon escape that he did not glance behind but skidded out on his hands and knees, thus fortunately presenting a poor target to the third man coming down the hall. Ross's shoulder hit the newcomer at thigh level, and they tangled in a strug-gling mass which saved Ross's life as the others burst out behind them.

Ross fought grimly, his hands and feet moving in blows he was not conscious of planning. His oppo-nent was no easy match and at last Ross was flattened, in spite of his desperate efforts. He was whirled over, his arms jerked behind him, and cold metal rings snapped about his wrists. Then he was rolled back, to lie blinking up at his enemies.

All three men gathered over him, barking questions which he could not understand. One of them disappeared and returned with Ross's former captive, his mouth a straight line and a light in his eyes Ross understood far better than words.

"You are the trader prisoner?" The man who looked like Assha leaned over Murdock, patches of red on his tanned skin where the gag and wrist bonds had been.

"I am Rossa, son of Gurdi, of the traders," Ross returned, meeting what he read in the other's expression with a ready defiance. "I was a prisoner, yes. But you did not keep me one for long then, nor shall you now."

The man's thin upper lip lifted. "You have done yourself ill, my young friend. We have a better prison here for you, one from which you shall not escape."

He spoke to the other men, and there was the ring of an order in his voice. They pulled Ross to his feet, pushing him ahead of them. During the short march Ross took note of things he could not identify in the rooms through which they passed. Men called questions and at last they paused long enough, Ross firmly in the hold of the fur-clad guard, for the other two to put on similar garments.

Ross had lost his cloak in the fight, but no fur shirt was given him. He shivered more and more as the chill which clung to that warren of rooms and halls bit into his half-clad body. He was certain of only one thing about this place: he could not possibly be in the crude buildings of the valley village. However, he was unable to guess where he was or how he had come there.

Finally, they went down a narrow room filled with bulky metal objects of bright scarlet or violet that gleamed weirdly and were equipped with rods ringed with all the colors of the rainbow. Here was a round door, and when one of the guards used both hands to tug it open, the cold that swept in was a frigid breath that burned as it touched bare skin.

11

The nearly opaque, dirty white walls of the tunnel were made of solid ice. Dark objects showed dimly through them here and there. A black wire hooked overhead and hung at regular intervals with lights did nothing to break the glacial cold about them.

Ross shuddered. Every breath he drew stung in his lungs. His bare shoulders and arms and the exposed section of thigh between kilt and boot grew numb. He could only move on stiffly, pushed ahead by his guards when he faltered. He guessed that were he to lose his footing here and surrender to the cold, he would forfeit the battle—and his life.

He had no way of measuring the length of the boring through the solid ice, but they were at last fronted by another opening, raggedly knocked out as if with an ax. They emerged from it into the wildest scene Ross had ever seen. Of course, he was familiar with ice and snow, but here was a world surrendered utterly to the brutal force of winter. It was a still, dead white-gray world in which nothing moved save the wind which curled the drifts.

Sunlight dazzled on the ice crest. The guards covered their eyes with the murky lenses they had worn pushed up on their foreheads within the shelter. Despite smarting eyes, Ross kept his gaze centered on his feet. He was given no time to look about. A rope was produced, a loop of it flipped in a noose about his throat, and he was towed along like a leashed dog. Before them was a path worn in the snow, not only by the passing of booted feet, but with more deeply scored marks as if heavy objects had been sledded there. Ross slipped and stumbled in the ruts, fearing to fall lest he be dragged. The numbness of his body reached into his head, he was dizzy, the world about him misting over now and again with a haze which arose from the long stretches of unbroken snow fields.

Tripping in a rut, he went down upon one knee, his flesh too numbed now to feel the additional cold of the snow, snow so hard that its crust delivered a knife's cut. Unemotionally, he watched a thin line of red trickle in a sluggish drop or two down the blue skin of his leg. The rope jerked him forward, and Ross scrambled awkwardly until one of his captors hooked a fur mitten in his belt and heaved him to his feet once more.

The purpose of that trek through the snow was obscure to Ross. In fact, he no longer cared, save that a hard rebel core deep inside him would not let him give up as long as his legs could move and he had a scrap of conscious will left in him. It was more difficult to walk now. He skidded and went down twice more. Then, the last time he slipped, he sledded past the man who led him, sliding down the slope of a glass-slick slope. He lay at the foot, unable to get up. Through the haze and deadening blanket of the cold he knew that he was being pulled about, shaken, generally mishandled, but this time he could not respond. Someone snapped open the rings about his wrists.

There was a call, echoing eerily across the ice. The fumbling about his body changed to a tugging and once more he was sent rolling down the slope. But the rope was now gone from his throat, and his arms were free. This time when he brought up hard against an obstruction he was not followed.

Ross's conscious mind—that portion of him that was Rossa, the trader—was content to lie there, to yield to the lethargy born of the frigid world about him. But the subconscious Ross Murdock of the Project prodded at him. He had always had a certain cold hatred which could crystallize into a spur. Once it had been hatred of circumstances and authority; now it became hatred for those who had led him into this wilderness with the purpose, as he knew now, of leaving him to freeze and die.

Ross pulled his hands under him. Though there was no feeling in them, they obeyed his will clumsily. He levered himself up and looked around. He lay in a narrow crevicelike cut, partly walled in by earth so frozen as to resemble steel. Crusted over it in long streaks from above were tongues of ice. To remain here was to serve his captors' purpose.

Ross inched his way to his feet. This opening, which was intended as his grave, was not so deep as the men had thought in their hurry to be rid of him. He believed that he could climb out if he could make his body answer to his determination.

Somehow Ross made that supreme effort and came again to the rutted path from which they had

tumbled him. Even if he could, there was no sense
in going along that rutted trail, for it led back to
the ice-encased building from which he had been
brought. They had thrust him out to die; they would
not take him in.

But a road so well marked must have some goal,
and in hopes that he might find shelter at the other
end, Ross turned to the left. The trace continued down
the slope. Now the towering walls of ice and snow
were broken by rocky teeth as if they had bitten deep
upon this land, only to be gnawed in return. Rounding
one of those rock fangs, Ross looked at a stretch of
level ground. Snow lay here, but the beaten-down trail
led straight through it to the rounded side of a huge
globe half buried in the ground, a globe of dark
material which could only be man-made.

Ross was past caution. He must get to warmth and
shelter or he was done for, and he knew it. Wavering
and weaving, he went on, his attention fixed on the
door ahead—a closed oval door. With a sob of
exhausted effort, Ross threw himself against it. The
barrier gave, letting him fall forward into a queer
glimmering radiance of bluish light.

The light rousing him because it promised more,
he crawled on past another door which was flattened
back against the inner wall. It was like making one's
way down a tube. Ross paused, pressing his lifeless
hands against his bare chest under the edge of his
tunic, suddenly realizing that there was warmth here.
His breath did not puff out in frosty streamers
before him, nor did the air sear his lungs when he
ventured to draw in more than shallow gulps.

With that realization a measure of animal caution
returned to him. To remain where he was, just inside
the entrance, was to court disaster. He must find a
hiding place before he collapsed, for he sensed he was

very near the end of his ability to struggle. Hope had given him a flash of false strength, the impetus to move, and he must make the most of that gift.

His path ended at a wide ladder, coiling in slow curves into gloom below and shadows above. He sensed that he was in a building of some size. He was afraid to go down, for even looking in that direction almost finished his sense of balance, so he climbed up.

Step by step, Ross made that painful journey, passing levels from which three or four hallways ran out like the radii of a spider's web. He was close to the end of his endurance when he heard a sound, echoed, magnified, from below. It was someone moving. He dragged his body into the fourth level where the light was very faint, hoping to crawl far enough into one of the passages to remain unseen from the stair. But he had gone only part-way down his chosen road when he collapsed, panting, and fell back against the wall. His hands pawed vainly against that sleek surface. He was falling through it!

Ross had a second, perhaps two, of stupefied wonder. Lying on a soft surface, he was enfolded by a warmth which eased his bruised and frozen body. There was a sharp prick in his thigh, another in his arm, and the world was a hazy dream until he finally slept in the depths of exhaustion.

There were dreams, detailed ones, and Ross stirred uneasily as his sleep thinned to waking. He lay with his eyes closed, fitting together odd bits of—dreams? No, he was certain that they were memories. Rossa of the Beaker traders and Ross Murdock of the project were again fused into one and the same person. How it had happened he did not know, but it was true.

Opening his eyes, he noticed a curved ceiling of soft blue which misted at the edges into gray. The

restful color acted on his troubled, waking mind like
a soothing word. For the first time since he had been
struck down in the night his headache was gone. He
raised his hand to explore that old hurt near his
hairline that had been so tender only yesterday that
it could not bear pressure. There remained only a thin,
rough line like a long-healed scar, that was all.

Ross lifted his head to look about him. His body
lay supported in a cradlelike arrangement of metal,
almost entirely immersed in a red gelatinous substance
with a clean, aromatic odor. Just as he was no longer
cold, neither was he hungry. He felt as fit as he ever
had in his life. Sitting up in the cradle, he stroked
the jelly away from his shoulders and chest. It fell
from him cleanly, leaving no trace of grease or dampness on his skin.

There were other fixtures in the small cylinderlike
chamber besides that odd bed in which he had lain.
Two bucketshaped seats were placed at the narrow
fore part of the room and before those seats was a
system of controls he could not comprehend.

As Ross swung his feet to the floor there was a click
from the side. This drew him around, ready for
trouble. But the noise had been caused by the opening
of a door into a small cupboard. Inside the cupboard
lay a fat package. Obviously this was an invitation to
investigate the offering.

The package contained a much folded article of
fabric, compressed and sealed in a transparent bag
which he fumbled twice before he succeeded in re-
leasing its fastening. Ross shook out a garment of
material such as he had never seen before. Its sheen
and satin-smooth surface suggested metal, but its stuff
was as supple as fine silk. Color rippled across it with
every twist and turn he gave to the length—dark blue
fading to pale violet, accented with wavering streaks

of vivid and startling green.

Ross experimented with a row of small, brilliant-green studs which made a transverse line from the right shoulder to the left hip, and they came apart. As he climbed into the suit the stuff modeled to his body in a tight but perfect fit. Across the shoulders were bands of green to match the studs, and the stockinglike tights were soled with a thick substance which formed a cushion for his feet.

He pressed the studs together, felt them lock, and then stood smoothing that strange, beautiful fabric, unable to account for either it or his surroundings. His head was clear; he could remember every detail of his flight up to the time he had fallen through the wall. And he was certain that he had passed through not only one, but two, of the Russian time posts. Could this be the third? If so, was he still a captive? Why would they leave him to freeze in the open country one moment and then treat him this way later?

He could not connect the ice-encased building from which the Russians had taken him with this one. At the sound of another soft noise Ross glanced over his shoulder just in time to see the cradle of jelly, from which he had emerged, close in upon itself until its bulk was a third of its former size. Compact as a box, it folded up against the wall.

Ross, his cushioned feet making no sound, advanced to the bucket-chairs. But lowering his body into one of them for a better look at what vaguely resembled the control of a helicopter—like the one in which he had taken the first stage of his fantastic journey across space and time—he did not find it comfortable. He realized that it had not been constructed to accommodate a body shaped precisely like his own.

A body like his own . . . That jelly bath or bed or whatever it was . . . The clothing which adapted so skillfully to his measurements . . .

Ross leaned forward to study the devices on the control board, confirming his suspicions. He had made the final jump of them all! He was now in some building of that alien race upon whose existence Millaird and Kelgarries had staked the entire project. This was the source, or one of the sources, from which the Russians were getting the knowledge which fitted no modern pattern.

A world encased in ice and a building with strange machinery. This thing—a cylinder with a pilot's seat and a set of controls. Was it an alien place? But the jelly bath—and the rest of it . . . Had his presence activated that cupboard to supply him with clothing? And what had become of the tunic he was wearing when he entered?

Ross got up to search the chamber. The bed-bath was folded against the wall, but there was no sign of his Beaker clothing, his belt, the hide boots. He could not understand his own state of well being, the lack of hunger and thirst.

There were two possible explanations for it all. One was that the aliens still lived here and for some reason had come to his aid. The other was that he stood in a place where robot machinery worked, though those who had set it up were no longer there. It was difficult to separate his memory of the half-buried globe he had seen from his sickness of that moment. Yet he knew that he had climbed and crawled through emptiness, neither seeing nor hearing any other life. Now Ross restlessly paced up and down, seeking the door through which he must have come, but there was not even a line to betray such an opening.

"I want out," he said aloud, standing in the center

of the cramped room, his fists planted on his hips, his eyes still searching for the vanished door. He had tapped, he had pushed, he had tried every possible way to find it. If he could only remember how he had come in! But all he could recall was leaning against a wall which moved inward and allowed him to fall. But where had he fallen? Into that jelly bath?

Ross, stung by a sudden idea, glanced at the ceiling. It was low enough so that by standing on tiptoes he could drum his fingers on its surface. Now he moved to the place directly above where the cradle had swung before it had folded itself away.

Rapping and poking, his efforts were rewarded at last. The blue curve gave under his assault. He pushed now, rising on his toes, though in that position he could exert little pressure. Then as if some faulty catch had been released, the ceiling swung up so that he lost his footing and would have fallen had he not caught the back of one of the bucket-seats.

He jumped and by hooking his hands over the edge of the opening, was able to work his way up and out, to face a small line of light. His fingers worked at that, and he opened a second door, entering a familiar corridor.

Holding the door open, Ross looked back, his eyes widening at what he saw. For it was plain now that he had just climbed out of a machine with the unmistakable outline of a snub-nosed rocket. The small flyer—or a jet, or whatever it was—had been fitted into a pocket in the side of the big structure as a ship into a berth, and it must have been set there to shoot from that enclosing chamber like a bullet shot from a rifle barrel. But why?

Ross's imagination jumped from fact to theory. The torpedo craft could be a plane. All right, he had been in bad shape when he fell into it by chance and the bed machine had caught him as if it had been created for just such a duty. What kind of a small plane would be equipped with a restorative apparatus? Only one intended to handle emergencies, to transport badly injured living things who had to leave the building in a hurry.

In other words, a lifeboat!

But why would a building need a lifeboat? That would only be standard equipment for a ship. Ross stepped into the corridor and stared about him with open and incredulous wonder. Could this be some form of ship, grounded here, deserted and derelict, and now being plundered by the Russians? The facts fitted! They fitted so well with all he had been able to discover that Ross was sure he was right. But he determined to prove it beyond all doubt.

He closed the door leading to the lifeboat berth, but not so securely that he could not open it again. That was too good a hiding place. On his cushioned feet he padded back to the stairway, and he stood there listening. Far below were sounds, a rasp of metal against metal, a low murmur of muted voices. But from above there was nothing, so he would explore above before he ventured into that other danger zone.

Ross climbed, passing two more levels, to come out into a vast room with a curving roof which must fill the whole crown of the globe. Here was such a wealth of machines, controls, things he could not understand that he stood bewildered, content for the moment merely to look. There were—he counted slowly—five control boards like those he had seen in the small escape ship. Each of these was faced by two or three of the bucket-seats, only these swung in webbing. He put his hand on one, and it bobbed elastically.

The control boards were so complicated that the one in the lifeboat might have been a child's toy in comparison. The air in the ship had been good; in the lifeboat it had held the pleasant odor of the jelly; but here Ross sniffed a faint but persistent hint of corruption, of an old stench.

He left the vantage point by the stairs and paced between the control boards and their empty swinging seats. This was the main control room, of that he was certain. From this point all the vast bulk beneath him had been set in motion, sailed here and there. Had it been on the sea, or through the air? The globe shape suggested an air-borne craft. But a civilization so advanced as this would surely have left some remains. Ross was willing to believe that he could be much farther back in time than 2000 B.C., but he was still sure that traces of those who could build a thing like this would have existed in the twenty-first century A.D.

Maybe that was how the Russians had found this. Something they had turned up within their country— say, in Siberia, or some of the forgotten corners of Central Asia—had been a clue.

Having had little schooling other than the intensive cramming at the base and his own informal education, the idea of the race who had created this ship overawed Ross more than he would admit. If the project could find this, turn it over to the guys who knew about such things . . . But that was just what they were striving for, and he was the only project man to have found the prize. Somehow, someway, he had to get back—out of this half-buried ship and its ice-bound world—back to where he could find his own people. Maybe the job was impossible, but he had to try. His survival was considered impossible by the men who had thrown him into the crevice, but here he was. Thanks to the men who had built this ship, he was alive and well.

Ross sat down in one of the uncomfortable seats to think and thus avoided immediate disaster, for he was hidden from the stairs on which sounded the tap of boots. A climber, maybe two, were on their way up, and there was no other exit from the control cabin.

12

Ross dropped from the web-slung chair to the floor and made himself as small as possible under the platform at the front of the cabin. Here, where there was a smaller control board and two seats placed closely together, the odd, unpleasant odor clung. It became stronger to Ross's senses as he waited tensely for the climbers to appear. Though he had searched, there was nothing in sight even faintly resembling a weapon. In a last desperate bid for freedom he crept back to the stairwell.

He had been taught a blow during his training period, one which required a precise delivery and, he had been warned, was often fatal. He would use it now. The climber was very close. A cropped head arose through the floor opening. Ross struck. He knew as his hand chopped against the folds of a fur hood that he had failed.

But the impetus of that unexpected blow saved him after all. With a choked cry the man disappeared, crashing down upon the one following him. A scream and shouts were heard from below, and a shot ripped up the well as Ross scrambled away from it. He might have delayed the final battle, but they had him cornered. He faced that fact bleakly. They need only sit below and let nature take its course. His session in the lifeboat had restored his strength, but a man could not live forever without food and water.

However, he had bought himself a bit of time which must be put to work. Turning to examine the seats, Ross discovered that they could be unhooked from their webbing swings. Freeing all of them, he dragged their weight to the stairwell and jammed them together to make a barricade. It could not hold long against any determined push from below, but, he hoped, it would deflect bullets if some sharpshooter tried to wing him by ricochet. Every so often there was the crash of a shot and some shouting, but Ross was not going to be drawn out of cover by that.

He paced around the control cabin, still hunting for a weapon. The symbols on the levers and buttons were meaningless to him. They made him feel frustrated because he imagined that among that countless array were some that might help him out of the trap if he could only guess their use.

Once more he stood by the platform thinking. This was the point from which the ship had been launched—in the air or on some now frozen sea. These control boards must have given the ship's master the means not only of propelling the vast bulk, but of unloading and loading cargo, lighting, heating, ventilation, and perhaps defense! Of course, every control might be dead now, but he remembered that in the lifeboat the machines had worked and fulfilled expertly the duty for which they had been constructed.

The only step remaining was to try his luck. Having made his decision, Ross simply shut his eyes as he had in a very short and almost forgotten childhood, turned around three times, and pointed. Then he looked to see where luck had directed him.

His finger indicated a board before which there had been three seats, and he crossed to it slowly, knowing that once he touched the controls he might inaugurate a chain of events he could not stop. The crash of a shot underlined the fact that he had no other recourse.

Since the symbols meant nothing, Ross concentrated on the shapes of the various devices and chose one which vaguely resembled the type of light switch he had always known. Since it was up, he pressed it down, counting to twenty slowly as he waited for a reaction. Below the switch was an oval button marked with two wiggles and a double dot in red. Ross snapped it level with the panel, and when it did not snap back, he felt somehow encouraged. When the two levers flanking that button did not push in or move up and down, Ross pulled them out without even waiting to count off.

This time he had results! A cracking of noise with a singsong rhythm, the volume of which, low at first, arose to a drone filled the cabin. Ross, deafened by the din, twisted first one lever and then the other until he had brought the sound to a less piercing howl. But he needed action, not just noise; he moved from behind the first chair to the next one. Here were five oval buttons, marked in the same vivid green as that which trimmed his clothing—two wiggles, a dot, a double bar, a pair of entwined circles, and a crosshatch.

Why make a choice? Recklessness bubbled up and Ross pushed all the buttons in rapid succession. The results were, in a measure, spectacular. Out of the top of the control board rose a triangle of screen which steadied and stood firm while across it played a rippling wave of color. Meanwhile the singsong became a squawk of angry protest.

Well, he had something, even if he didn't know what it was! And he had also proved that the ship was alive. However, Ross wanted more than a squawk of exasperation, which was exactly what the noise had become. It almost sounded, Ross decided as he listened, as if he were being expertly chewed out in another language. Yes, he wanted more than a series of squawks and a fanciful display of light waves on a screen.

At the section of board before the third and last seat there was less choice—only two switches. As Ross flicked up the first, the pattern on the screen dwindled into a brown color streaked with cream in which there was a suggestion of a picture. Suppose one didn't put the switch all the way up? Ross examined the slot in which the bar moved and now noted a series of tiny point marks along it. Selective? It would not do any harm to see. First he hurried back to the plug of chairs he had jammed into the stairwell. The squawks were now coming only at intervals, and Ross could hear nothing to suggest that his barrier was being forced.

He returned to the lever and moved it back two notches, standing open-mouthed at the immediate result. The cream-and-brown streaks were making a picture! Moving another notch down caused the picture to skitter back and forth on the screen. With memories of TV tuning to guide him, Ross brought the other lever down to a matching position, and the dim and shadowy images leaped into clear and complete focus. But the color was still brown, not the black and white he had expected.

And he was now looking into a face! Ross swallowed, his hand grasping one of the strings of chair webbing for support. Perhaps because in some ways it did resemble his own, that face was more preposterously nonhuman. The visage on the screen was sharply triangular with a small, sharply pointed chin and a jaw line running at an angle from a broad upper face. The skin was dark, covered largely with a soft and silky down, out of which hooked a curved and shining nose set between two large round eyes. On top of that astonishing head the down rose to a peak not unlike a cockatoo's crest. Yet there was no mistaking the intelligence in those eyes, nor the other's amazement at sight of Ross. They might have been staring at each other through a window.

Squawk . . . squeek . . . squawk . . . The creature in the mirror—on the vision plate—or outside the window—moved its absurdly small mouth in time to those sounds. Ross swallowed again and automatically made answer.

"Hello." His voice was a weak whistle, and perhaps it did not reach the furry-faced one, for he continued his questions, if questions they were. Meanwhile Ross, over his first stupefaction, tried to see something of the creature's surroundings. Though the objects were slightly out of focus, he was sure he recognized fittings similar to those about him. He must be in communication with another ship of the same type and one which was not deserted!

Furry-face had turned his head away to squawk rapidly over his shoulder, a shoulder which was crossed by a belt or sash with an elaborate pattern. Then he got up from his seat and stood aside to make room for the one he had summoned.

If Furry-face had been a startling surprise, Ross was now to have another. The man who now faced him on the screen was totally different. His skin registered as pale—cream-colored—and his face was far more human in shape, though it was hairless as was the smooth dome of his skull. When one became accustomed to that egg slickness, the stranger was not bad-looking, and he was wearing a suit which matched the one Ross had taken from the lifeboat.

This one did not attempt to speak. Instead, he took a long and measuring stare at Ross, his eyes growing colder and less friendly with every second of that examination. Ross had resented Kelgarries back at the project, but the major could not match Baldy for the sheer weight of ominousness he could pack into a look.

Ross might have been startled by Furry-face, but now his stubborn streak arose to meet this implied challenge. He found himself breathing hard and glaring back with an intensity which he hoped would communicate to Baldy that he would not have everything his own way if he proposed to tangle with Ross.

His preoccupation with the stranger on the screen betrayed Ross into the hands of those from below. He heard their attack on the barricade too late. By the time he turned around, the plug of seats was heaved up and a gun was pointing at his middle. His hands went up in small reluctant jerks as that threat held him where he was. Two of the fur-clad Russians climbed into the control chamber.

Ross recognized the leader as Ashe's double, the man he had followed across time. He blinked for just an instant as he faced Ross and then shouted an order at his companion. The other spun Murdock around, bringing his hands down behind him to clamp his wrists together. Once again Ross fronted the screen and saw Baldy watching the whole scene with an expression suggesting that he had been shocked out of his complacent superiority.

"Ah . . ." Ross's captors were staring at the screen and the unearthly man there. Then one flung himself at the control panel. His hands whipped back and forth, restoring to utter silence both screen and room.

"What are you?" The man who might have been Ashe spoke slowly in the Beaker tongue, drilling Ross with his stare as if by the force of his will alone he could pull the truth out of his prisoner.

"What do you think I am?" Ross countered. He was wearing the uniform of Baldy, and he had clearly established contact with the time owners of this ship. Let that worry the Russian!

But they did not try to answer him. At a signal he was led to the stair. To descend that ladder with his hands behind him was almost impossible, and they had to pause at the next level to unclasp the handcuffs and let him go free. Carefully keeping a gun on him, they hurried along, trying to push the pace while Ross delayed all he could. He realized that in his recognition of the power of the gun back in the control chamber, his surrender to its threat, he had betrayed his real origin. So he must continue to confuse the trail to the project in every possible way left to him. He was sure that this time they would not leave him in the first convenient crevice.

He knew he was right when they covered him with a fur parka at the entrance to the ship, once more manacling his hands and dropping a noose on him as a leash.

So, they were taking him back to their post here. Well, in the post was the time transporter which could return him to his own kind. It would be, it must be possible to get to that! He gave his captors no more trouble but trudged, outwardly dispirited, along the rutted way through the snow up the slope and out of the valley.

He did manage to catch a good look at the globe-ship. More than half of it, he judged, was below the surface of the ground. To be so buried it must either have lain there a long time or, if it were an air vessel, crashed hard enough to dig itself that partial grave. Yet Ross had established contact with another ship like it, and neither of the creatures he had seen were human, at least not in any way he knew.

Ross chewed on that as he walked. He believed that those with him were looting the ship of its cargo, and by its size, that cargo must be a large one. But cargo from where? Made by what hands, what *kind* of hands? Enroute to what port? And how had the Russians located the ship in the first place? There were plenty of questions and very few answers. Ross clung to the hope that somehow he had endangered the Russians' job here by activating the communication system of the derelict and calling the attention of its probable owners to its fate.

He also believed that the owners might take steps to regain their property. Baldy had impressed him deeply during those few moments of silent appraisal, and he knew he would not like to be on the receiving end of any retaliation from the other. Well, now he had only one chance, to keep the Russians guessing as long as he could and hope for some turn of fate which would allow him to try for the time transport. How the plate operated he did not know, but he had been transferred here from the Beaker age and if he could return to that time, escape might be possible. He had only to reach the river and follow it down to the sea where the sub was to make rendezvous at intervals. The odds were overwhelmingly against him, and Ross knew it. But there was no reason, he decided, to lie down and roll over dead to please the Russians.

As they approached the post Ross realized how much skill had gone into its construction. It looked as if they were merely coming up to the outer edge of a glacier tongue. Had it not been for the track in the snow, there would have been no reason to suspect that the ice covered anything. Ross was shoved through the white-walled tunnel to the building beyond.

He was hurried through the chain of rooms to a door and thrust through, his hands still fastened. It was dark in the cubby and colder than it had been outside. Ross stood still, waiting for his eyes to adjust to the gloom. It was several moments after the door had slammed shut that he caught a faint thud, a dull and hollow sound.

"Who is here?" he used the Beaker speech, determining to keep to the rags of his cover, which probably was a cover no longer. There was no reply, but after a pause that distant beat began again. Ross stepped cautiously forward, and by the simple method of running fullface into the walls, discovered that he was in a bare cell. Discovering that the noise lay behind the left-hand wall, he stood with his ear flat against it, listening. The sound did not have the regular rhythm of a machine in use—there were odd pauses between some blows, other came in a quick rain. It was as if someone were digging!

Were the Russians engaged in enlarging their ice-bound headquarters? Having listened for a considerable time, Ross doubted that, for the sound was too irregular. It seemed almost as if the longer pauses were used to check on the result of labor—was it to note the extent of the excavation or the continued preservation of secrecy?

Ross slipped down along the wall, his shoulders still resting against it, and rested with his head twisted so he could hear the tapping. Meanwhile he flexed his wrists inside the hoops which confined them, and folding his hands as small as possible, tried to slip them through the rings. All he did was chafe his skin raw to no advantage. They had not taken off his parka, and in spite of the chill about him, he was too warm. Only that part of his body covered by the suit he had taken from the ship was comfortable; he could almost believe that it possessed some built-in temperature control mechanism.

With no hope of relief Ross rubbed his hands back and forth against the wall, scraping the hoops on his wrists. The distant pounding had ceased, and this time the pause lengthened into so long a period that Ross fell asleep. His head fell forward on his chest, with his raw wrists still pushed against the surface behind him.

He was hungry when he awoke, and that hunger sparked his rebellion into flame. Awkwardly he got to his feet and lurched along to the door through which he had been thrown, where he proceeded to kick at the barrier. The cushiony stuff forming the soles of his tights muffled most of the force of those blows, but some noise was heard outside, for the door opened and Ross faced one of the guards.

"Food! I want to eat!" He put into the Beaker language all the resentment boiling in him.

The fellow ignoring him, reached in a long arm, and nearly tossing the prisoner off balance, dragged him out of the cell. Ross was marched into another room to face what appeared to be a tribunal. Two of the men there he knew—Ashe's double and the quiet man who had questioned him back in the other time station. The third, clearly one of greater authority, regarded Ross bleakly.

"Who are you?" the quiet man asked.

"Rossa, son of Gurdi. And I would eat before I make talk with you. I have not done any wrong that you should treat me as a barbarian who has stolen salt from the trading post—"

"You are an agent," the leader corrected him dispassionately, "of whom, you will tell us in due time. But first you shall speak of the ship, of what you found there, and why you meddled with the controls . . . Wait a moment before you refuse, my young friend." He raised his hand from his lap, and once again Ross faced an automatic. "Ah, I see that you know what I hold—odd knowledge for an innocent Bronze Age trader. And please have no doubts about my hesitation to use this. I shall not kill you now," the man continued, "but there are certain wounds which supply a maximum of pain and little serious damage. Remove his parka, Kirschov."

Once more Ross was unmanacled, the fur stripped from him. His questioner carefully studied the suit he wore under it. "Now you will tell us exactly what we wish to hear."

There was a confidence in that statement which chilled Ross; Major Kelgarries had displayed its like. Ashe had it in another degree, and certainly it had been present in Baldy. There was no doubt that the speaker meant exactly what he said. He had at his command methods that would wring from his captive the full sum of what he wanted. And there would be no consideration for that captive during the process.

His implied threat struck as cold as the glacial air, and Ross tried to meet it with an outward show of uncracked defenses. He decided to pick and choose from his information, feeding them scraps to stave off the inevitable. Hope dies very hard, and Ross having been pushed into corners long before his work at the project, had had considerable training in verbal fencing with hostile authority. He would volunteer nothing . . . Let it be pulled from him reluctant word by word! He would spin it out as long as he could and hope that time might fight for him.

"You are an agent . . ."

Ross accepted this statement as one he could neither affirm nor deny.

"You came to spy under the cover of a barbarian trader," smoothly, without pause, the man changed language in mid-sentence, slipping from the Beaker speech into English.

But long experience in meeting danger with an expression of incomprehension was Ross's weapon now. He stared somewhat stupidly at his interrogator with that bewildered, boyish look he had so long cultivated to bemuse enemies in his past.

Whether he could have held out long against the other's skill—for Ross possessed no illusions concerning the type of examiner he now faced—he was never to know. What happened next saved for Ross a measure of self-esteem.

A distant boom thundered. Underneath and around them the floor, walls, and ceiling of the room moved as if they had been pried from their setting of ice and were being rolled about by the exploring thumb and forefinger of some impatient giant.

13

Ross swayed against a guard, was shoved back, and bounced against the wall as the man shouted words Ross could not understand. A determined roar from the leader brought a semblance of order, but it was plain that they had not been expecting this. Ross was hustled out of the room back to his cell. His guards were opening the cell door when a second shock was felt and he was thrust into safekeeping with no ceremony.

He half crouched against the questionable security of the wall, waiting through two more twisting earth waves, both of which were accompanied or preceded by dull sounds. Bombing! That last wrench was really bad. Ross found himself lying on the floor, feeling tremors rippling along the earth. His stomach knotted convulsively with a fear unlike any he had known before. It was as if the world had been jerked from under him.

But that last explosion—if it was an explosion—appeared to be the end. Ross sat up gingerly after several long moments during which no more shocks moved the floor and walls. A line of light marked the door, showing cracks where none had previously existed. Ross, not yet ready to try standing erect, was crawling toward it on his hands and knees when a sharp noise behind him brought him to a halt.

Darkness disoriented him, but he was certain that the scrape of metal against metal sounded from the far side of the wall. He crawled back and put his ear to the surface. Now he heard not only that scraping, but an undercurrent of clicks, chippings . . .

Under his exploring hands the surface remained as smooth as ever, however. Then suddenly, about a foot from his head, there sounded a rip of metal. The wall was being holed from the other side! Ross caught a weak flicker of light, and moving in it was the point of a tool pushing at the smooth surface of the wall. It broke away with a brittle sound, and a hand holding a light reached through the aperture.

Ross wondered if he should catch that wrist, but the hope that the digger might just possibly be an ally kept him motionless. After the hand with the light whipped back beyond the wall, a wide section gave away and a hunched figure crawled through, followed by a second. In the limited glow he saw the first tunneler clearly enough.

"Assha!"

Ross was unprepared for what followed his cry. The lean brown man moved with a panther's striking speed, and Ross was forced back. A hand like a steel ring on his throat choked the breath away from his bursting lungs. The other's muscular body held him flat in spite of his struggles. The light of a small flash glowed inches beyond his eyes as he fought to fill his lungs. Then the hand on his throat was gone and he gasped, a little dizzy.

"Murdock! What are you doing—?" Ashe's clipped voice was muffled by another sudden explosion. This time the earth tremors not only hurled them from their feet, but seemed to run along the walls and across the ceiling. Ross, burying his face in the crook of his arm, could not rid himself of the fear that the building was being slowly twisted into scrap. When the shock was over he raised his head.

"What's going on?" he heard McNeil ask.

"Attack." That was Ashe. "But why, and by whom— don't ask me! You are a prisoner, I suppose, Murdock?"

"Yes, sir." Ross was glad that his voice sounded normal enough.

He heard someone sigh and guessed it was McNeil. "Another digging party." There was tired disgust in that.

"I don't understand," Ross appealed to that section of the dark where Ashe had been. "Have you been here all the time? Are you trying to dig your way out? I don't see how you can cut out of this glacier that we're parked under—"

"Glacier!" Ashe's exclamation was as explosive as the tremors. "So we're inside a glacier! That explains it. Yes, we've been here—"

"On ice!" McNeil commented and then laughed. "Glacier—ice—that's right, isn't it?"

"We're collaborating," Ashe continued. "Supplying our dear friends with a lot of information they already have and some flights of fancy they never dreamed about. However, they didn't know we had a few surprise packets of our own strewn about. It's amazing what the boys back at the project can pack away in a belt, or between layers of hide in a boot. So we've been engaged in some research of our own—"

"But I didn't have any escape gadgets." Ross was struck by the unfairness of that.

"No," Ashe agreed, his voice even and cold, "they are not entrusted to first-run men. You might slip up and use them at the wrong moment. However, you appear to have done fairly well . . ."

The heat of Ross's rising anger was chilled by the noise which cracked over their heads, ground to them through the walls, flattened and threatened them. He had thought those first shocks were the end of this ice burrow and the world; he *knew* that this one was.

And the silence that followed was as threatening in its way as the clamor had been. Then there was a shout, a shriek. The space of light near the cell door was widening as that barrier, broken from its lock, swung open slowly. The fear of being trapped sent the men in that direction.

"Out!"

Before Ross could respond, they were stopped by the crackling sound of automatic weapons firing. Somewhere in this warren a fight was in progress.

Ross, remembering the arrogant face of the bald ship's officer, wondered if this was not an attack in force—the aliens against the looting Russians. If so, would the ship people distinguish between those found here? He feared not.

The room outside was clear, but not for long. As they lay watching, two men backed in, then whirled to stare at each other. A voice roared from beyond as if ordering them back to some post. One of them took a step forward in reluctant obedience, but the other grabbed his arm and pulled him away. They turned to run, and an automatic cracked.

The man nearest Ross gave an odd little cough, folded forward to his knees, and sprawled on his face. His companion stared at him wildly for an instant, and then skidded into the passage beyond, escaping by inches a shot which clipped the door as he lunged through it.

No one followed, for outside there was a crescendo of noise—shouting, cries of pain, an unidentifiable hissing. Ashe darted into the room, taking cover by the body. Then he came back, the fellow's gun in his hand, and with a jerk of his head summoned the other two. He motioned them on in a direction away from the sounds of battle.

"I don't get all this," McNeil commented as they reached the next passage. "What's going on? Mutiny? Or have our boys gotten through?"

"It must be the ship people," Ross answered.

"What ship?" Ashe caught him up swiftly.

"The big one the Russians have been looting—"

"Ship?" echoed McNeil. "And *where* did you get that rig?" In the bright light it was easy to see Ross's alien dress. McNeil fingered the elastic material wonderingly.

"From the ship," Ross returned impatiently. "But if the ship people are attacking, I don't think they will notice any difference between us and the Russians . . ."

There was a burst of ear-splitting sound. For the third time Ross was thrown from his feet. This time the burrow lights flickered, dimmed, and went out.

"Oh, fine," commented McNeil bitterly out of the dark. "I never did care for blindman's buff."

"The transfer plate—" Ross clung to his own plan of escape— "if we can reach that—"

The light which had served Ashe and McNeil in their tunneling clicked on. Since the earth shocks appeared to be over for a while, they moved forward, with Ashe in the lead and McNeil bringing up the rear. Ross hoped Ashe knew the way. The sound of fighting had died out, so one side or the other must have gained the victory. They might have only a few moments left to pass undetected.

Ross's sense of direction was fairly acute, but he could not have gone so unerringly to what he sought as Ashe did. Only he did not lead them to the room with the glowing plate, and Ross stifled a protest as they came instead to a small record room.

On a table were three spools of tape which Ashe caught up avidly, thrusting two in the front of his baggy tunic, passing the third to McNeil. Then he sped about trying the cupboards on the walls, but all were locked. His hand falling from the last latch, Ashe came back to the door where Ross waited.

"To the plate!" Ross urged.

Ashe surveyed the cupboards once more regretfully. "If we could have just ten minutes here—"

McNeil snorted. "Listen, you may yearn to be the filling in an ice sandwich, but I don't! Another shock and we'll be buried so deep even a drill couldn't find us. The kid is right. Let's get out now. If we still can."

Once more Ashe took the lead and they wove through ghostly rooms to what must have been the heart of the post—the transfer point. To Ross's unvoiced relief, the plate was glowing. He had feared that when the lights blew out the transfer plate might also have been affected. He jumped for the plate.

Neither Ashe nor McNeil wasted time in joining him there. As they clung together there was a cry from behind them, underlined by a shot. Ross, feeling Ashe sag against him, caught him in his arms. By the reflected glow of the plate he saw the Russian commander of the post. Behind him, his hairless face hanging oddly bodiless in the gloom, was the alien. Were those two now allies? Before Ross could be

sure that he had really seen them, the wracking of
space time caught him and the rest of the room
faded away.

" . . . free. Get a move on!"

Ross glanced across Ashe's bowed shoulders to
McNeil's excited face. The other was pulling at Ashe,
who was only half-conscious. A stream of blood from
a hole in his bare shoulder soaked the upper edge of
his Beaker tunic, but as they steadied him between
them, he gained some measure of awareness and
moved his feet as they pulled him off the plate.

Well, they were free if only for a few seconds, and
there was no reception committee waiting for them.
Ross gave thanks silently for those two small favors.
But if they were now returned to the Bronze Age
village, they were still in enemy territory. With Ashe
wounded, the odds against them were so high it was
almost hopeless.

Working hurriedly with strips torn from McNeil's
kilt, they managed to stop the flow of blood from
Ashe's wound. Although he was still groggy, he was
fighting, driven by the fear which whipped them all—
time was one of their foremost enemies. Armed with
Ashe's gun, Ross kept watch on the transfer plate,
ready to shoot at anything appearing there.

"That will have to do!" Ashe pulled free from
McNeil. "We must move." He hesitated, and then
pulling the spools of tape from his bloodstained tunic,
passed them to McNeil. "You'd better carry these."

"All right," the other answered almost absently.

"Move!" The force of that order from Ashe sent
them into the corridor beyond. "The plate . . ." But
the plate remained clear. And Ross noted that they
must have returned to the proper time, for the walls
about them were the logs and stone of the village he
remembered.

"Someone coming through?"

"Should be—soon."

They fled, the hide boots of the other two making only the faintest whisper of sound, Ross's foam-soled feet none at all. He could not have found the door to the outer world, but again Ashe guided them, and only once did they have to seek cover. At last they faced a barred door. Ashe leaned against the wall, McNeil supporting him, as Ross pulled the locking beam free. They let themselves out into the night.

"Which way?" McNeil asked.

To Ross's surprise Ashe did not turn to the gate in the outer stockade. Instead he gestured at the mountain wall in the opposite direction. "They'll expect us to try for the valley pass. So we had better go up the slope there."

"That has the look of a tough climb," ventured McNeil.

Ashe stirred. "When it becomes too tough for me"—his voice was dry— "I shall say so, never fear."

He started out with some of his old ease of movement, but his companions closed in on either side, ready to offer aid. Ross often wondered later if they could have won free of the village by their own efforts that night. He was sure their resolution would have been equal to the attempt, but their escape would have depended upon a fabulous run of luck such as men seldom encounter.

They had just reached a pool of shadow beside a small hut two buildings away from the one they had fled, when the fireworks began. As if on signal the three fugitives threw themselves flat. From the roof of the building at the center of the village a pencil of brilliant-green light pointed straight up into the sky, and around that spear of radiance the roof sprouted tongues of more natural red-and-yellow flames. Figures shot from doors as the fire lapped down the peak of the roof.

"Now!" In spite of the rising clamor, Ashe's voice carried to his two companions.

The three sprinted for the palisade, mingling with bewildered men who ran out of the other cabins. The waves of fire washed on, providing light, too much light. Ashe and McNeil could pass as part of the crowd, but Ross's unusual clothing might be easily noticed.

Others were running for the wall. Ross and McNeil boosted Ashe to the top, saw him over in safety. McNeil followed. Ross was just reaching to draw himself up when he was enveloped in a beam of light.

A high, screeching call, unlike any shout he had heard, split the clamor. Frantically Ross tried for a hold, knowing that he was presenting a perfect target for those behind. He gained the top of the stockade, looked down into a black block of shadow, not knowing whether Ashe and McNeil were waiting for him or had gone ahead. Hearing that strange cry again, Ross leaped blindly out into the darkness.

He landed badly, hitting hard enough to bruise, but thanks to the skill he had learned for parachuting, he broke no bones. He got to his feet and blundered on in the general direction of the mountain Ashe had picked as their goal. There were others coming over the wall of the village and moving through the shadows, so he dared not call out for fear of alerting the enemy.

The village had been set in the widest part of the valley. Behind its stockade the open ground narrowed swiftly, like the point of a funnel, and all fugitives from the settlement had to pass through that channel to escape. Ross's worst fear was that he had lost contact with Ashe and McNeil, and that he would never be able to pick up their trail in the wilderness ahead.

Thankful for the dark suit he wore which was protective covering in the night, he twice ducked into the brush to allow parties of refugees to pass him. Hearing them speak the guttural clicking speech he had learned from Ulffa's people, Ross deduced that they were innocent of the village's real purpose. These people were convinced they had been attacked by night demons. Perhaps there had only been a handful of Russians in that hidden retreat.

Pulling himself up a hard slope, Ross paused to catch his breath and looked back. He was not too surprised to see figures moving leisurely about the village examining the cabins, perhaps in search of the inhabitants. Each of those searchers was clad in a form-fitting suit that matched his own, and their bulbous hairless heads gleamed white in the firelight. Ross was astonished to see that they passed straight through the wall of flame, apparently unconcerned and unsinged by the heat.

The human beings trapped in the town wailed and ran, or lay and beat their heads and hands on the ground, helpless before the invaders. Each captive was dragged back to a knot of aliens near the main building. Some were hurled out again into the dark, unharmed; a few others were retained. A sorting of prisoners was plainly in progress. There was no question that the ship people had followed through into this time, and that they had their own arrangements for the Russians.

Ross had no desire to learn the particulars. He started climbing again, finding the pass at last. Beyond, the ground fell away again. Ross went forward into the full darkness of the night with a vast surge of thankfulness.

Finally, he stopped simply because he was too weary and hungry to keep on his feet without stumbling. A fall in the dark on these heights could be costly. Ross discovered a small hollow behind a stunted tree and crept into it as best he could, his heart laboring against his ribs, a hot stab of pain cutting into his side with every breath he drew.

He awoke all at once with the snap of a fighting man who is ever alert to danger. A hand lay warm and hard over his mouth, and above it his eyes met McNeil's. When he saw that Ross was awake McNeil withdrew his hand. The morning sunlight was warm about them. Moving clumsily because of his stiff, bruised body, Ross crawled out of the hollow. He looked around, but McNeil stood there alone. "Ashe?" Ross questioned him.

McNeil, showing a haggard face covered with several days' growth of rusty-brown beard, nodded his head toward the slope. Fumbling inside his kilt, he brought out something clenched in his fist and offered it to Ross. The latter held out his palm and McNeil covered it with a handful of coarse-ground grain. Just to look at the stuff made Ross long for a drink, but he mouthed it and chewed, getting up to follow McNeil down into the tree-grown lower slopes.

"It's not good." McNeil spoke jerkily, using Beaker speech. "Ashe is out of his head some of the time. That hole in his shoulder is worse than we thought it was, and there's always the threat of infection. This whole wood is full of people flushed out of that blasted village! Most of them—all I've seen—are natives. But they have it firmly planted in their minds now that there are devils after them. If they see you wearing that suit—"

"I know, and I'd strip if I could," Ross agreed. "But

I'll have to get other clothing first; I can't run bare in this cold."

"That might be safer," McNeil growled. "I don't know just what happened back there, but it certainly must have been plenty!"

Ross swallowed a very dry mouthful of grain and then stopped to scoop up some leftover snow in the shadow of a tree root. It was not as refreshing as a real drink, but it helped. "You said Ashe is out of his head. What do we do for him, and what are your plans?"

"We have to reach the river, somehow. It drains to the sea, and at its mouth we are supposed to make contact with the sub."

The proposal sounded impossible to Ross, but so many impossible things had happened lately he was willing to go along with the idea—as long as he could. Gathering up more snow, he stuffed it into his mouth before he followed the already disappearing McNeil.

14

". . . That's my half of it. The rest of it you know."
Ross held his hands close to the small fire sheltered
in the pit he had helped dig and flexed his cold-
numbed fingers in the warmth.

From across the handful of flames Ashe's eyes, too
bright in a fever-flushed face, watching him demand-
ingly. The fugitives had taken cover in an angle where
the massed remains of an old avalanche provided a
cave-pocket. McNeil was off scouting in the gray
drizzle of the day, and their escape from the village
was now some forty-eight hours behind them.

"So the crackpots were right, after all. They only
had their times mixed." Ashe shifted on the bed of
brush and leaves they had raked together for his
comfort.

"I don't understand—"

"Flying saucers," Ashe returned with an odd little
laugh. "It was a wild possibility, but it was on the
books from the start. This certainly will make
Kelgarries turn red—"

"Flying saucers?"

Ashe must be out of his head from the fever, Ross supposed. He wondered what he should do if Ashe tried to get up and walk away. He could not tackle a man with a bad hole in his shoulder, nor was he certain he could wrestle Ashe down in a real fight.

"That globe-ship was never built on this world. Use your head, Murdock. Think about your furry-faced friend and the baldy with him. Did either look like normal humans to you?"

"But—a spaceship!" It was something that had so long been laughed to scorn. When men had failed to go farther into space after the initial excitement of the moon landings, space flight had become a matter for jeers. On the other hand, there was the evidence collected by his own eyes and ears. The services of the lifeboat had been techniques outside of his experience.

"This was insinuated once"—Ashe was lying flat now, gazing speculatively up at the projection of logs and earth which made them a partial roof— "along with a lot of other bright ideas, by a gentleman named Charles Fort, who took a lot of pleasure in pricking what he considered to be vastly over-inflated scientific pomposity. He gathered together four book loads of reported incidents of unexplainable happenings which he dared the scientists of his day to explain. And one of his bright suggestions was that such phenomena as the vast artificial earthworks found in Ohio and Indiana were originally thrown up by space castaways to serve as SOS signals—an intriguing idea. We know that example was wrong, but others might not be."

"But if such spaceships were wrecked on this world, I still don't see why we didn't find traces of them in our own time."

"Because that wreck you explored was bedded in a glacial era. Do you have any idea how long ago that was, counting from our own time? There were at least three glacial periods—and we don't know in which one the Russians went visiting. That age began about a million years before we were born, and the last of the ice ebbed out of New York State some thirty-eight thousand years ago, boy. That was the early Stone Age, reckoning it by the scale of human development, with an extremely thin population of the first real types of man clinging to a few warmer fringes of wilderness.

"Climate changes, geographical changes, all altered the face of our continents. There was a sea in Kansas; England was part of Europe. So, even though as many as fifty such ships were lost here, they could all have been ground to bits by the ice flow, buried miles deep in quakes, or rusted away generations before the first true *homo sapiens* arrived to wonder at them. Certainly there couldn't be too many such wrecks to be found. What do you think this planet was, a flypaper to attract them?"

"But if ships crashed here once, why didn't they later when men were better able to understand them?" Ross countered.

"For several reasons—all of them possible and able to be fitted into the fabric of history as we know it on this world. Civilizations rise, exist, and fall, each taking with it into the limbo of forgotten things some of the discoveries which made it great.

"The Sumerians once had a well-traveled trade route to India. Bronze Age traders opened up roads down into Africa. The Romans knew China. Then came an end to each of these empires, and those trade routes were forgotten. To our European ancestors of the Middle Ages, China was almost a legend, and the fact that Chinese fleets had successfully sailed to East

Africa was unknown. Suppose our space voyagers represented some star-born confederacy or empire which lived, rose to its highest point, and fell again into planet-bound barbarism all before the first of our species painted pictures on a cave wall?

"Or take it that this world was an unlucky reef on which too many ships and cargoes were lost, so that our whole solar system was posted, and skippers of star ships thereafter avoided it? Or they might even have had some rule that when a planet developed a primitive race of its own, it was to be left strictly alone until it discovered space flight for itself."

"Yes." Every one of Ashe's suppositions made good sense, and Ross was able to believe them. It was easier to think that both Furry-face and Baldy were inhabitants of another world than to think their kind existed on this planet before his own species was born. "But how did the Russians locate that ship?"

"Unless the information is on the tapes we were able to bring along, we shall probably never know," Ashe said drowsily. "I might make one guess—the Russians have been making an all-out effort for three hundred years to open up Siberia. In some sections of that huge country there have been great climatic changes almost overnight in the far past. Mammoths have been discovered frozen in the ice with half-digested plants in their stomach. It's as if the beasts were given some deep-freeze treatment instantaneously. If in their excavations the Russians came across the remains of a spaceship, remains well enough preserved for them to realize what they had discovered, they might start questing back in time to find a better one intact at an earlier date. That theory fits everything we know now."

"But why would the aliens attack the Russians now?"

"No ship's officers ever thought gently of pirates." Ashe's eyes closed.

There were questions, a flood of them, that Ross wanted to ask. He smoothed the fabric on his arm, that stuff which clung so tightly to his skin yet kept him warm without any need for more covering. If Ashe were right, on what world, what kind of world, had that material been woven, and how far had it been brought that he could wear it now?

Suddenly McNeil slid into their shelter and dropped two hares at the edge of the fire.

"How goes it?" he said, as Ross began to clean them.

"Reasonably well," Ashe, his eyes still closed, replied to that before Ross could. "How far are we from the river? And do we have company?"

"About five miles—if we had wings." McNeil answered in a dry tone. "And we have company all right, lots of it!"

That brought Ashe up, leaning forward on his good elbow. "What kind?"

"Not from the village." McNeil frowned at the fire which he fed with economic handfuls of sticks. "Something's happening on the side of the mountains. It looks as if there's a mass migration in progress. I counted five family clans on their way west—all in just this one morning."

"The village refugees' stories about devils might send them packing," Ashe mused.

"Maybe." But McNeil did not sound convinced. "The sooner we head downstream, the better. And I hope the boys will have that sub waiting where they promised. We do possess one thing in our favor—the spring floods are subsiding."

"And the high water should have left plenty of raft material." Ashe lay back again. "We'll make those five miles tomorrow."

McNeil stirred uneasily and Ross, having cleaned and spitted the hares, swung them over the flames to broil. "Five miles in this country," the younger man observed, "is a pretty good day's march"—he did not add as he wanted to—"for a well man."

"I will make it," Ashe promised, and both listeners knew that as long as his body would obey him he meant to keep that promise. They also knew the futility of argument.

Ashe proved to be a prophet to be honored on two counts. They did make the trek to the river the next day, and there was a wealth of raft material marking the high-water level of the spring flood. The migrations NcNeil had reported were still in progress, and the three men hid twice to watch the passing of small family clans. Once a respectably sized tribe, including wounded men, marched across their route, seeking a ford at the river.

"They've been badly mauled," McNeil whispered as they watched the people huddle along the water's edge while scouts cast upstream and down, searching for a ford. When they returned with the news that there was no ford to be found, the tribesmen then sullenly went to work with flint axes and knives to make rafts.

"Pressure—they are on the run." Ashe rested his chin on his good forearm and studied the busy scene. "These are not from the village. Notice the dress and the red paint on their faces. They're not like Ulffa's kin either. I wouldn't say they were local at all."

"Reminds me of something I saw once—animals running before a forest fire. They can't all be looking for new hunting territory," McNeil returned.

"Russians sweeping them out," Ross suggested. "Or could the ship people—?"

Ashe started to shake his head and then winced.

"I wonder . . ." The crease between his level brows deepened. "The ax people!" His voice was still a whisper, but it carried a note of triumph as if he had fitted some stubborn jigsaw piece into its proper place.

"Ax people?"

"Invasion of another people from the east. They turned up in prehistory about this period. Remember, Webb spoke of them. They used axes for weapons and tamed horses."

"Tartars"—McNeil was puzzled— "This far west?"

"Not Tartars, no. You needn't expect those to come boiling out of middle Asia for some thousands of years yet. We don't know too much about the ax people, save that they moved west from the interior plains. Eventually they crossed to Britain; perhaps they were the ancestors of the Celts who loved horses too. But in their time they were a tidal wave."

"The sooner we head downstream, the better." McNeil stirred restlessly, but they knew that they must keep to cover until the tribesmen below were gone. So they lay in hiding another night, witnessing on the next morning the arrival of a smaller party of the red-painted men, again with wounded among them. At the coming of this rear guard the activity on the river bank rose close to frenzy.

The three men out of time were doubly uneasy. It was not enough for them to merely cross the river. They had to build a raft which would be water-worthy enough to take them downstream—to the sea if they were lucky. And to build such a sturdy raft would take time, time they did not have now.

In fact, McNeil waited only until the last tribal raft was out of bow shot before he plunged down to the shore, Ross at his heels. Since they lacked even the stone tools of the tribesmen, they were at a disadvantage, and Ross found he was hands and feet for Ashe, working under the other's close direction. Before night closed in they had a good beginning and two sets of blistered hands, as well as aching backs.

When it was too dark to work any longer, Ashe pointed back over the track they had followed. Marking the mountain pass was a light. It looked like fire, and if it was, it must be a big one for them to be able to sight it across this distance.

"Camp?" McNeil wondered.

"Must be," Ashe agreed. "Those who built that blaze are in such numbers that they don't have to take precautions."

"Will they be here by tomorrow?"

"Their scouts might, but this is early spring, and forage can't have been too good on the march. If I were the chief of that tribe, I'd turn aside into the meadow land we skirted yesterday and let the herds graze for a day, maybe more. On the other hand, if they need water—"

"They will come straight ahead!" McNeil finished grimly. "And we can't be here when they arrive."

Ross stretched, grimacing at the twinge of pain in his shoulders. His hands smarted and throbbed, and this was just the beginning of their task. If Ashe had been fit, they might have trusted to logs for support and swum downstream to hunt a safer place for their shipbuilding project. But he knew that Ashe could not stand such an effort.

Ross slept that night mainly because his body was too exhausted to let him lie awake and worry. Roused in the earliest dawn by McNeil, they both crawled down to the water's edge and struggled to bind stubbornly resisting saplings together with cords twisted from bark. They reinforced them at crucial points with some strings torn from their kilts, and strips of rabbit hide saved from their kills of the past few days.

They worked with hunger gnawing at them, having no time now to hunt. When the sun was well westward they had a clumsy craft which floated sluggishly. Whether it would answer to either pole or improvised paddle, they could not know until they tried it.

Ashe, his face flushed and his skin hot to the touch, crawled on board and lay in the middle, on the thin heap of bedding they had put there for him. He eagerly drank the water they carried to him in cupped hands and gave a little sigh of relief as Ross wiped his face with wet grass, muttering something about Kelgarries which neither of his companions understood.

McNeil shoved off and the bobbing craft spun around dizzily as the current pulled it free from the shore. They made a brave start, but luck deserted them before they had gotten out of sight of the spot where they embarked.

Striving to keep them in mid-current, McNeil poled furiously, but there were too many rocks and snagged trees with them, and coming up fast was a full-sized tree. Twice its mat of branches caught on some snag, holding it back, and Ross breathed a little more freely, but it soon tore free again and rolled on, as menacing as a battering ram.

"Get closer to shore!" Ross shouted the warning. Those great, twisted roots seemed aimed straight at the raft, and he was sure if that mass struck them fairly, they would not have a chance. He dug in with his own pole, but his hasty push did not meet bottom; the stake in his hands plunged into some pothole in the hidden river bed. He heard McNeil cry out as he toppled into the water, gasping as the murky liquid flooded his mouth, choking him.

Half dazed by the shock, Ross struck out instinctively. The training at the base had included swimming, but to fight water in a pool under controlled conditions was far different from fighting death in a river of icy water when one had already swallowed a sizable quantity of that flood.

Ross had a half glimpse of a dark shadow. Was it the edge of the raft? He caught at it desperately, skinning his hands on rough bark, dragged on by it. The tree! He blinked his eyes to clear them of water, to try to see. But he could not pull his exhausted body high enough out of the water to see past the screen of roots; he could only cling to the small safety he had won and hope that he could rejoin the raft somewhere downstream.

After what seemed like a very long time he wedged one arm between two water-washed roots, sure that the support would hold his head above the surface. The chill of the stream struck at his hands and head, but the protection of the alien clothing was still effective, and the rest of his body was not cold. He was simply too tired to wrest himself free and trust again to the haphazard chance of making shore through the gathering dusk.

Suddenly a shock jarred his body and strained the arm he had thrust among the roots, wringing a cry out of him. He swung around and brushed footing under the water; the tree had caught on a shore snag. Pulling loose from the roots, he floundered on his hands and knees, falling afoul of a mass of reeds whose roots were covered with stale-smelling mud. Like a wounded animal he dragged himself through the ooze to higher land, coming out upon an open meadow flooded with moonlight.

For a while he lay there, his cold, sore hands under him, plastered with mud and too tired to move. The sound of a sharp barking aroused him— an imperative, summoning bark, neither belonging

to a wolf nor a hunting fox. He listened to it dully
and then, through the ground upon which he lay,
Ross felt as well as heard the pounding of hoofs.

Hoofs—horses! Horses from over the hills—horses
which might mean danger. His mind seemed as dull
and numb as his hands, and it took quite a long time
for him to fully realize the menace horses might bring.

Getting up, Ross noticed a winged shape sweeping across the disk of the moon like a silent dart.
There was a single despairing squeak out of the grass
about a hundred feet away, and the winged shape
arose again with its prey. Then the barking sound once
more—eager, excited barking.

Ross crouched back on his heels and saw a smoky
brand of light moving along the edge of the meadow
where the band of trees began. Could it be a herd
guard? Ross knew he had to head back toward the
river, but he had to force himself on the path, for he
did not know whether he dared enter the stream
again. But what would happen if they hunted him with
the dog? Confused memories of how water spoiled
scent spurred him on.

Having reached the rising bank he had climbed so
laboriously before, Ross miscalculated and tumbled
back, rolling down into the mud of the reed bed.
Mechanically he wiped the slime from his face. The
tree was still anchored there; by some freak the current had rammed its rooted end up on a sand spit.

Above in the meadow the barking sounded very
close and now it was answered by a second canine
belling. Ross wormed his way back through the reeds
to the patch of water between the tree and the bank.
His few poor efforts at escape were almost half-con-
sciously taken; he was too tired to really care now.

Soon he saw a four-footed shape running along the
top of the bank, giving tongue. It was then joined by

a larger and even more vocal companion. The dogs
drew even with Ross, who wondered dully if the animals could sight him in the shadows below, or whether
they only scented his presence. Had he been able,
he would have climbed over the log and taken his
chances in the open water, but now he could only
lie where he was—the tangle of roots between him
and the bank serving as a screen, which would be
little enough protection when men came with torches.

Ross was mistaken, however, for his worm's progress
across the reed bed had liberally besmeared his dark
clothing and masked the skin of his face and hands,
giving him better cover than any he could have wit-
tingly devised. Though he felt naked and defenseless,
the men who trailed the hounds to the river bank,
thrusting out the torch over the edge to light the sand
spit, saw nothing but the trunk of the tree wedged
against a mound of mud.

Rose heard a confused murmur of voices broken
by the clamor of the dogs. Then the torch was raised
out of line of his dazzled eyes. He saw one of the
indistinct figures above cuff away a dog and move off,
calling the hounds after it. Reluctantly, still barking,
the animals went. Ross, with a little sob, subsided
limply in the uncomfortable net of roots, still undis-
covered.

15

It was such a small thing, a tag of ragged stuff looped about a length of splintered sapling. Ross climbed stiffly over the welter of drift caught on the sand spit and pulled it loose, recognizing the string even before he touched it. That square knot was of McNeil's tying. As Murdock sat down weakly in the sand and mud, nervously fingering the twisted cord, he stared vacantly at the river. His last small hope died. The raft must have broken up, and neither Ashe nor McNeil could have survived the ultimate disaster.

Ross Murdock was alone, marooned in a time which was not his own, with little promise of escape. That one thought blanked out his mind with its own darkness. What was the use of getting up again, or trying to find food for his empty stomach, or warmth and shelter?

He had always prided himself on being able to go it alone, had thought himself secure in that calculated loneliness. Now that belief had been washed away in the river along with most of the will power which had kept him going these past days. Before, there had always been some goal, no matter how remote. Now, he had nothing. Even if he managed to reach the mouth of the river, he had no idea of where or how to summon the sub from the overseas post. All three of the time travelers might already have been written off the rolls, since they had not reported in.

Ross pulled the rag free from the sapling and wreathed it in a tight bracelet about his grimed wrist for some unexplainable reason. Worn and tired, he tried to think ahead. There was no chance of contacting Ulffa's tribe again. Along with all the other woodland hunters they must have fled before the advance of the horsemen. No, there was no reason to go back, and why make the effort to advance?

The sun was hot. This was one of those spring days which foretell the ripeness of summer. Insects buzzed in the reed banks where a green sheen showed. Birds wheeled and circled in the sky. Some flock was disturbed, their cries reaching Ross in hoarse calls of warning.

He was still plastered with patches of dried mud and slime, the reek of it thick in his nostrils. Now Ross brushed at a splotch on his knee, picking loose flakes to expose the alien cloth of his suit underneath, seemingly unbefouled. All at once it became necessary to be clean again at least.

Ross waded into the stream, stooping to splash the brown water over his body and then rubbing away the resulting mud. In the sunlight the fabric had a brilliant glow, as if it not only drew the light but reflected it. Wading farther out into the water, he began to swim, not with any goal in view, but because it was easier than crawling back to land once more.

Using the downstream current to supplement his

skill, he watched both banks. He could not really hope to see either the raft or indications that its passengers had won to shore, but somewhere deep inside him he had not yet accepted defeat.

The effort of swimming broke through that fog of inertia which had held him since he had awakened that morning. With a somewhat healthier interest in life Ross came ashore again on an arm of a bay or inlet angling back into the land. Here the banks of the river were well above his head, and believing that he was well sheltered, he stripped, hanging his suit in the sunlight and letting the unusual heat of the day soothe his body.

A raw fish, cornered in the shallows and scooped out, furnished one of the best meals he had ever tasted. He had reached for the suit draped over a willow limb when the first and only warning that his fortunes had once again changed came, swiftly, silently, and with deadly promise.

One moment the willows had moved gently in the breeze, and then a spear suddenly set them all quivering. Ross clutching the suit to him with a frantic grab, skidded about in the sand, going to one knee in his haste.

He found himself completely at the mercy of the two men standing on the bank well above him. Unlike Ulffa's people or the Beaker traders, they were very tall, with heavy braids of light, sunbleached hair swinging forward on their wide chests. Their leather tunics hung to mid-thigh above leggings which were bound to their limbs with painted straps. Cuff bracelets of copper ringed their forearms, and necklaces of animal teeth and beads displayed their personal wealth. Ross could not remember having seen their like on any of the briefing tapes at the base.

One spear had been a warning, but a second was held ready, so Ross made the age-old signal of surrender, reluctantly dropping his suit and raising his hands palm out and shoulder high.

"Friend?" Ross asked in the Beaker tongue. The traders ranged far, and perhaps there was a chance they had had contact with this tribe.

The spear twirled and the younger stranger effortlessly leaped down the bank. He paddled over to Ross to pick up the suit he had dropped and held it up while he made some comment to his companion. He seemed fascinated by the fabric, pulling and smoothing it between his hands. Ross wondered if there was a chance of trading it for his own freedom.

Both men were armed, not only with the long-bladed daggers favored by the Beaker folk, but also with axes. When Ross made a slight effort to lower his hands the man before him reached to his belt ax, growling what was plainly a warning. Ross blinked, realizing that they might well knock him out and leave him behind, taking the suit with them.

Finally, they decided in favor of including him in their loot. Throwing the suit over one arm, the stranger caught Ross by the shoulder and pushed him forward roughly. The pebbled beach was painful to Ross's feet, and the breeze which whipped about him as he reached the top of the bank reminded him only too forcibly of his ordeal in the glacial world.

Murdock was tempted to dash out on the point of the bank and dive into the river, but it was already too late. The man who was holding the spear had moved behind him, and Ross's wrist, held in a vise grip at the small of his back, kept him prisoner as he was pushed on into the meadow. There three shaggy horses grazed, their nose ropes gathered into the hands of a third man.

A sharp stone half buried in the ground changed the pattern of the day. Ross's heel scraped against it, and the resulting pain triggered his rebellion into explosion. He threw himself backward, his bruised heel sliding between the feet of his captor, bringing them both to the ground with himself on top. The other expelled air from his lungs in a grunt of surprise, and Ross whipped over, one hand grasping the hilt of the tribesman's dagger while the other, free of that prisoning wristlock, chopped at the fellow's throat.

Dagger out and ready, Ross faced the men in a half crouch as he had been drilled. They stared at him in open-mouthed amazement, then too late the spears went up. Ross placed the point of his looted weapon at the throat of the now quiet man by whom he knelt, and he spoke the language he had learned from Ulffa's people.

"You strike—this one dies."

They must have read the determined purpose in his eyes, for slowly, reluctantly, the spears went down. Having gained so much of a victory, Ross dared more. "Take—" he motioned to the waiting horses— "take and go!"

For a moment he thought that this time they would meet his challenge, but he continued to hold the dagger above the brown throat of the man who was now moaning faintly. His threat continued to register, for the other man shrugged the suit from his arm, left it lying on the ground, and retreated. Holding the nose rope of his horse, he mounted, waved the herder up also, and both of them rode slowly away.

The prisoner was slowly coming around, so Ross only had time to pull on the suit; he had not even fastened the breast studs before those blue eyes opened. A sunburned hand flashed to a belt, but the dagger and ax which had once hung there were now in Ross's possession. He watched the tribesman carefully as he finished dressing.

"What you do?" The words were in the speech of the forest people, distorted by a new accent.

"You go—" Ross pointed to the third horse the others had left behind— "I go—" he indicated the river—"I take these"—he patted the dagger and the ax. The other scowled.

"Not good . . ."

Ross laughed, a little hysterically. "Not good you," he agreed, "good—me!"

To his surprise the tribesman's stiff face relaxed, and the fellow barked a laugh. He sat up, rubbing at his throat, a big grin pulling at the corners of his mouth.

"You hunter?" The man pointed northeast to the woodlands fringing the hills.

Ross shook his head. "Trader, me."

"Trader," the other repeated. Then he tapped one of the wide metal cuffs at his wrist. "Trade—this?"

"That. More things."

"Where?"

Ross pointed downstream. "By bitter water—trade there."

The man appeared puzzled. "Why you here?"

"Ride river water, like you ride," he said, pointing to the horse. "Ride on trees—many trees tied together. Trees break apart—I come here."

The conception of a raft voyage apparently got across, for the tribesman was nodding. Getting to his feet, he walked across to take up the nose rope of the waiting horse. "You come camp—Foscar. Foscar chief. He like you show trick how you take Tulka, make him sleep—hold his ax, knife."

Ross hesitated. This Tulka seemed friendly now, but

would that friendliness last? He shook his head. "I go to bitter water. My chief there."

Tulka was scowling again. "You speak crooked words—your chief there!" He pointed eastward with a dramatic stretch of the arm. "You chief speak Foscar. Say he give much these—" he touched his copper cuffs—"good knives, axes—get you back."

Ross stared at him without understanding. Ashe? Ashe in this Foscar's camp offering a reward for him? But how could that be?

"How you know my chief?"

Tulka laughed, this time derisively. "You wear shining skin—your chief wear shiny skin. He say find other shiny skin—give many good things to man who bring you back."

Shiny skin! The suit from the alien ship! Was it the ship people? Ross remembered the light on him as he climbed out of the Red village. He must have been sighted by one of the spacemen. But why were they searching for him, alerting the natives in an effort to scoop him up? What made Ross Murdock so important that they must have him? He only knew that he was not going to be taken if he could help it, that he had no desire to meet this "chief" who had offered treasure for his capture.

"You will come!" Tulka went into action, his mount flashing forward almost in a running leap at Ross, who stumbled back when horse and rider loomed over him. He swung up the ax, but it was a weapon with which he had no training, too heavy for him.

His blow met only thin air as the shoulder of the mount hit him. Ross went down, avoiding by less than a finger's breadth the thud of an unshod hoof against his skull. Then the rider landed on him, crushing him flat. A fist connected with his jaw, and for Ross the sun went out.

He found himself hanging across a support which moved with a rocking gait, whose pounding hurt his head, keeping him half dazed. Ross tried to move, but he realized that his arms were behind his back, fastened wrist to wrist, and a warm weight centered in the small of his spine to hold him face down on a horse. He could do nothing except endure the discomfort as best he could and hope for a speedy end to the gallop.

Over his head passed the cackle of speech. He caught short glimpses of another horse matching pace to the one that carried him. Then they swept into a noisy place where the shouting of many men made a din. The horse stopped. Ross was pulled from its back and dropped to the trodden dust, to lie blinking up dizzily, trying to focus on the scene about him.

They had arrived at the camp of the horsemen, whose hide tents served as a backdrop for the fair long-haired giants and the tall women hovering about to view the captive. The circle about him then broke, and men stood aside for a newcomer. Ross had been impressed with the size of his original captors, but this one was their master. Lying on the ground at the chieftain's feet, Ross felt like a small and helpless child.

Foscar, if Foscar this was, looked strong as a bear. Heavy muscles rippled across his arms and shoulders as he leaned over to inspect Tulka's prize. Ross glared up at him, that same hot rage which had led to his attack on Tulka now urging him to the only defiance he had left—words.

"Look well, Foscar. Free me, and I would do more than *look* at you," he said in the speech of the woods hunters.

Foscar's blue eyes widened and he lowered a fist which could have swallowed in its grasp both of Ross's hands. Linking those great fingers in the stuff of the suit he drew the captive to his feet, with no sign that his act had required any effort. Even standing, Ross was a good eight inches shorter than the chieftain. Yet he put up his chin and eyed the other squarely, without giving ground.

"So—yet still my hands are tied." He put into that all the taunting inflection he could summon. His reception by Tulka had given him one faint clue to the character of these people; they might be brought to acknowledge the worth of one who stood up to them.

"Child—" The fist shifted from its grip on the fabric covering Ross's chest to his shoulder, and now under its compulsion Ross swayed back and forth.

"Child?" From somewhere Ross raised that short laugh. "Ask Tulka. I be no child, Foscar. Tulka's ax, Tulka's knife—they were in my hand. A horse Tulka had to use to bring me down."

Foscar regarded him intently and then grinned. "Sharp tongue," he commented. "Tulka lost knife—ax? So! Ennar," he called over his shoulder, and one of the men stepped out a pace beyond his fellows.

He was shorter and much younger than his chief, with a boy's rangy slimness and an open, good-looking face. His eyes shone on Foscar, bright with eager excitement. Like the other tribesmen he was armed with belt dagger and ax, and since he wore two necklaces and both cuff bracelets and upper armlets as did Foscar, Ross thought he might be a relative of the older man.

"Child!" Foscar clapped his hand on Ross's shoulder and then withdrew the hold. "Child!" He indicated Ennar, who reddened. "You take from Ennar ax, knife," Foscar ordered, "as you took from Tulka." He made a sign, and someone cut the thongs about Ross's wrists.

Ross rubbed one numbed hand against the other, setting his jaw. Foscar had stung his young follower with that contemptuous "child," so the boy would be eager to match all his skill against the prisoner. This would not be as easy as his taking Tulka by surprise. But if he refused, Foscar might well order him killed out of hand. He had chosen to be defiant; he would have to do his best.

"Take—ax, knife—" Foscar stepped back, waving at his men to open out a ring encircling the two young men.

Ross felt a little sick as he watched Ennar's hand go to the haft of the ax. Nothing had been said about Ennar's not using his weapons in defense, but Ross noted that there was some sense of sportsmanship in the tribesmen after all. It was Tulka who pushed to the chief's side and said something which made Foscar roar bull-voiced at his youthful companion.

Ennar's hand came away from the ax hilt as if that polished wood were white-hot, and he transferred his discomfiture to Ross as the other understood. Ennar had to win now for his own pride's sake, and Ross felt *he* had to win for his life. They circled warily, Ross watching his opponent's eyes rather than those half-closed hands held at waist level.

Back at the base he had been matched with Ashe, and before Ashe with the tough-bodied, skilled, and merciless trainers in unarmed combat. He had had beaten into his bruised flesh knowledge of holds and blows intended to save his skin in just such an encounter. But then he had been well-fed, alert, prepared. He had not been knocked silly and then transported for miles slung across a horse after days of exposure and hard usage. It remained to be learned—was Ross Murdock as tough as he always thought himself to be? Tough or not, he was in this until he won—or dropped.

Comments from the crowd aroused Ennar to the first definite action. He charged, stooping low in a wrestler's stance, but Ross squatted even lower. One hand flicked to the churned dust of the ground and snapped up again, sending a cloud of grit into the tribesman's face. Then their bodies met with a shock, and Ennar sailed over Ross's shoulder to skid along the earth.

Had Ross been fresh, the contest would have ended there and then in his favor. But when he tried to whirl and throw himself on his opponent he was too slow. Ennar was not waiting to be pinned flat, and it was Ross's turn to be caught at a disadvantage.

A hand shot out to catch his leg just above the ankle, and once again Ross obeyed his teaching, falling easily at that pull, to land across his opponent. Ennar, disconcerted by the too-quick success of his attack, was unprepared for this. Ross rolled, trying to escape steel-fingered hands, his own chopping out in edgewise blows, striving to serve Ennar as he had Tulka.

He had to take a lot of punishment, though he managed to elude the powerful bear hug in which he knew the other was laboring to engulf him, a hold which would speedily crush him into submission. Clinging to the methods he had been taught, he fought on. Only now he knew, with a growing panic, that his best was not good enough. He was too spent to make an end. Unless he had some piece of great good luck, he could only delay his own defeat.

Fingers clawed viciously at his eyes, and Ross did what he had never thought to do in any fight—he snapped wolfishly, his teeth closing on flesh as he brought up his knee and drove it home into the body wriggling on his. There was a gasp of hot breath in his face as Ross called upon the last few rags of his strength, tearing loose from the other's slackened hold.

He scrambled to one knee. Ennar was also on his knees, crouching like a four-legged beast ready to spring. Ross risked everything on a last gamble. Clasping his hands together, he raised them as high as he could and brought them down on the nape of the other's neck. Ennar sprawled forward facedown in the dust where seconds later Ross joined him.

16

Murdock lay on his back, gazing up at the laced hides which stretched to make the tent roofing. Having been battered just enough to feel all one aching bruise, Ross had lost interest in the future. Only the present mattered, and it was a dark one. He might have fought Ennar to a standstill, but in the eyes of the horsemen he had also been beaten, and he had not impressed them as he had hoped. That he still lived was a minor wonder, but he deduced that he continued to breathe only because they wanted to trade him for the reward offered by the aliens from out of time. It was not a pleasant prospect to contemplate.

His wrists were lashed over his head to a peg driven deeply into the ground; his ankles were bound to another. He could turn his head from side to side, but any further movement was impossible. He ate only bits of food dropped into his mouth by a dirty-fingered slave, a cowed hunter captured from a tribe overwhelmed in the migration of the horsemen.

"Ho—taker of axes!" A toe jarred his ribs, and Ross bit back the grunt of pain which answered that rude bid for his attention. He saw in the dim light Ennar's face and was savagely glad to note the discolorations about the right eye and along the jaw line, the signatures left by his own skinned knuckles.

"Ho—warrior!" Ross returned hoarsely, trying to lade that title with all the scorn he could summon.

Ennar's hand, holding a knife, swung into his limited range of vision. "To clip a sharp tongue is a good thing!" The young tribesman grinned as he knelt down beside the helpless prisoner.

Ross knew a thrill of fear worse than any pain. Ennar might be about to do just what he hinted! Instead, the knife swung up and Ross felt sawing at the cords about his wrists. He endured the pain in the raw gouges the bands had cut in his flesh with gratitude that it was not mutilation which had brought Ennar to him. He knew that his arms were free, but to draw them down from over his head was almost more than he could do, and he lay quiet as Ennar loosed his feet.

"Up!"

Without Ennar's hands pulling at him, Ross could not have reached his feet. Nor did he stay erect once he had been raised, crashing forward on his face as the other let him go, hot anger eating at him because of his own helplessness.

In the end, Ennar summoned two slaves who dragged Ross into the open where a council assembled about a fire. A debate was in progress, sometimes so heated that the speakers fingered their knife or ax hilts when they shouted their arguments. Ross could not understand their language, but he was certain that he was the subject under discussion. Foscar had the deciding vote but had not yet given the nod to either side.

Ross sat where the slaves had dumped him, rubbing his smarting wrists, so deathly weary in mind and beaten in body that he was not really interested in the fate they were planning for him. He was content merely to be free of his bonds. It was a small favor, but one he savored dully.

He did not know how long the debate lasted, but at length Ennar came to stand over him with a message. "Your chief—he give many good things for you. Foscar take you to him."

"My chief is not here," Ross repeated wearily, making a protest he knew they would not heed. "My chief sits by the bitter water and waits. He will be angry if I do not come. Let Foscar fear his anger—"

Ennar laughed. "You run from your chief. He will be happy with Foscar when you lie again under his hand. You will not like that—I think it so!"

"I think so, too," Ross agreed silently.

He spent the rest of that night lying between the watchful Ennar and another guard, though they had the humanity not to bind him again. In the morning he was allowed to feed himself, and he fished chunks of venison out of a stew with his unwashed fingers. But in spite of the messiness, it was the best food he had eaten in days.

The trip, however, was anything but comfortable. He was mounted on one of the shaggy horses, a rope run under the animal's belly to loop one foot to the other. Fortunately, his hands were bound so he was able to grasp the coarse, wiry mane and keep his seat after a fashion. The nose rope of his mount was passed to Tulka, and Ennar rode beside him with only half an eye for the path of his own horse and the balance of his attention for the prisoner.

They headed northwest, with the hills as a green-and-white goal against the morning sky. Though Ross's sense of direction was not too acute, he was certain that they were making for the general vicinity of the hidden village, which he believed the ship people had destroyed. He tried to discover how contact had been made between the aliens and the horsemen.

"How find other chief?" he asked Ennar.

The young man tossed one of his braids back across his shoulder and turned his head to face Ross squarely. "Your chief come our camp. Talk with Foscar—two—four sleeps ago."

"How talk with Foscar? With hunter talk?"

For the first time Ennar did not appear altogether certain. He scowled and then snapped, "He talk—Foscar, us. We hear right words—not woods creeper talk. He speak to us good."

Ross was puzzled. How could the alien out of time speak the proper language of a primitive tribe some thousands of years removed from his own era? Were the ship people also familiar with time travel? Did they have their own stations of transfer? Yet their fury with the Russians had been hot. He was mystified.

"This chief—he look like me?"

Again Ennar appeared at a loss. "He wear covering, like you."

"But was he like me?" persisted Ross. He didn't know what he was trying to learn. But it seemed important at that moment to press home to at least one of the tribesmen that he *was* different from the man who had put a price on his head and to whom he was to be sold.

"Not like!" Tulka spoke over his shoulder. "You look like hunter people—hair, eyes— Strange chief no hair on head, eyes not like—"

"You saw him too?" Ross demanded eagerly.

"I saw. I ride to camp—they come so. Stand on rock, call to Foscar. Make magic with fire—it jump up!" He pointed his arm stiffly at a bush before them on the trail. "They point little, little spear—fire come out of the ground and burn. They say burn our camp if we do not give them man. We say—not have man. Then they say many good things for us if we find and bring man—"

"But they are not my people," Ross cut in. "You see, I have hair, I am not like them. They are bad—"

"Maybe you taken in war by them—chief's slave." Ennar had a reply to that which was logical according to the customs of his own tribe. "They want slave back—it is so."

"My people strong too, much magic," Ross pushed. "Take me to bitter water and they pay much—more than stranger chief!"

Both tribesmen were amused. "Where bitter water?" asked Tulka.

Ross jerked his head to the west. "Some sleeps away—"

"Some sleeps!" repeated Ennar jeeringly. "We ride some sleeps, maybe many sleeps where we know not the trails—maybe no people there, maybe no bitter water—all things you say with split tongue so that we not give you back to master. We go this way not even one sleep—find chief, get good things. Why we do hard thing when we can do easy?"

What argument could Ross offer in rebuttal to the simple logic of his captors? For a moment he raged inwardly at his own helplessness. But long ago he had learned that giving way to hot fury was not good unless one did it deliberately to impress, and then only when one had the upper hand. Now Ross had no hand at all.

For the most part they kept to the open, whereas Ross and the other two agents had skulked in wooded areas on their flight through this same territory. So they approached the hills from a different angle, and though he tried, Ross could pick out no familiar landmarks. If by some miracle he was able to free himself from his captors, he could only head due west and hope to strike the river.

At midday their party made camp in a grove of trees by a spring. The weather was as unseasonably warm as it had been the day before. Flies, brought out of cold-weather hiding, attacked the stamping horses and crawled over Ross. He tried to keep them off with swings of his bound hands, for their bites drew blood.

Having been tumbled from his mount, he remained fastened to a tree with a noose about his neck while the horsemen built a fire and broiled strips of deer meat.

It would seem that Foscar was in no hurry to get on, since after they had eaten, the men continued to lounge at ease, some even dropping off to sleep. When Ross counted faces he learned that Tulka and another had both disappeared, possibly to contact and warn the aliens they were coming.

It was midafternoon before the scouts reappeared, as unobtrusively as they had gone. They went before Foscar with a report which brought the chief over to Ross. "We go. Your chief waits—"

Ross raised his swollen, bitter face and made his usual protest. "Not my chief!"

Foscar shrugged. "He say so. He give good things to get you back under his hand. So—he your chief!"

Once again Ross was boosted on his mount, and bound. But this time the party split into two groups as they rode off. He was with Ennar again, just behind Foscar, with two other guards bringing up the rear. The rest of the men, leading their mounts, melted into the trees. Ross watched that quiet withdrawal thoughtfully. It argued that Foscar did not trust those he was about to do business with, that he was taking certain precautions of his own. Only Ross could not see how that distrust, which might be only ordinary prudence on Foscar's part, could be any sort of advantage for him.

They rode at a pace hardly above a walk into a small open meadow narrowing at the east. Then for the first time Ross was able to place himself. They were at the entrance to the valley of the village, about a mile away from the narrow throat above which Ross had lain to spy and had been captured, for he had come from the north over the spurs of rising ridges.

Ross's horse was pulled up as Foscar drove his heels into the ribs of his own mount, sending it at a brisker pace toward the neck of the valley. There was a blot of blue there—more than one of the aliens were waiting. Ross caught his lip between his teeth and bit down on it hard. He had stood up to the Russians, to Foscar's tribesmen, but he shrank from meeting those strangers. He feared that the worst the men of his own species could do would be only a pale shadow to the treatment he might meet at their hands.

Foscar was now a toy man astride a toy horse. He halted his galloping mount to sit facing the handful of strangers. Ross counted four of them. They seemed to be talking, though there was still a good distance separating the mounted man and the blue suits.

Minutes passed before Foscar's arm raised in a wave to summon the party guarding Ross. Ennar kicked his horse to a trot, towing Ross's mount behind, the other two men thudding along more discreetly. Ross noted that they were both armed with spears which they carried to the fore as they rode.

They were perhaps three quarters of the way to join Foscar, and Ross could see plainly the bald heads of the aliens as their faces turned in his direction. Then the strangers struck. One of them raised a weapon shaped similarly to the automatic pistol Ross knew, except that it was longer in the barrel.

Ross did not know why he cried out, except that Foscar had only an ax and dagger which were both still sheathed at his belt. The chief sat very still, and then his horse gave a swift sidewise swerve as if in fright. Foscar collapsed, limp, bonelessly, to the trodden turf, to lie unmoving face down.

Ennar whooped, a cry combining defiance and despair in one. He reined up with enough violence to set his horse rearing. Then, dropping his hold on the leading rope of Ross's mount, he whirled and set off in a wild dash for the trees to the left. A spear lanced across Ross's shoulder, ripping at the blue fabric, but his horse whirled to follow the other, taking him out of danger of a second thrust. Having lost his opportunity, the man who had wielded the spear dashed by at Ennar's back.

Ross clung to the mane with both hands. His greatest fear was that he might slip from the saddle pad and since he was tied by his feet, lie unprotected and helpless under those dashing hoofs. Somehow he managed to cling to the horse's neck, his face whipped by the rough mane as the animal pounded on. Had Ross been able to grasp the dangling rope, he might have had a faint chance of controlling that run, but as it was he could only hold fast and hope.

He had only broken glimpses of what lay ahead. Then a brilliant fire, as vivid as the flames which had eaten up the Russian village, burst from the ground a few yards ahead, sending the horse wild. There was more fire and the horse changed course through the rising smoke. Ross realized that the aliens were trying to cut him off from the thin safety of the woodlands. Why they didn't just shoot him, as they had Foscar, he could not understand.

The smoke of the burning grass was thick, cutting between him and the woods. Might it also provide a curtain behind which he could hope to escape both parties? The fire was sending the horse back toward the waiting ship people. Ross could hear a confused shouting in the smoke. Then his mount miscalculated, and a tongue of red licked too close. The animal screamed, dashing on blindly straight between two of the blazes and away from the blue-clad men.

Ross coughed, almost choking. His eyes watered as the stench of singed hair thickened the smoke. But he had been carried out of the fire circle and was shooting back into the meadow-land. Mount and unwilling rider were well away from the upper end of that cleared space when another horse cut in from the left, matching speed to the uncontrolled animal to which Ross clung. It was one of the tribesmen riding easily.

The trick worked, for the wild race slowed to a gallop. The other rider, in a feat of horsemanship at which Ross marveled, leaned from his seat to catch the dangling nose rope, bringing the runaway against his own steady steed. Ross shaken, still coughing from the smoke and unable to sit upright, held to the mane. The gallop slowed to a rocking pace and finally came to a halt. Both horses stood blowing, white-foam patches on their chests and their riders' legs.

Having made his capture, the tribesman seemed indifferent to Ross, looking back instead at the wide curtain of grass smoke, frowning as he studied the swift spread of the fire. Muttering to himself, he pulled the lead rope and brought Ross's horse to follow in the direction from which Ennar had brought the captive less than a half hour earlier.

Ross tried to think. The unexpected death of their chief might well mean his own, should the tribe's desire for vengeance now be aroused. On the other hand, there was a faint chance that he could now better persuade them that he was indeed of another clan and that to aid him would be to work against a common enemy.

But it was hard to plan clearly, though wits alone could save him now. The parley which had ended with Foscar's murder had bought Ross a small measure of time. He was still a captive, although of the tribesmen and not the unearthly strangers. Perhaps to the ship people these primitives scarcely counted higher than the forest animals.

Ross did not try to talk to his present guard, who towed him under the western sun of late afternoon. They halted at last in that same small grove where they had rested at noon. The tribesman fastened the mounts and then inspected the animal Ross had ridden. With a grunt he loosened the prisoner and spilled him unceremoniously on the ground while he examined the horse. Ross levered himself up to see the burn mark across the horse's hide where the fire had blistered the skin.

Thick handfuls of mud from the side of the spring were brought and plastered over the seared strip. Then, having rubbed down both animals with twists of grass, the man came over to Ross, pushed him back to the ground, and studied his left leg.

Ross understood. By rights, his thigh should also have been scorched where the flame had hit, yet he felt no pain. Now as the tribesman examined him for a burn, he could not see even the faintest discoloration of the strange fabric. He remembered how the aliens had strolled unconcerned through the burning village. As the suit had insulated him against the cold of the ice, it seemed that it had also protected him against the fire, for which he was duly thankful. His escape from injury was a puzzle to the tribesman, who, failing to find any trace of burn on him, left Ross alone and went to sit well away from his prisoner as if he feared him.

They did not have long to wait. One by one, those who had ridden in Foscar's company gathered at the grove. The very last to come were Ennar and Tulka, carrying the body of their chief. The faces of both men were smeared with dust and when the others sighted the body they, too, rubbed dust into their cheeks, reciting a string of words and going one by one to touch the dead chieftain's right hand.

Ennar, resigning his burden to the others, slid from his tired horse and stood for a long moment, his head bowed. Then he gazed straight at Ross and came across the tiny clearing to stand over the man of a later time. The boyishness which had been a part of him when he had fought at Foscar's command was gone. His eyes were merciless as he leaned down to speak, shaping each word with slow care so that Ross could understand the promise—that frightful promise:

"Woods rat, Foscar goes to his burial fire. And he shall take a slave with him to serve him beyond the sky—a slave to run at his voice, to shake when he thunders. Slave-dog, you shall run for Foscar beyond the sky, and he shall have you forever to walk upon as a man walks upon the earth. I, Ennar, swear that Foscar shall be sent to the chiefs in the sky in all honor. And that you, dog-one, shall lie at his feet in that going!"

He did not touch Ross, but there was no doubt in Ross's mind that he meant every word he spoke.

17

The preparations for Foscar's funeral went on through the night. A wooden structure, made up of tied fagots dragged in from the woodland, grew taller beyond the big tribal camp. The constant crooning wail of the women in the tents was enough to drive a man to the edge of madness. Ross had been left under guard where he could watch it all, a refinement of torture which he would earlier have believed too subtle for Ennar. Though the older men carried minor commands among the horsemen, because Ennar was the closest of blood kin among the adult males, he was in charge of the coming ceremony.

The pick of the horse herd, a roan stallion, was brought in to be picketed near Ross as sacrifice number two, and two of the hounds were in turn leashed close by. Foscar, his best weapons to hand and a red cloak lapped about him, lay waiting on a bier. Nearby squatted the tribal wizard, shaking his thunder rattle and alternately chanting and shrieking. This wild activity might have been a scene lifted directly from

197

some tape stored at the project base. It was very difficult for Ross to remember that this was reality, that he was to be one of the main actors in the coming event, with no timely aid from Operation Retrograde to snatch him to safety.

Sometime during that nightmare he slept, his weariness of body overcoming him. He awoke, dazed, to find a hand clutching his mop of hair, pulling his head up.

"You sleep—you do not fear, Foscar's dog-one?"

Groggily Ross blinked up. Fear? Sure, he was afraid. Fear, he realized with a clarity such as he had seldom experienced before, had always stalked beside him, slept in his bed. But he had never surrendered to it, and he would not now if he could help it.

"I do not fear!" He threw that creed into Ennar's face in one hot boast. He *would* not fear!

"We shall see if you speak so loudly when the fire bites you!" The other spat, yet in that oath there was a reluctant recognition of Ross's courage.

"When the fire bites . . ." That sang in Ross's head. There was something else—if he could only remember! Up to that moment he had kept a poor little shadow of hope. It is always impossible—he again felt that strange clarity of mind—for a man to face his own death honestly. A man always continues to believe to the last moment of his life that something will intervene to save him.

The men led the horse to the mound of fagots which was now crowned with Foscar's bier. The stallion went quietly, until a tall tribesman struck true with an ax, and the animal fell. The hounds were also killed and laid at their dead master's feet.

But Ross was not to fare so easily. The wizard danced about him, a hideous figure in a beast mask, a curled fringe of dried snakeskins swaying from his belt. Shaking his rattle, he squawked like an angry cat as they pulled Ross to the stacked wood.

Fire—there was something about fire—if he could only remember! Ross stumbled and nearly fell across one leg of the dead horse they were propping into place. Then he remembered that tongue of flame in the meadow grass which had burned the horse but not the rider. His hands and his head would have no protection, but the rest of his body was covered with the flame-resistant fabric of the alien suit. Could he do it? There was such a slight chance, and they were already pushing him onto the mound, his hands tied. Ennar stooped, and bound his ankles, securing him to the brush.

So fastened, they left him. The tribe ringed around the pyre at a safe distance, Ennar and five other men approaching from different directions, torches aflame. Ross watched those blazing knots thrust into the brush and heard the crackle of the fire. With hard and measuring eyes he studied the flash of flame from dried brush to seasoned wood.

A tongue of yellow-red flame licked up at him. Ross hardly dared to breathe as it wreathed about his foot, his hide fetters smoldering. The insulation of the suit did not cut all the heat, but it allowed him to stay put for the few seconds he needed to make his escape spectacular.

The flame had eaten through his foot bonds, and yet the burning sensation on his feet and legs was no greater than it would have been from the direct rays of a bright summer sun. Ross moistened his lips with his tongue. The impact of heat on his hands and face was different. He leaned down, held his wrists to the flame, taking in stoical silence the burns which freed him.

Then, as the fire curled up so that he seemed to

stand in a frame of writhing red banners, Ross leaped
through that curtain, protecting his bowed head with
his arms as best he could. But to the onlookers it
seemed he passed unhurt through the heart of a roaring fire.

Keeping his footing, he stood facing that part of
the tribal ring directly before him. A cry rose and a
blazing torch flew through the air and struck his hip.
Although he felt the force of the blow, the burning
bits of the head merely slid down his thigh and leg,
leaving no mark on the smooth blue fabric.

"Ahhh!"

Now the wizard capered before him, shaking his
rattle to make a deafening din. Ross struck out, slapping the sorcerer out of his path. He stooped to pick
up the smoldering brand which had been thrown at
him. Whirling it about his head, though every movement was torture to his scorched hands, he set it
flaming once more. Holding it in front of him as a
weapon, he stalked directly at the men and women
before him.

The torch was a poor enough defense against spears
and axes, but Ross did not care—he put into this last
gamble all the determination he could summon. Nor
did he realize what a figure he presented to the tribesmen. A man who had crossed a curtain of fire without apparent hurt, who appeared to bathe in tongues
of flame without harm, and who now called upon fire
in turn as a weapon, was no man but a demon!

The wall of people wavered and broke. Women
screamed and ran; men shouted. But no one threw
a spear or struck with an ax. Ross walked on, a man
possessed, looking neither to the right or left. He was
in the camp now, stalking toward the fire burning
before Foscar's tent. He did not turn aside for that
either, but holding the torch high, strode through the

heart of the flames, risking further burns for the sake of insuring his ultimate safety.

The tribesmen melted away as he approached the last line of tents, with the open land beyond. The horses of the herd, which had been driven to this side to avoid the funeral pyre, were shifting nervously. The scent of burning was making them uneasy.

Once more Ross whirled the dying torch about his head. Recalling how the aliens had sent his horse mad, he tossed it behind him into the grass between the tents and the herd. The tinder-dry stuff caught immediately. Now if the men tried to ride after him, they would have trouble.

Without hindrance he walked across the meadow at the same even pace, never turning to look behind. His hands were two separate worlds of smarting pain; his hair and eyebrows were singed, and a finger of burn ran along the angle of his jaw. But he was free, and he did not believe that Foscar's men would be in any haste to pursue him. Somewhere before him lay the river, the river which ran to the sea. Ross walked on in the sunny morning while behind him black smoke raised a dark beacon to the sky.

Afterward he guessed that he must have been light-headed for several days, remembering little save the pain in his hands and the fact that it was necessary to keep moving. Once he fell to his knees and buried both hands in the cool, moist earth where a thread of stream trickled from a pool. The muck eased a little of the agony while he drank with a fever thirst.

Ross seemed to move through a haze which lifted at intervals during which he noted his surroundings, was able to recall a little of what lay behind him, and to keep to the correct route. However, the gaps of time in between were forever lost to him. He stumbled along the banks of a river and fronted a

bear fishing. The massive beast rose on its hind legs
and growled, but Ross walked by it uncaring, unmen-
aced by the puzzled animal.

Sometimes he slept through the dark periods which
marked the nights, or he stumbled along under the
moon, nursing his hands against his breast, whimpering
a little when his foot slipped and the jar of that mishap
ran through his body. Once he heard singing, only to
realize that it was himself who croaked a melody which
would be popular thousands of years later in the world
through which he wandered. But always Ross knew
that he must go on, using that thick stream of running water as a guide to his final goal, the sea.

After a long while those spaces of mental clarity
grew longer, appearing closer together. He dug small
shelled things from under stones along the river and
ate them avidly. Once he clubbed a rabbit and feasted.
He sucked birds' eggs from a nest hidden among some
reeds—just enough to keep his gaunt body going,
though his gray eyes were now set in a death's-head
of a face.

Ross did not know just when he realized that he
was again being hunted. It started with an uneasiness
different from his previous fever-bred hallucinations.
This was an inner pulling, a growing compulsion to
turn and retrace his way back toward the hills to meet
something, or someone, waiting for him on the backward path.

But Ross kept on, fearing sleep now and fighting it. For once he had lain down to rest and had
wakened on his feet, heading back as if that compulsion had the power to take over his body when
his waking will was off guard.

So he rested, but dared not sleep. The desire
constantly tore at his will, striving to take over his
weakened body and draw it back. Against all reason

he believed that it was the aliens who were trying to control him. Ross did not even venture to guess why they were so determined to get him. If there were tribesmen on his trail as well, he did not know, but he was sure that this was now purely a duel of wills.

As the banks of the river were giving way to marshes, he had to wade through mud and water, detouring the boggy sections. Great clouds of birds whirled and shrieked their protests at his coming. Sleek water animals paddled and poked curious heads out of the water as this two-legged thing walked mechanically through their green land. Always that pull was with him, until Ross was more aware of fighting it than of traveling.

Why did they want him to return? Why did they not follow him? Were they afraid to venture too far from where they had come through the transfer? Yet the unseen rope tugging at him grew no thinner as he put more distance between himself and the valley. Ross could understand neither their motives nor their methods, but he could continue to fight.

The bog was endless. He found an island and lashed himself with his suit belt to the single willow which grew there, knowing that he must have sleep, or he could not hope to last through the next day. Then he slept, only to waken cold, shaking, and afraid. Shoulder deep in a pool, he was aware that in his sleep he must have opened the belt buckle and freed himself. Only the mishap of falling into the water had brought him around to sanity.

Somehow he got back to the tree, rehooked the buckle and twisted the belt around the branches so that he was sure he could not work it free until daybreak. He lapsed into a deepening doze, and awoke, still safely anchored, at the morning cries of the birds. Ross considered the suit as he untangled the belt. Could the strange clothing be the tie by which the aliens held to him? If he were to strip, leaving the garment behind, would he be safe?

He tried to force open the studs across his chest, but they would not yield to the slight pressure which was all his seared fingers could exert, and when he pulled at the fabric, he was unable to tear it. So, still wearing the livery of the off-world men, Ross continued on his way, hardly caring where he went or how. The mud plastered on him by his frequent falls was some protection against the swarm of insect life his passing stirred into attack. However, he was able to endure a swollen face and slitted eyes, being far more conscious of the wrenching feeling within him than the misery of his body.

The character of the marsh began to change once more. The river was splitting into a dozen smaller streams spreading like a fan. Looking down at this from one of the marsh hillocks, Ross knew a faint surge of relief. Such a place had been on the map Ashe had made him memorize. He was close to the sea at last. For the moment that was enough.

A salt-sharpened wind cut at him with the force of a fist in the face. In the absence of sunlight the leaden clouds spread winterlike gloom across the countryside. To the constant sound of birdcalls Ross tramped heavily through small pools, forcing a path through tangles of marsh grass. He stole eggs from nests, sucking his nourishment eagerly with no dislike for the fishy flavor, and drinking from brackish ponds.

Suddenly Ross halted, at first thinking that the continuous roll of sound he heard was thunder. Yet the clouds overhead were massed no more than previously and he saw no sign of lightning. Continuing on, he realized that the mysterious sound was the pounding of surf—he was near the sea!

Willing his body to run, he reeled forward at a trot, pitting all his energy against the incessant pull from behind. His feet skidded out of marsh mud and into sand. Ahead of him were dark rocks surrounded by the white lace of spray.

Ross headed straight toward that spray until he stood knee-deep in the curling, foam-edged water and felt its tug on his body almost as strong as that other tug upon his mind. He knelt, letting the salt water sting to life every cut, every burn, sputtering as it filled his mouth and nostrils, washing from him the slime of the bog lands. It was cold and bitter, but it was the sea! He had made it!

Ross Murdock staggered back and sat down suddenly in the sand. Glancing about, he saw that his refuge was a rough triangle between two of the small river arms, littered with the debris of the spring floods. Although there was plenty of material for a fire, he had no means of kindling a flame, having lost the flint all Beaker traders carried for such a purpose.

This was the sea, and against all odds he had reached it. He lay back, his self-confidence restored to the point where he dared once more to consider the future. He watched the swooping flight of gulls drawing patterns under the clouds above. For the moment he wanted nothing more than to lie here and rest.

But he did not surrender to this first demand of his overdriven body for long. Hungry and cold, sure that a storm was coming, he knew he had to build a fire—a fire on shore could provide him with the means of signaling the sub. Hardly knowing why—because one part of the coastline was as good as another—Ross began to walk again, threading a path in and out among the rocky outcrops.

So he found it, a hollow between two such wind-breaks within which was a blackened circle of small stones holding charred wood, with some empty shells piled near-by. Here was unmistakable evidence of a camp! Ross plunged forward, thrusting a hand impetuously into the black mass of the dead fire. To his astonishment, he touched warmth!

Hardly daring to disturb those precious bits of charcoal, he dug around them, then carefully blew into what appeared to be dead ashes. There was an answering glow! He could not have just imagined it.

From a pile of wood that had been left behind, Ross snatched a small twig, poking it at the coal after he had rubbed it into a brush on the rough rock. He watched, all one ache of hope. The twig caught!

With his stiff fingers so clumsy, he had to be very careful, but Ross had learned patience in a hard school. Bit by bit he fed that tiny blaze until he had a real fire. Then, leaning back against the rock, he watched it.

It was now obvious that the placement of the original fire had been chosen with care, for the outcrops gave it wind shelter. They also provided a dark backdrop, partially hiding the flames on the landward side but undoubtedly making them more visible from the sea. The site seemed just right for a signal fire—but to what?

Ross's hands shook slightly as he fed the blaze. It was only too clear why anyone would make a signal on this shore. McNeil—or perhaps both he and Ashe—had survived the breakup of the raft, after all. They had reached this point—abandoned no earlier than this morning, judging by the life remaining in the coals—and put up the signal. Then, just as arranged, they had been collected by the sub, by now on its way back to the hidden North American post. There was no hope of any pickup for him now. Just as he had believed them dead after he had found that rag on the sapling, so they must have thought him finished after his fall in the river. He was just a few hours too late!

Ross folded his arms across his hunched knees and rested his head on them. There was no possible way he could ever reach the post or his own kind—ever again. Thousands of miles lay between him and the temporary installation in this time.

He was so sunk in his own complete despair that he was long unaware of finally being free of the pressure to turn back which had so long haunted him. But as he roused to feed the fire he got to wondering. Had those who hunted him given up the chase? Since he had lost his own race with time, he did not really care. What did it matter?

The pile of wood was getting low, but he decided that did not matter either. Even so, Ross got to his feet, moving over to the drifts of storm wrack to gather more. Why should he stay here by a useless beacon? But somehow he could not force himself to move on, as futile as his vigil seemed.

Dragging the sun-bleached limbs of long-dead trees to his half shelter, he piled them up, working until he laughed at the barricade he had built. "A siege!" For the first time in days he spoke aloud. "I might be ready for a siege . . ." He pulled over another branch, added it to his pile, and kneeled down once more by the flames.

There were fisherfolk to be found along this coast, and tomorrow when he was rested he would strike south and try to find one of their primitive villages. Traders would be coming into this territory now that the Russian-inspired raiders were gone. If he could contact them . . .

But that spark of interest in the future died almost as soon as it was born. To be a Beaker trader as an agent for the project was one thing, to live the role for the rest of his life was something else.

Ross stood by his fire, staring out to sea for a sign he knew he would never see again as long as he lived. Then, sharp as a spear between his shoulder blades, the attack came.

The blow was not physical, but came instead as a tearing, red pain in his head, a pressure so terrible he could not move. He knew instantly that behind him now lurked the ultimate danger.

18

Ross fought to break that hold, to turn his head, to face the peril which crept upon him now. Unlike anything he had ever met before in his short lifetime, it could only have come from some alien source. This strange encounter was a battle of will against will! The same rebellion against authority which had ruled his boyhood, which had pushed him into the orbit of the project, stiffened him to meet this attack.

He was going to turn his head; he was going to see who stood there. He *was*! Inch by inch, Ross's head came around, though sweat stung his seared and bitten flesh, and every breath was an effort. He caught a half glimpse of the beach behind the rocks, and the stretch of sand was empty. Overhead the birds were gone—as if they had never existed. Or, as if they had been swept away by some impatient fighter, who wanted no distractions from the purpose at hand.

Having successfully turned his head, Ross decided to turn his body. His left hand went out, slowly, as if it moved some great weight. His palm gritted painfully

on the rock and he savored that pain, for it pierced
through the dead blanket of compulsion that was
being used against him. Deliberately he ground his
blistered skin against the stone, concentrating on the
sharp torment in his hand as the agony shot up his arm.
While he focused his attention on the physical pain,
he could feel the pressure against him weaken. Summoning all his strength, Ross swung around in a movement which was only a shadow of his former feline
grace.

The beach was still empty, except for the piles of
driftwood, the rocks, and the other things he had
originally found there. Yet he knew that something was
waiting to pounce. Having discovered that for him pain
was a defense weapon, he had that one resource. If
they took him, it would be after besting him in a fight.

Even as he made this decision, Ross was conscious
of a curious weakening of the force bent upon him.
It was as if his opponents had been surprised, either
at his simple actions of the past few seconds or at his
determination. Ross leaped upon that surprise, adding it to his stock of unseen weapons.

He leaned forward, still grinding his torn hand
against the rock as a steadying influence, took up a
length of dried wood, and thrust its end into the fire.
Having once used fire to save himself, he was ready
and willing to do it again, although at the same time,
another part of him shrank from what he intended.

Holding his improvised torch breast-high, Ross
stared across it, searching the land for the faintest sign
of his enemies. In spite of the fire and the light he
held before him, the dusk prevented him from seeing too far. Behind him the crash of the surf could
have covered the noise of a marching army.

"Come and get me!"

He whirled his brand into bursting life and then

hurled it straight into the drift among the dunes. He was grabbing for a second brand almost before the blazing head of the first had fallen into the twisted, bleached roots of a dead tree.

He stood tense, a second torch now kindled in his hand. The sharp vise of another's will which had nipped him so tightly a moment ago was easing, slowly disappearing as water might trickle away. Yet he could not believe that this small act of defiance had so daunted his unseen opponent as to make him give up the struggle this easily. It was more likely the pause of a wrestler seeking for a deadlier grip.

The brand in his hand—Ross's second line of defense—was a weapon he was loath to use, but would use if he were forced to it. He kept his hand mercilessly flat against the rock as a reminder and a spur.

Fire twisted and crackled among the driftwood where the first torch had lodged, providing a flickering light yards from where he stood. He was grateful for it in the gloom of the gathering storm. If they would only come to open war before the rain struck . . .

Ross sheltered his torch with his body as spray, driven inward from the sea, spattered his shoulders and his back. If it rained, he would lose what small advantage the fire gave him, but then he would find some other way to meet them. They would neither break him nor take him, even if he had to wade into the sea and swim out into the lash of the cold northern waves until he could not move his tired limbs any longer.

Once again that steel-edge will struck at Ross, probing his stubbornness, assaulting his mind. He whirled the torch, brought the scorching breath of the flame across the hand resting on the rock.

Unable to control his own cry of protest, he was not sure he had the fortitude to repeat such an act.

He had won again! The pressure had fallen away in a flick, almost as if some current had been snapped off. Through the red curtain of his torment Ross sensed a surprise and disbelief. He was unaware that in this bizarre duel he was using both a power of will and a depth of perception he had never known he possessed. Because of his daring, he had shaken his opponents as no physical attack could have affected them.

"Come and get me!" He shouted again at the barren shoreline where the fire ate at the drift and nothing stirred, yet something very much alive and conscious lay hidden. This time there was more than simple challenge in Ross's demand—there was a note of triumph.

The spray whipped by him, striking at his fire, at the brand he held. Let the sea water put both out! He would find another way of fighting. He was certain of that, and he sensed that those out there knew it too and were troubled.

The fire was being driven by the wind along the crisscross lines of bone-white wood left high on the beach, forming a wall of flame between him and the interior. Not that the barrier would keep out whatever lurked there.

Again Ross leaned against the rock, studying the length of beach. Had he been wrong in thinking that they were within the range of his voice? The power they had used might carry over a great distance.

"Yahhhh—" Instead of a demand, he now voiced a taunting cry, screaming his defiance. Some wild madness had been transmitted to him by the winds, the roaring sea, his own pain. Ready to face the worst they could send against him, he tried to hurl that thought back at them as they had struck with their united will at him. No answer came to his challenge, no rise to counter-attack.

Moving away from the rock, Ross began to walk forward toward the burning drift, his torch ready in his hand. "I am here!" he shouted into the wind. "Come out—face me!"

It was then that he saw those who had tracked him. Two tall thin figures, wearing dark clothes, were standing quietly watching him, their eyes dark holes in the white ovals of their faces.

Ross halted. Though they were separated by yards of sand and rock and a burning barrier, he could feel the force they wielded. The nature of that force had changed, however. Once it had struck with a vigorous spear point; now it formed a shield of protection. Ross could not break through that shield, and they dared not drop it. A stalemate existed between them in this strange battle, the like of which Ross's world had not known before.

He watched those expressionless white faces, trying to find some reply to the deadlock. There flashed into his mind the certainty that while he lived and moved, and they lived and moved, this struggle, this unending pursuit, would continue. For some mysterious reason they wanted to have him under their control, but that was never going to happen if they all had to remain here on this strip of water-washed sand until they starved to death! Ross tried to drive that thought across to them.

"Murrrrdock!" That croaking cry borne out of the sea by the wind might almost have come from the bill of a sea bird.

"Murrrrdock!"

Ross spun around. Visibility had been drastically curtailed by the lowering clouds and the dashing spray, but he could see a round dark thing bobbing on the waves. A sub? A raft?

Sensing a movement behind him, Ross wheeled about as one of the alien figures leaped the blazing drift, heedless of the flames, and ran light-footedly toward him in what could only be an all-out attempt at capture. The man had ready a weapon like the one that had felled Foscar. Ross threw himself at his opponent in a reckless dive, falling on him with a smashing impact.

In Ross's grasp the alien's body was fragile, but he moved fluidly as Murdock fought to break his grip on the hand weapon and pin him to the sand. Ross was too intent upon his own part of the struggle to heed the sounds of a shot over his head and a thin, wailing cry. He slammed his opponent's hand against a stone, and the white face, inches away from his own, twisted silently with pain.

Fumbling for a better hold, Ross was sent rolling. He came down on his left hand with a force which brought tears to his eyes and stopped him just long enough for the other to regain his feet.

The blue-suited man sprinted back to the body of his fellow where it lay by the drift. He slung his unconscious comrade over the barrier with more ease than Ross would have believed possible and vaulted the barrier after him. Ross, half crouched on the sand, felt unusually light and empty. The strange tie between him and the strangers had been severed.

"Murdock!"

A rubber raft rode in on the waves, two men aboard it. Ross got up, pulling at the studs of his suit with his right hand. He could believe in what he saw now— the sub had not left, after all. The two men running toward him through the dusk were of his own kind.

"Murdock!"

It did not seem at all strange that Kelgarries reached him first. Ross, caught up in this dream, appealed to the major for aid with the studs. If the strangers from the ship did trace him by the suit, they were not going to follow the sub back to the post and serve the project as they had the Russians.

"Got—to—get—this—off—" He pulled the words out one by one, tugging frantically at the stubborn studs. "They can trace this and follow us—"

Kelgarries needed no better explanation. Ripping loose the fastenings, he pulled the clinging fabric from Ross, sending him reeling with pain as he pulled the left sleeve down the younger man's arm.

The wind and spray were ice on his body as they dragged him down to the raft, bundling him aboard. He did not at all remember their arrival on board the sub. He was lying in the vibrating heart of the undersea ship when he opened his eyes to see Kelgarries regarding him intently. Ashe, a coat of bandage about his shoulder and chest, lay on a neighboring bunk. McNeil stood watching a medical corpsman lay out supplies.

"He needs a shot," the medic was saying as Ross blinked at the major.

"You left the suit—back there?" Ross demanded.

"We did. What's this about them tracing you by it? Who was tracing you?"

"Men from the space ship. That's the only way they could have trailed me down the river." He was finding it difficult to talk, and the protesting medic kept waving a needle in his direction, but somehow in bursts of half-finished sentences Ross got out his story—Foscar's death, his own escape from the chief's funeral pyre, and the weird duel of wills back on the beach. Even as he poured it out he thought how unlikely most of it must sound. Yet Kelgarries appeared to accept every word, and there was no expression of disbelief on Ashe's face.

"So that's how you got those burns," said the major slowly when Ross had finished his story. "Deliberately searing your hand in the fire to break their hold—" He crashed his fist against the wall of the tiny cabin and then, when Ross winced at the jar, he hurriedly uncurled those fingers to press Ross's shoulder with a surprisingly warm and gentle touch. "Put him to sleep," he ordered the medic. "He deserves about a month of it, I should judge. I think he has brought us a bigger slice of the future than we had hoped for . . ."

Ross felt the prick of the needle and then nothing more. Even when he was carried ashore at the post and later when he was transported into his proper time, he did not awaken. He drifted into a dreamy state in which he ate and drowsed, unable to care about anything beyond his own bunk.

But there came a day when he did care, sitting up to demand food with a great deal of his old self-assertion. The doctor looked him over, permitting him to get out of bed and try out his legs. They were exceedingly uncooperative at first, and Ross was glad he had tried to move only from his bunk to a waiting chair.

"Visitors welcome?"

Ross looked up eagerly and then smiled, somewhat hesitatingly, at Ashe. The older man wore his arm in a sling but otherwise seemed his usual imperturbable self.

"Ashe, tell me what happened. Are we back at the main base? What about the Russians? We weren't traced by the ship people, were we?"

Ashe laughed. "Did Doc just wind you up, Ross? Yes, this is home, sweet home. As for the rest—well, it is a long story, and we are still picking up pieces of it here and there."

Ross pointed to the bunk in invitation. "Can you tell me what we know?" He was still somewhat at a loss, his old secret awe of Ashe tempering his outward show of eagerness. Ross still feared one of those snubs the other so well knew how to give. But Ashe did come in and sit down, none of his old formality now in evidence.

"You have been a surprise package, Murdock." His observation had some of the ring of the old Ashe, but there was no withdrawal behind the words. "Rather a busy lad, weren't you, after you were bumped off into that river?"

Ross's reply was a grimace. "You heard all about that!" He had no time for his own adventures, already receding into a past which made them both dim and unimportant. "What happened to you—and to the project—and—"

"One thing at a time, and don't rush your fences." Ashe surveyed him with an odd intentness which Ross could not understand. He continued to explain in his "instructor" voice. "We made it down the river—how, don't ask me. That was something of a 'project' in itself," he laughed. "The raft came apart piece by piece, and we waded most of the last couple of miles, I think. I'm none too clear on the details; you'll have to get those out of McNeil, who was still among those present then. Other than that, we cannot compete with your adventures. We built a signal fire and sat by it toasting our shins for a few days, until the sub came to collect us—"

"And took you off." Ross experienced a fleeting return of that hollow feeling he had known on the shore when the still-warm coals of the signal fire had told him the story of his too-late arrival.

"And took us off. But Kelgarries agreed to spin out our waiting period for another twenty-four hours, in case you did manage to survive that toss you took into the river. Then we sighted your spectacular display of fireworks on the beach, and the rest was easy."

"The ship people didn't trace us back to the post?"

"Not that we know of. Anyway, we've closed down the post on that time level. You might be interested in a very peculiar tale our modern agents have picked up, floating over and under the border. A blast went off in the Baltic region of this time, wiping some installation clean off the map. The Russians have kept quiet as to the nature of the explosion and the exact place where it occurred. But we can pinpoint it."

"The aliens followed *them* all the way up to our time!"—Ross half rose from the chair—"But why? And why did they trail me?"

"That we can only guess. But I don't believe that they were moved by any private vengeance for the looting of their derelict. There is some more compelling reason why they don't want us to find or use anything from one of their cargoes—"

"But they were in power thousands of years ago. Maybe they and their worlds are gone now. Why should things we do today matter to them?"

"Well, it does matter, and in some very important way. And we have to learn that reason."

"How?" Ross looked down at his left hand, encased in a mitten of bandage under which he very gingerly tried to stretch a finger. Maybe he should have been eager to welcome another meeting with the ship people, but in all honesty, he had to admit that he was not. He glanced up, sure that Ashe had read his hesitation and scorned him for it. But there was no sign that the other man had noticed.

"By doing some looting of our own," Ashe answered.

"Those tapes we brought back are going to be a big help. More than one derelict was located. We were right in our first surmise that the Russians first discovered the remains of one in Siberia, but it was in no condition to be explored. They already had the basic idea of the time traveler, so they applied it to hunting down other ships, with several way stops to throw people like us off the scent. So they found an intact ship, and then several others. At least three are on *this* side of the Atlantic where they couldn't get at them very well. Those we can deal with now—"

"Won't the aliens be waiting for us to try that?"

"As far as we can discover they don't know where any of these ships crashed. Either there were no survivors, or passengers and crew took off in lifeboats while they were still in space. They might never have known of the Russians' activities if you hadn't triggered that communicator on the derelict."

Ross was reduced to a small boy who badly needed an alibi for some piece of juvenile mischief. "I didn't mean to." That excuse sounded so feeble that he laughed, only to see Ashe grinning back at him.

"Seeing as how your action also put a very effective spike in the opposition's wheel, you are freely forgiven. Anyway, you have also provided us with a pretty good idea of what we may be up against with the aliens, and we'll be prepared for that next time."

"Then there will be a next time?"

"We are calling in all time agents, concentrating our forces in the right period. Yes, there will be a next time. We have to learn just what they are trying so hard to protect."

"What do you think it is?"

"Space!" Ashe spoke the word softly as if he relished the promise it held.

"Space?"

"That ship you explored was a derelict from a galactic fleet, but it was a ship and it used the principle of space flight. Do you understand now? In these lost ships lies the secret which will make us free of all the stars! We must claim it."

"Can we—?"

"Can *we*?" Ashe was laughing at Ross again with his eyes, though his face remained sober. "Then *you* still want to be counted in on this game?"

Ross looked down again at his bandaged hand and remembered swiftly so many things—the coast of Britain on a misty morning, the excitement of prowling the alien ship, the fight with Ennar, even the long nightmare of his flight down the river, and lastly, the exultation he had tasted when he had faced the alien and had locked wills—to hold steady. He knew that he could not, would not, give up what he had found here in the service of the project as long as it was in his power.

"Yes." It was a very simple answer, but when his eyes met Ashe's, Ross knew that it would serve better than any solemn oath.

Galactic
Derelict

1

Hot—it sure was stacking up to be a hot one today.

He'd better check on the spring in the brakes before the sun really boiled up the country ahead. That was the only water in this whole frying pan of baking rock—or was it?

Travis Fox hitched forward in his saddle. He studied the pinkish yellow of the desert strip between him and that distant line of green juniper against the buff of sagebrush which marked the cuts of the brakes. This was a barren land, forbidding to anyone unused to its harshness.

It was also a land frozen into one color-streaked mold of unchanging rock and earth. In that it was probably now rare upon the rider's planet. Elsewhere around the world deserts had been flooded with sea water purified of salt. Ordered farms beat ancient sand dunes into dim memories. Mankind was fast breaking free of the whims of weather or climate. Yet here the free desert remained unaltered because the nation within which it lay could afford to leave land undeveloped.

Someday this, too, would be swept away, taking with it the heritage of such as Travis Fox. For five hundred years, or maybe a thousand now—no one could rightly say when the first Apaches had come questing into this territory—they had dominated these canyons and sand wastes, valleys and mesas. His tough, desert-born breed could travel, fight, and live off bleakness no other race dared face without supplies from outside. His ancestors had waged war for almost four centuries across this country. And now the survivors wrested a living from the region with the same determination.

That spring in the brakes . . . Travis' brown fingers began to count off seasons in taps on his saddle horn. Nineteen . . . twenty . . . This was the twentieth year after the last big dry, and if Chato was right, that meant the water which should be there was due to fail. And the old man had already been correct in his prediction of an unusually arid summer this year.

If Travis rode straight there and found the spring dry, he'd lose most of the day. And time was precious. They *had* to move the breeding stock to a sure water supply. On the other hand, if he cut back into the Canyon of the Hohokam on a hunch and was wrong—then his brother Whelan would have every right to call him a fool. Whelan stubbornly refused to follow the Old Ones' knowledge. And in that his brother was himself a fool.

Travis laughed softly. The White-eyes—deliberately he used the old warrior's term for a traditional enemy, saying it aloud, "Pinda-lick-o-yi"—the White-eyes didn't know *everything*. And a few of them were willing to admit it once in a while.

Then he laughed again, this time at himself and his own thoughts. Scratch the rancher—and the Apache was right under the surface of his sun-dried hide. But there was a bitter note in that second laugh. Travis booted his pinto into a lope with more force than was necessary. He didn't care to follow the trail of those particular thoughts. He'd make for the place of the Hohokam and he'd be Apache for today. Nothing would spoil that as his other dreams had been spoiled.

Whelan thought that if an Apache lived like the White-eyes, and set aside all the old things, then he would prosper like the White-eyes. To Whelan there was nothing good in the past. Even to consider the Old Ones, what they did and why they did it, was a foolish waste of time. Travis bit again on disappointment, to find it as fresh and bad-tasting as it had been a year earlier.

The pinto threaded a way between boulders along a dried stream bed. Odd that a land now so arid could carry so many signs of past water. There were miles of irrigation ditches used by the Old Ones, marking off sun-baked pans of open land which had not known the touch of moisture for centuries. Travis urged his mount up a sharp slope and headed west, feeling the heat bore into his back through the faded shirt fabric.

He doubted if Whelan knew the Canyon of the Hohokam. That was one of the things from the old days, a story preserved by such as Chato. And there were now two kinds of Apache—Chato and Whelan. Chato denied the existence of the White-eyes, living his own life behind a shutter which he dropped between him and the outside world of the whites. And Whelan denied the existence of the Apache, striving to be all white.

Once Travis had seen a third way, that of blending the white man's learning with Apache lore. He thought he had discovered those who agreed with him. But it had all gone, as quickly as a drop of water poured upon a rock would vanish here. Now he tended to agree with Chato. Knowing that, Chato had freely given him information Whelan did not have, about Whelan's own range land.

Chato's father—again Travis counted, fingertip against saddle horn—why, Chato's father would be a hundred and twenty years old if he were alive today! And his grandfather had been born in the Hohokam's valley while his family were hiding from the U.S. Cavalry.

Chato had guided Travis to the lost canyon when he was so small he could barely grip a horse's barrel with his short legs. And he had returned there again and again through the years. The houses of the Hohokam had intrigued him, and the spring there never failed. There were piñons with nuts to be gathered in season, and some stunted fruit trees still yielding a measure of fruit. Once it had been a garden; now it was a hidden oasis.

Travis was working his way into the maze of canyons which held the forgotten trail of the Old Ones when he heard an unfamiliar hum. Instinctively he drew rein, knowing that he was concealed by the shadow of a cliff, and glanced skyward.

"'Copter!" he said aloud in sheer surprise. The ageless desert country had claimed him so thoroughly during the past few hours that sighting a modern mode of travel came as a shock.

Could it be Whelan, checking up on him? Travis' mouth tightened. But when he had left the ranch house at sunup, Bill Redhorse, Chato's grandson, had been tinkering with the engine of the ranch bus. Anyway, Whelan couldn't waste fuel on desert coasting. With the big war scare on again, rationing had tightened up and a man kept his 'copter for emergencies, using horses again for daily work.

The war scare . . . Travis thought about it as he watched the strange machine out of sight. Ever since he could remember there had been snapping and snarling in the news. Little scrimmages bursting out, smoldering, talk and more talk. Then, some months back, something odd had happened in Europe—a big blast set off in the north. Though the Russians had clamped down their tight screen of secrecy, rumor said that some kind of new bomb had gone wrong. All this might be leading up to an out-and-out break between East and West.

The government must believe that. They'd tightened up regulations all along the line and slapped on additional fuel rationing. Tension filled the air and whispers of trouble to come.

Out here it was easy enough to shove all that stuff out of one's mind. The desert silenced the bickering of men. These cliffs had stood the same before the brown-skinned men of his race had trickled down from the north. They would probably be standing when the White-eyes blasted both white and brown men out of it again.

The sight of the 'copter had triggered memories Travis did not like. He continued to wonder, as the machine disappeared in the direction he himself was following, what its mission was here.

He did not sight it again, so it must not be carrying a local rancher. If the pilot had been hunting strays, he would circle. Prospectors? But there had been no news of a government expedition, and no one else had been permitted to prospect for years.

Travis located the entrance of the hidden canyon and studied the ground as he rode. There was no sign that anyone had passed that way for a long time. He clicked his tongue and the horse quickened pace. They had gone about two miles along that snaking path when Travis brought his mount to a halt.

A puff of breeze tickling his nose had warned him. This was no desert wind laden with heat and grit, for it carried the scent of juniper and pine. The pinto nickered and mouthed its bit—water ahead. But the land before them was not empty of men.

Travis swung out of the saddle, taking his rifle with him. Unless the terrain had altered in the past year, there was a good cover on the lip of the hidden canyon's entrance. Without being seen, he would be able to survey the camp whose smells of wood smoke, coffee, frying bacon were now reaching him.

The ascent to his chosen spy post was easy. From below the pine scent rose, heavier now, drawn out by the sun's rays. Small, busy birds twittered about their own concerns. There was a cup of green lying there, around a spring-fed pool which mirrored the hot blue of the sky. Between that water and the vast shallow cave holding the city of the Old Ones, stood the 'copter. A man was tending a cooking fire while another had gone to the pool for water.

Travis did not believe they were ranchers. But they wore sturdy outdoor clothing and moved about the business of camping with assurance. He began to inventory what he could see of their supplies and equipment.

The 'copter was a late model. And in the shade offered by a small stand of trees he could make out bedrolls. But he did not sight any digging tools or other indication that this was a prospecting team. Then the man walked back from the pool, set his filled bucket down by the fire. He dropped cross-legged before a big package and unwrapped its canvas covering. Travis watched him uncover what had to be a portable communicator of advanced design.

The operator was patiently inching up the antenna rod, when Travis heard the pinto nicker. Age-old instinct brought him around, still on his knees, with rifle ready. But he found himself fronting another weapon aimed directly and mercilessly at his middle.

The oddly designed barrel did not waver. Above it gray eyes watched him with a chill detachment worse than any vocal threat. Travis Fox considered himself a worthy descendant of the toughest warriors this stretch of country had ever seen. Yet he knew that neither he nor any of his kind had ever faced a man quite like this one. This man was young, no older than himself. Subtle menace did not altogether fit with his slender body or calm, boyish face.

"Drop it!" The intruder expected no resistance.

Travis obeyed, allowing the rifle to slip from his hands and slide across his leg to the gravel.

"On your feet. Make it snappy. Down there . . ." The gentle voice and even tone of the orders oddly increased the menace Travis sensed.

The Apache stood up, turned downslope and walked forward with his hands up. He did not know what he had stumbled on, but that it was important—and dangerous—Travis did not doubt.

The man cooking and the man at the com set both sat back on their heels, calmly surveying Travis as he advanced. To his eyes they were little different from the white ranchers he knew in the district. Yet the cook . . . ?

Travis studied him in puzzlement, certain that he had seen the man or his likeness before under very different circumstances.

"Where did you flush this one, Ross?" asked the man at the com.

"Lying up on the ridge, getting an eyeful," Travis' captor replied.

The cook stood up, wiped his hands on a cloth, and started toward them. Eldest of the three strangers, his skin was deeply tanned, his eyes a startlingly bright blue against that brown. He radiated authority which did not suit his present employment but which marked him, for Travis, as the leader of the party. The Apache guessed his own reception would depend upon this man's reaction. Only why did some faint twist of memory persist in outlining the cook's head with a black square?

Since the stranger seemed to be in no hurry to ask questions, Travis met him eye to eye, drawing on his own brand of patience. There was danger in this man, too, the same controlled force his younger companion had revealed when trapping the Apache on the heights.

"Apache." It was a statement, rather than a question. And it raised Travis' estimation of the stranger. There were few men nowadays who would or could distinguish Apache from Hopi, Navajo, or Ute in one brief glance.

"Rancher?" That was a question this time and Travis gave it a truthful answer. He sensed that using evasive tactics with this particular White-eye would only lead to his own disadvantage.

"Rider for the Double A."

The man by the com unit had unrolled a map. He ran a forefinger along a wavy mark and nodded, not at Travis, but to the interrogator.

"Nearest range to the east. But he can't be hunting strays this far into the desert."

"Good water." The other nodded at the pool. "The Old Ones used it."

Obliquely that was another inquiry. And Travis found himself replying to it.

"The Old Ones knew. Not those only." With his chin

he pointed to the ruins in the great shallow cave. "But the People in turn. Never dry, even in bad years."

"And this is a bad year." The stranger rubbed his hand along his jaw, his blue eyes still holding Travis'. "A complication we didn't foresee. So Double A runs a herd in here in dry years, son?"

Against his will, Travis found himself replying with the exact truth. "Not yet. Few of the riders know of it now. Not many care to listen to the stories of the old men." He was still puzzling over the teasing memory of seeing this man's lean face before. That black border about it—a frame! A picture frame! And the picture had hung over Dr. Morgan's desk at the university.

"But you do . . ." There came another of those measuring stares like the one which had stripped away his rancher's clothing to display the Apache underneath. Now those eyes were trying to sort out the thoughts in his head, thoughts of Dr. Morgan's study. This man's picture had hung there, but with a stepped pyramid behind him.

"It is so." Absently he used another speech pattern as he tried to remember more.

"The problem is, buster"—the man by the com unit stood up, spoke lazily—"just what are we going to do with you now? How about it, Ashe? Does he go in cold storage—maybe up there?" He jerked a thumb at the ruins.

Ashe! Dr. Gordon Ashe! He'd put a name to the stranger at last. And with the name came a reason for the man's presence there. Ashe was an archaeologist. Only Travis did not have to look at the com unit or at the camp to guess that this was no expedition to hunt ancient relics. He had had firsthand knowledge of those. What were Dr. Ashe and his companions really doing in the Canyon of the Old Ones?

"You can put your hands down, son," Dr. Ashe said. "And you can make it easy for yourself if you agree to stay here peaceably for a time."

"For how long?" countered Travis.

"That depends," Ashe hedged.

"I left my horse up there. He needs water."

"Bring the horse down, Ross."

Travis turned his head. The young man holstered his strange-looking weapon and climbed upslope, to reappear shortly leading the pinto. Travis unsaddled his mount and turned the animal loose. He returned to find Ashe awaiting him.

"So not many people know of this place?"

Travis shrugged. "One other man on the Double A—he is very old. His grandfather was born here, long ago when the Apaches were fighting the army. Nobody else is interested any more."

"Then there was never any digging done in the ruins?"

"A little—once."

"By whom?"

Travis pushed back his hat. "Me." His answer was short and hostile.

"Oh?" Ashe produced a package of cigarettes, offered them. Travis took one without thinking.

"You came here for a dig?" he counter-questioned.

"In a manner of speaking." But when Ashe glanced at the cliff house, Travis thought it was as if he saw something far more interesting behind or beyond those crumbling blocks of sun-dried brick.

"I thought your main interest was pre-Mayan, Dr. Ashe." Travis squatted on his heels, brought out a smoldering twig from the fire to light his smoke, and was inwardly satisfied to note that he had startled the archaeologist with that observation.

"You know me!" He made a challenge of the words.

Travis shook his head. "I know Doctor Prentiss Morgan."

"So that's it! You're one of his bright boys!"

"No." That was short, a bitten-off warning not to probe. And the other man must have been sensitive enough to understand at once, for he asked no other question.

"Chow ready, Ashe?" asked the man with the com. Behind him the youngster Ashe called "Ross" came to the fire, reached out for the frying pan. Travis stared at his hand. The flesh was seamed with scars. Once before the Apache had seen healed wounds like those—from a deep and painful burn. He looked away hurriedly as the other apportioned food onto plates, and he got his own lunch from his saddlebags.

They ate in oddly companionable silence. The first tension of their meeting eased from the range rider. His interest in these men, his desire to know more about them and what they were doing here, dampened his annoyance at the way he had been captured. That young Ross was a slick tracker. He had to be experienced to trap Travis so neatly. The Apache longed for a closer look at the other's weapon. It was not a conventional pistol. Wearing it ready for use said that they expected attack—from whom?

The longer Travis studied the three men he sensed a distinction between Ashe and Ross on one hand and Grant, the com operator on the other. Ashe and Ross were alike in more than their heavy tans, their silent walk, their keen watchfulness. As Travis watched them go through the natural business of eating and policing camp, the surer he was that they had *not* come to this place to explore cliff ruins. They had to be engaged in some more serious—and perhaps deadly—action.

He asked no questions, content to let the others

now make the first move. It was the com unit which broke the peace of the small camp. A warning cackle brought its tender on the run. He snapped on earphones and relayed a message.

"Procedure has to be stepped up. They'll start bringing the stuff in tonight!"

2

"Well?" Ross's glance swept over Travis, settled on Ashe.

"Anybody know you were coming here?" the older man asked the range rider.

"I came out to check the springs. If I don't return to the ranch within a reasonable time, they'll hunt me up, yes." Travis saw no reason to enlarge upon that with two other bits of information. One, that Whelan would not be unduly alarmed if he did not return within twenty-four hours, and the other, that he was supposed to be in the brakes to the south.

"You say that you know Prentiss Morgan—how well?"

"I was in one of his classes at the U—for a while."

"Your name?"

"Fox. Travis Fox."

The com operator cut in, again consulting his map. "The Double A belongs to a Fox—"

"My brother. But I work for him, that's all."

"Grant"—Ashe turned now to the com man—"mark

this top priority and send it to Kelgarries. Ask him to check Fox—all the way."

"We can ship him out when the first load comes in, chief. They'll store him at headquarters as long as you want," Ross offered, as if Travis had ceased to be a person and was merely an annoying problem.

Ashe shook his head. "Look here, Fox, we don't want to make it hard for you. It's pure bad luck that you trailed in here today. Frankly, we can't afford to attract any attention to our activities at present. But if you'll give me your word not to try and go over the hill, we'll leave it at that for the present."

The last thing Travis wanted to do was leave. His curiosity was thoroughly aroused. He had no intention of going unless they removed him bodily. And that, he promised himself silently, would take a lot of doing.

"It's a deal."

But Ashe was already on another track. "You say you did some digging over there. What did you uncover?"

"The usual stuff—pottery, a few arrowheads. These mountain ruins are filled with such things."

"What did you expect, chief?" Ross asked.

"Well, there was a slim chance," the other returned ambiguously. "This climate preserves. We've found baskets, fabrics, fragile things lasting—"

"I'll take the bones and baskets—in place of some other things." Ross held his scarred hand against his chest. He rubbed its seamed flesh with the other, as if soothing a wound that still ached. "Better get out the lights if the boys are going to drop in tonight."

The pinto continued to graze in the center of the meadow while Ross and Ashe paced out two lines and spaced small plastic canisters at intervals. Travis, watching, guessed they were marking a landing site. But it was twice the size needed by a 'copter such as the one now standing beyond. Then Ashe settled with his back against a tree, reading a bulging notebook, while Ross brought out a roll of felt and opened it.

What he uncovered was a set of five stone points, beautifully fashioned, too long to be arrowheads. Travis recognized their distinctive shape by the pattern of their flaked edges! Far better workmanship than the later productions of his own people, yet much older. He had held their like in his hands, admired the artistry of the forgotten weapon maker who had patiently chipped them into being. Folsom points! They were intended to head the throwing spears of men who went up against mammoth, giant bison, cave bear, and Alaskan lion.

"Folsom man here?" He saw Ross glance toward him, Ashe's attention lift from the notebook.

Ross picked up the last point in that row, held it out to Travis. He took it carefully. The head was perfect, fine. He turned it over between his fingers and then paused—not sure of what he knew, or why.

"Fake."

Yet was it? He had handled Folsom points and some, in spite of their great age, had been as perfectly preserved as this one. Only—this did not feel right. He could give no better reason for his judgment than that.

"What makes you think so?" Ashe wanted to know.

"That one was certified by Stefferds." Ross took up the second point from the line. But Travis, instead of being confounded by that certification from the authority on prehistoric American remains, remained sure of his own appraisal.

"Not the right feel to it."

Ashe nodded to Ross, who picked up the third stone head, offering it in exchange for the one Travis still held. The new point was, to all examination by eye, a copy of the first. Yet, as he ran a forefinger along the fine serrations of the flaked edge, Travis knew that this was the real thing, and he said so.

"Well, well." Ross studied his store of points. "Something new had been added," he informed the empty space before him.

"It's been done before," Ashe said. "Give him your gun."

For a moment it seemed as if Ross might refuse. He frowned as he drew the weapon. The Apache, putting down the Folsom point with care, took the weapon and examined it closely. Though it looked much like a pistol, Travis noted enough differences to set it totally apart. He sighted it at a tree trunk and found that when held correctly for firing, the grip was not altogether comfortable. The hand for which it had been fashioned was not quite like his own.

Another difference grew in his mind the longer he held the weapon. He did not like that odd sensation . . .

Travis laid the gun down beside the flint point, staring at them with astonished eyes. From both of them he had gained a common impression of age—a wide expanse of time separating him from the makers of those two very dissimilar weapons. For the Folsom point that feeling was correct. But how could the gun give him the same answer? He had come to rely on that peculiar unnamed sense of his. Its apparent failure now was disconcerting.

"How old is the gun?" asked Ashe.

"It can't be—" Travis protested. "I won't believe that it is as old—or older—than the spearhead!"

"Brother"—Ross regarded him with an odd expression—"you can call 'em!" He reholstered the gun. "So now we have a time guesser, chief."

"Such a gift is not too uncommon," Ashe commented absently. "I've seen it in operation before."

"But a gun can't *be* that old!" Travis still objected. Ross's left eyebrow raised in a sardonic arc as he gave a half-smile.

"That's all you know about it, brother," he observed. "New recruit?" That was addressed to Ashe. The latter was frowning, but at Ross's inquiry he smiled with a warmth that for a second or two made Travis uncomfortable. It so patently advertised that those two were a long-established team, shutting him outside.

"Don't rush things, boy." Ashe stood up and went over to the com unit. "Any news from the front?"

"Cackle-cackle, yackety-yak," snorted the operator. "Soon as I tune out one band interference, we hit another. Someday maybe they'll make these gadgets so they'll operate without overloading a guy's eardrums. No, nothing for us yet."

Travis wanted to ask questions, a lot of them. But he was also sure that most would receive evasive answers. He tried to fit the gun into the rest of his jigsaw of surmises, hints, and guesses, and found it wouldn't. But he forgot that when Ashe sat down once more and began to talk archaeologist's shop. At first Travis only listened, but soon he was being drawn more and more into answering, into giving opinions and once or twice daring to contradict the other. Apache lore, cliff ruins, Folsom man—Ashe's conversation ranged widely. It was only after Travis had been led to talking freely with the pent-up eagerness of one who has been denied expression for too long, that he understood the other man must have been testing his knowledge.

"Sounds rugged, the way they lived then," Ross observed at the conclusion of Travis' story of the use of their present camp site by Apache holdouts in the old days.

"That, from you, is good," Grant laughed. He

snapped on his earphones once more as the com came to life. With one hand he steadied a pad on his knee and copied the message.

Travis studied the shadows on the cliffs. It was close to sundown now, and he was growing impatient. This was like being in a theater waiting for the curtain to go up—or lying in wait for trouble to come pounding around some bend.

Ashe took the scribbled page from Grant, checked it against more scribbles in his notebook. Ross was chewing on a long stem of grass, outwardly relaxed and almost sleepy. Yet Travis suspected that if he were to make a wrong move, Ross would come alert in an instant.

"You know this country must have been popping once," Ross commented lazily. "That looks like a regular apartment house over there—with maybe a hundred, two hundred people living in it. How *did* they live, anyway? This is a small valley."

"There's another valley to the northwest with irrigation ditches still marked," Travis replied. "And they hunted—turkey, deer, antelope, even buffalo—if they were lucky."

"Now if a man had some way to look back into history he could learn a lot—"

"You mean by using Vis-Tex?" Travis asked with careful casualness, and had the satisfaction of seeing the other's calm crack. Then he laughed, with an edge on his humor. "We Indians don't wear blankets or feathers in our hair any more, and some of us read and watch TV, and actually go to school. But the Vis-Tex I saw in action wasn't too successful." He decided on a guess. "Planning to test a new model here?"

"In a way—yes."

Travis had not expected a serious answer like that.

And it had come from Ashe, plainly to the surprise of Ross. But his assent opened startling possibilities.

The Vis-Tex process for photographing the past from radiation echoes had been under development for more than twenty years. The process had been perfected to the stage where objects would appear on films exposed a week after they had disappeared from a given point. And Travis had been present on one occasion when an experimental Vis-Tex had been demonstrated by Dr. Morgan. But if they *did* have a new model which could produce a real reach back into history—! He drew a deep breath and stared at the cave-enclosed ruins before him. What would it mean to see the past again! Then he grinned.

"A lot of history will have to be rewritten in a hurry if you have one that works."

"Not history as we know it." Ashe drew out cigarettes and passed them. "Son, you're a part of this now, whether or no. We can't afford to let you go, the situation is too critical. So—you'll be offered a chance to enlist."

"In what?" countered Travis warily.

"In Project Folsom One." Ashe lit his cigarette. "Headquarters checked you out all along the line. I'm inclined to think that providence had a hand in your turning up here today. It all fits."

"Too well?" There was a frown line between Ross's brows.

"No," Ashe replied. "He's just what he said he is. Our man reported from the Double A and from Morgan. He can't be a plant."

What kind of a plant? wondered Travis. Apparently he was being drafted, but he demanded to know why and for what. He thought he wasn't hearing correctly when Ashe answered.

"We're here to see the Folsom hunters' world."

"That's a tall order, Doctor Ashe. You've got a super Vis-Tex if you can take a peek ten thousand years back."

"Even farther back than that," Ashe corrected him. "We aren't sure yet."

"Why the hush-hush? A look at some roaming primitive tribe should bring out the newsmen—"

"We're more interested in other things than primitive tribesmen."

"Such as where that gun came from," agreed Ross. He was again rubbing his scarred hand. His eyes held the same bleakness Travis had noted in their first meeting on the rim of the canyon. It was the look of a fighter preparing for battle.

"You'll have to take us on faith for a while," Ashe cut in. "This is a strange business and a necessarily top-secret one, to use the patter of our times."

They ate supper and Travis moved the pinto to the narrow lower end of the canyon, well away from the improvised landing field. Dusk had hardly closed in before the first of the cargo 'copters touched down. Soon he found himself as one of a line of men passing packages and boxes from the machine back to the shelter of the small grove. They worked without any waste motion at a speed which suggested that time was of the essence. Travis found that he had caught that need for haste from them. The first machine was stripped of its load, rose, and was gone only minutes before a second one came in to take its place. Again an unloading chain formed, this time for heavier boxes which required two men to handle them.

Travis' back ached, his hands were raw by the time the fourth 'copter was freed and left. Four more men had joined their party, one coming in with each load, but there was little talk. All were concentrating on the unloading and storing of the material. In a period of lull after the departure of the fourth machine, Ashe came up to Travis accompanied by another man.

"Here he is." Ashe's hand closed on Travis' shoulder, drawing him out to face the newcomer.

He was taller than Dr. Ashe, and there was no mistaking the air of command, or the power of those eyes which bored straight into the Apache. But after a long moment the big man smiled briefly.

"You're quite a problem for us, Fox."

"Or the missing ingredient," corrected Ashe. "Fox, this is Major Kelgarries, at present our commanding officer."

"We'll have a talk later," Kelgarries promised. "Tonight's rather busy."

"Clear the field!" called someone from the flare line. "Setting down."

They plunged out of the path of the fifth 'copter and work started again. The Major, Travis noted, was right in line with the others when it came to tossing boxes around. There was no more time for talking.

Seven or eight loads, which was it? Travis tried to count them up, wriggling stiff fingers. It was still night but the flares had been extinguished. The men who had worked together now sat around the fire drinking coffee and wolfing sandwiches which had been delivered with their last cargo. They did not talk much and Travis knew they were as tired as he was.

"Bedtime, brother. And am I glad to hit the sack!" Ross said between yawns. "Need the makings— blankets—anything?"

Half stupid with fatigue, Travis shook his head. "Got my bedroll with m'saddle." And he was asleep almost before he was fully stretched out.

In the day light of morning the camp looked disorganized. But men were already sorting out the material, working as if this was a task they had often done before. As Travis was helping to shift a large crate, he looked up to see the Major.

"Spare me a moment, Fox." He led the way from the scene of activity.

"You've got yourself—and us—in a muddle, young man. Frankly, we can't turn you loose—for your own sake, as well as ours. This project has to be kept under wraps and there are some very tough boys who would like to pick you up and learn what they could from you. So, we either take you all the way in—or put you on ice. It's up to you which it is going to be. You've been vouched for by Doctor Morgan."

Travis tensed. What had they raked up now? Memories cramped his belly. But if they'd been asking questions of Prentiss Morgan, they must know what happened last year—and why. Apparently they did, for Kelgarries continued:

"Fox, the time when anyone can afford prejudices is past—way past. I know about Hewitt's offer to the University and what happened when he pressured to have you fired from the expedition staff. But prejudices can stretch both ways—you didn't stand up to him very long, did you?"

Travis shrugged. "Maybe you've heard the term 'second-class citizen,' Major. How do you suppose Indians rate with some people in this country? To that crowd we are and we'll always be dirty, ignorant savages. You can't fight when the other fellow has all the weapons. Hewitt gave that grant to the University to do some important work. When he wanted me off, that was that. If I'd let Doctor Morgan fight to keep me on his staff, Hewitt would have snatched his check away again so fast the friction would have burnt the paper. I know Hewitt and what makes him tick. And Doctor Morgan's work was more important—" Travis stopped short. Why in the world had he told the Major all that? It was none of Kelgarries' business why he had quit and come back to the ranch.

"There aren't many like Hewitt left—fortunately. And I assure you we do not follow his methods. If you choose to join us after Ashe briefs you, you're one of a team. Lord, man"—the Major slapped his hand vigorously against his dusty breeches—"I don't care if a man is a blue Martian with two heads and four mouths—if he can keep those mouths shut and do his job! It's the job which counts here, and, according to Morgan, you have something useful to contribute. Make up your mind and let me know. If you don't want to play—we'll ship you out tonight, tell your brother that you're on government work, and keep you quiet for a while. Sorry, but that's the way it will have to be."

Travis smiled at that promise. He thought he could get out of here safely on his own if he really wanted to. But now he prodded the Major a little.

"Expedition back to catch a Folsom man—" But Kelgarries might not have heard, for he had already turned away. Travis followed, to come upon Ashe.

The latter was engaged in assembling a tripod of slender rods. His care proclaimed the objects as brittle and precious. He glanced up as Travis' shadow fell across his work.

"Decided to join us for a look-see into the past?"

"Do you really mean you *can* do that?"

"We've done more than look." Ashe adjusted a screw delicately. "We've been there."

Travis stared. He could accept the fact of a new and greatly improved Vis-Tex to provide a peephole into history and prehistory. But time travel was something else.

"It's perfectly true," Ashe finished with the screw.

His attention passed from the tripod to Travis. His manner carried conviction.

"And we're going back again."

"After a Folsom man?" demanded the Apache incredulously.

"After a spaceship."

3

This was no dream, not even a realistic one. There was Ashe, his fingers busy, his brown face outlined against the red and yellow walls of the cliff and the crumbling ruins they enclosed. This was here and now—yet what Ashe was saying, soberly, and in detail, was the wildest fantasy.

" . . . so we discovered the Russians had time travel and were prospecting back into the past. What they dredged up there couldn't be explained by any logic based on the history we knew and the prehistory we had pieced out. What we didn't know then was that they had found the remains—badly smashed—of a spaceship. It was encased in the ice of Siberia, along with preserved mammoth bodies and a few other pertinent clues to suggest the proper era for them to explore. They muddied the trail as well as they could by establishing way stations in other periods of time. Then we chanced on one of those middle points. And the Russians themselves, by capturing our time agents, showed us the ship they were plundering some thousands of years earlier."

The story made sense—in a crazy kind of way. Travis mechanically handed Ashe the small tool he was groping for in the tangled grass.

"But how did the ship get there?" he asked. "Was there an early civilization on earth which had space travel?"

"That was what we thought—until we found the ship. No, it was from the outside—a cargo freighter lost from some galactic run. Either this world was an astrogation menace of the same type as a reef at sea, or there was some other reason to cause forced landings here. We brought film from the Russian time station pinpointing about a dozen such wrecks. And some of those were on this side of the Atlantic."

"You're planning to dig for one of those *here*?"

Ashe laughed. "What d'you think we'd find after about fifteen thousand years and a lot of land upheaval, even local volcanic activity? We want our ship in as good condition as possible."

"To study?"

"With caution. If you'd check with Ross Murdock he'd give you a good reason for the caution. He was one of our agents who was actually aboard the ship the Russians were plundering. When they cornered him in the control cabin, he accidentally activated the com system and called in the real owners. They weren't too pleased with the Russians—came down and destroyed their time base on that level and then followed them through the other way stations, destroying each. Remember that hush-hush bang in the Baltic early this year? That was the 'space patrol,' or whatever they call themselves, putting finis to the Russian project. So far as we know they didn't discover that we were and are interested in the same thing. So if we find our ship here, we walk softly along its corridors."

"You want the cargo?"

"In part. But mostly we want the knowledge—what its designers had—the key to space."

The thrill of that touched Travis. Mankind had reached for the stars for three generations. Men had had small successes, many searing failures. Now—what were missions to the barren moon compared to star flight and what lay far out?

Ashe, reading his expression, smiled. "You feel it too, don't you?"

The Apache nodded absently, gazing down the canyon. He tried to believe that somewhere around here, trapped in time, a wrecked star ship lay waiting for them. But he could not even visualize this country as it must have been in pluvial times. When rain fell most of the year, it must have made a morass of these lands. The retreating arms of shrinking glaciers lay not too far northward.

"But why the Folsom points?" Out of the welter of facts and half facts he picked that as a starting point.

"We've sent back agents disguised as pre-Celts, as Tartars—or their remote ancestors—as Bronze Age Beaker Traders, and in half a hundred other character parts. Now there's a chance we may have to produce a few Folsom spearmen. One of the first and most important rules of this game, Fox, is that one does not interfere with time by introducing any modernisms. There must be no hint of our agents' real identity. We have no idea what might happen if one meddled with the stream of history as we know it, and we trust we'll never have to find out the hard way."

"Hunters," Travis said slowly, hardly aware at that moment that he spoke at all. "Mammoth—mastodon—camels—the dire wolf—sabertooth—"

"Why do all those interest you?"

"Why?" Travis echoed and then stopped to examine his reasons. Why *had* his reaction to Ashe's picture of the drifting prehistoric hunters in disguise been his own quick inner vision of a land peopled with strange beasts his own race had never hunted? Or had they? Had the Folsom hunters been his remote ancestors, as the pre-Celt and Beaker Trader Ashe mentioned been the other's forefathers? He only knew that he had experienced a sudden thrust of excitement that lingered. He longed to see that world his own age knew only by the dim and often contradictory evidence of rocks, a handful of flint points, broken bones, the ancient smears of vanished cooking fires.

"My people were hunters—long after yours followed another way of life," he said, making the best answer he could.

"Right." Ashe's tone held a note of satisfaction. "Now—just reach me that rod." He went back to the job at hand and Travis settled down as his somewhat bewildered assistant. The Apache knew that he had made the choice Kelgarries wanted—that he was going to be a part of this whole incredible adventure.

The one thing he was sure of during the next two crowded days was that they were indeed working under pressure and against deadlines. Whether the unexplained threat which seemed to overhang the whole project came from outside the country or from fear of a policy change here at home, no one bothered to make clear. But Travis was willing to let it go at that. It was far more interesting and absorbing to work with Ross Murdock. They set the proper kind of shafts to the pseudo-Folsom spear points and then experimented with the spear thrower. This made the efficient weapons they finally turned out twice as powerful. A seven-foot javelin could be hurled a good hundred and fifty yards or more by the use of that two-foot shaft of the thrower. Travis knew that in close infighting it would add tremendous thrusting power. No wonder a party of hunters so armed dared to go against mammoth and other giant mammals of the period.

In addition to the spears they had flint knives, the counterparts of those found in the debris of Folsom camp sites across most of western America. Travis did not know why he was so sure that he was actually going to use knife and spears and play the role of a wandering prehistoric hunter. Still, he was sure. He learned from Ross that the rest of the time agents' equipment would not be assembled at the base until the experts had taped film reports out of the past to use as samples.

On the third day Kelgarries and Ashe took a three-man expedition out of the canyon in one 'copter loaded to its limit. They were gone almost a week, and upon their return they hurriedly sent off tapes.

Ashe joined Travis and Ross that same night. He lay down beside their fire with a sigh of weary pleasure.

"Hit pay dirt?" Ross wanted to know.

His chief nodded. There were dark smudges under his eyes and a fine, drawn look to his features. "The wreck is there, all right. And we located hunters on the fringe of the territory. But I think we can follow Plan One. The tribe is small and there doesn't appear to be more than one. Our guess that the district was thinly populated must be correct. It won't be necessary to really establish our scouts with the tribe—just let them keep track of wandering hunters."

"And the transfer?"

Ashe glanced at the watch on his wrist. "Harvey and Logwood are assembling the new one. I give them about forty-eight hours. Headquarters will fly in the extra power packs tonight. Then our men go through. We haven't the time to spend on finer points now. A working crew follows as soon as the scouts give the 'all clear.' H.Q. is analyzing the film reports. They'll have the rest of the equipment to us as soon as possible."

Travis stirred. Who was going to be part of that scouting team into the far past? He wanted to ask that—to hope that he might be one. But what had happened a year ago to smash other plans, kept him tongue-tied now. Ross voiced that all-important question.

"Who makes the first jump, chief?"

"You—me—we're on the spot. Our friend here, if he wants to."

"You mean that?" Travis asked slowly.

Ashe reached for the waiting coffeepot. "Fox, as long as you don't go loping off on your own to test that flint-tipped armory you've been constructing on the first available mammoth, you can come along. Mainly because you look the part, or will when we get through with you. And maybe you can adapt better than we can. Briefing for a time run used to take weeks. Ask Ross here; he can tell you what a cram course in our work is like. But today we haven't weeks to spare. We've only days and they grow fewer with each sunrise. So we're gambling on you, on Ross, on me. But get this—I'm your section leader, the orders come from me. And the main rule is—the job comes first! We keep away from the natives, we don't get involved in any happenings back there. Our only reason for going through is to make as sure as we can that the technical boys are not going to be disturbed while they work on that wreck. And that may not be an easy job."

"Why?" Ross asked.

"Because this ship didn't make as good a landing as the one you saw the Russians stripping. According to the films we took through the peeper, there was a bad smash when it hit dirt. We may have to let it go altogether and track down Number Two on our list. Only, if we *can* come up with just one good find on board this one, we can stave off the objections of the Committee and get the appropriation for future exploration."

"Might do to run one of the Committee through," Ross remarked.

Ashe grinned. "Want to lose your job, boy? Give 'em a good look around in some of the spots we've prospected and they'd turn up their toes—quick."

Just three days later a bright shaft of sunlight pierced a small side pocket of the canyon to spotlight the three as they worked under the critical eyes of a small, neat man. He regarded them intently through the upper half of his bifocals and made terse suggestions in a dry, precise voice. Stripping, they meticulously rubbed their skins with the cream their instructor had provided. That treatment turned their tanned, or naturally dark, skins into the leathery uniform brownness of men who wore very little clothing in any kind of weather.

Ashe and Ross had been provided with contact lenses so that their eyes were now as dark brown as Travis'. And their closely cropped hair was hidden under wigs of straggling, coarse black locks which fell shoulder-length at the sides and descended like a pony's mane between their shoulder blades.

Then each took his turn flat on his back while the

make-up artist, working from film charts, proceeded to supply his victims with elaborate patterns of simulated tattoos on chests, upper arms, chins, and upper cheekbones. Travis, undergoing the process, studied Ashe, who now represented the finished product. Had he not seen all the steps in that transformation, he would not have guessed that under that savage exterior now existed Dr. Gordon Ashe.

"Glad we're allowed sandals," the same savage commented as he tightened the thongs which held about him a loincloth-kilt of crudely dressed hide.

Ross had just thrust his bare feet into a pair of such primitive footwear. "Let's hope they'll stay on if we have to scramble, chief," he said, eyeing them dubiously.

Finished at last, the three stood in line to be checked by the make-up man and Kelgarries. The Major carried some furred skins over his arm, and now he tossed one to each of the disguised men.

"Better hold on to those. It gets cold where you're going. All right—the 'copter's waiting."

Travis slung a hide pouch over his shoulder and gathered up the three spears he had headed with pseudo-Folsom points. All the men were armed with the same weapons and there was a supply bag for each man.

The 'copter took them up and out, swinging away from the Canyon of the Hohokam into a wide sweep of desert land, bringing them down again before a carefully camouflaged installation. Kelgarries gave Ashe his last instructions.

"Take a day—two if you have to. Make a circle about five miles out, if you can. The rest is up to you."

Ashe nodded. "Can do. We'll signal in as soon as we can give an 'all clear.'"

The concealed structure housed a pile of material

and an inner compartment of four walls, one floor, no roof. Together the three agents crowded into it. They watched the panel slide shut behind them while radiance streamed around their bodies. Travis felt a tingling through bone and muscle, and then a stab of panic as the breath was squeezed from his lungs by a weird wrenching that twisted his insides. But he kept his feet, held on to his spears. There was a second or two of blackness. Then once again he gulped air, shook himself as he might have done climbing out of a strong river current. Ross's dot-bordered lips curved in a smile and he signaled "thumbs up" with his scarred hand.

"End of run—here we go . . ."

As far as Travis could see they were still in the box. But when Ashe pushed open the door panel, the stacked boxes which had lain there before had been replaced by an untidy heap of rocks. And clambering over those in the wake of his companions, the Apache did find a very strange world before him.

Gone was the desert with its burden of sun-heated rock. A plain of coarse grass, thigh- or even waist-high, rolled away to some hills. And that grassy plain was cut by the end of a lake which stretched northward beyond the horizon. Travis saw brush and clumps of small trees. Although too distant for him to distinguish their species, he could make out slowly moving lumps which had to be grazing animals.

There was a sun overhead, but an icy wind lashed Travis' three-quarters-bare body. He pulled the hide robe about his shoulders, and saw that his companions had copied that move. The air was not only chilly, it was dank with a wealth of moisture. And each puff of breeze carried new, rank smells, which his nostrils could not identify. This world was as harsh and grim as his own, but in an entirely different fashion.

Ashe stooped and rolled aside one of the nearby rocks to disclose a small box. From his supply bag he produced three small buttons and gave one to each of the younger men.

"Plant that in your left ear," he ordered, and did so with his own. Then he pushed a key on the side of the box. A low chirruping sound was instantly audible. "This is our homing signal. It acts as radar to bring you back here."

"What's that?"

A plume of wind-whipped smoke bannered to the north. Travis could not believe that the long trail of grayish vapor marked a forest fire, yet it surely signalized a conflagration of some size.

Ashe glanced up casually. "Volcano," he returned. "This part of the world hasn't settled down yet. We head northwest, around the lake tip, and we should strike the wreck." He started off at a steady lope which told Travis that this was not the first time the time agent had played the role of primitive hunter.

The grass brushed against them, leaving drops of cold moisture on their bare legs and thighs. Travis concluded that there must have been rain just before their arrival. And from the look of the massing clouds to the east, a second storm might catch them soon.

As they came away from the hill marking the time transfer, the chirruping in his ear grew fainter, varying in intensity as Ashe twisted and turned about the hooked end of the lake. The wide reach of lush grass continued. This was truly game country although they had not yet passed close enough to any of the grazers to identify them.

About a half mile from the curving shore of the lake rested an object that Nature never made. Half a globe of metallic material had been rammed into the ground. Two jagged rents gaped in its side. The blackened earth around it bore random clumps of new grass. But what impressed Travis chiefly was the object's size. He deduced that only half of the thing was visible—if its form had originally been a true globe. Yet that half now above the earth was at least six stories tall. The complete vessel must have been a veritable monster, far larger than the largest aircraft of his own time.

"She certainly got it!" observed Ross. "Bad crack up at landing—"

"Or else she had it before landing." Ashe leaned on a spear to survey the hulk.

"What—?"

"Those holes might have been caused by shell fire. We'll leave that to the experts to determine. This could be a wreck from a space battle. But look! That storm's coming fast. I say we'd better circle west ahead of it and find some shelter in the hills. If the first reports are correct, we'll be caught in a rain worse than we've ever known!"

Ashe's lope lengthened into a trot, and the trot into a run. He was heading away from the wrecked ship to the distant hills. To reach them they had to round the narrow end of the lake.

They were carefully threading their way through a marshy spot when a scream halted them. Travis knew that it was a death cry, but the sound ahead was followed by a yowling squall which could come from no throat, animal or human, of his own time. The squall was answered in turn by grunts that might have issued from the deep chest of a great pig. And that grunting was echoed on a higher note almost directly behind them!

"Down!" Obeying the order from Ashe, Travis threw himself flat on the muddy ground, wriggling to the left. A moment later all three scouts huddled in a growth of tough brush. They paid no attention to the bramble scratches on their arms and shoulders, for they had front-row seats on a wild drama which held them enthralled.

Crumpled on the ground was a mound of heaving flesh. It was plainly in the death throes for its long, shaggy yellow hair was sodden with blood. Crouched at bay behind that body was another animal. Travis identified it when he caught sight of those long, curved fangs: sabertooth. It was slightly shorter than a lion of Travis' own day, and its muscular legs and powerful shoulders had the power to daunt a larger beast. But now it was facing a giant . . .

The opponent, whose cub had been killed, was a mountain of flesh, rearing almost eighteen feet above the ground. Balanced on large-boned hind feet and thick tail, it confronted the sabertooth with powerful forearms, each tipped with a gigantic single claw. As the narrow head twisted and turned above the slender forebody, its thick brown hair rippled constantly.

A rank animal smell was blown to the men in the brush as a second monstrous ground sloth moved in to give battle. And the sabertooth spat like the enraged cat it was.

4

A hand closed on Travis' arm, jerking his attention from the shaping battle. Ashe pointed westward and pulled again. Ross was already creeping in that direction. The wind was at their back so that they caught the fetor of the beasts without danger of being scented by them in turn.

"Get to it!" Ashe ordered. "We don't want that cat on our trail. It can't take on two adult sloths and it'll be one mighty disappointed diner—out looking for another meal pretty quick."

They wormed their way forward, trying to gauge from the squalls of the cat and the grunting of the sloths whether battle had yet reached the stage of actual blows. If the cat was smart, Travis thought it would let itself be driven off. And knowing the tactics of mountain lions of *his* southwest, he believed that was what would happen.

"Okay—run!" Ashe scrambled to his feet and set a good pace across the open lands, the other two thudding behind him. The sun had completely disappeared now, and the grayness under those lowering clouds approached twilight. The thin chirrup of their homing device sounded very lonely and far away.

Brown-gray lumps swung up heads with wide stretches of horns. Save that those horns were straight and not curved, the animals might have been the bison of the historic plains. Catching the scent of the scouts, they tossed those horned heads and set off northward across the open land at a lumbering gallop. Large-headed horses with spectacularly striped coats ran among them with more speed, and far more grace. This was plainly a hunter's paradise.

The rain raced behind the men, making a visible curtain of water. When that enfolded them, Travis gasped, choked and fought for breath under the pounding flood. But his legs kept the striding pace Ashe had set, and the three continued to head for the hills which were now scarcely visible through the downpour.

A rising slope slowed them, and twice they had to leap runnels of streams carrying water from the heights above them. A vicious crack of lightning lit up the scene. A hand pulled Travis to the left, and so into partial shelter from the storm.

He crowded together with Ashe and Ross, half crouching in the lee of some rocks. It was not quite a cave, but the crevice was better than the open slope.

"How long will this last?" Ross growled.

Ashe's answer offered little hope, "Anywhere from an hour to a couple of days. Let's hope we're lucky."

They squatted, drawing their hide robes about them, pressing together for the warmth of body contact in the midst of that damp cold. Perhaps they dozed, for Travis came alert with a jerk of his head which hurt neck and shoulder. He knew that the rain *had* stopped, though there was night outside their inadequate shelter. He asked:

"Do we move on?"

But the world outside their hiding place replied with a roar loud enough to split eardrums. Travis, his nails digging into the wooden shaft of his spear, could not stop shuddering after that menacing blast.

"We do if we want to provide a midnight snack for our friend out there," Ashe commented. "The rain probably spoiled hunting for somebody. Hereabouts we have sabertooth, the Alaskan lion, the cave bear, and a few other assorted carnivores I don't want to meet without, say, a tank in reserve."

"Cheery spot," Ross remarked. "I'd say our playmate upridge hasn't had much luck tonight. Any chance of his coming down to scoop us out—or try for a taste?"

"If he, she or it does, he'll get a pawful of spear points," Ashe replied. "One advantage of this hole, nothing can get in if we're firm in saying No!"

There was a second roar, from farther away, Travis noted with relief. Whatever meat hunter on the hoof prowled the hills, it would not have followed their trail. The rain must have cleansed their scent from grass and earth. Huddling there, stiff and cold, they managed now and then to change position of arms or legs so that morning would not find them too cramped to move. They remained until the sky did lighten with the first sign of dawn.

Travis crawled out and straightened up painfully. He bit back a stinging word or two, as a below zero morning breeze cut in under the flap of his cloak blanket. He decided that to properly prepare for roaming the Pleistocene world in the garb of its rightful inhabitants, one should practice beforehand by spending a month or so in a deep freeze stripped to one's shorts. And he was pleased to see that neither Ashe nor Ross was any more agile when he emerged from the hole of refuge.

They mouthed food-concentrate bars from their storage bags. Travis, though knowing the energy-building uses of those small squares, longed for real meat, hot and juicy, straight from the fire. There was no taste to these concentrate things.

"Up we go." Ashe wiped the back of his hand across his mouth and slung his bag over his shoulder. He studied the way before them to find the best ascent. But Travis had already started, winding in and out between boulders which marked the debris of a land-slide.

When the scouts at last reached the summit, they turned back to look into the valley of the lake. That smooth sheet of water occupied perhaps half of the basin. And it seemed to Travis that the mirror surface reached closer to the wrecked ship today than it had when they passed it the afternoon before. He said as much, and Ashe agreed.

"Water has to go somewhere and these rains feed all the streams heading down there. Another reason why we must make this a fast job. So—let's get moving."

But when they turned again to follow the line of the heights, Travis halted. Thin, watery sunlight broke through the clouds, carrying with it little or no warmth as yet, but providing more light. And—he peered intently westward and downslope on the other side of the hills . . . No, he had not been mistaken! That sunlight, feeble as it was, was reflecting from some point in the second valley. From water? No, the answering spark was too brilliant.

Ashe and Ross, following his direction, saw it too.

"Second ship?" Ross suggested.

"If so, it is not marked on our charts. But we'll take a look. I agree that's too bright to be sun on water."

Had there been survivors from the other crash? Travis wondered. If so, had they established a camp down there? He had heard enough during the past few days to judge that any contact with the original owners of the galactic ships could be highly dangerous. Ross had been pursued by one of their patrols across miles of wilderness. He had escaped from the mind compulsion they exerted only by deliberately burning his hand in a fire and using pain to counter their mental demand for surrender. They were not human, those ship people. What powers or weapons they possessed were so alien as to defy human understanding so far.

So the three took to cover, making expert use of every bit of brush, every boulder, as they advanced to locate that source of reflection. Again Travis was amazed by the skill of his companions. He had hunted mountain lion, and lion in the beast's native ground is very wary game. He could read trail with all the skill imparted to him by Chato who knew the ways of the old raiding warriors. But these two were equal to him at what he always considered a red man's rather than a white man's game.

They came at last to lie in a fringe of trees, parting the grass cautiously to look out on an expanse of open land. In the middle of it rested another globe-shaped ship. But this one was entirely above ground and it was small, a pygmy compared to the giant in the other valley. At first superficial examination it looked to have been landed normally, not crashed. Halfway up, the curve facing them showed the dark hole of an open entrance port, and from it dangled a ladder. Someone *had* survived this landing, come to earth here!

"Lifeboat?" Ashe's voice was the slightest of whispers.

"It is not shaped like the one I saw before," Ross hissed. "That was like a rocket."

Wind sang across the clearing. It set the ladder clanging against the side of the globe. From the foot of the strange ship some birds tried to rise. But they moved sluggishly, awkwardly flopping their wings. And the wind brought to the three in hiding a sweetish, stomach-turning odor that could never be mistaken by those who had ever smelled it. Something lay dead there, very dead.

Ashe stood up, watching those birds narrowly. Then he stepped forward. A snarl rose from ground level. Travis' spear came up. It sang through the air and a brown-coated, four-footed beast yelped, leaped pawing in the air, and crashed back into the grass. More of the gorged carrion birds fluttered and hopped away from their feast.

What lay about the foot of the ladder was not a pretty sight. Nor could the scouts tell at first glance how many bodies there had been. Ashe attempted to make a closer examination and came away, white-faced and gagging. Ross picked up a tatter of blue-green material.

"Baldies' uniforms, all right." He identified it. "This is one thing I'll never forget. What happened here? A fight?"

"What ever it was, it happened some time ago," Ashe, livid under tan and skin stain, got out the words carefully. "Since there was no burial, I'd say the crew must all have been finished."

"Do we go in?" Travis laid a hand on the ladder.

"Yes. But don't touch anything. Especially any of the instruments or installations."

Ross laughed on a slightly hysterical high note.

"That you do not need to underline for me, chief. After you, sir, after you."

Thus, Ashe leading the way, they climbed the ladder and entered the gaping hole of the port. There was a second door a short distance inside, doubly thick and reinforced with heavy braces. But it, too, was ajar. Ashe pushed it back and then they were in a well from which another ladder-like stair arose.

Somehow Travis had expected darkness, since there were no windows or wall openings in the outer skin of the globe. But a blue light seeped from the walls about them, and not only light, but a comforting warmth.

"The ship's still alive," Ross commented. "And if she *is* intact—"

"Then," Ashe finished softly for him, "we've made the *big* find, boys. We never hoped for luck like this." He started to climb the inner ladder.

They came to a landing, or rather a platform from which opened three oval doors, all closed. Ross pushed against each, but they all held.

"Locked?" Travis asked.

"Might be—or else we don't know how to turn the right buttons. Going on up, chief? If this follows the pattern of that other one, the control cabin is on top."

"We'll take a look. But no experiments, remember?"

Ross stroked his scarred hand. "I'm not forgetting that."

A second ladder section brought them through a manhole in the floor of a hemisphere chamber occupying the whole top of the ship. And, before they were through that entrance, they knew that death had come that way before them.

There was only one body, crumpled forward against the straps of a seat which hung on springs and cords from the roof. The rigid corpse, clad in the blue-green material, had slumped toward a board crowded with dials, buttons, levers.

"Pilot—died at his post." Ashe walked forward, stooped over the body. "I don't see any sign of a wound. Could be an epidemic which attacked the whole crew. We'll let the doctors figure it out."

They did not linger to explore farther, for this find was too important. It was too necessary that the news of this second ship be relayed to Kelgarries and his superiors. But Ashe took the precaution of drawing the ladder into the globe's port after his two younger companions had descended. He made his way down by rope.

"Who do you think is going to snoop?" Ross wanted to know.

"Just a little insurance. We know there are primitives in the northern end of this country. They may be the type to whom everything strange is taboo. Or they may be inquisitive enough to explore. And I don't fancy someone touching off a com again and calling in the galactic patrol or whoever those chaps wearing blue are. Now, let's get to the transfer on the double!"

The weak sunlight of the early morning had increased in strength. The air was growing noticeably warmer, and danker, too, as the moisture-laden grass about them gave up its burden of last night's rain. Travel resembled running through a river choked with slimy, slapping reeds, save that the ground underfoot was firm. The men panted up the heights and down past their refuge of the stormy night to the plain of the lake. They skirted the glade where scavengers were busy with the remains of the sabertooth's kill.

As they came out into the open Ashe broke stride and swept one hand down in an emphatic order to take cover. That mixed herd of bison and horses which they had startled the night before was in movement once more, cutting diagonally across their path. And the animals were plainly fleeing some menace. Saber-tooth again? The huge bison appeared able to take care of themselves with those sweeping horns.

Only when the wind bore to Travis high, far-off sounds which his ears translated into human shouts did he understand that the hunters were out in force. The primitive tribesmen had stampeded the herd in order to cut down the weaker stragglers.

The scouts were pinned down, as an ever-thickening stream of animals cut across the road they must take in order to reach the time transport. Before they had attained their present position, the main body of the herd had caught up, headed by the fleeter horses that whirled ahead of the heavier bison. Now the men caught sight of other harriers, using the general disturbance to their own advantage. Five dark shapes broke cover a hundred yards or so away. They wove in to cut around a lumbering, half-grown calf on the edge of the bison herd.

"Dire wolves," Ashe identified.

They were stocky, large-headed animals, running without giving tongue, but clearly familiar with this game. Two darted in to snap at the calf's head, while the others rushed in for a crippling tendon slash at the hind legs which would make the bison easy prey.

"Oooooo-yahhh!"

That small drama so near to them had absorbed Travis almost to the point of his forgetting what must lie beyond. There was no chance yet of sighting those who called and made the stragglers their targets. But at that moment a horse staggered on past the bison being attacked by the wolves. Its large head had sunk close to knee level and a rope of bloody foam hung from muzzle to trampled grass. Driven deeply into its

barrel was a spear. And even as the animal came fully
into view it tried to lift its head, faltered, and crashed
to earth.

One of the wolves straightway turned attention to
this new prey. It trotted away from the battle with
the calf to sniff inquiringly at the still-breathing horse.
With a growl, it launched itself at the animal's throat.
The wolf was feeding when the hunter of that kill
retaliated for his brazen theft.

Another spear, lighter, but as deadly and well aimed,
sped through the air, caught the dire wolf behind the
right shoulder. The wolf gave a convulsive leap and
collapsed just beyond the body of the horse. At the
same time other spears flashed, bringing down its pack
mates and, last of all, the young bison they had been
worrying.

Most of the fleeing herd had passed by now. There
were other animals lying on the flattened grass of the
back trail. The three scouts crouched low, unable to
withdraw lest they attract the notice of the hunters
now coming in to collect their booty.

There were twenty or more males, medium-sized
brown-skinned men with ragged heads of black hair
like the wigs provided the scouts. Their clothing consisted of the same hide loincloth-kilts fastened about
their sweating bodies with string belts and lacings of
thongs. Studying them, Travis could see how well their
own make-up matched the general appearance of the
Folsom hunters.

Behind the men trudged the women and children,
stopping to butcher the kill. They outnumbered the
hunters. Whether those they saw represented the full
strength of a small tribe, there was no telling. The
men shouted to each other hoarsely, and the two who
had accounted for the wolves seemed especially
pleased. One of them squatted on his heels, pried

open the mouth of the wolf which had killed the horse, and inspected its fangs with a critical eye. Since a necklace of just such trophies strung on a thong thumped across his broad chest with every movement of his body, it was plain he was considering a new addition to his adornment.

Ashe's hand fell on Travis' shoulder. "Back," he breathed into the Apache's ear. They retreated, wriggling out of the grass into the edge of the morass at the end of the lake. Flies and other stinging insects avidly attacked their muck-covered bodies. They moved away from the scene of the hunt with every bit of stalker's skill they possessed, glad there was a wealth of meat to occupy the tribesmen.

Clumps of willow-like trees thickened enough to provide cover, allowing them to run in a crouch until Ashe dived panting into a convenient brush pile. With hot pain stabbing him at every breath, Travis threw himself down beside Ashe and Ross collapsed between them.

"That was nearly it," Ross got out between rasping intakes of air. "Never a dull moment in this business . . ."

Travis raised his head from his bent arm and tried to locate landmarks. They had been headed for the concealed time transport when the hunt cut across their path. But they had had to swing north to avoid the butchering parties. So their goal must now lie southeast.

Ashe was on his knees, peering northward to where the bulk of the wrecked ship was embedded in the plain.

"Look!"

They drew up beside him to watch a party of the hunters patter around the wreckage. One of them raised a spear and clanged it against the side of the spaceship.

"They didn't avoid it." Travis got the significance of the casual assault.

"Which means—we'll have to move fast with the smaller one! If they discover it, they may try to explore. Time's growing shorter."

"Only open country between us and the transfer now." Travis pointed out the obvious. To cut directly across to that cluster of masking rocks would put them in the open, to be instantly sighted by any tribesman looking in the right direction.

Ashe gazed at him thoughtfully. "Do you think you could make it without being spotted?"

Travis measured distances, tried to pick out any scrap of cover lying along the shortest route. "I can try," was all he could say.

5

He made for the rise at the southern point of the pile of rocks masking the installation. A brindled shape slunk out of his path, showing fangs. The dire wolf trotted on to the nearest carcass, where the women had stripped only the choicest meat, to seek food for which it would not have to fight.

Travis worked his way along the foot of the rise. The main path of the stampede was to the west and he believed himself in the clear, when snorting exploded before him. A bulk heaved through small bushes and he found himself confronting a bison cow. A broken spear shaft protruded too high on her shoulder to cause a disabling wound. And the pain had enraged her to a dangerous state.

In such a situation even a range cow would be perilous for a man on foot, and the bison was a third again larger than the animals he knew. Only the bushes around them saved Travis from death at that first meeting. The cow bellowed and charged, bearing down on him at a speed which he would have

thought impossible for her weight. He hurled himself
to the left in a wild scramble to escape and landed
in a thorny tangle. The cow, meanwhile, burst past
him close enough for her coarse hair to rasp against
one outflung arm.

Travis' head rang with the sound of her bellowing
as he squirmed around in the bush to bring up his
heaviest spear. The cow had skidded to a stop, gouged
matted grass and turf with her hoofs as she wheeled.
Then the spear haft in her shoulder caught in one of
the springy half-trees. She bellowed again, lurching
forward to fight that drag. The broken spear ripped
loose and a great gout of blood broke, to be sopped
up in the heavy tangle of shoulder hair.

That slowed her. Travis had time to get on his feet,
ready his spear. There was no good target in that wide
head confronting him. He jerked off his supply bag,
swung it by its carrying thong, and flung it at the cow's
dripping muzzle. His trick worked. The bison charged,
not for him, but after the thing that had teased her.
And Travis thrust home behind her shoulder with all
the force he had.

The weight of the bison and the impetus of the
animal's charge tore the shaft from his hold. Then the
cow went to her knees, coughing, and the big body
rolled on one side. He hurdled the mount of her hind-
quarters, fearing that the noise of battle might attract
the hunters.

Forcing a way through the brush, he made most
of the remainder of his journey on hands and knees.
At last he crouched in the shelter of the rock pile,
his ribs heaving, careless of the bleeding scratches
which laced his exposed flesh.

With his body pressed to earth, Travis scanned his
back trail and saw that he had been wise to leave the
scene of battle quickly. Three of the hunters were

running across the plain toward the brush, trailing spears. But they showed caution enough to suggest that this was not the first time they had had to deal with wounded stragglers from a stampeded herd.

Having scouted the brush, the brown men ventured into its cover. And seconds later a surprised shout informed Travis his kill had been located. Then that shout was answered by a long eerie wail from some point up the hill above the rocks. Travis stirred uneasily.

The spear he had been forced to leave in the body of the cow resembled their own—but did it look enough like theirs for them to believe the kill had been made by a tribesman? Had these people some system of individual markings for personal weapons, such as his own race had developed in their roving days? Would they try to track him down?

He snaked his way into the crevice of the rocks. The alerting signal was there, a second box set in beside the radar guide which now hummed its signal in his ear. He plunged down the lever set in its lid, then moved the tiny bit of metal rapidly up and down in the pattern he had been drilled on only the day before. In the desert of the twenty-first century that call would register on another recording device, relaying to Kelgarries the need for a hasty conference.

Travis edged out from the rocks and looked about him warily. He flattened against a boulder taller than his wiry body and listened, not only with his ears but with every wilderness-trained sense he possessed. His flint knife was in his fist as he caught that click of warning. And his other hand went out to grab at an upraised forearm as brown and well muscled as his own. The smell of blood and grease hit his nostrils as they came together chest to chest, and the stranger spat a torrent of unintelligible words at him. Travis brought up the fist with the knife, not to stab the other's flesh, but in a sharp blow against a thick jaw-bone. It rocked the shaggy black head back for a moment.

Pain scored along Travis' own ribs as the two men broke apart. He aimed another blow at the jaw, brought up his knee as the native sprang in, knife ready. It was dirty fighting by civilized rules, but Travis wanted a quick knockout with no knife work. He staggered the hunter, and was going in for a last telling blow when another figure darted around the rocks and hit the back of the tribesman's head, sending him limp and unconscious to the ground.

Ross Murdock wasted no time in explanations. "Come on. Help me get him under cover!"

Somehow they crowded into the shelter of the transfer, the Folsom man between them. With quick efficiency, Ross tied the wrists and ankles of their captive and inserted a strip of hide for a gag between his slack jaws.

Travis inspected a dripping cut across his own ribs and decided it was relatively unimportant. He faced about as Ashe joined them.

"Looks as if you've been elected target for today." Ashe pushed aside Travis' hands to inspect the cut critically. "You'll live," he added, as he rummaged in his supply bag for a small box of pills. One he crushed on his palm, to smear the resulting powder along the bloody scratch, the other he ordered his patient to swallow. "What did you do to touch this off?"

Travis sketched his adventure with the bison cow.

Ashe shrugged. "Just one of those unlucky foul-ups we have to expect now and then. Now we have this fellow to worry about." He surveyed the captive bleakly.

"What do we do?" Ross's nose wrinkled. "Start a zoo with this exhibit one?"

"You got the message through?" Ashe asked.

Travis nodded.

"Then we'll sit it out. As soon as it gets dark we'll carry him out, cut the cords, and leave him near one of their camps. That's the best we can do. Unfortunately the tribe seems to be heading west—"

"West!" Travis thought of that other ship.

"What if they try to board that spacer?" Ross seemed to share his concern. "I've a feeling this isn't going to be a lucky run. We've had trouble breathing down our necks right from the start. But we should keep watch on that other ship—"

"And what *could* we do to prevent their exploring it?" Travis wanted to know. He was feeling low, willing to agree with any forebodings.

"We'll hope that they will follow the herd," Ashe answered. "Food is a major preoccupation with such a tribe and they'll keep near to a good supply as long as they can. But it does make sense to watch the ship. I'll have to wait here to report to Kelgarries. Suppose you two take our friend here for his walk and then keep on going to that ridge between the valleys. Then you can let us know in time to keep our men under cover if the tribe drifts that way."

Ross sighed. "All right, chief. When do we start?"

"At dusk. No use courting trouble. There will be prowlers out there after nightfall."

"Prowlers!" Ross grinned without much humor. "That's a mild way of putting it. I don't intend to meet up with any eleven-foot lion in the dark!"

"Moon tonight," corrected Travis mildly, and settled himself for what rest he could get before they ventured to leave.

Not only the moon gave light that night. The dusky

sky was riven by the sullen fire of the distant volcano—or volcanoes. Travis now believed that there was
more than one burning mountain to the north. And
the air had a distinct metallic taste, which Ashe
ascribed to an active eruption miles away.

Somehow, between them they got their captive on
his feet and marched him along. He seemed to be
in a dazed state, slumping again to the ground while
Travis went ahead to scout out a group about a fire.

The Folsom men—and women—were gorging on
meat lightly seared by the fire. The odor of it reached
Travis and filled him with an urge to dart into that
company and seize a sizzling rib or two for himself.
Concentrates might provide the scientific balance of
energy and nourishment which his body needed, but
they were no substitute, as far as he was concerned,
for the contents of the feast he was watching.

Fearing to linger lest his appetite overpower his
caution, he flitted back to Ross and reported that there
were no sentries out to spoil their simple plan. So they
hauled their charge to the edge of the firelight,
removed his bonds and gag, and gave him a light
push. Then they quickly raced out of range.

If any natives did follow, they did not find the right
trail, and the two made the ridge without further bad
luck.

"We're the stupid ones," Ross observed as they drew
up the last incline and found a reasonably sheltered
spot under an overhang. It was not quite a cave, but
had only one open side to defend. "Nobody in his right
senses is going to gallop around in the dark."

"Dark?" protested Travis, clasping his arms about
the knees pulled tightly to his chest, and staring northward. His suspicion about the volcanic activity there
was borne out now by the redness of the sky and the
presence of fumes in the wind. It was a spectacular

display, but not one to instill confidence. His only satisfaction lay in the miles which must stretch between that angry mountain and the ridge on which he was now stationed.

Ross made no answer. Since Travis had the first watch, his companion had rolled in his hide cloak and was already asleep.

It was a night of broken sleep. When Travis rose in the dawn he discovered a thin skim of gray dust on his skin and the surrounding rocks. At the same time a sulphuric blast made him cough raggedly.

"Anything doing?" he croaked.

Ross shook his head and offered the gourd water bottle. The small spaceship rested peacefully below. The only change in the picture from the previous day was that there was less activity among the scavengers below the open port.

"What are they like—those men from space?" Travis asked suddenly.

To his surprise Ross, whom he had come to regard as close to nerveless, shivered.

"Pure poison, fella, and don't you ever forget it! I saw two kinds—the baldies who wear the blue suits, and a furry-faced one with pointed ears. They may look like men—but they aren't. And believe me, anyone who tangles with those boys in blue is asking to be chopped up like hamburger!"

"I wonder where they came from." Travis raised his head. The few stars were dim pinpoints of light in the dawn sky. To think of those as suns nourishing other worlds such as the solid earth now under him—where men, or at least thinking creatures, carried on lives of their own—was a huge leap of imagination.

Ross waved a hand skyward. "Take your pick, Fox. The big brains running this show of ours believe there was a whole confederation of different worlds tied together in a United Something-or-other then—" He blinked and laughed. "Me—saying 'then' when I mean 'now!' This jumping back and forth in time mixes a guy's thinking."

"And if someone were to take off in that ship down there, he'd run into them outside?"

"If he did, he'd regret it!"

"But if he took off in our time—would he still find them waiting?"

Ross played with the thongs fastening the supply bag. "That's one of the big questions. And nobody'll have the right answer until we do go and see. Twelve-fifteen thousand years is a long time. Do you know any civilization here that's lasted even a fraction of that? From painted hunters to the atom here. Out there it could be the atom back to painted hunters—or to nothing—by now."

"Would you like to go and see?"

Ross smiled. "I've had one brush with the blue boys. If I could be sure they weren't still on some star map, I might say yes. I wouldn't care to meet them on their home ground—and I'm no trained space man. But the idea does eat into a fella . . . Ha—company!"

There was movement down in the valley—to the north. But what were issuing from the woods at a leisurely and ponderous pace were not Folsom hunters. Ross whistled very softly between his teeth, watching that advance eagerly, and Travis shared his excitement.

The bison herd, the striped horses, the frustrated sabertooth confronting the giant ground sloths, none had been as thrilling a sight as this. Even the elephant of their own time could generate a measure of awe in the human onlooker by the sheer majesty of its movement. And these larger and earlier members of the same tribe produced an almost paralyzing sense of wonder in the two scouts. "Mammoths!"

Tall, thick-haired giants, their backbones sloping from the huge dome of the skull to the shorter hind-quarters, dwarfed tree and landscape as they moved. Three of them towered close to fourteen feet at the shoulder. They bore the weight of the tremendous curled tusks proudly, their trunks swaying in time to their unhurried steps. They were the most formidable living things Travis had ever seen. And, watching them, he could not believe that the hunters he had spied upon in the other valley had ever brought down such game with spears. Yet the evidence that they had, had been discovered over and over again—scattered bones with a flint point between the giant ribs or splitting a massive spine.

"One—two—three—" Ross was counting, half under his breath. "And a small one—"

"Calf," Travis identified. But even that baby was nothing to face without a modern weapon to hand.

"Four—five—Family party?" Ross speculated.

"Maybe. Or do they travel in herds?"

"Ask the big brains. Ohhh—look at that tree go!"

The leader in the dignified parade set its massive head against a tree bole, gave a small push, and the tree crashed. With a squeal audible to the scouts, the mammoth calf hustled forward and began busily harvesting the leaves, while its elders appeared to watch it with adult indulgence.

Ross pushed the wind-blown tails of wig hair out of his eyes. "We may have a problem here. What if they don't move on? I can't see a crew working down there with those tons of tusks skipping about in the background."

"If you want to haze 'em on," Travis observed, "don't let me stop you. I've drag-herded stubborn

cows—but I'm not going down there and swing a rope
at any of those rumps!"

"They might take a fancy to bump over the ship."

"So they might," agreed Travis. "And what could
we do to stop 'em?"

But for the moment the mammoth family seemed
content at their own end of the valley, which was at
least a quarter of a mile from the ship. After an hour's
watch Ross tightened the thongs of his sandals and
gathered up his spears.

"I'll report in. Maybe those walking mountains will
keep hunters away—"

"Or draw them here," corrected Travis pessimisti-
cally. "Think you can find your way back?"

Ross grinned. "The trail is getting to be a regular
freeway. All we need is a traffic cop or two. Be seeing you . . ." He disappeared from their perch with that
uncanny ability to vanish silently into the surrounding landscape that Travis still found unusual in a white
man.

As Travis continued to lie there, chin supported
on forearm, idly watching the mammoths, he tried
again to figure out what made Ashe and Ross Murdock so different from the other members of their
race that he knew. Of course he had in a measure
felt the same lack of self-consciousness with Dr.
Morgan. To Prentiss Morgan a man's race and the
color of his skin were nothing—a shared enthusiasm
was all that really mattered. Morgan had cracked
Travis Fox's shell and let him into a larger world.
And then—like all soft creatures—he had been the
more deeply hurt when that new world had turned
hostile. He had then fled back into the old, leaving everything—even friendship behind.

Now he waited for that smoldering flame of past
anger to bite. It was there, but dulled, just as the night

fire of the volcano was now only a lazy smoke plume under the rising sun. The desert over which he had ridden to find water a week ago was indeed buried in time. What—?

The mammoths had moved, with the largest bull facing about. Trunk up, the beast shrilled a challenge that tore at Travis' ears. This was beyond the squall of the sabertooth, the grunting roar of a sloth prepared to do battle. It was the most frightening sound he had ever heard.

A second time the bull trumpeted. Sabertooth on the hunt? The Alaskan lion? What animal was large enough, or desperate enough, to stalk that walking mountain? Man?

But if there was a Folsom hunter in hiding, he did not linger. The bull paced along the edge of the wood and then butted over another tree, to tear loose leafy branches and crunch them greedily. The crisis was past.

An hour later a party guided by Ross climbed up to join him. Kelgarries and four others wearing camouflage coveralls, spread themselves on the ground to share the lookout.

"That's our baby!" The major's face was alight with enthusiasm as he sighted the derelict. "What can you do about her, boys?"

But one of the crew focused glasses in another direction. "Hey—those things are mammoths!" he shouted. As one, his fellows turned to follow his pointing finger.

"Sure," snapped the major. "Look at the ship, Wilson. If she is intact, can we possibly swing a direct transfer?"

Reluctantly the other man abandoned the mammoth family for business. He studied the derelict through his lenses. "Some job. Biggest transfer we ever did was the sub frame—"

"I know that! But that was two years ago, and Craw-
ford's experiments have proved that the grid can be
expanded without losing power. If we can take this
one straight through without any dismantling, we've
put the schedule ahead maybe five years! And you
know what that will mean."

"And who's going to go down there to set up a grid
with those outsize elephants watching him? We have
to have a clear field to work in and no interruptions.
A lot of the material won't stand any rough handling."

"Yeah," echoed one of the subordinates. Again the
lenses swung to the north. "Just how are you going
to shoo the mammoths out?"

"Scout job, I suppose." That resigned comment
came from Ashe as he joined the party. "Well, I'm admitting right here and now that I have no ideas, bright
or otherwise, on how to make a mammoth decide to
take a long walk. But we're open for suggestions."

They watched the browsing beasts in silence.
Nobody volunteered any ideas. It appeared that this
particular problem was not yet covered by any rule
on or off the book.

6

"What we need is a mine field—like the one planted around Headquarters," Ross said at last.

"Mine field?" repeated the man Kelgarries had called Wilson. Then he said again, "Mine field!"

"Got something?" demanded the major.

"Not a mine field," Wilson corrected. "We could fix it for those brutes to blow themselves up, all right, but they'd take the ship with them. However, a sonic barrier now—"

"Run it around the ship outside your work field—yes!" The major was eager again. "Would it take long to get it in?"

"We'd have to bring a lot of equipment through. Say a day—maybe more. But it is the only thing I can think of now which might work."

"All right. You'll get all the material you need—on the double!" promised Kelgarries.

Wilson chuckled. "Just like that, eh? No howls about expense? Remember, I'm not going to sign any orders I have to defend with my lifeblood about two years from now before some half-baked investigating committee."

"If we pull this off," Kelgarries returned with convincing force, "we'll never have to defend anything before anyone! Man—you get that ship through intact and our whole project will have paid for itself from the day it was nothing but a few wishful sentences on the back of an old envelope. This is it—the big pay-off!"

That was the beginning of a hectic period in Travis' life which he was never able to sort out neatly in his head afterward. With Ashe and Ross he patrolled a wide area of hill and valley, keeping watch upon the camps of the wandering hunters, marking down the drifting herds of animals. For two days men shuttled back and forth and then erected a second time transfer within the valley of the smaller ship.

Wilson's sonic barrier—an invisible yet nerve-shattering wall of high-frequency impulses—was in place around the ship. And while its signals did not affect human ears, the tension it produced did reach any man who strayed into its influence. The mammoth family withdrew into the small woodland from which they had come. The men working on the globe did not know whether that retreat was the result of the vibrations or not—but at least the beasts were gone.

Meanwhile more sonic broadcasters were set up on every path in and out of the valley, sealing it from invasion. Kelgarries and his superiors were throwing every resource of the project into this one job.

About the ship arose a framework of bars as fast as the men could fit one to another. Travis, watching the careful deliberation of the fitting, understood that delicate and demanding work was in progress. He learned from overheard comments that a new type of time transfer was in the process of being assembled here. One so large had never been attempted before. If the job was successful, the globe would be carried intact through to his own era for detailed study.

In the meantime another small crew of experts explored the ship, taking care not to activate any of its machines, and also made a detailed study of the remains of the crew. Medical men did what they could to discover the cause for the mass death of the space men. And their final verdict was a sudden attack of disease or food poisoning, for there were no wounds.

Three days—four—Travis, weary to his very bones, dragged back from a scouting trip southward. He hunched down by the fire in the camp the three field men kept on the heights above the crucial valley. A metallic taste in the air rasped throat and lungs when he breathed deeply. For the past two days volcanic activity in the north had intensified. During the previous night they had all been awakened by a display— luckily miles away—in which half a mountain must have blown skyward. Twice torrents of rain had hit, but it was warm rain and the sultriness of the air made conditions now almost tropical. He would be very glad when that fretwork of bars was in place and they could leave this muggy hotbox.

"See anything?" Ross Murdock tossed aside the hide blanket he had pulled about head and shoulders. He coughed raspingly as one of the sulphur-tinged breezes curled about them.

"Migration—I think," Travis qualified his report. "The big bison herd is already well south and the hunters are following it."

"Don't like the fireworks, I suppose." Ross nodded to the north. "And I don't blame them. There's a forest burning up there today."

"Seen anything more of the mammoths?"

"Not around here, I was northeast anyway."

"How long before they'll be through down there?"
Travis went to look down at the ship. There was a
murky haze gathering about the valley and it was
spoiling the clearness of the view. But men were still
aloft on the scaffolding of rods—hurrying to the
final capping of the skeleton enclosure around the
sphere.

"Ask one of the brains. The other crew—the
medics—finished their poking this afternoon. They
went through transfer an hour ago. I'd say tomorrow
they'll be ready to throw the switch on that gadget.
About time. I have a feeling about this place . . ."

"Maybe rightly." Ashe loomed out of the growing
murk. "There's trouble popping to the north." He
coughed, and Travis suddenly noted that the mat of
wig was missing from the older man's head. He saw
that there was a long red burn mark down Ashe's
shoulder, crossing the white seam of an earlier scar.
Ross, seeing it too, jumped to his feet and turned
Ashe toward the light of the fire to inspect that burn
closer.

"What did you do—try to play boy on the burning deck?" His voice held an undernote of concern.

"I miscalculated how fast a stand of green timber
can burn—when conditions are right. The top of a
mountain did blow off last night, and it may have an
encore soon. We're moving down nearer to the transfer. And we may have visitors—"

"Hunters? I saw them moving south—"

Ashe shook his head in answer to Travis.

"No, but we may have been too clever about rig-
ging that sonic screen. Those mammoths have been
holed up in a small sub-valley to the north. If the hell
I'm expecting now breaks loose, sonics won't hold
them back, but breaking through such a barrier will

make them really wild. They might just charge straight down through here. Kelgarries will have to try his big transfer if that happens."

The scouts reached the floor of the valley in time to see the technicians dropping from the grillwork and hurrying to the time transfer. But they had not gotten to the grill when the world went mad. With flame, noise and thunder from the north, a great surge of fire leapt up to scorch the underside of lowering clouds. Travis was thrown off his feet as the ground crawled sickeningly. He saw the grid sway around the globe, heard cries and shouts.

"—quake!" The volcanic outburst was being matched by earthquake. Travis stared up at the grid fascinated, expecting every moment to see the rods fly apart and come crashing down on the dome of the ship. But although the framework swayed, it did not fall.

In the thickening murk Kelgarries drove his men to the personnel transfer. Travis knew that he should join that line, but he was simply too amazed by the scene to stir. The smoke grew denser. Out of it arose a shout in a familiar voice. Getting to his feet, he ran to answer that plea for help.

Ashe lay on the ground. Ross was bending over him, trying to get him to his feet. As Travis blundered up, his spears thrown away, the smoke closed in and provoked strangled coughing. Travis' sense of direction faltered. Which way was the time transfer? Light ashes drifting through the air blurred air and ground alike. It was like being caught in a snowstorm.

He heard a scream of sheer terror, scaling up. A black shape, bigger than any nightmare, pounded into sight. The mammoths were charging down-valley as Ashe had feared.

"—get out!" Ross pulled Ashe to the right. Now the older man was between them, stumbling dazedly along.

They skirted the wall of rods about the globe and squeezed through to the ball. A mammoth trumpeted behind them. There was little hope now of reaching the personnel transfer in time. Ashe must have realized that. He pulled free of the other two and staggered around the ship, one hand on its surface for guide.

Travis guessed his reason—Ashe wanted to find the ladder which led to the open port, use the ship as a refuge. He heard Ashe call, and slipped behind him to find that the other held the ladder.

Ross gave his officer a boost, then followed after him, while Travis steadied the dangling ladder as best he could. He had started to ascend when he saw Ashe, only a dark blot, claw through the port above. Again he heard a mammoth trumpet and wondered that the beasts had not already smashed into the framework surrounding the ship. Then Travis in turn scrambled through the port, and lay inside gasping and coughing as the irritation carried in the fog bit into his nose and throat.

"Shut it!" Someone shoved Travis roughly away from the door and pushed past him. The outer hatch closed with a clang. Now the fog was only a wisp or two, and utter silence took the place of the bedlam outside.

Travis drew a long breath, one that did not rasp in his throat. The bluish light from the walls of the ship was subdued, but it was bright enough to reveal Ashe. The older man lay half propped against a wall. A bruise was beginning to rise on his forehead, which was no longer covered by any wig. Ross returned from the outer hatch.

"Kind of close quarters here," he commented. "We might as well spread out some."

They went out the inner door of the lock. Murdock

swung that shut behind them, a move which was to save their lives.

"In here—" Murdock indicated the nearest door. The barriers which had been tightly closed on their first visit to the ship had been opened by the technicians. And the cabin beyond was furnished with a cross between a bunk and a hammock. It was both fastened to the wall and swung on straps from the ceiling. Together they guided Ashe to it and got him down, still dazed. Travis had time for no more than a quick glance about when a voice rang down the well of the stair.

"Hey! Who's down there? What's going on?"

They climbed to the control cabin. In front of them stood a wiry young man in technician's coveralls, who stared at them wide-eyed.

"Who are you?" he demanded, as he backed away raising his fists in defense.

Travis was completely bewildered until he caught sight of a reflection on the shiny control board—a dirty, nearly naked savage. And Ross was his counterpart—the two of them must certainly look like savages to the stranger. Murdock peeled off his ash-encrusted wig, a gesture Travis copied. The technician relaxed.

"You're time agents." He made that recognition sound close to an accusation. "What's going on, anyway?"

"General blowup." Ross sat down suddenly and heavily in one of the swinging chairs. Travis leaned against the wall. Here in this silent cabin it was difficult to believe in the disaster and confusion outside. "There's a volcanic eruption in progress," Murdock continued. "And the mammoths charged—just before we made it in here—"

The technician started for the stairwell. "We've got to get to the transfer."

Travis caught his arm. "No getting out of the ship now. You can't even see—ash too thick in the air."

"How close were they to taking this ship through?" Ross wanted to know.

"All ready, as far as I know," the technician began, and then added quickly, "d'you mean they'll try to warp her through now—with us inside?"

"It's a chance, just a chance. If the grid survived the quake and the mammoths." Ross's voice thinned. "We'll have to wait and see."

"We can *see*—a little." The technician stepped to one of the side panels his hand going to a button there.

Ross moved, leaping from his seat in a spring which rivaled a sabertooth's for quickness. He struck the other, sending him sprawling on the floor. But not before the button was pressed home. A flat screen rose from the board, glowing. Then, over the head of the angry technician who was still on his knees, they beheld swirling ash-filled vapor, as if they were looking through a window into the valley.

"You fool!" Ross stood over the technician, and the menace Travis had seen in him at their first meeting was very much alive. "Don't touch anything in here!"

"Wise guy, eh?" The technician, his face flushed and hard, was getting up, his fists ready. "I know what I'm doing—"

"Look—out there!" Travis' cry broke them apart before they tangled.

The fogged picture still held. But there was something else to see there now. Yellow-green lines of light built up, bar by bar, square by square, bright and brutal as lightning. The pattern grew fast, superimposed on the gray of the drifting ash.

"The grid!" The technician broke away from Ross. Grasping the back of one of the swinging seats, he leaned forward eagerly to watch the screen. "They've turned the power on. They're going to try to pull us through!"

The grid continued to glow—to scream with light. They could not watch it now because of its eye-searing brilliance. Then the ship rocked. Another earthquake— or something else? Before Travis could think clearly he was caught up in a fury of sensation for which no name was possible. It was as if his flesh and his mind were at war with each other. He gasped and writhed. The brief discomfort he had felt when he used the personnel transfer was nothing compared to this wrenching. He groped for some stability in a dissolving world.

Now he was on the floor. Above him was the window on the outside. He lifted his head slowly because his body felt as if he had been beaten. But that window display—there was no gray now—no ashes falling as snow. All was blue, bright, metallic blue—a blue he knew and that he wanted above him in safety. He staggered up, one hand stretching toward that promise of blue. But that feeling of instability remained.

"Wait!" The technician's fingers caught his wrist in a hard, compelling grasp. He dragged Travis away from the screen, tried to push him down in one of the chairs. Ross was beyond, his scarred hand clenched on the edge of a control panel until the seams in the flesh stood out in ugly ridges. Losing that look of cold rage, his expression grew wary.

"What's going on?" Ross asked harshly.

It was the technician who gave a sharp order. "Get in that seat! Strap down! If it's what I think, fella—" He shoved Ross back into the nearest chair. The other obeyed tamely as if he had not been at blows with the man only moments earlier.

"We're through time, aren't we?" Travis still watched that wonderful, peaceful patch of blue sky.

"Sure—we're through. Only how long we're going to stay here . . ." The technician stumbled to the third chair, that in which they had discovered the dead pilot days earlier. He sat down with a suddenness close to collapse.

"What do you mean?" Ross's eyes narrowed. His dangerous look was coming back.

"Dragging us through by the energy of the grid did something to the engines here. Don't you feel that vibration, man? I'd say this ship was preparing for a take-off!"

"What?" Travis was half out of his seat. The technician leaned forward and shoved him back into the full embrace of the swinging chair. "Don't get any bright ideas about a quick scram out of here, boy. Just look!"

Travis followed the other's pointing finger. The stairwell through which they had climbed to the cabin was now closed.

"Power's on," the other continued. "I'd say we're going out pretty soon."

"We can't!" Travis began and then shivered, knowing the futility of that protest even as he shaped it.

"Anything you can do?" Ross asked, his control once more complete.

The technician laughed, choked, and then waved his hand at the array on the control board. "Just what?" he asked grimly. "I know the use of exactly three little buttons here. We never dared experiment with the rest without dismantling all the installations and tracing them through. I can't stop or start anything. So we're off to the moon and points up, whether we like it or not."

"Anything they can do out there?" Travis turned

back to that patch of blue. He knew nothing about the machines, even about the science of mechanics. He could only hope that somewhere, somehow, someone would end this horror they faced.

The technician looked at him and then laughed again. "They can clear out in a hurry. If there's a backwash when we blast off, a lot of good guys may get theirs."

That vibration, which Travis had sensed on his revival from the strain of the time transport, was growing stronger. It came not only from the walls and floor of the cabin, but seemingly from the very air he was gulping in quick, shallow breaths. The panic of utter helplessness sickened him, dried his mouth and gripped his middle with twisting pain.

"How long—?" he heard Ross ask, and saw the technician shake his head.

"Your guess is as good as mine."

"But why? How?" Travis asked hoarsely.

"That pilot, the one they found sitting here . . ." The technician rapped the edge of the control board with his fingers. "Maybe he set automatic controls before he crashed. Then the time transfer—that energy triggered action somewhere . . . But I'm only guessing."

"Set automatic controls for where?" Ross's tongue swept over his lips as if they were dry.

"Home, maybe. This is it, boys—strap in!"

Travis fumbled with the straps of the seat and pulled them across his body clumsily. He, too, felt that last quiver of extra vibration.

Then a hand, an invisible force as large, as powerful as a mammoth's foot, crushed down upon him. Under his body the seat straightened out into a swaying bed. He was fastened on it, unable to breathe, to think, to do more than feel, endure somehow the pain of flesh and bone under the pressure of that take-off. The blue square was one moment before his aching eyes—and then there was only blackness.

7

Travis came back to consciousness slowly, painfully aware of inner bruising. He tasted stale blood when he tried to swallow and found it hard to focus his eyes. That screen which had last been blue was now a dull black. As he moved the seat-bed under him swung violently, though the effort he had made was small. He raised his body, more cautiously pushing up with both hands.

On another swinging cot lay Ross Murdock. The lower part of his face was caked with blood, his eyes closed, his skin greenish white under the heavy tan and stain. The technician seemed to be in no better state. But under them, around them, the cabin was now quiet, devoid of either sound or vibration. Recognizing that, Travis fumbled with the strap across his middle and tried to get up.

This attempt brought disaster. His efforts drove him away from his support, right enough. But his feet did not touch the floor. Instead, he plunged out, weightless, to strike the edge of the main control board with force enough to raise a little yelp of pain. Panic-stricken, he held on to the board, pulling himself along until he could reach the technician. He tried to rouse the other, his methods growing rougher when they did not rouse signs of returning consciousness.

Finally the man groaned, turned his head, and opened his eyes. As awareness grew in their depths, so did surprise and fear.

"What—what happened?" The words were slurred. "You hurt?"

Travis drew the back of his hand across mouth and chin, brought it away clotted with blood. He must look as bad as Ross.

"Can't walk." He introduced the foremost problem of the moment. "Just—float . . ."

"Float?" repeated the technician, then he struggled up, unfastened his belt. "Then we *are* through—out of earth's gravity! We're in space!"

Jumbled fragments of articles he had read arose out of Travis' memory. Free of gravity—no up, down— no weight— He was nauseated, his head spinning badly, but keeping hold of the board he worked his way past the technician to Ross. Murdock was already stirring, and as Travis laid his hand on his seat he moaned, his fingers sweeping aimlessly across his chest as if to soothe some hurt there. Travis gently caught the other's bloody chin, shaking his head slowly from side to side as the gray eyes opened.

" . . . and that's it, we're out!" Case Renfry, the technician, shook his head at the flood of questions from the time scouts. "Listen, fellas, I was loaned to this project to help with the breakdown appraisal. I can't fly any ship, let alone this one—so it must be on automatic controls."

"Set by the dead pilot. Then it should go back to his base," Travis suggested gloomily.

"You are forgetting one thing." Ross sat up with care, keeping firm hold on his mooring with both hands. "That pilot's base is twelve thousand years or so in the past. They warped us through time before we took off—"

"And we can't go home?" Travis demanded again of the technician.

"I wouldn't try meddling with any key on that board," Renfry said, shaking his head. "If we're flying on automatic controls, the best thing is to keep on to the destination and then see what we can do."

"Only there are a few other things to consider—such as food, water, air supplies," Travis pointed out.

"Yes—air," Ross underlined with chilling soberness. "How long might we be on the way?"

Renfry grinned weakly. "Your guess is as good as mine. The air supply is all right—I think. They had a recycling plant in the ship and Stefferds said it was in perfect working order. Something like algae in a sealed section keeps it fresh. You can look in at it but you can't contaminate the place. And they breathed about the same mixture as we do. But as to food and water—we'd better look around. Three of us to feed . . ."

"Four! There's Ashe!" Ross, forgetting where he was, tried to jump free of his seat. He swam forward in a tangle of flailing legs and arms until Renfry drew him down.

"Take it easy, mighty easy, fella. Hit the wrong button while you're thrashing that way and we could be worse off than we are. Who's Ashe?"

"Our section chief. We stowed him in a cabin down below, he had had a bad knock on the head."

Travis aimed for the well leading to the center section of the globe. He overshot, bounced back, and was thankful when his fingers closed on the bar of its cover. They got it open and made their way clumsily in a direction Travis still thought of—in spite of the evidence of his eyes—as "down."

To descend into the heart of the ship required an agility that tormented their bruised and aching bodies. But when they at last reached the cabin they found Ashe still safely stowed in the bunk, far better tended against the force of the take-off than they had been. For only his peaceful face showed above a thick mass of a jelly substance which filled the interior of the bunk-hammock.

"He'll be all right. That's the stuff they keep in their lifeboats to patch up the injured—saved my life once," Ross identified. "A regular cure for anything."

"How do you know so much?" Renfry began, and then, he eyes wonderingly on Ross, he added, "why— you must be the guy who was with the Russians on that ship they were stripping!"

"Yes. But I'd like to know a little more about this one. Food—water . . ."

They went exploring in Renfry's wake, discovering adaptation to weightlessness a hard job, but determined to learn what they could about the best, and the worst, of their predicament. The technician had been all through the ship and now he displayed to them the air-renewal unit, the engine room, and the crew's quarters. They made a detailed examination of what could only be a mess cabin combined with kitchen. It was a cramped space in which no more than four men—or man-like beings—could fit at one time.

Travis frowned at the rows of sealed containers racked in the cupboards. He extracted one, shook it near his ear, and was rewarded by a gurgle which made him run a dry tongue over his blood-stained lips. There must be liquid of a sort inside, and he could not remember now when he had had a really satisfying drink.

"This is water—if you want a drink." Renfry brought a Terran canteen out of a corner. "We had four of these on board, used 'em while we were working."

Travis reached for the metal bottle, but did not uncap it after all. "Still have all four?" Perhaps more than any of the rest on board he knew the value of water, the disaster of not having it.

Renfry brought them out, shaking each. "Three sound full. This one's about half—maybe a little less."

"We'll have to go on rations."

"Sure," the technician agreed. "Think there're some concentrate food bars here, too. You fellas have any of those?"

"Ashe still had his supply bag with him, didn't he?" Travis asked Ross.

"Yes. And we'd better see how many of the bars we can find."

Travis looked at the alien container which had gurgled. At the moment he would have given a great deal to be able to force the lid, to drink its contents and ease both thirst and hunger.

"We may have to come to trying these." Renfry took the container from the scout, fitted it back into the holder space.

"I'd guess we'll have to try a lot of things before this trip is over—if it ever is. Right now I'd like to try a bath, or at least a wash." Ross surveyed his own scratched, half-naked, and very dirty body with disfavor.

"That you can have. Come on."

Again Renfry played guide, bringing them to a small cubbyhole beyond the mess cabin. "You stand on that—maybe you can hold yourself in place with those." He pointed to some rods set in the wall. "But get your feet down on that round plate and then press the circle in the wall."

"Then what happens? You roast or broil?" Travis inquired suspiciously.

"No—this really works. We tried it on a guinea pig yesterday. Then Harvey Bush used it after he upset a can of oil all over him. It's rather like a shower."

Ross jerked at the ties of his disreputable kilt and kicked off his sandals, his movements sending him skidding from wall to wall. "All right. I'm willing to try." He got his feet on the plate, holding himself in position by the rods, and then pressed the circle. Mist curled from under the edge of the floor plate, enveloped his legs, rose steadily. Renfry pushed shut the door.

"Hey!" protested Travis, "he's being gassed!"

"It's okay!" Ross's disembodied voice came from beyond. "In fact—it's better than okay!"

When he came out of the fogged cubby a few minutes later, the grime and much of the stain were gone from his body. Moreover, scratches that had been raw and red were now only faint pinkish lines. Ross was smiling.

"All the comforts of home. I don't know what that stuff is, but it peels you right down to your second layer of hide and makes you like it. The first good thing we've found in this mousetrap."

Travis shucked his kilt a little more slowly. He didn't relish being shut into that box, but neither did he enjoy the present state of his person. Gingerly he stepped onto the floor disk, got his feet flattened on its surface, and pressed the circle. He held his breath as the gassy substance puffed up to enfold him.

The stuff was not altogether a gas, he discovered, for it was thicker than any vapor. It was as if he were immersed in a flood of frothy bubbles that rubbed and

slicked across his skin with the effect of vigorous tow-
eling. Grinning, he relaxed and, closing his eyes,
ducked his head under the surface. He felt the smooth
swish across his face, drawing the sting out of scratches
and the ache out of his bruises and bumps.

When the bubbles ebbed and Travis stepped out
of the cubby, he was met by a changed Ross. The
latter was just hitching up over his broad shoulders
the upper part of a tight, blue-green suit. It clung to
his body, modeling every muscle as he moved. Made
all in one piece, its feet were soled with a thick sponge
that cushioned each step. Ross picked another bundle
of blue-green from the floor and tossed it to the
Apache.

"Compliments of the house," he said. "I certainly
never thought I'd want to wear one of these again."

"Their uniforms?" Travis remembered the dead
pilot. "What is this—silk?" He rubbed his hand over
the sleek surface of a fabric he could not identify
and was attracted by the play of color—blue, green,
lavender—rippling from one shade to another as the
material moved.

"Yes. It has its good points, all right—insulated
against cold and heat, for one thing. For another, it
can be traced."

Travis paused, his arm half through the right sleeve.
"Traced?"

"Well, I was trailed over about fifty miles of pretty
rugged territory because I was wearing one like this.
And they tried to get at me mentally, too, when I had
it on. Went to sleep one night and woke up heading
right back to the boys who wanted to collect me."

Travis stared, but it was plain Ross meant every
word he said. Then the Apache glanced down again
at the silky stuff he was wearing, with an impulse to
strip it off. Yet Murdock, in spite of his story, was

fastening the studs which ran from one shoulder to the other hip of his own garment.

"If we were in their time, I wouldn't touch this with a fifty-foot pole," Ross continued, smiling wryly. "But, seeing as how we are some thousands of years removed from the rightful owners, I'll take the chance. As I said, these suits do have some points in their favor."

Travis snapped his own studs together. The material felt good, smooth, a little warm, almost as soothing as the foam bubbles which had scoured and energized his tired body. He was willing to chance wearing the uniform. It was infinitely better than the hide garment he had discarded.

They were learning to navigate through weightlessness. The usual technique approached swimming, and they found convenient handholds to draw them along. If Travis could forget that the ship was boring on into the unknown, their present lodging had a lot to recommend it. But when the four of them gathered in the control cabin an hour or so later, they prepared to consider the major problem with what objectivity they could summon.

Ashe, alertly himself again, fresh from the healing of the aliens' treatment, was their leader by unspoken consent. Only it was to Renfry that the three time scouts looked for hope. The technician had little to offer.

"The pilot must have set the ship's controls on some type of homing device just before he died. I'm just guessing at this, you understand, but it is the only explanation to make sense now. When we explored here, my chief, working from what he knew of the tape records from the Russian headquarters, traced three installations; the one giving outside vision," he began, tapping lightly on the screen which had been

blue for those few precious moments before their
involuntary take-off. "Another which is the inside com
system connecting speakers all over the ship. And a
third—this." He pushed a lever to its head in a slot.
Three winks of light showed on the board and out of
the air above their heads came a sound which might
have been a word in an unknown tongue.

"And what *is* that?" Ashe watched the lights with
interest.

"Guns! We have four ports open now, and a weapon
in each ready to fire. It was the chief's guess that this
was—is—a small military scout, or police patrol ship."
He clicked the lever back into place and the lights
were gone.

"Not very helpful now," Ross commented. "What
about the chances for getting back home?"

Renfry shrugged. "Not a chance that I can see so
far. Frankly, I'm afraid to do any poking around these
controls while we're in space. There is too good a
chance of stopping and not getting started again—
either forward or back."

"That makes sense. So we'll just have to keep on
going to whatever port for which your controls are now
set?"

Renfry nodded. "Not *my* controls, sir. This—all
of this—is far advanced, and different—beyond our
planes. Maybe, if I had time, and we were safely
on ground, I could discover how the engines tick,
but what makes them do so would still be another
problem."

"What's the fuel?"

"Even that I can't say. The engines are completely
sealed. We didn't dare pry too far."

"And home port may be anywhere in the universe,"
mused Ashe. "They had some type of distance-time
jump—voyages couldn't have lasted centuries."

Renfry was studying the banks of buttons and levers with an expression of complete exasperation. "They could have every gadget in a fiction writer's imagination, sir, and we wouldn't know it—until the thing did or didn't work!"

"Quite a prospect." Ashe got up with caution, the careful motions of a novice in weightlessness. "I think a detailed exploration of the rest of our present home is now in order."

There were three of the small living cabins, each equipped with two bunk-hammocks. And by experimenting with the wall panels they discovered clothing, personal effects of the crew. Travis did not like to empty those shallow cupboards and handle those possessions of dead men. But he did his share during the hunt for some clue which might mean the difference between life and death for the present passengers. He had opened a last small cavity in one locker when he caught a promising glitter. He picked up the object and found himself holding a rectangle of some slick material that felt like glass. It was milky white, blank when he picked it up. But the chill of the first touch faded as he turned it over curiously. The rim was bordered in a band of tiny flashing bits of yellow which might be gem stones—framing blankness instead of a picture.

A picture! If he could hold a picture of a far place—what sort would it be? Family—home—friends? He watched the plain surface within the border. Plain—? There *was* something there! Color was seeping up to the surface and spreading. Outlines were becoming solid. Bewildered, almost frightened, Travis studied that changing scene.

He did have a picture now. And one he knew. It was an entirely familiar scene—a stretch of desert and mountains. Why, he might be standing on the cliffs looking toward Red Horse Canyon! He wanted to throw the thing from him. How could an alien who lived twelve thousand years ago carry among his belongings a picture of the country Travis knew as home? It was unbelievable—unreal!

"What is it, son?" Ashe's hand was real on his arm, Ashe's voice warmed the chill congealing inside him as he continued to stare at the thing he held, the thing which, in spite of its familiar beauty, was wrong, terrible . . .

"Picture . . ." he mumbled. "Picture of my home— here."

"What?" Ashe stepped closer and gave an exclamation, took the block out of Travis' hands. The younger man wiped his sweating palms down his thighs, trying to wipe away the touch of that weird picture.

But, as he watched the desert scene, he cried out. For it was fading away, the colors were absorbed in the original white. The outlines of the cliffs and mountains were gone. Ashe held the plaque up in both of his hands. And now there was a new stirring in the depths, a murky flowing as again a scene grew into sharp brilliance.

Only this was not the desert, but a stand of tall, green trees Travis recognized as pines. Below them was a strand of gray-white sand, and beyond the pound of waves lashing high in foam against fanged rocks. Above that restless water white birds soared.

"Safeharbor!" Ashe sat down suddenly on the bunk and the picture shook as his hands trembled. "That's the beach by my home in Maine—in Maine, I tell you! Safeharbor, Maine! But how did this get here?" His expression was one of dazed bewilderment.

"To me it showed my home also," Travis said slowly. "And now to you another scene. Perhaps to the man who once lived in this cabin it also showed his home.

This is a magic thing, I think. Not the magic which your people have harnessed to do their will, nor the magic of my Old Ones either." Somehow the thought that this object bewildered the white man as much as it did him took away a little of the fear. Ashe raised his eyes from the scene of shore and sea to meet Travis'. Slowly he nodded.

"You may be guessing, but I'll stake a lot on your guess being right. What they knew, these people—what wonders they knew! We must learn all we can, follow them."

Travis laughed shakily. "Follow them we are, Doctor Ashe. About the learning—well, we shall see."

8

A figure edged along the narrow corridor, his
cushioned feet barely touching the floor. In the time-
less interior of the spaceship where there was no
change between day and night, Travis had had to wait
a long time for this particular moment. His brown
hands, too thin nowadays, played with the fastening
of his belt. Under that was a gnawing ache which
never left him now.

They had stretched their water supply with strict
rationing, and the concentrate bars the same way. But
tomorrow—or in the next waking period they would
arbitrarily label "tomorrow"—they would have only
four of those small squares. And Travis was keenly
aware not only of that indisputable fact but of something which Ross had said when they had argued out
the need for experiment with alien food supplies.

"Case Renfry," the younger time agent had pointed
out the obvious, "is certainly not going to be your
tester. If we are ever going to be able to find out what
makes this bus tick and get it started home again, he's

the one to do it. And, chief"—he had then turned
upon Ashe—"you've the best brain"—it's up to you to
help him. Maybe somewhere in this loot we've found
you can locate a manual, or a do-it-yourself tape that'll
give us a fair break."

They had been pulling over the material they had
found in the cabins. Objects such as the disappearing picture were set aside on the hope that Ashe, with
his archaeologist's training in the penetration of age-
old mysteries, might understand them through study.

"Which," Ross had continued, "leaves the food problem up to a volunteer—me."

Travis had remained quiet, but he had also made
plans. He had already followed Ross's reasoning to
a logical end, but his conclusion differed from Murdock's. Of the four men on board he, not Murdock,
was certainly the most expendable. And the history
of his people testified that Apaches possessed remark-
ably tough digestions. They had been able to live off
a land where other races starved. So—he was now
engaged in his own private project.

Last sleep period he had tackled the first container
chosen from the supply cupboard, the one which had
sloshed when shaken. He had swallowed two large
mouthfuls of a sickly sweet substance with the consistency of stew. And, while the taste had not been
pleasant, Travis had suffered no discomfort afterward.
Now he chose a small round can, prying off the lid
quickly while listening for any warning from the
corridor.

He had left Ross asleep in the small cabin they
shared and had looked in upon Renfry and Ashe
before he made this trek. There was so little time
and he had to wait a reasonable period between each
tasting.

Travis wanted a drink, but he knew better than to

take one. He had palmed his concentrate bar at the last "meal," held the canteen to his mouth but not drunk, keeping his stomach empty. Now he studied his new selection with disgust.

It was a brown jelly that quivered slightly with the movement of the cylinder in his hand, its surface reflecting the light. Using the edge of the lid as an improvised spoon, Travis ladled a portion into his mouth. Unlike the stew, the stuff had little flavor, though he did not relish the greasy feel on his tongue. He swallowed, took a second helping. Then he chose a third sample—a square box. He would wait. If there were no ill effects from the jelly—then this. If he could prove four or five of these different containers held food the humans could stomach, they might have enough to outlast the voyage.

He did not return to his bunk. The magnetic bottoms of each container clung to the surface of the table, just as the thick soles of his suit feet clung to the walking surfaces in the ship when he planted them firmly. They had all adapted in a measure to the lack of gravity and the actual conditions of space flight. But Travis had a struggle to conceal his dislike of the ship itself, of the confinement forced upon them. And now, to sit alone brought him a fraction of comfort, for he dared to relax that strict control.

He had enjoyed the venture into time. The prehistoric world had been an open wilderness he could understand. But the ship was different. It seemed to him that the taint of death still clung to its small cabins, narrow corridors, and ladders. The very alienness of it was a menace far more acute than a sabertooth or a charging mammoth.

Once he had believed that he wanted to know more about the Old Ones. He had wanted to probe the mysteries which could be deduced from bits of broken pottery or an arrowhead pried from a dust-filled crevice. But those Old Ones had been distantly akin to him; those who had built this ship were not. For a moment or two his claustrophobia welled up, shaking his control, making him want to batter the walls about him with his fists, to beat his way out of this shell into the light, the air, into freedom.

But outside these walls there was no light, no air, and only the freedom of vacuum—or of the mysterious hyperspace that canceled the distance between the stars. Travis fought his imagination. He could not face that picture of the ship hanging in emptiness without even the frigid points of light to mark the stars—where there was nothing solid and stable.

The travelers could only hope that sometime they would reach the home port for which the dying alien pilot had set controls. But that course had been set twelve thousand—perhaps more—years ago. What port would they find waiting beyond the wall of time? Twelve-fifteen thousand years . . . These were figures too great for ordinary comprehension. At that time on earth, the first mud-walled villages had not yet been built, nor the first patch of grain sown to turn man from a wandering hunter into a householder. What had the Apache been then—and the white man? Roving hunters with skill in spear and knife and chasing game. Yet at that time the aliens had produced this ship, voyaged space, not only between the planets of a single system, but from star to star!

Travis tried to think of their future, but his thoughts kept sliding back to his craving for open space. He yearned to stand under the sun with wind—yes, even a desert wind hot and laden with grit—blowing against him. That longing was as acute as a pain—a pain!

His hands went to his middle. A sudden thrust of pure agony that rent him was not born out of any homesickness. The cramping was physical and very real. He bent half double, trying to ease that hot clawing in his insides as the cabin misted before his eyes. Then the stab was gone, and he straightened—until it caught him again. This was it. His luck at his second attempt with the alien food was bad.

Somehow he got to his feet, lurching against the table as a third bout of cramps caught him. The torture ebbed, leaving his hands and face wet. And in the few moments before the next pang he made it halfway along the corridor, reaching the haven he sought just as his outraged stomach finally revolted.

Travis would not have believed that two mouthfuls of a greasy jelly could so weaken a man. He pulled his spent body back to the mess cabin, dropping limply into a chair. More than anything now he wanted water, to cleanse the foulness from his mouth, to slake the burning in his throat. The canteens mocked him for he dare not take one up, knowing just how little of the precious liquid still remained.

For a while he hunched over the table, weakly glad of his freedom from pain. Then he drew the can of jelly to him. This must be marked poisonous. Only two containers had been tested—and how many more would prove impossible?

Only five concentrate bars were left, counting the one he had hidden that day. Nothing was going to multiply that five into ten—or into two hundred. If they were to survive the voyage of unknown duration, they *must* use some of this other food. But Travis could not control the shaking of his hands as he worked to free the lid of the square box. Maybe he was rushing things, taking another sample so soon after the disastrous effects of the other. But he knew that if he did not, right now, he might not be able to force himself to the third attempt later.

The lid came free and he saw inside dry squares of red. To his questing finger these had the texture of something between bread and a harder biscuit. He raised the can to sniff. For the first time the odor was faintly familiar. Tortillas paper-thin and crisp from the baking had an aroma not unlike this. And because the cakes did arouse pleasant memories, Travis bit into one with more eagerness than he would have believed possible moments earlier.

The stuff crumbled between his teeth like corn bread, and he thought the flavor was much the same, in spite of the unusual color. He chewed and swallowed. And the mouthful, dry as it was, appeared to erase the burning left by the jelly. The taste was so good that he ventured to take more than a few bites, finishing the first cake and then a second. Finally, still holding the box in one hand, he slumped lower in his seat, his eyes closing as his worn body demanded rest.

He was riding. There was the entrance to Red Horse Canyon, and the scent of juniper was in the air. A bird flew up—his eyes followed that free flight. An eagle! The bird of power, ascending far up into a cloudless sky. But suddenly the sky was no longer blue, but black with a blackness not born of night. It was black, and caught in it were stars. The stars grew swiftly larger—because he was being drawn up into the blackness where there were only stars . . .

Travis opened heavy-lidded eyes, looked up foggily at a blue figure. Looming over him was a thin, drawn face, slight hollows marked the cheeks, dark smudges under cold gray eyes.

"Ross!" The Apache lifted his head from his arm, wincing at the painful crick in his back.

The other sat down across the table, glanced from the array of supply containers to Travis and back again.

"So this is what you've been doing!" There was accusation in his tone, almost a note of outrage.

"You said yourself it was a job for the most expendable."

"Trying to be a hero on the quiet!" Now the accusation was plain and hot.

"Not much of a one." Travis rested his chin on his fist and considered the containers lined up before him. "I've sampled three so far—exactly three."

Ross's eyelids flickered down. His usual control was back in place, though Travis did not doubt the antagonism was still eating at him.

"With what results?"

"Number one"—Travis indicated the proper can—"too sweet, kind of a stew—but it stays with you in spite of the taste. This is number two." He tapped the tin of brown jelly. "I'd say its only use was to get rid of wolves. This"—he cradled the can of red cakes—"is really good."

"How long have you been at it?"

"I tried one last sleep period, two this."

"Poison, eh?" Ross picked up the tin of jelly, inspecting its contents.

"If it isn't poison, it puts up a good bluff," Travis shot back a little heatedly, stung by the suggestion of skepticism.

Ross set it down. "I'll take your word for it," he conceded. "What about this little number?" He had arisen to stand before the cupboard, and now he turned, holding a shallow, round canister. It was hard to open, but at last they looked at some small dark balls in yellow sauce.

"D'you know, those might just be beans," Ross observed. "I've yet to see any service ship where beans in some form or other didn't turn up on the menu. Let's see if they eat like beans." He scooped up a good mouthful and chewed thoughtfully. "Beans—no—I'd say they taste more like cabbage—which had been spiced up a bit. But not bad, not bad at all!"

Travis found himself nursing a small wicked desire to have the cabbage-beans do their worst to Ross, not with as devastating results as the jelly—he wouldn't wish *that* on anyone! But if they would just make themselves felt enough to prove to Murdock that food testing was not as easy as all that . . .

"Waiting for them to turn me inside out?" Ross grinned.

Travis flushed and then the stain spread and deepened on his cheeks as he realized how he had given himself away. He pushed the cracker-bread to one side and got up to select with inward—if not outward—defiance a tall cylinder which sloshed as he pried at its cap.

"Misery loves company," Ross continued. "What does that smell like?"

Travis had been encouraged by his discovery of the bread. He sniffed hopefully at the cone opening, then snatched the holder away from his nose as a white froth began to puff out.

"Maybe you have the push-button soap," Ross commented unhelpfully. "Give the stuff a lick, fella, you have only one stomach to lose for your country."

Travis, so goaded, licked—suspicious and expecting something entirely unpalatable. But, to his surprise, though it was sweet, the froth was not so sickly as the stew had been. Rather, the result on the tongue was refreshing, carrying satisfaction for his craving for water. He gulped a bigger mouthful and sat waiting, a little tensely, for fireworks to begin inside him.

"Good?" Ross inquired. "Well, your luck can't be rotten all the time."

"This luck is mixed." Travis capped the foam which

had continued to boil wastefully from the bottle. "We're alive—and we're still traveling."

"Traveling is right. A little more information as to our destination would be useful and comforting—or the reverse."

"The world the builders of this ship owned can't be too different from ours," Travis repeated observations made earlier by Ashe. "We can breathe their air without discomfort, and maybe eat some of their food."

"Twelve thousand years . . . D'you know, I can say that but I can't make it mean anything real." Ross's hostility had either vanished or been submerged. "You say the words but you can't stretch your imagination to make them picture something for you—or do you know what I mean?" he challenged.

Travis, rasped on an ancient raw spot, schooled his temper before he replied. "A little. I did four years at State U. There's more to us than beads and feathers."

Ross glanced up, a flicker of puzzlement in those cold gray eyes.

"I didn't mean it like that—for what it's worth." Then he smiled and for the first time there was nothing superior or sardonic in that expression. "Want the whole truth, fella? I picked up what education I had before I went into the Project the hard way— no State U. But you studied the chief's racket— archaeology—didn't you?"

"Yes."

"So—what does twelve thousand years mean to you? You deal with time in big doses, don't you?"

"That's a long span on our world, jumps one clear back to the cave period."

"Yeah—before they put up the pyramids of Egypt— before they learned to read and write. Well, twelve thousand years ago, these blue boys had the stars for theirs. But I'm betting they haven't kept them! There hasn't been a single country on our world, not even China, that has had a form of civilization lasting that long. Up they climb and then—" he snapped his fingers. "It's kaput for them, and another top dog takes over the power. So maybe when we get to this port Renfry believes we're homing for, we'll find nothing, or else someone else waiting for us there. You can bet one way or another and have a good chance of winning on either count. Only, if we do find nothing— then maybe our number's up for sure."

Travis had to accept the logic of that. Suppose they did come into a port which had ceased to exist, set down on a strange world from which they could not lift again because they had not the skill to pilot the ship. They would be exiles for the rest of their lives in a space uncharted by their kind.

"We're not dead yet," Travis said.

Ross laughed. "In spite of all our efforts? No—that's our private battle cry, I think. As long as a man's alive he's going to keep kicking. But it would be good to know just how long we're going to be shut up in this ship." His usual flippancy of tone thinned at that last remark as if his carefully cultivated self-sufficiency was beginning to show the slimmest of cracks.

In the end their experiments with the food were partially successful. The crackers Travis continued to label "corn"; the foam and Ross's cabbage-beans could be digested by a human being without difficulty. And they added to that list a sticky paste with the consistency of jam and a flavor approaching bacon, and another cake-like object which, despite a sour tang that puckered the mouth, was still edible. Greatly daring, Travis tapped the aliens' water supply and drank. Though the liquid had an unpleasant metallic aftertaste, it was not harmful.

In addition the younger members of the involuntary crew made themselves useful in the cautious investigations carried on by Ashe and Renfry. The technician was in an almost constant state of frustration during the hours he spent in the control cabin trying to study machines he dared not activate or dismantle for the fuller examination he longed to make. Travis was seated behind him one morning— at least it was ten o'clock by Renfry's watch, their only method of time-keeping—when there *was* a change to report, to report and take action on.

A shrill buzz pierced the usual silence, beeping what must be a warning. Renfry grabbed at the small mike of the ship's com circuit.

"Strap down!" He rasped the order with rising excitement. "There's an alert sounding here—we may be coming in to land. Strap down!"

Travis grabbed at the protecting bands on his chair. Below they must be scrambling for the bunks. There was vibration again—he was sure he could not mistake that. The ship no longer felt inert and drifting— she was coming alive.

What followed was again beyond his powers of description. It came in two stages, the first a queasy whirl of sensation not far removed from what they had experienced when the ship had been whirled through the time transfer. Limp from that, Travis lay back, watching the screen which had been blank for so long. And when his eyes caught what was now appearing there, he gave a cry of recognition.

"That's the sun!"

A point of blazing yellow set a beacon in the black of space.

"A sun," Renfry corrected. "We've made the big hop. Now it's the homestretch—into the system . . ."

That blaze of yellow-red was already sliding away

from the screen. Travis had an impression that the ship must be slowly rotating. Now that the brighter glare of the sun was gone he could pick up a smaller dot, far smaller than the sun which nurtured it. That held steady on the screen.

"Something tells me, boy," Renfry said in a small and hesitant voice, "that's where we're going."

"Earth?" A warm surge of hope spread through Travis.

"An earth maybe—but not ours."

9

"We're down." Renfry's voice, thin, harsh, broke the silence of the control cabin. His hands moved to the edge of the panel of levers and buttons before him, fell helplessly on it. Though he had had nothing to do with that landing, he seemed drained by some great effort.

"Home port?" Travis got the words out between dry lips. The descent had not been as nerve- and body-wracking as their take-off from his native world, but it had been bad enough. Either the aliens' bodies were better attuned to the tempo of their ships, or else one acquired, through painful experience, conditioning to such jolts.

"How would I know?" Renfry flared, plainly eaten by his own frustration.

Their window on the outside world, the screen, did mirror sky again. But not the normal Earth sky with its blue blaze which Travis knew and longed to see again. This was a blue closer to the green hue of turquoise mined in his hills. There was something cold and inimical in that sky.

Piercing the open space was a structure which glinted like metal. But the smoothness of those dull red surfaces ended in a jagged splinter, raw against the blue-green, plainly marking a ruin.

Travis unfastened his seat straps and stumbled to his feet, his body once more adjusting clumsily to the return of gravity. As much as he had come to dislike the ship, to want his freedom from it, at this moment he had no desire to emerge under that turquoise sky and examine the ruin pictured on the screen. And just because he felt reluctance, he fought against it by going.

In the end they all gathered at the space lock while Renfry opened the fastening, then went on to the outer door. The technician glanced back over his shoulder.

"Helmets fastened?" His voice boomed hollowly inside the sphere now resting on Travis' shoulders and secured by a close-fitting harness. Ashe had discovered those and had tested them, preparing for this time when they might dare a foray into the unknown. The bubble was equipped with no cumbersome oxygen tanks. It worked on no principle Renfry was able to discover, but the aliens had used these and the humans must trust to their efficiency now.

The outer port swung back into the skin of the ship. Renfry kicked out the landing ladder and backed down it. But each of them, as he emerged from the globe, glanced quickly around.

What lay below was a wide sweep of hard white surface which must cover miles of territory. This was broken at intervals by a series of structures of the dull red, metallic material set in triangles and squares. In the center of each of those was a space marked with black rings. None of the red structures was whole, and the landing field—if that was what it was—had the sterile look of a place long abandoned.

"Another ship . . ." Ashe's arm swung up, his voice came to Travis through the helmet com.

There was a second globe, all right, reposing about a quarter of a mile away on one of the squares among the buildings. And beyond that Travis spotted a third. But nowhere was there any sign of life. He felt wind, soft, almost caressing, against his bare hands.

They descended the ladder and stood in a group at the foot of their own ship, a little uncertain as to what to do next.

"Wait!" Renfry caught at Ashe. "Something moved— over there!"

They had found weapons in the ship; now they drew those odd guns, twins to the one Ross had worn when Travis had first met him. The wind blew a fragment of long-dead vegetation before it. It caught against the globe and then was whirled away in a dreary dance.

But out of an opening at the foot of the red tower nearest to them something stirred. And Travis, watching that coil heading straight for them, froze. A snake? A snake unwinding to such a length that its questing head was approaching their stand while the end of its tail still lay within the ruin where it denned?

He took aim at that swaying coil. Then Renfry struck his wrist pads, knocking away the barrel of the weapon. And in that moment the Apache saw what the other had noticed first, that the snake was not a thing of flesh, skin, and supple bones, but of some manufactured material.

Something else moved through the door from which the snake had crawled. This newcomer strode forward by jerks, paused, came on, as if compelled to advance despite the limitations of ancient fabric and long wear. The thing was vaguely manlike in form, in that it advanced on stilt legs. But it had four upper appendages now folded against its central bulk, and where the head should have been there was a nodding stalk resembling the antennae of a com unit.

Its jerky walk with the many pauses conveyed internal discord, rust and wear, and the deterioration of time. How much time? The four humans stepped away from the ship, giving free passage to the strange partners from the tower.

"Robots!" Ross said suddenly. "They're robots! But what are they going to do?"

"Refuel, I think." Ashe rather than Renfry answered that.

"You've hit it!" The technician pushed forward. "But do they have fuel—now?"

"We'd better hope there is some left." Ashe sounded bleak. "I'd say we aren't supposed to stay here—better get back on board."

The threat of being trapped here, of locked controls raising the ship and leaving them marooned, induced something close to panic in all three hearers. They raced to the ladder and began to climb. But when they reached the air lock, Renfry remained at the open door, relating the movements of the robots.

"I think that animated pipeline's been connected—underneath. Can't see what the walker's doing—maybe he just stands by in case of trouble. And there's something coming through the hose—you can see it swell! We're taking on whatever we're supposed to have!"

"A fueling station." Ashe looked out over the wide stretch of crumbling towers and checkerboard landing spaces. "But look at the size of this place. It must have been constructed to handle hundreds, even thousands, of ships. And since they couldn't *all* be in to refuel at the same time, that presupposes a fleet"—he drew a deep breath of wonder—"a fleet almost beyond comprehension. We were right—this civilization was galaxy-wide. Maybe it spread to the next galaxy."

But Travis' eyes rested on the splintered cap of the tower from which the robots had come. "It looks like no one has been here for some time," he observed.

"Machines," Renfry answered, "will go on working until they run down. I'd say that walking one down there is close to its final stop. We triggered some impulse when we landed on the right spot. The robots were activated to do their job—maybe their last job. How long since they worked the last time? This may have kept going for a long part of that twelve thousand years you're always talking about—an empire dying slowly. But I wouldn't try to measure the time. These aliens knew machinery, and their materials are better than our best."

"I'd like to see the interior of one of those towers," Ashe said wistfully. "Maybe they kept records, had something we could understand to explain it all."

Renfry shook his head. "Wouldn't dare try it. We might raise before you got inside the door. Ahh—the walker is going back now. I'd say get ready for take-off."

They snugged the open port and the inner door of the space lock. Renfry, out of habit, went on up to the control cabin. But the other three took to their bunks. There was a waiting period and then once more the blast into space. This time they did not lose consciousness as they endured the stress of reentering space.

"Now what?" Hours later they squeezed into the mess cabin to hold a rather aimless conference concerning the future. Since no one had anything more than guesses to offer, none of them answered Renfry's question.

"I read a book once," Ross said suddenly with the slightly embarrassed air of one admitting to a minor social error, "that had a story in it about some Dutch sea captain who swore he'd get around the horn in one of those old-time sailing ships. He called up the Devil to help him and he never got home—just went on sailing through the centuries."

"The Flying Dutchman," Ashe identified.

"Well, we haven't called up any Devil," Renfry remarked.

"Haven't we?" Travis had spoken his thoughts, without realizing until they all stared at him that he was done so aloud.

"Your Devil being?" Ashe prompted.

"We were trying to get knowledge out of this ship— and it wasn't our kind of knowledge," he floundered a little, attempting to put into words what he now believed.

"Scavengers getting their just desserts?" Ashe summed up. "If you follow that line of reasoning, yes, you have a point. The forbidden fruit of knowledge. That was an idea planted so long ago in mankind's conscience that it lingers today as guilt."

"Planted," Ross repeated the word thoughtfully, "planted . . ."

"Planted!" Travis echoed, his mind making one of those odd jumps in sudden understanding of which he had only recently become conscious. "By whom?"

Then glancing around at the alien ship which was both their transport and their prison, he added softly, "By these people?"

"They didn't want us to know about them." Ross's words came in a rush. "Remember what they did to that Russian time base—traced it all the way forward and destroyed it in every era. Suppose they *did* have contacts with primitive man on our world—planted ideas—or gave them such a terrifying lesson at one time or other that the memory of it was buried in all their descendants?"

"There are other tales beside your Flying Dutchman, Ross," Ashe squirmed a little in his seat. None of the chairs in the ship quite fitted the human frame or provided comfort. "Prometheus and the fire—the man who dared to steal the knowledge of the gods for the use of mankind and suffered eternally thereafter for his audacity, though his fellows benefited. Yes, there are clues to back such a theory, faint ones." His eagerness grew as he spoke. "Maybe—just maybe—we'll find out!"

"The supply port was long deserted," Travis pointed out. "There may be nothing left of their empire anywhere."

"Well, we've not found the home port yet." Renfry got to his feet. "Once we set down there—I hadn't intended to say this, but if we ever get to the end of this trip, there's a chance we may get back, providing—" He drummed his fingers against the door casing. "Providing we have more than our share of luck."

"How?" demanded Ashe.

"The controls must now be set with some sort of a guide—perhaps a tape. Once we are grounded and I can get to work, that might just be reversed. But there are a hundred 'ifs' between us and earth, and we can't count on anything."

"There's this, too," Ashe added thoughtfully to that faintest of hopes. "I've been studying the material we have found. If we can crack their language tapes—some of the records we have discovered here must deal with the maintenance and operation of the ship."

"And where in space are you going to find a Rosetta Stone?" returned Travis. He did not dare to believe that either of the two discoveries might be possible. "No common word heritage."

"Aren't mathematics supposed to be the same, no matter what language? Two and two always add to four, and principles such as that?" puzzled Ross.

"Please find me some symbols on any of those tapes you've been running through the reader that have the smallest resemblance to any numbers seen on earth." Renfry had swung back to the pessimistic side of the balance. "Anyway—I'm not meddling with the machines in that control cabin while we're still in space."

Still in space—how long were they going to keep on voyaging? And somehow they found this second lap of their journey into nowhere worse than the first. All of them had been secretly convinced that there was only one goal, that their first star port would be their last. But the short pause to refuel now promised a much longer trip. Their only way of telling time was by the hours marked on the dial of Renfry's watch. Days—Ashe made a record of those by counting hours. It was one week since they had left the fuel port— two days more.

Out of the sheer necessity for keeping their minds occupied, they pried at the puzzles offered them in the ship. Ashe had already mastered the operation of a small projector which "read" the wire-kept records, and so opened up not a new world, but worlds. The singsong speech which went with the pictures meant nothing to the humans. But the pictures—and such pictures! Three-dimensional, in full color, they allowed one a window on the incomprehensible life of a complex starfaring civilization.

Races, cultures, and only a third of them humanoid—were these factual records? Or were they fiction meant to divert and amuse during the long hours of space travel? Or real reports of some service action?

They could guess at any answer to what they saw unrolled on the screen of the small machine.

"If this was a police ship and those are authentic reports of past cases," commented Ross, "they sure had their little problems." He had watched with rapt attention a lurid battle through a jungle on a water-logged planet. The enemy there was represented by white amphibious things with a distracting ability to elongate parts of their bodies at will—to the discomfiture of opponents they were thus able to ensnare. "On the other hand," he went on, "these may be just cheer-for-the-brave-boys-in-blue story writing to amuse the idle hour. How are we to know?"

"There's one which I discovered this morning—of more interest to us personally." Ashe sorted through the plate-shaped containers of record wire. "Take a look at this now." He drew out the coil of the jungle battle and inserted the new spool.

Then they saw a sky, gray, lowering with thick clouds. Below it stretched a waste of what could only be snow such as they knew on their own world. A small party moved into the range of the picture, and the familiar blue suits of those in it were easy to distinguish against the gray-white of the monotonous background.

"Suggest anything to you?" Ashe asked of Ross.

Murdock was leaning forward, studying the picture with a new intentness that argued an unusual interest in so simple a scene.

There were four blue-suited, bald-headed humanoids. They wore no outer clothing and Travis remembered Ross's remarks concerning the insulating qualities of the strange material. Over their heads they did have the bubble helmets, and they were traveling at a slow pace which suggested treacherous footing.

The tape blinked in one of those quick changes to which the viewers had become accustomed. Now they must be surveying the same country from the viewpoint of one of the four blue-clad travelers. There was a sudden, breath-taking drop; the camera must have skimmed at top speed down into a valley. Before them lay a second descent—and the perspectives were out of proportion.

They were not distorted enough, however, to hide what the photographer wanted to record. The viewers were gazing down onto a wide, level space and in that, half buried in banks of drifted snow, was one of the large alien freighters.

"It can't be!" Ross's expression was one of startled surprise.

"Keep watching," Ashe bade.

At a distance, around the stranded half globe, black dots moved. They trailed off on a line marked clearly in the beaten snow. The path had been worn by a good amount of traffic. There was another disconcerting click and again they saw ice—a huge, murky wall of it, rearing into the gray sky. And directly to that wall of ice led the beaten path.

"The Russian time post! It must be! And this ship"—Ross was almost sputtering—"this ship must have been mixed up in that raid on the Russians!"

There was a last click and the screen went blank.

"Where's the rest?" Ross demanded.

"You've seen all there is. If they recorded any more, it's not on this spool." Ashe fingered the colored tag fastened to the container from which he had taken the coil. "Nothing else with a label matching this, either."

"I wonder if the Russians got back at them some way. If that was what killed off the crew later. Bio warfare . . ." Ross jiggled the switch of the projector back and forth. "I suppose we'll never know."

Then, over their heads, blasting the usual quiet of the ship, came the warning from the control cabin where Renfry kept his self-imposed watch.

"She's triggering for another break-through, fellas. Strap down! I'd say we're due for the big snap very soon!"

They hurried to the bunks. Travis pulled at his protecting webbing. What would they find this time? Another robot-inhabited way stop—or the home port they were longing to reach? He set himself to endure the wrench of the break-through from hyperspace to normal time, hoping that familiarity would render the ordeal easier.

Once more the ship and the men in it were wracked by that turnover which defied natural sensations.

"Sun ahead." Travis, opening his eyes, heard Renfry's voice, a little sharpened, through the ship-wide com. "One—two—four planets. We seem to be bound for the second."

More waiting time. Then once more descent into atmosphere, the return of weight, the vibration singing through walls and floors about them. Then the set-down, this time with a slight grating bump, as if the landing had not been so well controlled as it had at the fueling port.

"This is different . . ." Renfry's report trailed into silence, as if what he saw in the screen had shocked him into speechlessness.

They climbed to the control cabin and crowded below that window on the new world. It must be night—but a night which was alive with reddish light, as if some giant fire filled the sky with the reflection of its fury. And that light rippled even as flames would ripple in their leaping.

"Home?" This time Ross asked the question.

Renfry, entranced as he still watched that display of fiery light, made a usual cautious answer.

"I don't know—I just don't know."

"We'll try a look-see from the port." Ashe took up his planet-side command.

"Might be a volcano," Travis hazarded from his experience in the prehistoric world.

"No, I don't think so. I've only seen one thing like that—"

"I know what you mean." Ross was already on the ladder. "The Northern Lights!"

10

The checkerboard spread of the fueling port, different as its architecture had been, was yet not too far removed from their own experience. But this—Travis gazed at the wild display beyond the outer door—this was the most fantastic dream made real.

That flickering red played in tongues along the horizon, filling about a quarter of the sky, ascending in licks up into the heavens. It paled stars and battled the moon which hung there—a moon three times the size of the one which accompanied his home planet.

Rippling out from about the ship was a stretch of cracked, buckled field that had once been smoothly surfaced. There was a faint crackling in the air which did not come from any wind but from static electricity. And the lurid light with its weaving alternately illuminated and reduced to shadow the whole countryside.

"Air's all right." Renfry had cautiously slipped off his helmet. At his report the others freed their own heads. The air was dry, as arid as desert wind.

"Buildings of some sort—in that direction." They turned heads to follow Ross's gesture.

Whereas the towers of the fueling field, ruined as they were, had fingered straightly into the sky, these structures, or structure, hugged the earth, the tallest portion not topping the globe. And nowhere in the red light could Travis sight anything suggesting vegetation. The desolation of the fuel port had been apparent, but here the barrenness was menacing.

None of them was inclined to go exploring under that fiery sky, and nothing moved in turn toward the ship. If this was another break in their journey, intended for the purpose of servicing their transport, the mechanics had broken down. At last the humans withdrew into the ship and closed the port, waiting for day.

"Desert . . ." Travis said that half to himself but Ashe glanced at him inquiringly.

"You mean—out there?"

"There's a feel in the air," Travis explained. "You learn to recognize it when you've lived most of your life with it."

"Is this the end of the trip?" Ross asked Renfry again.

"I don't know." They had climbed back to the control cabin. Now the technician was standing in front of the main control panel. He was frowning at it. Then he turned suddenly to Travis.

"You feel desert out there. Well, I feel machines— I've lived with them for most of *my* life. We've set down here, there's no indication that we're going to take off again. Nothing but a sense that I have— that we're not finished yet." He laughed, a little self-consciously. "All right, now tell me that I'm seeing ghosts and I'll have to agree."

"On the contrary, I agree with you so thoroughly

that I'm not going too far from the ship." Ashe smiled
in return. "Do you suppose this is another fuel stop?"

"No robots out," Ross objected.

"Those could have been immobilized or rusted away
long ago," Renfry replied. He appeared sorry now that
he had raised that doubt.

They went at last to their bunks, but if any of
them slept, it was in snatches. To Travis, lying on
the soft mattress which fitted itself to the comfort
of his body, there was no longer any security—the
ambiguous security offered by the ship while in flight.
Now outside the shell he could rest his hand against
was an unknown territory more liable to offer
danger than a welcome. Perhaps the display of
fiery lights in the night, perhaps the dry air worked
on him to produce the conviction that this was not
a world of machines left to carry out tasks set them
before his kind had evolved. No, there *was* life here
and it waited—outside.

He must have dozed, for it was Ross's hand on his
shoulder which brought him awake. And he trailed
after the other to the mess. He ate, still silent, but
with every nerve in his gaunt body alert, convinced
that danger lay outside.

They went armed, strapping on the belts supporting the aliens' weapons. And they issued into a merciless sunlight, as threatening with its white brilliance
as the flames of the night before.

Ashe shielded his eyes with his hand. "Try wearing the helmets," he ordered. "They might just cut
some of the glare."

He was right. When they fastened down the
bubbles, the material cut that daylight so that their
eyes were unaffected.

Travis had been right, too, in his belief that they
were in desert country. Sand—dunes of white sand,

glittering with small sun-reflecting particles which must be blinding to unshielded eyes—crept over the long-deserted landing space. Here were no other grounded ships like the ones at the first galactic port, only lonely sweeps of sand, unbroken by the faintest hint of vegetation.

Sand—and buildings, low, earth-hugging buildings—perhaps a quarter of a mile away.

The four from the ship hesitated at the foot of the ladder. It was not only Renfry's hunch that their voyage was not completed that kept them tied to the globe. The barrenness of the countryside certainly was no invitation to explore. And yet there was always a chance that some discovery might help to solve the abiding riddle of their return.

"We do it this way." Ashe, the veteran explorer, took over with decisive authority. "You stay here, Renfry—up at the door. Any sign the ship is coming to life again and you fire—on maximum."

A bolt of the force spewed from the narrow muzzle of the alien weapon would produce crackling blue fire which should be visible for miles. They were not sure of the range of the helmet coms, but they could be certain of the effectiveness of a force bolt as a warning.

"Can do!" Renfry was already swinging up the ladder, displaying no disappointment in not being one of the explorers.

Then, with Ashe in the center and the lead, the other two flanking him a little behind and to the right and left, the humans headed for the buildings. Travis mechanically studied the sand under foot. What he was searching for he could not have told, nor would that loose sand have held tracks—tracks! He glanced back. The faint depressions which marked his footsteps were already almost indistinguishable. There was certainly nothing to indicate that anyone—

or *anything*—had passed over that portion of the forgotten base for days, months, years, generations.

But the sand was not everywhere. He stepped aside to avoid a broken block of the pavement tilted up to one side and forming a hollow—a concealing hollow. Travis hesitated, gazing down into that hollow.

Last night a wind had swept across this field; he had felt it up at the port of the ship. Today the air was dead, not a breeze troubled the lightest drift of sand. And that hollow was free of sand. He did not know why his instincts told him that this was wrong. But because he was nudged by that subconscious uneasiness, he went down on his knees to study the interior of the pocket with the close scrutiny of a hunter-tracker.

So he saw what he might otherwise have missed— a depression marked in the soil where the sand had not drifted. On impulse he rubbed his fingertips hard across that faint mark. There was a greasy feel. He unfastened his helmet long enough to raise those same investigating fingers to his nostrils.

A rank odor—sweat of something alive—something with filthy body habits. He was sure of it! And because that thing must have crouched here for a long time in its well-chosen hiding place to watch the ship undetected, he could also believe it possessed intelligence—of a kind. Snapping down his helmet once more, he reported his find over the com.

"You say it must have been there for some time?" Ashe's voice floated back.

"Yes. And it can't have been gone long either." He was basing all his deductions upon that lingering taint which had been imparted by a warm body to the dusty earth within the small shelter.

"No tracks?"

"They wouldn't show in this stuff." Travis scuffed

his foot across a small fan of sand. No, no tracks. But there could only be one place from which the hidden watcher had come—those buildings half concealed by the creeping dunes. He stood up, walked forward, his hand swinging very close to the weapon at his belt. The sense of danger was very strong.

Ashe stood before the midpoint of the buildings—there was really only one as they could see now. Each of its two outlying wings was connected by a low-lying, windowless passage to the main block. Travis was familiar with the effects of wind and blown-sand erosion upon rock outcrops. Here the same factors had operated to pit surfaces, round and polish away corners and edges, until the walls were like the dunes rising about them.

There were no windows—no visible doorways. But at the end of the wing before Travis there was a dip in the sand dune, breaking the natural line chiseled by the wind. It was a break unusual enough to catch his alerted attention.

"Over here," he called softly, forgetting that the helmet com and not the air waves carried his voice. Slowly, with the caution of a stalker after wary game, he moved toward that break in the dune. There were no tracks, yet he was almost certain that the disturbance had been recent and made by the passage of something moving with a purpose—not just the result of a vagary of the night wind.

He rounded the pointing finger of one dune which rose at his shoulder height against the wall, and knew he was right. The sand had obviously been thrust back—blocked loosely on either side—as if some door had opened outward from the building, pushing the sand drift before it.

"Cover him!" Ashe's shadow crossed the sun-drenched sand of the dune, met the other one cast by Ross. With the two time agents at his back, the Apache began a detailed inspection of that length of wall.

Although his eyes could detect no difference in that surface, his fingers did when he ran them along about waist level. There was a strip here, extending down to the ground, which was not of the same texture as the substance above and to the sides. But though he pressed, pulled, and applied his weight to move it in every way he could think to try, there was no yielding. He was sure that that portion could open, to cause the marks in the sand.

At last, getting down on his hands and knees, Travis crawled along, trying to force fingertips under at ground's edge. And so he discovered a harsh tuft of protruding hair. Combined efforts of knife tip and fingers worked the wisp loose. It was coarse stuff, coarser than any animal's he had ever seen, each separate hair was larger than six strands of a horse's mane. And it was gray-white in color, melting into the shade of the sand so it could not be distinguished against the dunes.

Having a greasy feel, it clung to Travis' fingers. He did not really need the evidence of his nose to tell him that it was rankly odorous. He brought it back to Ashe, his distaste in handling it growing steadily. The latter put the trophy away in one of his belt pockets.

"Any chance of opening that?" Ashe indicated the hidden door in the wall.

"Not that I can see," Travis returned. "It is probably secured on the inside."

They studied the building dubiously. Behind its length, as far as they could judge, there was only a waste of sand dunes reaching out and out to the sky rim where the fire had played the night before. If there was any riddle to be solved, its answer lay inside this locked box and not in the desert countryside.

"Ross, you stay here. Travis, move on to the end of the wing. Stay there where you can see Ross—and me, as I go along the back."

Ashe used the same care as the Apache had done, running his hands along the eroded surface, seeking any indication of another door which might possibly be forced. He went the entire length of the building and came back—with nothing to report.

"There were windows once and a door. But they were all walled up a long time ago, sealed tight now. We might pick out the sealing, given time and the right tools."

Ross's voice came through the helmet coms. "Any chance of getting in through the roof, chief?"

"If you're game to try—up with you!"

Travis stood against the wall which refused to give up its secrets and Ross used him as a ladder, mounting to the roof. He moved inward and the two left on the ground lost sight of him. But on Ashe's orders he made a running commentary of what he saw through the com.

"Not much sand—you'd think there would be more . . . Hulloo!" There was an eagerness in that sudden exclamation. "This *is* something! Round plates set in circles all over—about the size of quarters. They are solid and you can't move them."

"Metal?"

"Nooo . . ." The reply was hesitant. "Seem more like some kind of glass, opaque rather than transparent."

"Windows?" suggested Travis.

"Too small," Ross protested. "But there are a lot of them—all over. Wait!" The urgency in that last cry alerted both the men on the ground. "Red—they're turning red!"

"Get out of there! Jump!" Ashe's order barked loudly in all their helmets.

Ross obeyed without question, landing with a para-trooper's practiced roll on one of the dune crests. The others scrambled to join him, all their attention focused on the roof of the sealed building. Perhaps something in the sun-repelling qualities of their helmets enabled them to see those rays as faint reddish lines cutting up from the roof far into the sky.

The skin on Travis' bare hands tingled with a pins-and-needles sensation as if the circulation in it had been arrested and was not coming back to duty. Ross scrambled up out of the sand and shook himself vigorously.

"What in the world is going on?" There was an unusual note of awe in his tone.

"I think—some fireworks to discourage you. I believe that we may assume whoever lives in there is definitely not at home to curious callers. Not only that, but the householder has some mighty unpleasant gadgets to back up his desire for privacy. Probably just as well we didn't find his, her, or its front door unlocked."

Travis could no longer see those thin fiery lines. Either the power had been shut off, or the rays were now past the point of detection by human eyes, even with the aid of the helmet. That coarse hair, the repulsive odor—and now this. Somehow the few facts did not add properly. The hair, of course, could have been left by a watchdog, or the equivalent on this particular planet of a watchdog. That supposition would also fit with the low entrance into the building. But a watchdog that kept to carefully chosen cover, the best in the whole landscape, and stayed to spy, maybe for hours, on the ship—? Those facts did not fit with the nature of any animal he had ever known. Rather, that action matched with intelligence, and intelligence meant man.

"I believe they are nocturnal," Ashe said suddenly. "That fits with all we've seen so far. This sun glare may be as painful for them as it is for us without helmets. But at night—"

"Going to sit up and watch what happens?" Ross asked.

"Not out in the open. Not until we know more."

Silently Travis agreed to that. There was a furtiveness about the last night's spying which made him wary. And to his mind this world was far more frightening and sinister than the fueling port. Its very arid barrenness held a nebulous threat he had never sensed in the desert lands of his own planet.

They walked back to the ship, climbed the ladder, and were glad to close the port upon the dead white glare, to unhelm in the blue glow of the interior.

"What did you see?" Ashe asked Renfry.

"Murdock taking a high dive from the roof and then some red lines, very faint, shooting up from all over its surface. What did you do, push the wrong doorbell?"

"Probably waked somebody up. I don't think that's a very healthy place to go visiting. Lord—what a stink!" Ross ended, sniffing.

Ashe held on his palm the tuft of hair. The odor rising from it was not only noticeable in the usual scentless atmosphere of the ship, but penetrating in its foulness.

They carried the lock into the small cubbyhole which might once have been the quarters of the commander and where Ashe had assembled his materials for study. In spite of the noisome effluvia of their trophy, they gathered around as he pulled the tuft apart hair by hair and spread it flat.

"Those hairs—so thick!" Renfry marveled.

"If they *are* hairs. What I wouldn't give for a lab!" Ashe folded a clear sheet of the aliens' writing materials to imprison the lock.

"That smell—" Travis, remembering how he had handled the noisome find, rubbed his hand back and forth across his thigh.

"Yes?" Ashe prompted.

"Well—I think that comes from just plain filthiness, sir. Or, part might be because the hairs are from a creature we don't know."

"Alien metabolism." Ashe nodded. "Each human group has a distinctive body odor far more apparent to others than to one of his own breed. But what are you getting at, Travis?"

"Well, if that does come from some—some man," he used the term because he had no other—"and not from an animal, then I'd say he was living in a regular sty. And that means either a pretty low type of primitive, or a degenerate."

"Not necessarily," Ashe pointed out. "Bathing entails water, and we haven't seen any store of water here."

"Sure, there's no water we can see. But they must have some. And I think—" Only there were few proofs he could offer to bolster his argument.

"Might be. Anyway, tonight we'll watch and see what *does* come out of the booby-trapped box over there."

They napped during the day, Renfry in the control cabin as usual. None of them could see any reason why the ship had earthed on this sand pile, and the very barrenness of the place reinforced Renfry's belief that this could not be their ultimate goal. It was only logic that the ship must have originally voyaged from some center of civilization—and this was not that.

The glare of the sun was gone and dusk clothed the mounds of creeping sand when they gathered again at the door in the outer skin to watch the building and the stretch of ground lying between them and that enigmatic block.

"How long do you suppose we'll have to wait?" Ross shifted position.

"No time at all," Ashe answered softly. "Look!"

From behind the dune which marked the low doorway Travis had discovered, there showed a very faint reddish glow.

11

Had the flaming display of the late evening before been in progress, they could not have spotted that. And now, in the dusk, with the shapes of the dunes distorting vision, it was difficult to see. Ashe was counting slowly under his breath. As he reached "twenty" the glow vanished with a sudden completeness which suggested the slamming of a door.

Travis strained his eyes, watching the end of that masking dune. If the thing which had spied upon them the night before was coming back to the old position, the shortest route to take would cross that point. But he had seen nothing so far.

There was a very thin sound, but that came from the opposite direction, a whispering from the open country. Then a pat of arid air touched his cheek, wind rising with the coming of night. And the whispering must be sand grains moving under its first tentative stir.

"We could ambush one scout," Ross observed wistfully.

"Their senses may be more acute than ours. Certainly if they are nocturnal, their night sight will be. And we can believe that they are already suspicious of us. Also, I'd like to know a little more about the nature of something or someone I'm going to lay a trap for."

Travis only half heard Ashe. Surely he had seen a flicker of movement out there. Yes! His fingers closed on the older man's arm in swift warning pressure. A blob of shadow had slipped from the end of the dune, skidded quickly into hiding, heading straight for the hollow behind the upended block of masonry. Was the spy now settled in for a long spell of duty in that improvised observation post? Or tonight would he, she or it venture closer to the ship?

The dusk deepened and with the coming of true dark the tongues of fire danced in the sky. Though the light afforded by that display was not steady, it did illuminate the smoother ground immediately about the globe. Any attack on the part of the unknown natives could be sighted by the men on guard above. The humans knew, though, that with the ladder up and open port some dozen feet removed from ground level, they had little to fear from any actual attempt to force their stronghold. Unless the creatures out there possessed weapons able to cut down the distance advantage.

"Close the inner-lock door," Ashe said suddenly. "We'll shut off the ship's light, make it hard for them to spot us here."

With the lock shut and the blue light of the ship blanked out, they lay flat on the floor of the cramped space, trying not to hamper each other, awaiting the next move on the part of the lurker or lurkers below.

"Something there," Ross warned softly. "To the left—right at the end of that last dune."

The lurker was impatient. A blob of dark, which might have been a head, moved against the white sand. Wind sang around the ship, gathering up grit. The men snapped down their helmets in protection against that. But those whirls of sand devils did not appear to bother the native.

"I think there are more than one of them," Travis said. "That last movement came too far away from the first I sighted."

"Could they be getting ready to rush us?" Ross wondered.

Oddly enough, none of the humans had drawn his weapon. Their perch was so high above the surface over which the attackers must advance, and the smooth rounding of the unclimbable globe was so apparent, that both gave them a sense of security.

The dark thing made a dart toward the globe. And it either ran bent almost double—or else on all fours! One of the startling jumps of the sky's light spotlighted the form, and the watchers exclaimed.

Man or animal? The thing had four long limbs, and two more projections at mid-body. The head was round, down-held as it darted, so that they could not sight any features. But the whole body was matted with hair—dark hair, not light to match the tuft Travis had found. There was no sign of clothing, nor did the creature appear to be carrying weapons.

For a single moment that flitting shadow paused, facing the ship. Then it scurried back into hiding among the dunes once more. There was another flash of movement which the watchers could hardly detect, as this time the body of the runner merged in color with the sand about it.

"That might have been your hair shedder," remarked Ashe. "It certainly was lighter in color than the first one."

"They come in different colors—but all about the same size," Ross added. "And what in the world are they?"

"Nothing in our world." Ashe was definite about that. "We can believe, though, that they are interested in this ship and that they are trying to find some way of getting to it undetected."

"The way they move," Travis said, "as if they feared attack . . . They must have enemies."

"Enemies to be associated with such a ship as this?" Ashe jumped to the point with his usual speed of understanding. "Yes, that could be. Only I don't believe that there has been a ship here for a long, long time."

"Memories passed down—"

"Memories would mean they are men!" Travis was not aware until he voiced those words out of a sense of outrage that he abhorred association with those half-seen creatures in the dunes.

"To themselves they may be men," Ashe returned, "and we might represent monsters. All relative, son. At any rate, I believe that they do not regard us with kindness."

"What I wouldn't give for a flashlight now," Ross said wistfully. "I'd like to catch one of them in a beam for a really good look."

They were treated to a wealth of half glimpses of the natives moving through the sand hills as the minutes crawled on, but never did they have a chance really to study one.

"I think they're working their way around to come in behind the globe—on our blind side," Travis offered, having traced at least two in that possible direction.

"Won't do them any good—this is the only opening." Ross sounded close to smug.

But the thought of the natives coming in behind the globe could not be accepted so easily by Travis. Every buried instinct of hunter and desert warrior argued that such a chance threatened his own security. Reason told him, though, that there was only this one door to the ship, and that it was easily defended. They need only close it and nothing could reach them.

"What was the reason for this port anyway?" Ross pursued the big question a few seconds later. "There must have been some purpose for stopping here. Do we have to find something—or do something—before we can leave again?"

That thought had ridden all their minds, but Ross had brought fear into the open. And what if the solution lay over there, in that building to which there was no entrance—unless one could be forced at night? A nighttime entrance guarded by the flitting hairy things which could see in the dark and whose home hunting-ground it was . . .

"The building—?" Travis made a question of it. He felt Ashe stir beside him.

"Might just be," the other assented. "If we are hung up here much longer, we can try burning our way in by day. These weapons pack a pretty hefty charge when set at maximum."

Travis' hand shot out, clamped down on Ashe's shoulder. His helmet was locked against the grit drift in the wind, but his hand had been resting on the edge of the door casing and had caught that thud-thud transmitted by the outer skin of the globe. Below the bulge which kept the humans from viewing the ground directly under the curve of the side, something was beating on the metallic outer casing of the vessel— for what purpose and with what result, he could not guess. He groped for Ashe's hand, drew it out beside his own and pressed the palm flat to get the same message.

"Pounding, I think." He realized that the messages in helmet coms could not reach the ears of lurkers below. "But why?"

"Trying to hole the ship?" Ross hung over the other two. "They've no chance of getting through the hull—or have they?" His concluding flash of anxiety was shared by the rest. What did they know of the resources of the natives?

Coiled beside Travis was the ladder. Dare he push that out, climb over to see what the night creepers were doing below? The thud of the pounding appeared to him to be taking on both speed and intensity. Suppose by some miracle, or the use of some unknown tool, the hairy things could pierce the outer skin of the globe? Then there would be no possible hope of escape from this forgotten desert.

He began to edge the ladder forward. Ashe made a grab which the younger man fended away.

"We have to see," he said, "we *have* to!"

Ross and Ashe moved together and in that narrow space blocked each other long enough for Travis to squeeze through the door, swing over the lip and climb down the length of his own body. Then he felt the ladder catch tight and knew that the other two were preventing its descent to ground level.

Gripping the rungs tightly, holding his body as close as he could to the surface of the ship, Travis looked down. The play of red flashes against the sky furnished a weird light for the activity below, for there *was* activity. He had been right. The hairy things had crept in unseen from behind the ship, and a group of them were now clustered about the base of the globe. But what they were doing he could not make out in the constant flickering of the light. Then one reared from its usual quadrupedal stance, and raised its forearms over its hump of head. The appendages at its mid-section gave a twist, writhed out in a manner which suggested bonelessness, and clasped tight to the ship.

The creature gave a bound into the air and then hung, its hind feet now a foot or so off the ground. Apparently it held on by the grip of waist tentacles against the globe, while the fists or paws on its fore-limbs pounded vigorously against that surface. There was something about that hitching climb, squirming upward as Travis watched, that spelled purposeful malevolence.

Now a second creature had hitched itself to the hull by midsection tentacles and was beginning to ascend. Travis could sight no weapons, nothing but those steadily pounding fists. But neither did he have any wish to battle the slow climbers. He reported to Ashe and was ordered back into the ship. They closed the port, took the precaution of sealing it as if making ready for flight, and then loosened their helmets.

Neither the pounding nor the sound of the climbers could reach them now. But Travis did not believe that the creatures had ceased their efforts to win into the ship, futile as those efforts might seem. The humans climbed to the control cabin to watch the outer world on the limited view of the screen. Renfry looked puzzled.

"I don't get it. I still say that I'm sure this isn't the end of the flight. But I can't tell you why, or the why of this port, either. If the answer lies in that build-ing, you'll have to crack it open. But we may have a better cracker than just those hand weapons."

Ross caught his meaning first. "The ship's guns!"

"Might be."

"*Can* we use them?" Ashe wanted to know.

"Well, they're less a top secret than the rest of the

stuff around here. Remember this?" He pressed a lever. Lights winked, that word from a vanished language spoke out of the thin air. It was all as it had been on their exploration of the ship.

"And you can fire them?"

"The chief—my chief—doped out that this does that"—Renfry fingered another switch he did not depress. "As far as I deduce, one of those king-sized blasters should just about clip across the roof of your strongbox. We can try it on for size any time you're ready."

But Ashe was rubbing his jaw in that absent-minded way which meant he had not yet come to a decision. "Too much guessing in all of this. We don't know that we have to crack that place open in order to lift ship again. In fact, if we did crack it and couldn't find what we needed—we wouldn't be any better off. These natives must depend upon that shelter for their lives. Break it open and they're just as dead as if we mowed them down with guns. They may not be anything or anybody we'd care to live with, but this is their world and we're intruders. I'd like to wait a little before I try anything as drastic as blowing up the place."

None of them was inclined to push him into action. Outside the flames beat into the night sky, and the white of the moon they had noted the night before was marred by a more yellow gleam from a smaller satellite trailing behind the larger. But of the activity of the dune skulkers the screen gave them no clue.

That came not by sight but by a startling shifting of the ship itself. How had the creatures outside achieved that movement? Perhaps, Travis imagined, by the sheer weight of many creeping bodies plastered to the hull. The globe canted from its landing position. And maybe that triggered the flying controls. For the now-familiar warnings of a take-off alerted them all.

"No!" Renfry protested, "we can't—not yet—not until we know why."

But the engines the humans did not understand, and could not hope to control, had no ears for that feeble defiance. Perhaps only a time limit had governed their visit, a full day and night of planetary time. Or maybe it was the strange attack of the hairy things.

And those creatures—would they free themselves in time, drop to the ground as the ship lifted, warned by the vibrations? Or would they cling in stupid concentration upon their attack, to be carried out into the freezing blackness of the eternal night?

The unwilling crew of the ship followed the old routine of strap down and wait for the wrench of blast-off, the break into hyperspace. Again they were being carried into the unknown with perhaps a long voyage ahead.

But it was not to be the same this time. Travis noticed the first departure from the usual routine. The take-off was not so severe—or else he had adjusted to it far better than he ever had before. He did not black out completely, nor did he have to undergo that terrible inner twisting. And he heard Renfry's voice exclaim in wonder:

"I don't think we went into hyper! What happened?"

They were up and about, watching the screen of the ship. Renfry's guess was right. For instead of the complete blackness which closed in upon them when they made a big inter-system jump, they saw now the receding orb of the desert planet, its face a mass of shifting color as they withdrew from it.

"Must be heading for another planet in this same system," Ashe supplied one answer. And, as the hours wore on, they believed that was the right one. The ship now appeared to be on course for the third planet of that unknown sun.

"Do we visit them all?" inquired Ross with some of his old flippancy. "If so—why? Parcel delivery?"

Three days went by, four. They ate the alien food and moved restlessly about the ship, unable to pay attention for any length of time to anything but the screen in the control cabin. Then on the sixth day, came the signals of an approaching landing.

On the screen the goal showed a vivid blue-green, patched here and there with orange-red under clouds. They had drawn lots for the occupancy of the three seats in the control cabin, and the odd man to be relegated to the bunk below. So Travis now lay alone and unseeing in the heart of the throbbing globe, wondering what new future they must confront.

The ship set down this time in the planet's day. The Apache freed himself from his straps, stumbled in the return clutch of gravity to the ladder and climbed up to share the others' view of the new world.

"No—!"

The ruined towers standing starkly to portion off the expanse of the fueling port had speared as straightly into the sky—but they had not been like this one. Against a background of cloudless, delicate pink, was an opaline dome. It curved in flowing lines which spiraled up in turn to a fragile frosting of lace. It was nothing like a human construction.

Torn lace . . . As he studied those lifting spans, Travis could mark the breaks which spoiled the perfect pattern. Yet in spite of that damage there was still the fantastic beauty of form and light and play of rainbow color. It rose out of dark foliage tinged with blue unlike the green of his own world's leaves.

And those leafy branches stirred almost languidly

as if light breezes pulled at them, showing here and there a touch of other colors. Fruit? Flowers?

Renfry brought their attention away from the scene which was so ethereal as to seem unreal.

"Look!"

He was on his feet before the main control board, his hands grasping the back of the pilot's seat so tightly that the muscles stood out on his taut arms. For the board had taken on life. They had witnessed the flickers of light which had heralded the readying of the ship's guns. This was something else—a line of small winks of brilliance flowing unevenly down the rows of levers and buttons. And where each flashed a lever arose, a button sank or snapped above the level of the board. There was a final burst of light from a spot Travis could have covered with his thumb. And there a lid opened and a cavity beneath disgorged a small, coin-shaped bit of red metal that tinkled out, to roll across the floor.

Renfry came to life, dove to catch it up. He held it in his hand as if the disk was something very precious indeed.

"Home port!" He swung about to face them, his eagerness lighting a flame in his eyes. "This is the home port! And I think I am holding the course tape!"

There could be no other explanation for what they had just witnessed. The journey plotted by a dying man had come to its full conclusion. That small button of metal Renfry had closed his fist upon, held now not only the secret of their arrival—but of their return. If they were ever to regain their own world, it would be because they had solved the workings of that disk.

Yet Travis' eyes went from the technician's clenched hand and what it held, back to the screen. The picture there showed a gentle wind lifting flowering branches about a tower of opal against a sky of palest rose. And the immediate future seemed at that moment more entrancing than the more distant one.

Perhaps Ashe shared that feeling at the moment. For the senior time agent moved toward the inner ladder. He paused at the well and looked back over his shoulder, to say with a strange simplicity:

"Let us go out—now."

12

If there had once been a wide landing strip here, the space was long since swallowed by a cover of green. From the mass crushed by the landing of the ship came the scent of growing things, some spicy, some rank.

The humans had not worn their helmets, nor did they need to here. A sunlight no stronger than that of early summer in the temperate zone of their own world greeted them. And there was no burden of sand in the soft wind which whirled flower petals and torn leaves from the wreckage under their feet.

Now that they had a wider view than that offered by the screen, they noted other breaks in the luxuriance of growing things. The opal tower with its fantastic form was flanked by another building as strange and as far removed from the style of its companion as the desert world was from this green one. For those massive blocks of dull red, geometric in their solidity, could not have sprung from the same creative imagination—or perhaps from even the same race or age.

And beyond that was another, with knife-sharp gables and secretive windows piercing its gray walls. It had a pointed roof of some rough material, dull under the sun, and gave rootage in places to vines, even a small tree. But again it was not of the same origin as the fairylike dome or the massive blocks.

"Why—?" Ross's head turned slowly as he looked from one of those totally dissimilar buildings to the next. All were tall, dwarfing the globe, and all had their lower stories hidden by the vegetation.

Travis thought back to a past which seemed a little blurred by all which had happened lately. There were places on his own world where a Zuñi village in miniature stood beside a Sioux lodge or an Apache wickiup.

"A museum?" He ventured the only explanation he could see.

Ashe's face was pale under his fading tan. He stared raptly from dome to block, block to sharply accented gables. "Or else a capital where each embassy built in their home style."

"And now it is all dead," Travis added. For that was true. This was as deserted as the fueling port.

"Capital perhaps—of a galactic empire. What there is to be learned here! A treasure house—" Ashe was breathing fast. "We may have the treasures of a thousand worlds to uncover here."

"And who will ever know—or care?" Ross asked. "Not that I'm not ready to go and look for them."

Travis tensed. There was a stirring in the mass of tangled vegetation where the grounding of the globe had flattened some of the fern trees, along with others tied to them by vines. He watched that shaking of bruised and broken branches. Something alive was working its way from a point about a hundred yards away from the ship toward the wall of still-standing plants. And the fugitive thing must be fairly large by the amount of displacement its progress caused.

Had that unseen crawling thing been injured in the crash of the tree ferns? Was it now dragging itself off to die? Travis listened, striving to hear more than the rustling of the leaves. But if the thing was hurt, it made no complaint. Animal? Or—something else? Something as alien as the dune lurkers, more than animal, yet different from man as they knew men?

"It's in cover now," breathed Ross. "Couldn't have been too hurt or it wouldn't have moved so lively."

"I think we can believe that this world isn't as empty as it might look to the first glance," Ashe said a little dryly. "And what about those?"

"Those" came lightly, drifting across the torn clearing caused by the descent of the globe. They flapped gossamer wings once or twice to keep air-borne, but their attention was manifestly centered on the ship.

And what were they? Birds? Insects? Flying mammals? Travis could almost believe the four small creatures were a weird combination of all three. Their long narrow wings, prismatic and close to transparent, resembled those of an insect. Yet they had bodies equipped with three legs, two smaller ones in front ending in clawshaped digits, one larger limb in back with an even more pronounced talon. Their heads seemed to be set directly on their shoulders with no visible neck. These were round at the top, narrowing to a curved beak, while their eyes—four of them!—protruded on short stalks, two in front and two in back. And their triangles of bodies were clothed in plushy fur of pale and frosted blue.

Slowly, in a solemn, silent procession, they drifted toward the ship. The second in line broke out of formation, dipped groundward. Its hind claws found anchorage on a stub of broken branch and its wings

folded together above its back, resembling a butter-
fly on Earth.

The two last in line flapped back and forth across
the open port twice and then wheeled, flew off,
mounting into the sky to clear the treetops. But the
leader came on, until it hung, beating wings now and
then to maintain altitude, directly before the entrance
of the ship.

It was impossible to read any expression in those
brilliantly blue stalked eyes. But none of the four
humans felt any repulsion or alarm as they had upon
their encounter with the nocturnal desert people.
Whatever the flyer was, they could not believe that
it was either aggressive or potentially dangerous.

Renfry expressed their common reaction to the
creature first:

"Funny little beggar, isn't he? Like to see him
closer. If they're all the same as him here, we don't
have to worry."

Why the technician should refer to the winged
thing as "he" was obscure. But the creature was
attractive enough to hold their interest. Ross snapped
his fingers and held out his hand in welcome.

"Here, boy," he coaxed.

Those brilliant bits of blue winked as the eye stalks
moved, the wings beat, and the flyer approached the
port. But not close enough for the humans to touch.
It hung there, suspended in mid-air for a long moment. Then with a flurry of beating wings, sparking
rainbows, it mounted skyward, its partner taking off
from the brush below at the same moment to join it.
A few seconds later they vanished as if they had never
been.

"Do you suppose it is intelligent?" Ross watched
after the vanished flyer, his disappointment mirrored
on his usually impassive face.

"Your guess is as good as mine," Ashe replied. "Renfry," he spoke to the technician, "you have your journey tape now. Can you reset it?"

"I don't know. Wish I had a manual—at least some type of guide. Do you suppose you can find such a thing here?"

"Why are you in such a big hurry to leave, chief? We only got here and it looks like a pretty good vacation spot to me." Ross raised his head a little to eye the dome where opal lights played under the sun's rays.

"That is just why," Ashe replied quietly. "There are too many temptations here."

Travis understood. To Ashe the appeal of those waiting buildings, of the knowledge which they might contain, must be almost overpowering. They could postpone work on the ship, delay and delay, fascinated by this world and its secrets. He knew the same pull, though perhaps in a lesser degree. Before it trapped them all, they must struggle against that enveloping desire to plunge into the green jungle, slash a path to the opal dome, and see for themselves what wonders it housed.

Ashe was sorely tempted. And because he was the man he was, he must be fighting that temptation now, believing that if he once plunged wholeheartedly into exploration, he might not be able to stop. Also, Renfry was offering them an excuse to do just that by wishing for some aid in the problem of the tape.

An hour later the three of them did leave the ship, Renfry remaining in charge there. Using the lowest beam of the weapons, they cut a path into the woods. Travis picked up a flower head. Five wide petals, fluted, crinkled a little at the tips, were a deep cream in color, shading orange at the heart. Resting on his palm, those petals began to move visibly, closing until he held a bud instead of a flower. He could not toss away the blossom. Its color was too arresting, its spicy scent too appealing. He worked the short stem into one of the latches of a belt pouch, where, the heat of his hand removed, the flower opened once again. Nor did it fade or droop in spite of the shortness of its stem.

Now, out of the direct rays of the sun, the humans found the air cool, moist, heavy with the odor of luxuriant vegetation. Not that those odors were unpleasant—in fact, they were overpoweringly good. Spicy scents warred with perfumes and the sharper smell of earth as their feet scuffed through the mass of dead leaves.

"Whew!" Ross waved his hand back and forth in front of his face as if to set up a reviving current of air. "Perfume factory—or what have you! I feel as if I were burrowing through about a ton of roses!"

Ashe appeared to have lost some of his somberness since they had left the ship. "With another of carnations thrown in," he agreed. "I think I can detect"— he sniffed and then sneezed—"some cloves and maybe a few nutmegs into the bargain."

Travis breathed shallowly. He had welcomed the mixture of perfumes minutes earlier. Now he found himself wishing instead to face a wind with a burden of sage and piñon in place of these cloying scents in their thick abundance.

The jungle grew clear up to the base of the opaline building. And the structure itself loomed far higher from ground level than had appeared true from the port of the ship. They worked their way along, hunting the entrance which must exist somewhere, unless the inhabitants had all worn wings. Oddly enough—though there were windows in plenty of stories above, many opening on small airy balconies—

the first story showed no openings at all. Here were panels set in carved frames alternating with solid blocks of the opal material. And each panel was clad in gleaming mosaic, not forming any recognized design but merely wedding color to color in vivid shades.

The humans cut their way through underbrush and reached the end of the wall. This was a large building occupying the space of a normal Terran city block. But around the corner they found the door, at the head of a curling ramp. The portal extended almost the full height of the first story and it was open, a carved archway. The frame was like frozen lace, with here a curve and there a point cracked and gone.

They hesitated. Save for the sighing of the wind, the sound of leaf against moving leaf, and some small twitters and squeaks from the unseen inhabitants of the green world surrounding the foot of the ramp, there was quiet—the quiet of the forgotten.

Ashe stepped onto the ramp, his soft-shod feet making not the slightest noise. He climbed the gentle slope almost reluctantly, as if he did not really want to know what waited within.

Travis and Ross came behind. There were pockets of dead leaves caught in the curves of the ramp, and more drifted inside the open portal. They shuffled through them, to come into a hall which was breathtaking in its height. For it went up and up, until they were dizzied when they tried to follow its inner spiral with their eyes. And covering this expanse was the great opaline dome. The sunlight shone through it, painting rainbows on walls and on the ramp which climbed in a coil along the walls, serving other lacy archways on every floor level.

Here there was none of the brilliance of the outside mosaics. The spread of color was sharply reduced to soft, faded shades: dusky violet, pallid green, dusty rosy, pale cream . . .

" . . . forty-eight—forty-nine—fifty! Fifty doors up and down that ramp at least." Ross kept his voice to a murmur and yet that echo of a whisper carried eerily back to them. "Where do we start?" Now his tone was definitely louder in challenge to that echo and the stillness which deadened it. Ashe left them and crossed the expanse of hall, stretching out his hands to a niche. When they hurried after him they discovered he was holding a small statuette carved of a dusky violet stone. Like the blue flyers, the subject bore baffling resemblances to living things they knew, and yet its totality was alien.

"Man?" Ross wondered. "Animal?"

"Totem? God?" Travis added out of his own knowledge and background.

"All or any," conceded Ashe. "But it is a work of art."

That they could all recognize, even if the subject still puzzled them. The figure was posed erect on two slender hind limbs, both of which terminated in feet of long, narrow, widely separated, clawed digits. The body, also slender but with a well-defined waist and broad shoulders, was closer to the human in general appearance, and there were two arms held aloft, as if the creature was about to leap outward into space. But it would have a better chance of survival in such a leap than those now passing the statuette from hand to hand. For the arms supported skin wing-flaps, extended on ribs not unlike those possessed by bats on Earth.

The head was the least human, almost grotesque in its ugliness to the time agents' eyes. There were sharply pointed ears, overshadowing in their size and extension the rest of the features which were crowded together in the forepart of the face. Eyes were set deep within cavities under heavy skull ridges, the nose was simply a vertical slit above a mouth from which thin vestiges of lips curled back to display a frightening set of fangs. And yet its ugliness was not repulsive, nor horrifying. There was no clothing to suggest that it represented an intelligent being. Yet all of them were certain, the longer they examined the figure, that it had not been meant to portray an animal.

To the touch the violet stone was smooth and cool, and when Travis held it out into a patch of light from the dome, the statuette sparkled gemlike. The careful detail of the figure contrasted with the abstraction of the murals on the outer walls, more akin to the carvings on the dome and about the doorways.

Ross drew his finger along the interior of the niche where Ashe had found the image. Dust piled there dribbled out to the floor. How long had the winged one stood there undisturbed?

Ashe carried it in the crook of his arm as they went on—not up the spiral of the ramp, but into the first of the open doorways on ground level. But the room beyond was empty, lighted through slits high on the wall. They wandered on. More empty rooms, no trace of those who had once lived here—if this indeed had been a dwelling place and not a building for public use. It was as if the inhabitants had stripped it bare when they had at last withdrawn, forgetting only the little statue in the hall.

As they came from the last bare chamber, Ross sighed and leaned against the wall.

"I don't know how you feel about it," he announced. "But I've swallowed more than my share of dust this past hour or so. Also breakfast was a long time back. A coffee break right now—providing we had coffee— might be heartening."

They didn't have coffee, but they had come provided with the foam drink from the ship. So, sitting in a row across the ramp, they sucked in turn from containers of that and ate some of the "corn" cakes they carried for trail rations.

"Be good to have some fresh food," Travis said wistfully. The rather monotonous diet from the ship's stores satisfied hunger but did not appeal to his taste. He allowed himself the luxury of visualizing a sizzling steak and all that would accompany it back at the ranch.

"Maybe some on the hoof—out there." Ross, his hands full, pointed with his chin toward the riot of greenery they could sight from their present perch. "We could go hunting . . ."

"How about that?" Travis roused and turned to Ashe eagerly. "Dare we try?"

But the older agent did not warm to the suggestion. "I wouldn't kill—until I knew what I was killing."

For a moment Travis did not understand, and then the meaning of the rather ambiguous statement sank in. How could they be sure that the prey was not— man! Or man's equivalent here? But he still wanted that steak, with a longing which gnawed at him.

"Do we climb?" Ross stood up. "This'll be an all-day job right here, if we stick to it. I'd say the cupboard's bare, though."

"Maybe." Ashe cradled his bat-thing in his arm. "We can take a quick look through the ground floor of that big red block to the north."

They fought their way through the thick wall of brush, grass, tree and vine to the monolithic building. Here again they faced an open door, this one narrow as the window slits, as if grudging any entrance at all.

"I'd say the guys who built this one didn't like their

neighbors too well," Ross commented. "This could make a pretty good fort if you had to have one. That domed place is wide open."

"Different peoples . . ." Travis had been a little in advance, lingering for a moment before he took the step which would bring him over the threshold. Once inside he froze.

"Trouble!" His weapon was out, ready to fire.

There was a wide hall before him, as there had been in the dome building. But where that had been clean and bare, this one was different.

A series of partitions some five or six feet high cut back and forth, chopping the floor space into a crazy quilt of oddly shaped and sized spaces, with little chance to see from one to the next. But that did not bother Travis so much as the message recorded by his nose.

The odor of the night creatures had been something like this. It was the taint of a lair—a lair long in use. It smelled of decay, alien body reek, dried and rotted vegetation, and animal matter. Something denned here and had used this place freely for a long time.

It was the eagerness of the strange hunter which betrayed it. A low, throaty murmur, such as a cat might utter when intent upon unsuspecting prey, carried across the shadows.

Travis spun around. He saw the hunched shape balancing on top of a partition, knew it was about to launch straight for him. And he pressed the firing button of the weapon as he brought it up.

The attacker was caught in mid-air. A terrible yowl of rage, and pain, echoed and re-echoed about the massive walls. A flailing limb, well provided with claws, raked across Travis' body from the waist down, sending him reeling from the door into the greater gloom. Just then Ross and Ashe burst in, to center the full beams of their weapons on the rolling, caterwauling thing making a second attempt at Travis.

Whatever it was, the creature possessed abnormal vitality. It was not until their blast rays met and crossed in its body that it lay still. Travis scrambled to his feet, shaken. He knew that if he had not had that split second of warning, he would be dead—or so badly mauled he would have longed for death.

He limped back toward the door, his thigh and leg feeling numb from the force of that smashing stroke. But under his questing hand the fabric of the suit was untorn, and there seemed to be no open wound.

"Did it get you?" Ashe came to meet him, pushing aside his hands to look at his body. Travis, still shaken, winced under the exploring probe of the other's fingers.

"Just bruised. What was it?"

Ross arose from a gingerly inspection of the remains. "After the blasting we gave it, your guess is as good as mine. But it is sure sudden death on six legs—and that's no overstatement."

The weapons had not left too much to identify, that was true. But the thing had been six-legged, furred, and carnivorous—and it was about eight feet long with fangs and claws in proportion to the size.

"Sabertooth, local variety," Ross remarked.

Ashe nodded to the outside world. "I suggest we make a strategic withdrawal. These may be nocturnal, too, but I'd rather not tangle with another in the jungle."

13

"Did you think we'd find *no* nasty surprises?" Ross drummed on the mess table with his scarred hand, his eyes showing amusement, even if his lips did not curve into a smile. "Let me share with you a small drop of good common sense, fella. It's just when things look smoothest that there's a big trap waiting ahead on the trail."

Travis rubbed his bruised thigh. The other's humor grated. And since he had had time to consider the late battle, he began to suspect that he *had* been a little too sure of himself when he had entered the red-walled building. That didn't make him more receptive to Ross's implied criticism, though—or what he chose to believe was criticism.

"You know"—Renfry came in from the corridor talking to Ashe—"those blue flying things came back twice while you were gone. They flew almost up to the port, but not inside."

Travis, recalling the claws with which those were equipped, grunted. "Might be just as well," he commented.

"Then," Renfry said, paying not attention to his interruption, "just before you came back I found this—inside the outer lock."

"This" was clearly no natural curiosity left on their doorstep by some freak of the wind. Three green leaves possessing yellow ribs and veins had been pinned together with two-inch thorns into a cornucopia holder, a holder filled with oval, pale-green objects about the size of a thumbnail.

They could be fruit, seeds, a form of grain. Oddly enough, Travis was sure they were food of a sort. And plainly, too, they were an offering—a gesture of friendship—an overture on the part of the blue flyers. Why? For what purpose?

"You didn't see a flyer leave it?" questioned Ashe.

"No. I went to the port—and there it was."

One of the seed things had dropped out of the packet, rolled across the table. Travis put a fingertip to it and the globe promptly burst as an over-ripe grape does when pressed. Without thinking, he raised his sticky finger to his mouth. The taste was tart, yet sweet, with the fresh cleanness of mint or some similar herb.

"Now you've done it," observed Ross. "Well, we can watch while you break out in purple spots, or turn all green and shrivel up." His words were delivered in his usual amused tone, but there was a heat beneath that Travis did not understand. Unless once more Ross believed the Apache had taken too much on himself in that unthinking experiment.

"Good flavor," he returned with stolid defiance. And deliberately he chose another, transferring it to his mouth and breaking the skin with his teeth. The berry, or seed, or whatever it was, did not satisfy his desire for fresh meat, but it was not a concentrate or something out of one of the aliens' cans and the taste was good.

"That is enough!" Ashe swept up the leaf bag and its contents. "We'll have no more unnecessary chances taken."

But when Travis experienced no ill effects from his sampling, they shared out the rest of the gift at the evening meal, relishing the flavor after their weeks of the ship's supplies.

"Maybe we can trade for some more of these," Ross had begun almost idly. Then he gave a start and sat straighter in the uncomfortable mess seat.

Ashe laughed. "I wondered just when that possibility was going to dawn on you."

Ross grinned. "You may well ask. You'd think nothing stuck long between my ears, wouldn't you? All right—so we set up as traders again. I never did get a good chance to try out my techniques when we were on the Beaker run—too many interruptions."

Travis waited patiently for them to explain. This was another of those times when their shared experiences from the past shut him out, to remind him that only chance had brought him into this adventure, after all.

"There ought to be some things among all that stuff we routed out to study which should attract attention." Ross wriggled around Ashe to leave the mess cabin. "I'll see."

"Trade, eh?" Renfry nodded. "Heard how you boys on the time runs play that angle."

"It's a good cover, one of the best there is. A trader moves around without question in a primitive world. Any little strangeness in his speech, his customs, his dress, can be legitimately accounted for by his profession. He is supposed to come from a distance, his contacts don't expect him to be like their fellow tribesmen. And a trader picks up news quickly. Yes, trade was a cover the project used from the first."

"You were a trader, back in time?" Travis asked.

Ashe appeared willing enough to talk of his previous ventures. "D'you ever hear of the Beaker Folk?
There *were* traders for you—had their stations from
Greece to Scotland during the early Bronze Age. That
was my cover, in early Britain, and again in the Baltic. You can really be fascinated by such a business.
My first partner might have retired a millionaire—or
that period's equivalent to one." Ashe paused, his face
closing up again, but Travis asked another question.

"Why didn't he?"

"The Russians located our station in that era. Blew
it up. And themselves into the bargain because they
gave us our fix on their own post when they did that."
He might have been discussing some dry fact in a
report—until you saw his eyes.

Travis knew that Ross was dangerous. He thought
now that Ashe probably could surpass his young sub-
ordinate in ruthless action, was there any need to do
so. Ross came back, his hands full. He set out his
selections for their appraisal.

There was a length of material—perhaps intended
for a scarf—which they had found in one of the crew
lockers. A small thread of a vivid purple barred the
green length, both colors bright enough to rivet
attention. Then there were four pieces of carved
wood, a coral-shaded wood with flecks of gold. They
were stylized representations of fern fronds or feathers,
as far as the humans could tell, and Ashe believed they
might be part of some game, though playing board
and other pieces had not been located. Lastly was the
plaque which could so mysteriously reproduce a picture of home for the one holding it. That Ashe pushed
aside with a shake of his head.

"That's too important. We needn't be too generous
the first time, anyway. After all, we've only a small
offering to top. Try the scarf and two of these."

"Put them in the port?" Ross asked.

"I'd say no. No use encouraging visitors. Use your judgment in picking out some place below."

Ashe might have told Ross to take the initiative in that venture, but he followed him out. Travis, his leg having given him a sudden severe twinge, retired to his bunk, to try out the healing properties that resting pad had to offer in the circumstances. He stripped off his suit, stretched out with a grimace or two, and relaxed.

He must have gone to sleep under the narcotic influence of the healing jelly which seeped out and over him, triggered by his need. When he roused, it was to find Ross pulling at him.

"What's the matter?"

Ross allowed him no time for protest. "Ashe's gone!" His face might be schooled and impassive, but twin cold devils looked out of his eyes.

"Gone?" The drowsiness induced by the healing of the bunk did not make quick thinking easy. "Gone where?"

"That's what we have to find out. Get moving!"

Travis, his bruises and aches gone, dressed and buckled the arms belt Ross pushed into his hands. "Let's have the story."

Ross was already in the corridor, every line of his taut body expressing his impatience.

"We were out there—fixed up a trading stone. There were a couple of flyers watching us and we waited to see if they would come down. When they didn't, Ashe said we had better take cover, as if we were going on to the buildings. Ashe detoured around a fallen tree—I saw him go. I tell you—I saw him! Then he wasn't there—or anywhere!" Ross was clearly shaken well out of his cultivated imperviousness.

"A ground trap?" Travis gave the first answer

probable as he followed Ross to the air lock. Renfry was there making fast two lengths of silky cord barely coarser than knitting yarn but which, as they had discovered earlier, was surprisingly strong. Thus hitched to the ship, they could prowl the vicinity and yet leave a guide to their whereabouts.

"I crawled over that ground inch by inch," Ross said between set teeth. "Not so much as a worm or ant hole showing. He was there one minute—the next he wasn't!"

Making fast their lines and leaving Renfry as lookout, they descended into the trampled and blasted area about the globe where the green was now withering under a late afternoon sun. Darkness would complicate their search. They had better move swiftly, find some clue before they were hampered further.

Ross took the lead, balancing along a fallen tree trunk to its crown of dropping fern fronds, now crushed and broken. "He was right here."

Travis swung down into the crushed foliage. The sharp smell of sticky sap, as well as the heavy scents of flowers and leaves, was cloying. But Ross was right. The vegetation on the ground had been pulled away in a wide sweep, and there was no sign that the dank earth beneath had been disturbed. He sighted a round-toed track, but it was twin to the ones he was leaving in the mold and could have been pressed there by either Ashe or Ross. But, because it was the only possible trace, he turned in the direction it pointed.

A moment or two later, at the very edge of the clearing Ross had made during his search, Travis saw something else. There was another tree trunk lying there, the remains of a true forest giant. And it had not been brought down by the landing of the ship, but had lain there long enough for soil and fallen leaves to build up around it, to grow a skin of red-capped moss or fungi.

Across that moss there were now two dark marks, ragged scars, suggesting that someone or something had clawed for a desperate hold against irresistible force. Ashe? But how had he been captured without Ross's seeing or hearing his struggles?

Travis vaulted the tree trunk. There was his confirmation—another footprint deep in the mold. But beyond it—nothing—absolutely nothing! And no living creature could have continued along that stretch of soft earth without leaving a trace. From this point it did appear that Ashe had vanished into thin air.

Air! Not on the ground but above it was where they would have to search. Travis called to Ross. There were tall trees about them now, trees with twenty feet or more of smooth bole before their first fern branches broke from the trunks. The wind rustled here, but they could sight no movement that was not normal, hear no sounds aloft.

Then one of the blue flyers came along, hovering over Travis, watching him with all four of its stalked eyes. The flyers—had they taken Ashe? He couldn't believe that. A man of Ashe's weight and strength, undoubtedly struggling hard into the bargain—at least the scraping on the moss suggested that—could not have been airborne unless by a large flock of the blue creatures working together. But the Apache believed as completely as if he had witnessed it, that Ashe had been taken away either through the air or along a road of treetops.

"How did they get him up?" Ross puzzled. He appeared willing to accept Travis' idea, but the Apache, in turn, was forced to agree such a maneuver would be difficult. "And getting up," the time agent continued, "where in the world did they take him?"

"This lies in the opposite direction from the three nearest buildings," Travis pointed out. "To transport a prisoner might force them to travel in a direct line to their own quarters—speed would matter more than concealment."

"Which means a direct strike out into the jungle." Ross eyed the wilderness of trees, vines and brush with disfavor. "Well, there's one little trick—let me have your belt. This was something they showed us in basic training—good old basic." He took Travis' belt, made it fast to his own, increasing its expansion to the last hole before he measured it about the tree. But the girth of the bole was too great. Ross untied his cord connection with the ship, slashed off a length to incorporate in the circle of belts. This time it served, linking him to the bole. With the belt to support him, he hitched up the trunk which overhung the signs of struggle.

The fronds shook as he forced his way between them. "Here's your clue," he called down. "There's been a rope strung about this limb—worn a groove in the bark. And—Well, well, well—they're not so bright, after all—or they don't think we are. Here's a way to travel, all right—by the upper reaches. Come and see!"

A line made of cord and belts slapped down the trunk and Travis caught at it, making the climb with less agility than Ross had shown, to join the other at his perch among the fronds. He found the agent folding up between his hands another rope, a supple green one which aped the vines native to this aerial place.

"You do a Tarzan act." Ross flipped the rope end for emphasis. "Swing over to that tree, probably find another rope end there—and so on. I still don't see how they boosted Ashe along. Though"—his eyes narrowed—"maybe they waited to go until I went back to the ship for you."

Travis eyed the rope. "Leaving that here means one thing—"

"That they intend to return?" Ross nodded. "They may have some bright plans about scooping us up one by one. But who are 'they'? Not those blue flyers . . ."

"Those might act as their hounds." Travis tried not to glance at the ground, for his present perch inspired little confidence in him.

"And that fruit present was bait for a trap," Ross agreed. "It fits. The fruit to get us out of the ship, the flyers to report when we came. Then—pounce!— one of us is snaffled! Only Ashe isn't going to stay a prisoner."

"This could be a trap, too," Travis reminded him as he gave the rope a jerk and discovered Ross had been right, the line was very firmly attached to its tree anchorage.

"True enough. But we'll find some way."

"At night?" The sun was close to setting. Travis wanted to be on the trail just as much as Ross, but common sense would pay off better than a reckless dash to the rescue.

"Night—" Ross squinted at the patches of sunlight. "These things move around in the daytime. And they're used to heights."

"Which suggests there may be good reasons for not travelling on the ground or in the dark." Travis was growing a little tired of talking. "Our friend in the red house may be one of those reasons. What is your solution?"

"We go back to the domed place—up to the top. There is a balcony around the dome itself, and we can take our bearings from there."

Travis could agree with that. But they had to argue down the protests of Renfry. The technician's demands to accompany them Ross was able to overcome by pointing out crisply that alone of their party Renfry possessed the knowledge, or fraction of knowledge, which might mean their eventual control of the ship, and so of their future. And the need for a scouting party before dark urged the necessity of speed in their try to locate landmarks which might guide them on a hunt for Ashe.

They trod the path they had cut that morning. Travis glanced now and then at the sky when they crossed small glades. He half expected to find the blue flyers on the lookout. But none appeared.

Ross took the inner ramp under the dome at a rapid trot. His pace, however, slowed as they wound their way up past five levels, then six, seven, eight, nine and finally ten. There was no sound in the building, nothing to break the echoing emptiness of the fantastically beautiful shell.

They reached the balcony, a narrow walk curving completely around the bulk of the dome, protected by a breast-high parapet of the carved lace. The wind, now rising in intensity, pulled at their hair, sang weirdly through the openwork. Ross took the lead. He hurried to the vantage point from which they could obtain an unrestricted view in the direction they thought Ashe's captors had headed.

There were other buildings, or the remains of buildings, rising out of the jungle. Some of them were smaller than the dome, with three or four—at a greater distance—taller. And the taller ones had a certain similarity of outline which suggested that they must have had a common architectural origin.

It was one of those which Ross indicated now. "If they were headed for the nearest building across the treetops—that must be it." He sighted along his pointed finger as if it were a rifle barrel.

Travis was listing all possible landmarks—though from ground level three-quarters of them would not be of much use. "To the right of that funnel-shaped turret, and the left of the pile of blocks. It may be several miles from here."

To cut a trail along the ground was possible—using their weapons. But such action would certainly advertise their coming. If they wanted to locate the enemy—provided, of course, that the enemy *was* roosting in the structure Ross had just chosen—the process must entail a more complicated bit of trail craft. And that kind of scouting could not be done at night.

"There's one way of checking," Ross said, as if he were thinking aloud. "If we stay here until dark, we'd know."

"How?"

"Lights. If we see any lights out there—they would be proof."

"Slim chance. They'd be fools to use lights."

"Could be trap-setting again," Ross demurred. "More bait to pull us in."

"That's just guessing. How can we tell what makes their minds tick? We don't even know what they are. You didn't like the type who first wore this uniform." Travis plucked at the blue fabric crossing his chest. "If this was their home planet, wouldn't they be able to play games with us the way they did with you—by mental control?"

"Look out there!" Ross's sweep of hand included half the landscape, the sea of untroubled jungle, the buildings rising in isolated islands out of it. "Whatever they had—it's dead now—long dead. And maybe they're dead, too—or back at the primitive stage. If they're primitives, Ashe can handle them to a point; he's been taught to do just that. I've seen him in action. Give me an hour up here past sundown. Then if we see no lights—I'll go . . ."

Travis drew his weapon. Dark, or even heavy dusk, here might unleash things to lurk in the shadows along their trail. But he could understand Ross's point, and they had a well-marked path to the ship.

"All right."

They walked slowly around the dome waiting for the murk of evening to gather. And so they counted at least fifty more fantastic buildings, all different, some even appearing to defy the laws of gravity. Beyond them were those others, tall, thin, of a common mold. Were those the native structures and these others embassies, examples of trans-galactic architecture as Ashe had suggested? If not all of them were stripped, what a wealth of knowledge lay—

Travis was jerked out of speculation by a cry from Ross. There was still a reflection of sunlight in the sky at their backs. But—Murdock's hunch had paid off. A wink of light flashed across the green from the first of the distant tall towers. Flashed on—off—on.

Was it meant to be an enticing signal?

14

They held a council of war in the ship, the outer hatch closed against the night, that simple precaution taught them by the desert world.

"It'll be difficult to go straight through the tangle in that direction," Renfry observed. "They'd be waiting for you to try it."

"Sometimes the fastest way is around, not straight," Ross agreed. He had a map drawn on a sheet of material from the aliens' stores, the crosses and squares on it marking the various buildings they had sighted. "See here—they bunch, those tall towers. But here, and here, and here, are other buildings. Suppose we head for this one which looks like an outsized oil can, then beyond that there's a pile of blocks. The one we want is between them. So—move to the funnel top, then start beyond to the block pile—and cut back. If we can make them believe we're just searching everything in that direction, it'll buy us time. Reach a point about here"—his forefinger dug into the surface of the improvised map—

"and then do a right-about-face and go at top speed." He looked up challengingly. "Anybody got a better idea?"

Renfry shrugged. "This is your party, you've had the training for this type of thing. But I'll go along."

"And let some joker take the ship behind our backs?" Ross wanted to know. "They've a line on us—they must have or they wouldn't have scooped up the chief so neatly. He's no recruit at this type of fun and games, remember. I've seen him in action."

"Through the treetops," Travis mused. "If that's their regular mode of travel, then maybe we have another point in our favor. Once we're really into the jungle, there's a lot of cover which will give us protection. They can't watch us from above all the time."

"You're both set on this then?" Renfry still studied the map.

Ross stood up. "I don't propose to let them snatch the chief and get away with it. And the quicker we are on the move—the better!"

But even Ross had to admit that they must wait until dawn to put their plan to the test. They rummaged the ship for supplies and assembled a small pack apiece. Each wore a belt supporting alien weapons. In addition, a coil of the supple cord was wound from shoulder to hip about their bodies, and they had retained the flint knives from their hunter disguise. Brittle though the flint might be, the finely chipped blades could be deadly in close combat. They slung packsacks with food and the froth containers.

Renfry disputed his staying with the ship. But he was forced to admit that there was no way to lock the port behind them and so a guard must remain. However, he insisted upon triggering the armament of the spacer. So when they descended the ladder to the ground in the first dull rose of the early morning, the black mouths of those sinister tubes were thrust from the shell of the globe.

They took turns cutting a path. And, where they could, they pushed through the underbrush, saving the power of the weapons. It was Travis who led when they thrust completely through a fern wall into a green tunnel.

The ground here had been worn into a shallow trough and beaten hard. Travis needed only one look to know that slot for what it was—a game trail, leading either to water or to some favorite grazing ground. It had been well traveled, and for some length of time.

There were tracks here, pads with the pinprick indentations of claws well beyond them, a cloven hoof with so deep a cleavage that the hoof must be almost split in two, and some smaller tracings too alien to be identified.

"This goes in the right direction. Do we follow it?" Travis was in two minds about such an action himself. On one hand they could greatly increase speed and speed might be important. But a well-used game trail not only provided a road for animals—it was as well a lure for creatures who preyed upon such travelers.

Ross moved out on the narrow path. It had twists and turns, but the way did run in the direction of the funnel top which was their first goal.

"We do," he decided.

Travis dropped into a loose trot which fitted his feet into the slot of the track. He caught small sounds in the vegetation about them—twitters, squeaks, sometimes a harsh, croaking call. But he saw nothing of the creatures that voiced them.

The trail took a dip into a shallow ravine. At the bottom a stream trickled lazily over brown-green gravel and above them the sky was open. There they disturbed a fisher.

Travis' hand went to the grip of his weapon, dropped away again. Like the blue flyers, this inhabitant of the unknown world gave no impression of hostility. The beast was about the size of a wild cat, and somewhat similar to a cat in appearance. At least, it possessed a round head with eyes set slightly aslant. But the ears were very long and sharply pointed with heavy tufts of—feathers at their tips. Feathers! The blue flyer had been furred, provided with insect wings. The fisher, plainly a ground dweller, was fluffily clothed in soft feathers of the same blue-green shade as the foliage around it. Had it not been crouched on the rock in the open, it would have passed unseen.

Its haunches and hind legs were heavy and it squatted back upon them. Two pairs of far more slender and longer front limbs held a limp, scaled thing which it had been methodically denuding of a series of fringe legs with its teeth and claws. Interrupted, the animal watched Travis with round-eyed interest, displaying neither alarm nor anger at his sudden appearance.

As the man edged forward, the creature freed one front leg, still clasping its prey in the other three, and flicked a fringe leg or two from its feather-clad paunch in absent-minded tidiness. Then folding its breakfast to its middle with the intermediary pair of forepaws, it leaped spectacularly from a sitting position, to be hidden in the brush.

"Rabbit—cat—owl—whatsis," Ross commented. "Wasn't afraid though."

"Means that it either hasn't any enemies—or none resembling us." Travis studied the curtain into which the fisher had plunged. "Yes, it's still watching—from over there," he added in a half whisper.

But the presence of the feather-clad feaster was in a way a promise of security along this road. Travis found the opening of the trail on the other side of the stream. And he was now better pleased to follow it, even though once more the tree ferns closed in overhead and he and Ross were swallowed in what was a tight tunnel of green.

The indications of a busy, hidden life about them continued to come in sounds. Twice they stumbled on evidence of some hunter or hunters working the trail. Once they found a fluff of plush-like gray fur still bedaubed with pinkish blood, then a clot of cream-yellow feathers and draggled skin.

There was an open apron about the funnel building. A fan of stone, dappled with red moss but not yet claimed in entirety by the jungle and the game trail, skirted this, running on past the building. If they were to continue to follow Ross's plan, they must strike back now into the jungle again and bull their way through its resilient mass. But first, for the benefit of any watchers, they crossed that moss-spattered apron to the building as if about to search its interior. Only there was no easy entrance here. A grill, of the same impenetrable material as that which formed the fan area before the door, forbade their entry. Through its bars they could see parts of the inside. Plainly this particular structure had been left furnished after a fashion, for objects, muffled in disintegrated coverings, crowded the floor.

Ross, his face pressed close to the bars, whistled. "I'd say they were getting ready for movers, only the vans never arrived. The chief'll want to break in here, might be some of his kind of pickings about."

"Better collect *him* first." Travis stood at the top of those four wide steps leading to the barred door. He could sight the tower which was their ultimate goal, though the fern trees shielded it for about three stories up. He saw no signs of life about it, nothing moved at any of the window holes. Yet there had been that light at yesterday's dusk.

"All right—we'll get to it!" Ross came away from the grill. He swung his arm wide in an extravagant gesture to mark not the goal of their choice but the block building beyond it.

They had to cut their way now, using weapons and their hands to pull and break a path between the small, isolated glades where the fall of some giant tree in the past had cleared a passable strip for them. Panting and floundering, they came to the fifth such clearing.

"This is it," Ross said. "We'll turn back from here."

Luckily the summit of the tower showed now and then as a guide. They were approaching it from the back, and by a freakish whim of nature there was less underbrush here. So they had to choose cover, watching the heights for any indication that some scout or spy might lurk aloft. Not that they could be certain of spotting an army under the circumstances, Travis decided gloomily, moving with the wariness of one expecting an ambush at any moment.

They had covered perhaps half of the distance which would bring them to the base of the tower when both of them were startled into immobility by a squall. The battle cry of the thing which had laired in the red hall! And the sound was so distorted by the jungle about them that Travis could not tell whether its source lay before or behind.

That first wail of battle was only the starting signal of a racket loud enough to split human eardrums. A bird thing boomed out of the brush, flew in blind panic straight for the two, blundered past them into safety. A graceful, slender creature with a dappled coat and a single curving horn flashed away before Travis was truly sure he had seen it.

But those howls of rage and blood hunger chorused on. There must be more than one of the beasts— perhaps a pack of them! And from the noise, they were engaged in combat. Travis could only think of Ashe cornered in the tower to face such an enemy. He began to run. Ross drew level with him before they plunged together into a hedge of brush, fighting their way in the straightest line to the base of the tower.

Travis tripped, staggered forward, fighting to regain his balance, and plowed on his hands and knees into the open. He was facing the entrance to the tower, a long, narrow slit of opening. From within came the sounds. Ross, weapon in hand, leaped past him, a blue streak of concentrated action.

The Apache scrambled up, was only a step or two behind the time agent as they entered, finding them- selves directly on the foot of an upward-leading ramp. One of those squalling roars, sounding above, ended in a cough. A mass of dull red fur and flashing legs rolled down. Its flat weasel's head snapped its jaws in convulsive death agony. Ross leaped aside.

"Blast beam got that one!" he shouted. "Chief! Ashe! You up there?"

If there was any answer to that hail, the words were drowned in the screech of the animals. The light was dusky here, but there was enough for the humans to spot the barrier across the ramp. It must have been there for some time. But now it showed a gap, choked by two of the red beasts struggling against each other in their eagerness to force the doorway. Behind them snarled a third.

Travis steadied the barrel of his weapon across his forearm and nicked a darting weasel-head with a sniper's expert aim. The thing did not even cry out, but reared and somersaulted backward down the ramp as the men jumped apart to give it room.

One of the creatures at the gap caught sight of the two below and pulled back, allowing its fellow through the barrier while it whirled to spring at Ross. His blast beam raked across its shoulders and it screamed hideously, collapsed and scratched frantically with its hind feet to gain footing. Ross fired again and the animal was still. But the rage of the fight beyond the barrier continued.

"Ashe!" Ross shouted. And Travis, catching his breath, echoed that call. To go through the gap in the barrier before them and perhaps be met by a blast from a friend was certainly not to be desired.

"Hullloooo!" The cry was weirdly echoed. It might be coming from ahead of them or above. But both of them had heard it. They pushed past the barrier into a wide hallway.

There was light here, coming from the white flames of smoking brands that lay on the floor at the far end as if tossed from a higher level. One of the red beasts lay dead. The men hurdled the body. Another, dragging useless hindquarters, crept with deadly purpose toward them and Travis picked it off. But the beam in his weapon died before he lifted finger from firing button. Another try proved his fears correct—the charge in the weapon was exhausted.

Something scrambled on the second ramp at the far end of the hall. Ross stood at the foot, his weapon up. Travis stooped to scoop up one of the torches. He whirled the brand in the air, bringing the smoldering end to life.

Ross aimed at a charging weasel-head, missed, flung himself to the side of the ramp and down to the floor to escape the rush. But the beast plunged insanely after him. Travis whirled the torch a second time, swinging its flaming end down against the snaky, darting head of the attacker.

One of those powerful forepaws aimed a vicious swipe that tore the torch from the Apache's hold. But Ross was up to his knees again, weapon ready. And the red animal died. Travis retreated, a little unsteadily, to pick up a second torch.

"Hullloooo!" Again that shout from overhead. Ross answered it.

"Ashe! Down here . . ."

There were no more squalls from the ramp. But Travis wondered if more of the beasts lay in wait. With a useless weapon he had no desire to climb into the unknown. A flint knife was nothing against the weasel-heads.

They waited, listening, at the foot of the ramp. But when there came no other attack, Ross pattered ahead and Travis followed, nursing his new torch. His hand shot out, closed on Ross's arm, as he caught up with the other. Something was waiting for them up there.

Travis thrust the torch into that pocket of gloom at the head of the ramp, saw Ross's weapon at ready—

"Come on in!" The words were ordinary enough, but Ashe's voice sounded a little breathless and in higher pitch than usual. But it *was* Ashe, unharmed and seeming his usual self, who stepped into the pool of light and waited for them to join him. Only he was not alone. Half-seen shadows moved behind him. Ross did not holster his weapon and Travis' hand rested on his knife hilt.

"You all right, chief?"

Ashe laughed in answer to Ross's demand. "Now that the space patrol has landed, yes. You boys introduced the right play at the proper moment. Come on and meet the gang."

The torch sputtered as those shadows moved in closer to Ashe. Then a new light blazed up well above floor level and Travis blinked at the company that fire revealed.

Ashe was six feet tall, giving Travis himself an inch or so. But in this company he towered, for the tallest of his companions came only a little above his shoulder.

"They have wings!"

Yes, with a sudden twitch a flap of wing—not feathered, but ribbed skin—had unfurled, pointing up above its owner's shoulder. Where had he seen a wing such as that? On the statue from the domed building!

However, the faces now all turned toward the humans were not as grotesque as the one of the image. The ears were not so large, the features were more humanoid, though the noses remained vertical slits. Either the statue had been a caricature, or it represented a far more primitive type.

The natives hung back, and from their narrow, pointed jaws came a low murmur, rising and falling, which Travis could not separate into distinct sounds or words.

"Local inhabitants?" Ross still held his weapon. "They the ones who kidnapped you, chief?"

"In a manner of speaking. I take it you accounted for the wild life below?"

"All we saw," Travis returned, still watching the winged people, for they were people, of that he was sure.

"Then we can get out of here." Ashe turned to the waiting shadows and holstered his own weapon with an emphatic slam. Two of the winged men beckoned and the rest stood back, allowing Ashe, Ross and Travis to pass them, to climb a third ramp. At the top the

humans saw open sunlight, and came out into a wide
hall with archways, not doors, down its length.

Travis' nostrils expanded as he caught a mixture
of scents, some pleasant, some otherwise. There was
activity here; there were indications of a permanent
settlement. The archways were hung with green nets
into which flowers had been tucked here and there.
Many were like the one he had found on his first
day of exploration. Hollowed logs made into troughs
stood about the walls. From these grew a mixture
of plants, all reaching toward the sun which came
through windows, forming a curtain of green from
floor to ceiling.

The people were no longer just shadows. And in
this brighter light their humanoid resemblance was
marked. The furled wings covering their backs might
have been folded cloaks. They wore no clothing save
ornaments of belt, collar or armlets. Their weapons,
which all within sight carried, were small spears—little
enough protection against the red killers who had
assailed them from below.

They watched the humans closely, keeping up their
murmur of speech, but making no threatening gestures. And since it was impossible for the humans to
read any expression on their faces, Travis did not know
whether the three from the ship were considered
prisoners, allies, or merely strange objects of general
interest.

"Here . . ." Ashe stopped before one of the cur-
tained archways and pursed his lips to give a gentle
hoot.

The curtain parted and he went in, signaling the
other two to follow him.

Under their feet was thick matting plaited from
vines and leaves. And there were low partitions of
latticework over which living plants climbed to form

dividing walls, cutting one large room into a series of smaller cubicles around a central space fronting the archway.

"Pay attention to nothing around the wall," Ashe said quickly. "Keep your eyes on the one at the table."

One of the winged men squatted by a table raised some two feet from the carpeted floor. Those they had seen in the outer hallway had had dusky lavender skins, close in shade to the stone from which the image had been carved. But this one was much darker, almost a deep purple. And the stiffness of his constrained movements suggested advanced age.

But when the native looked up to meet Ashe's gaze in welcome, Travis knew that this was not only a man, but a great man among his kind. It was there in his eyes, in the pride of his carriage, and in the slow deliberation with which he regarded the three humans.

15

"What a junkyard!" Ross stared about him in sheer stupefaction.

"Treasure house!" his chief corrected him almost sharply.

Travis simply stood between them and gazed. Perhaps both descriptions could apply in part.

"They kidnapped you to sort *this* out for them?" Ross demanded, as if he couldn't believe a word of that conclusion.

"That's the general idea," Ashe admitted. "Question is—where do we start, what do we have, and how can we get across to them the meaning of anything we do find—if we can make it out ourselves?"

"How long have they been collecting all this?" Travis wondered. There were paths through those piles of moldering materials, so one *could* investigate the contents of the heaps. But the general confusion of the mass was intimidating.

Ashe shrugged. "When your total method of

communication consists of gestures, a lot of ragged guessing, and pointing, how is anyone to know anything?"

"But why you? I mean—how are you supposed to know what makes all this tick, or thump, or otherwise run?" Ross asked again.

"We came in the ship. They may have some hazy tradition—legends—that the ship people knew everything."

"The Fair Gods," Travis threw in.

"Only we are not Cortez and his men," Ashe returned with a snap.

"They aren't the baldies, or that furry-faced operator I saw on the screen of the ship the Russians had. So where do they fit in?"

"Judging by that statue, their ancestors were known to the builders of the dome," Ashe replied. "But I think they are primitive, not decadent."

Travis' imagination made a sudden, swift leap.

"Pets?"

Both of the others looked at him. Ashe drew a deep breath.

"You might just be right!" The way he spaced his words gave them an impressive emphasis. "Give our world enough time and the right combination of conditions and see what could happen to our dogs or our cats."

"Are we prisoners?" Ross came back to the main point.

"Not now. Our handling of the weasels took care of that. A common enemy is an excellent argument for mutual peace. And we have a common purpose here, too. If we're going to find out anything which will help Renfry, it will be in just such a collection as this."

"It'd take a year just to shuffle through the top layer in this mess," Ross gave a gloomy opinion.

"We know what we are looking for—we have examples on the ship. Anything we can uncover in the process which might help our winged friends, we turn over to them. And who knows what we may find?"

Ashe was right about the attitude of the winged people. The chief or leader, who had first received them in the vine-walled room and brought them in turn into the huge chamber containing the loot gathered by his tribe, showed no unwillingness to let them return to the ship. But their path back, followed on ground and not by the aerial ways of the natives, was supervised by two of the blue flyers that had some link with the winged people—perhaps a relationship not unlike man and hound.

During his period of captivity Ashe had learned that the red weasels were the principal local menace and that the winged folk had tried to wall off the lower sections of their dwelling towers to baffle the hunters. These creatures had worked with sly cunning— which suggested a measure of intelligence on their part also—on the ramp barrier. But only a determined raid made by a whole pack had finally broken through that laboriously constructed wall to get at the living quarters of the flying people. Ashe's readiness to use his weapon on the behalf of his captors, plus the surprise attack by Ross and Travis had completely destroyed the marauding pack. These two things had also made a favorable impression upon the intended victims. As Ashe had commented, a common enemy was a firm base on which to build an alliance.

"But they can fly," Ross protested. "Why didn't they just take off—out the windows, and let those six-legged weasels have the place?"

"For a reason their chief was finally able to make plain. This is apparently the season during which their young are born. The males could have escaped, but the females and young could not."

They found Renfry awaiting their arrival at the ship in a fingernail-gnawing state of impatience. Relieved to see them whole and together, he greeted them with the news that he had managed to trace the routing of the trip tape through the control board. Whether he could reset another tape, or reverse the present one, he did not yet know.

"I don't know about rewinding this one." He tapped the coin-sized disk they had seen ejected from the board on the morning of their arrival. "If the wire breaks—" He shrugged and did not need to elaborate.

"So you'd like to have another to practice on." Ashe nodded. "All right, we all know what to look for when we start our digging into the treasure trove tomorrow."

"If any still exist." Renfry sounded dubious.

"Deduction number one." Ashe took a long pull from the froth-drink can. "I believe most of the stuff the winged folk have gathered came from towers such as the one that houses their village. And there are a number of towers here. The buildings of radically different design are not duplicated. Which leads you to surmise that the tower structures are native to this planet, while the other types represent imported architecture.

"When that pilot set the control tape to bring the ship here, he was setting course either for his home— or his service headquarters. Therefore, it is not too improbable to suppose that we can hope to come across something in that miscellaneous mixture of loot they've gathered which is allied to record tapes we have found on this ship. And I will not rule out journey wires among the litter."

"There are a lot of ifs, ands, and maybes in that," Renfry said.

Ashe laughed. "Man, I have been dealing with ifs and maybes for most of my adult life. Being a snooper into the past takes a lot of guessing—then the hard grind of working to prove your guesses are right. There are certain basic patterns which become familiar— which you can use as the framework for your guess."

"Human patterns," Travis reminded. "Here we do not deal with humans."

"No, we don't. Unless you widen the definition of human to include any entity with intelligence and the power to use it. Which I believe we shall have to do, now that we are no longer planet—or system—bound. Anyway, to hunt through the remains of the tower civilization is our first job.

The next morning found them all, Renfry included, back at the tower. And, in those patches of sunlight which entered the packed room, the job Ashe and the chief of the winged people had set them looked even more formidable.

That is—it did until the cubs, or chicks, or children of the natives turned up to offer busy hands and quick bright eyes to assist. Travis found himself the center of a small gathering of the winged halflings all watching him with eager attention as he tried to disentangle a pile of disintegrating objects. A pair of small hands swooped to catch a rolling container, another helper brought out a box. A third straightened a coil of flexible stuff which was snarled about the top layer of the pile. The Apache laughed and nodded, hoping that both gestures would be translated as thanks and encouragement. Apparently they were, for the youngsters dived in with a will, their small hands wriggling into places he could not reach. Twice, though, he had to hurriedly jerk some too-ambitious delver back from a threatened avalanche of heavy goods.

So much of what they uncovered, examined, and put to one side was either too badly damaged by time to be of any use, or else had no meaning for the humans. Travis struggled with the covers of crumbling containers and boxes. Sometimes he would see them go to dust with their contents under his prying hands; other times he would find their interiors filled only with powder that might have once been fabric.

Lengths of an alloy, fashioned into sections of pipe, he laid to one side. These seemed still intact and might be of use to the winged people, either as material for weapons more effective than their spears, or for tools. Once he came upon an oval box which flaked to bits in his hands. But it left mingled with the powder on his palm a glittering stone set in a scroll of metal, as untarnished and perfect as the day the jewel had been stored. His volunteer assistants hummed with wonder, so he gave it to the nearest, to see it passed from hand to hand and at last gravely returned to his keeping.

By noon none of the four humans, working in opposite corners of the big room, had found anything useful to their own purposes. They met under a window to share food supplies free of dust from the rubbish heap.

"I knew it was a year's job," Ross complained. "And what have we found so far? Some metal which hasn't rusted completely away, a few jewels—"

"And this." Ashe held out a round spool. "If I'm not mistaken, this is a record tape. And it may be intact. Looks something like those we found aboard the ship."

"Here comes the big boss," Ross said, glancing up. "Are you going to ask him for that?"

The chief who had brought them to this storeroom entered the far doorway with his escort. He moved slowly about the perimeter of the room to inspect the piles where the explorers had made such a small beginning. When he reached the humans they stood up, towering over both chief and escort. Though they did not share language and their communication was by gesture, Ashe went to work to suggest a few uses for the morning's salvage. The gems were understandable enough. And the metal tubes were examined politely without much interest.

Ashe spoke to Renfry across the chief's shoulder. "Any chance of working these into spears?"

"Given time—and tools—maybe." But the technician did not sound too certain.

Last of all Ashe displayed the spool, and for the first time the chief became animated. He took it into his own hands and hummed to one of the guards who went off at a trot. He tapped one finger on the red tape and then spread out all the digits several times, ending with a wide inclusive sweep of one arm.

"What's he trying to tell us, Ashe?" Renfry had been watching the performance closely.

"I think he means that this is only one of many. We may have made a real discovery."

The guard came back followed by a smaller, younger edition of himself. Taller than the children, the newcomer was apparently an adolescent. He saluted the chief with a clap of his wings and stood waiting until his leader held out the spool. Then, reaching out, the chief caught at Ashe's hand and put the youngster's in it—waving them off together.

"You going?" Ross wanted to know.

"I will. I think they want to show us where this came from. Renfry, you had better come too. You might be able to recognize a technical record better than I could."

When they were gone, the chief and his retinue after them, Ross looked about him with dissatisfaction written plain on his face.

"There's nothing worth grubbing for here."

Travis had picked up a length of the tubing, to examine it in the full light of the window. The section was four feet or so long and showed no signs of erosion or time damage. The alloy was light and smooth, and what its original use had been he did not know. But as he ran it back and forth through his hands an idea was born.

The winged men needed better weapons than the spears. And to make such weapons from the odds and ends of metals they had found in this litter required forging methods perhaps none of the visitors, not even Renfry, had the skill to teach. But there was one arm which could be made—and perhaps even the ammunition for it might also exist in the unclassified masses on the floor. It was not a weapon his own people had used, but to the south others of his race had developed it into a deadly and accurate arm.

"What's so special about that tube?" Ross asked.

"It might be special—for these people." Travis held it up, put one end experimentally to his lips. Yes, it was light enough to be used as he planned.

"In what way?"

"Didn't you ever hear of blowguns?"

"What?"

"The main part is a tube such as this—they're used mostly by South American Indians. A small splinter arrow is blown through and they are supposed to be accurate and deadly. Sometimes poisoned arrows are used. But the ordinary kind would do if you hit a vital point, say one of those weasel's eyes—or its throat."

"You begin to make sense, fella." Ross hunted for a section of pipe to match Travis'. "You plan to give these purple people a better way to kill red weasels. Can you make one to really work?"

"We can always try." Travis turned to the clustering children and gestured, getting across the idea that such sections of pipe were now of importance. The junior assistants scattered with excited hums as if he had loosed a swarm of busy bees in the room.

As Travis had hoped, he was also able to discover the necessary material for arrows there. Again their original use was unknown; but at the end of a half hour's search he had a handful of needle-slim slivers of the same light alloy as the pipes themselves. Since he had never built or used a blowgun and knew the principles of the weapon only through reading, he looked forward to a period of trial and error. But at last they gleaned from the room a wealth of raw materials for experiment. And they had not yet done when the youngster who had guided Ashe came back, to pull at Ross's sleeve and beckon the men to follow.

They wound from one ramp to another, passing the point where the weasels had breached. But they did not leave the tower. Instead their guide went to the back of the entrance hall, putting both hands to a seemingly blank wall and pushing. Travis and Ross, watching his effort, joined their strength to his and a panel slipped back into the wall.

Before them was not a room, but a more sharply inclined ramp descending into a well of shadow which increased in darkness until its foot could not be seen from their present stand. The winged boy took the downward path at a run. His wings expanded until they balanced his body and he skimmed at a speed neither of the humans was reckless enough to try to match.

Once they reached the foot of the descent, they

saw in the distance the smoky gleam of a native torch. And, guided by that, they ran along a narrow corridor where dust rose in puffs under their pounding feet.

The room of plunder in the tower above had housed unsorted heaps of bits and pieces. The place they now entered, where Ashe awaited them, was a monument to the precision and efficiency of the same race—or a kindred people—who had flown the ship.

Here were machines, banks of controls, dim, dark screens. And as the humans slowly advanced, the torch displayed racks and racks of containers, not only of record tapes, but of journey disks. Hundreds, thousands of those button spools which had brought them across space, were racked in cylinders with transparent tops and unknown symbols of the other people on their labels.

"Port control center—we think." Ashe may have temporized by adding those last two words, but there was a certainty in his tone which suggested he was sure. Renfry was filling the front of his suit with samples taken from both record containers and tape racks.

"Library . . ." Travis added an identification of his own.

Ashe nodded. "If we only knew what to take! Lord, maybe everything we want, we need—not only for now but for the whole future—is right here!"

Ross went to the nearest rack, began to follow Renfry's example.

"We can try to run these on the reader in the ship. And if we take enough of them, the odds are at least one or two should be helpful."

His logical approach to the problem was the sensible one. They went about the selection as methodically as they could, lifting samples from each rack of holders.

"A whole galaxy of knowledge must be stored here," Ashe marveled, as his fingers flicked one coil after another free.

They left at last, the fronts of their flexible suits bulging, their hands full. But before they left the tower, Travis also gathered up the lengths of pipe and the needle slivers. And when they were back in the ship, the reader set up, their plundered record rolls ready to feed, the Apache went to work on fashioning the weapon he hoped to offer to the winged people in return for their sharing of the stored wisdom.

Renfry, an array of small tools from the crew lockers aligned before him, was operating on one of the route disks. He pried off its cover and carefully unwound the thin wire spiral curled within. Twice he was doomed to disappointment, that fragile thread upon which a ship could cruise to the stars, snapped brittlely under his most careful handling. The second time that happened he looked up, his face drawn, his eyes red with strain.

"I don't think it can be done."

"There's this." Ashe reached for one of the waiting disk tapes. "Those you are working with are old. The one in the ship is new."

There it was again, the jog in time which might return them to their own world—or might not. But that reminder appeared to encourage Renfry. He checked the outside of his disks, pushing aside any which showed the pitting of years. His next choice did not look too different from the one which held their future locked into its spiral. For the third time he pried delicately to force off the case.

But it was not to be that night that they learned anything which was of value to them. The record tapes in the reader gave only a series of pictures, fascinating in themselves, but of no value now. And in addition there were others which merely flashed symbols—perhaps formulas, perhaps written accounts. At last Ashe snapped off the machine.

"We can't expect to be lucky all the time."

"There're thousands of those things stored in that place," Ross pointed out. "If we do find anything useful—it will have to be by luck!"

"Well, luck is what we have to count on in our game." Ashe's voice was tired, drained. He moved slowly, rubbing his hands across his eyes. "When you give up a belief in luck, you're licked!"

16

Travis set the mouthpiece of a blowgun to his lips and puffed. A thin, shining sliver, tipped with a fleecy tuft, sped—to hit on his improvised target of a red-veined leaf and pin it more securely to the trunk of a fern tree ten feet away. He was absurdly pleased with the success of his trial shot. He moved back another four feet and prepared for a second test. All the while the low humming of his enthralled native audience buzzed bee-fashion across the clearing.

When he was able to place a second dart almost beside the first, his satisfaction was close to complete. With a crooked finger Travis beckoned to the winged youth who had helped to carry the newly manufactured weapons to the testing ground. He handed over the tube he had just used, picking up a second, slightly longer, from the selection on the ground.

The young warrior laid his spear on the leaf mold, hooking his clawed toes over its shaft while he fumbled with the blowgun. Raising the weapon to his mouth, he gave a vigorous puff. Not as centered as Travis' shot had been, the sliver hit the tree slightly above the leaf. Two other natives, their wings unfolding slightly as they ran, hurried to inspect the target, and Travis, smiling and nodding, brought his hands together in a sharp clap of approval.

They needed no more urging to try this new weapon. Tubes were snatched, passed from hand to hand, with some squabbling on the outer fringes of the gathering. Then each took his turn to try shooting, with varying degrees of success. They halted from time to time to pick the target clean of ammunition, or put up another leaf over the tattered remnants of the last.

Several of Travis' pupils had sharpshooters' eyes, and the Apache believed that with practice they could far surpass his own efforts. When the midday sun bit down on the range, he left the blowguns with the enthusiastic marksmen and went to hunt up his crew mates.

Renfry was still buried in his study of journey tapes and the ship's circuits. But when Travis climbed to the control cabin he found Ashe there also. The reader was set up on the floor, and both of them were squatting before it, alternately watching some recording and making attacks on the main panel of the pilot's unit. The case of that had been removed, exposing an intricate wiring pattern. And from time to time Renfry traced one of those threads up or down and either beamed or frowned at the results of his investigation.

"What's going on?"

Ashe answered Travis. "We may have had our break! This record is a manual of sorts. It provides some wiring blueprints Renfry has been able to identify with that cat's cradle of cords up there."

"Some wiring." Renfry's enthusiasm did not match Ashe's at that moment. "About one line in ten! This is like trying to put together a missile head when all

your working instructions are written in Chinese code! Yeah—the red cord hits the plate there—but does it say anything about these white loop-de-loops to the left?"

Ashe squinted at the loops in question and consulted the record reader again. "Yes!" Renfry was down on his knees in an instant to see for himself the diagram on the picture screen.

"Anybody home?" Ross's voice floated up the well of the interior ladder, and Travis could feel the vibration of his footfalls on the rungs as he climbed.

His head and shoulders emerged from the stairwell. His dust-streaked face testified to his occupation of the morning as the investigator on duty in the crazy treasure house at the winged people's tower.

"Any luck?" Travis asked with some sympathy. Ross shrugged.

"A handful of stuff they may be able to use. I'm no big brain to string together some wire, nails and a couple of pieces of tin and produce a jet all set to fly. Saw your William Tells busy with those spitters of theirs. One of them had already bagged an addition to the dinner pot—not that the dear departed looked too edible. I don't care for things with about four dozen legs all clawing at once. But I could relish some more civilized food right now."

Travis glanced at Ashe and the dedicated Renfry. "If we have any today, looks as if you and I are elected to get it ready. They've discovered a record which shows the inside of the control board."

"Well—that's more like it!" Ross climbed the rest of the way into the cabin and stooped to look over Ashe's shoulder at the miniature screen. "I'd say it's closer to the plans for a demon-inspired highway system," he commented judiciously. "And I'll settle for a can of stew."

Renfry and Ashe were pried away and they ate in
the absent-minded fashion of men whose complete
interest was centered elsewhere. When they had gone,
Ross stretched and gazed at Travis.

"Care for a little look-see of our own?" he asked
with a casualness which aroused Travis' suspicion.

"In what direction?"

"That funnel place. Remember—the front hall is
packed as if the boys living there had been in a hurry
to move out, but had to leave their baggage behind?
I'd like to have a good look at the baggage."

"If I remember rightly, there is also a good stout
grill over the doorway," Travis reminded him.

"And I have a way to get around that. Come on."

Ross's way of passing the secured door was simple
enough. One of the natives flew to a second-story
window equipped with a coil of climbing cord from
the ship. He confronted a shutter across the window.
But prying with his spear point forced the latch on
that, and a few moments later the rope dangled down
the side of the building in open invitation to climb.

The gallery into which they so forced a way gave
many indications it had been hurriedly stripped. Some
ragged tatters of flimsy web, which fell to powder at
the touch of a finger, still hung on the walls. And there
were pieces of oddly shaped furniture shrouded in
dust. But the dust on the floor was marked in places
by tracks and, seeing those, their native companion
fingered his spear. Then, his eyes on the humans holding their attention, he drove it point down into the
pattern of that trail with the vigor of one making a
determined attack upon an enemy.

Another lair of the weasel things? Travis, studying
those tracks in the half gloom beyond the light from
the opened window, believed not. In fact, the marks
were disturbingly like a human footprint. And the

teasing picture provided by his imagination of some one of the old lords of this place lingering on to haunt its solitude, grew disturbingly in the back of his mind.

Here for the first time they found a stairway, though its treads were so narrow and steep as to make the humans believe that it had been built to accommodate bodies unlike their own. Ross, taking the lead, went down, his explorer's zeal well tempered with caution, in search of the crowded hall they had seen from without.

Travis sniffed. There was a faint fetid odor, not just the accumulated dust of centuries, leaf mold borne in by the wind, or the taint of some small animal lair. This was not only strong enough to be recent, but the stench was also vaguely familiar.

Warning of a weasel den? He did not think so. This was not quite so rank and compelling as the stench of the red-walled structure those beasts had taken for their own. And it was not the alien but inoffensive odor which clung to the winged people's quarters.

He noted that the nose flap of their native companion expanded, and the deep-set eyes in that lavender face glittered as they turned alertly from side to side. Not for the first time the Apache regretted the absence of a quick common form of communication. It had proved impossible for the humans to approximate the humming sounds which made up the natives' speech. And none of *them* in return appeared able to utter any recognizable word, in spite of all the coaxing and patient repetition of common nouns or action verbs.

The interior of the building was gloomy, though the hall into which they had descended received a greater measure of light from the door. Ross stepped out, skirting a pile of boxes. He laid his hand on the top one, his other hovering over the grip of his weapon.

Travis remained where he was. That smell—it tugged at his memory. They stood still, the winged youth freezing with them. Then a sudden gust of wind through the latticed doorway brought with it a warm, fresh reek and Travis knew—

"The sand people!" His words were a hiss of whisper but they carried the authority of a shout. What were the nocturnal creatures of the shrouded desert world doing here?

"You are sure?" To his surprise Ross questioned his identification no further than that.

"You don't forget a stink like that in a hurry." Travis' eyes were busy, surveying the pools of shadow about the crates and boxes piled in the hallway. Had anything moved out there? Were they being watched now by eyes which could see farther than their own in this dusk?

The hand of the native touched his arm, an appeal for attention. Travis' head swung slowly as he saw the other ready a spear. He fitted a dart in his blowgun.

"There is something—to the left." Ross's whisper was the thinnest trickle of sound. His blaster was pointed at that shadowy corner.

Then the hall came alive, a boiling up of forms from every likely and concealing cover. The attacking things shambled swiftly on four limbs like animals. Their silent advance carried with it an added horror in the fact that those slavering beasts—or their remote ancestors had once been—men!

A blast from Ross's weapon brought down three of the clumsy runners. A tentacle licked out and then a fourth attacker went down, a dart dancing in its hairy throat. Behind Travis the native ran back a few steps up stairs, launched out into the air with a beat of his wings. Wheeling over the enemy, he stabbed at the boneless middle limbs raised to drag him down with a concentration which hinted at a long enmity between the two species.

Ross cried out. A tentacle flicked from the shadows, coiled about his ankle and pulled, as he fought to keep his balance. He turned his weapon beam on that rope of living flesh. He was answered by a roar as the loop fell away. Then Travis' dart caught the thing which arose to its hind legs clawing for Ross's shoulders. The Apache shot as fast as he could insert darts into the pipe. Backed against the stairs, he now flailed out with his weapon as a club, clearing a space to drag Ross with him.

A tentacle had jerked the native's spear from his hold. Perching on one of the piles of boxes, he rocked back and forth on his refuge, beating his wings to hasten the tumble of the stack. He rose into the air just as the bulky containers crashed down across the foot of the stairway to provide the beginnings of a barricade.

"Weapon charge—exhausted," Ross panted. Gripping the barrel of the gun, he smashed the butt down on the round skull of a creature scrambling over the wreckage.

They retreated up the stairway. Travis kicked out, catching a hairy head under the chin, slamming its owner back and down to tangle with another eager attacker. The native sent a second pile of boxes crashing. Now he was flying back and forth over the ruck of the enemy's main body, bombing them with smaller packages snatched up from the heaps.

For a moment the humans were free. Taking advantage of that lull, they won back to the gallery where they had entered what might have proved a trap. The native shot up, over their heads. He stood on the sill of the open window to beckon them on, uttering excited hums which rose to a volume approaching squeaks.

Travis shouldered Ross behind him toward the exit. "I've only two more darts—get out quick!"

For a moment the other resisted, then his common sense took command and he ran for the window. Travis aimed a dart at a hunched shoulder and head just appearing above the stairs. But that missile only nicked a furred upper arm, and fangs showed in a gap which was no longer a man's mouth. Eyes, small, red with fury and yet alight—horribly so—with a spark of intelligence, spotted him.

He backed to the window. A lavender-skinned arm reached over his shoulder, a hand fastened on the blowgun, twisted at it, trying to pull the tube from his grasp. The native still kept his post on the sill; now he wanted the weapon.

And Travis, knowing that the other had a means of escape he himself did not possess, surrendered the blowgun, then boosted his body over and out on the rope. He watched the lavender back of their rear guard. Wings projected outside the frame of the window and they were raised, ready . . .

Then the native threw himself backward and out in a wild display of aerial gymnastics. His wings flapped wide, broke his fall and he soared again, spiraling upward as the first shaggy head protruded from the window. Hairy fists pawed at eyes which were apparently blinded by the sun. Ross had reached the ground, Travis was not far behind him. The rope swung vigorously, scraping him along the building, and he realized that those above were trying to draw him up.

The Apache let go, falling as relaxed as he could, and the lightened rope flapped wildly as it was jerked up into the window. But they were safely out in the day. He did not believe that the nocturnal creatures would pursue them into the light. However, as they crossed the strip of jungle to reach the ship, both of them applied their scoutcraft to discovering whether or not they were being tailed.

Ashe listened to their report frowningly. "It might be worse—if we were staying here."

Ross threw aside his useless weapon. "D'you mean we're getting out? When?"

"Another day—maybe two. Renfry is ready to try rewinding the tape."

For the first time Travis made himself face how much would depend upon the proper handling of that slender length of wire, how one small break would defeat their purpose and leave them exiled here forever. Or how a weakness which they could not see might develop in space, snapping their invisible tie with their home world, to set the ship drifting between solar systems an eternal derelict. *Could* Renfry rewind the spool? And if it were rewound—would it work in reverse? There could be no test flight. Once they raised ship from this spot, they were gambling with their lives on a very slender thread composed mainly of hope and an illogical belief in luck.

"You understand now?" Ashe asked. "Remember this—we can stay here."

They would be exiles for the rest of their lives, but they *would* be alive. There were enemies here, but they could set up an alliance with the winged natives, join them. Suddenly Travis got to his feet. He went to that compartment in the cabin where they had put the square of picture block which could tune in on a man's memory and make home visible to him. He had to know—whether the past had enough strength to push him into this greatest gamble of his life.

He held the slab between his hands, looked into its curdled depths. Soon he saw—red cliffs rising from the fringe of smoky green marking piñon—a blue sky—the hills of home. He could almost taste the bite of alkali dust in a rising wind, feel the swell of a horse's barrel between his legs. And he knew that he must take the chance . . .

In the end they all made the same choice. Ross summed up their feelings:

"Time travel—that is different. We're still on our own world. If something goes wrong and we're marooned back before history began—well, it'll give a guy a bad jolt, sure. Who wants to play around with mammoths when he's more used to jets? But still, he'd know pretty well what he was up against and that the people he'd meet would be his own species. But to stay here— No, not even if we get the job of playing gods for the winged people! They aren't our kind— we're visitors, not immigrants. And I don't want to be a lifetime visitor anywhere!"

They made a last trip to the record library transporting back to the ship and stowing away in every available storage place all the record tapes which appeared to be intact. The chief of the natives, delighted with the blowguns, allowed them to choose other objects from the tribe's treasure room. He only asked that they return in time, bringing with them new knowledge to share. They saw no more of the nocturnal creatures from the funnel-spired building— though they again took the precaution of sealing the ship at night.

"*Will* we be back?" Ross asked when Ashe came from his last meeting with the chief.

"Let us get home safely with this haul," Ashe returned dryly, "and someone will be back, all right. You can depend on that. Well, Renfry?"

The technician looked like a ghost of his usual self. Lines of tension that would probably never fade bracketed his mouth, marked the corners of his tired eyes.

His hands shook a little and he could not lift his drinking container to his mouth without hooking all ten fingers about it.

"The tape's rewound," he said flatly. "And the wire didn't break. Tomorrow I'll thread it ready to run. For the rest—we pray the trip out. That's all I can tell you."

Travis lay on his bunk that night—*his* bunk, *their* ship . . . The globe and its contents had grown progressively less alien when compared to what lay without. Around his wrist was a heavy band of red metal set with small sea-green stones in a pattern which suggested breaking waves, a gift presented to him by the winged chief at their formal farewell. He was sure that the lavender-skinned flying man had not fashioned that bracelet. How old was the ornament? And from what world, from the art of what forgotten and long-vanished race had it come?

They had not even scratched the surface of what was to be found in this ancient port. Had the jungle-cloaked city been the capital of some galaxy-wide empire, as Ashe suspected? They had had no time to explore very far. Yes, there would be a return—sometime. And men from his world would search and speculate, and learn, and guess—perhaps wrongly. Then, after a while there again would be a new city rising somewhere—maybe on his own world—which would serve as a storehouse of knowledge gained from star to star. Time would pass, and that city, too, would die. Until some representative of a race yet unborn would come to search and speculate—and guess. Travis slept.

He awoke swiftly, with a quick sense of urgency. Over his head he heard the sigh of the speaker from the control cabin.

"All ready," came Renfry's voice, thin, drained. Why,

the technician must have worked through the night, eager to prove his handiwork.

"All ready."

They still had time to say "no" to this crazy venture, to choose known perils against the unknown. Travis felt a surge of panic. His hands levered against the bunk, pushing his body up. He had to stop Renfry—they must not blast into space.

Then he lay down once more, made his hands clasp the bunk straps across his body, his lips pressed tightly together. Let Renfry push the proper button—soon! It was the waiting which always wore on a man. He felt the familiar vibration, singing through the walls, through his body. There was no going back now. Travis closed his eyes and tried not to stiffen his whole body in protest against that waiting.

17

"We're out—safely."

"So far—so good." Another voice made answer to
that over the com system.

Travis opened his eyes and wondered if anyone ever
became fully inured to the discomfort of a planetary
take-off. He had forgotten during the past days when
they had been comfortably earth-bound what it meant
to be wrenched into the heights beyond the atmos-
phere and gravity. But at least the tape had worked
to the extent that they had lifted safely off world.

And their flight continued, until at length they all
breathed easier and began to hold more confident
feelings than just hope concerning their future.

"If we simply repeat the pattern," Ashe observed
thoughtfully on the evening of the fifth day, "we set
down again on the desert world sometime tomorrow."

"Be better if we could eliminate that stop," Travis
remarked. There was something in the desolate waste
and the night things which repulsed him as nothing
else had during this fantastic voyage.

"I've been thinking . . ." Ross glanced across the swinging seat to the pilot's perch where Renfry spent most of his waking hours. "We refueled on the trip out—at the first port. Suppose—just suppose that we exhausted the supply there."

Renfry grinned, a death's-head stretch of skin across bones. His thumb jerked downward in the immemorial gesture of sardonic defeat. "Then we've had it, fella. Let's hope that we can stretch our luck past that particular point along with all the rest of the elastic tricks."

This time they downed on the desert port in the early morning, when the lavish display of flames along the horizon was paling into nothingness. They saw the blaze of the rising sun reflected too brightly from the endless drifts of sand.

"Two days here, roughly—*if* we do duplicate the pattern exactly."

Waiting two days, cooped up in the ship, not sure that they *would* take off again. At the thought of it, Travis shifted restlessly in his seat. And the specter Ross had evoked shared the narrow confines of the cabin with them all.

"Any walk-about?" Ross must be feeling it too—that goading desire to be busy, to drown in action everpresent fears.

"Not much reason for that," Ashe replied calmly enough. "We'll take a look outside—in daytime. Not that I believe there is much to see."

The sun-repelling helmets on, they opened the outer hatch. They surveyed the expanse where the winds might have whittled new patterns among the dunes, but where they could see no change since their last visit. The enigmatic sealed buildings still squatted beyond, with no sign of life about.

"What *did* they do here?" Ross's hands moved restlessly along the frame of the exit port. "There was some reason for this stop—there had to be. And why were those same things—people, animals, whatever they are—or were—on the other world, in the funnel-topped building?"

"Which are the exiles?" Ashe asked. "Is this their home world, while those others exist across the void and have for generations because they were not recalled in time? Or are these the exiles and the others are at home? We may never know the reason or answer to any questions about them." He studied the squat building among the creeping dunes. "They must live underground, with the building covering the entrance. Perhaps they live underground on the other planet also. Once they must have been here to service ships—to maintain some necessary outpost."

"And then," Travis said slowly, "the ships didn't come any more."

"Yes. There were no more ships. Perhaps a whole generation waited—hoping for ships—for recall. Then they either sank into apathy and stagnation, to slide down the hill of evolution, or they more consciously adapted to their surroundings."

"In the end, the result was the same," Ross observed. "I don't think those here are any different from the ones in the funnel building. And there they had a better world to adapt to."

"Wait!" Travis had been studying that sand-enclosed block with interest. Now he thought that his memory of the place as it had been weeks earlier did not match what he saw now. "Was that elevation on the left there before?"

Ross and Ashe leaned forward, their attention settling on the end of the structure he indicated.

"You're right, that's new!" Ross's affirmation came first. "And I don't think that projection is made of stone like the rest, either."

The block which had so oddly appeared on the corner of that distant roof did not flash like metal in the sun's rays. But neither was it dull. There was a sleek sheen to it, such as might be displayed by opaque glass or obsidian. The hump had no openings that they could see, and what its purpose might be remained as much of a mystery as the rest of this age-old puzzle.

It remained so for only a few moments. Then came action the watchers in the ship did not expect. They had seen the rays which protected the roof of the building against assault or investigation. Now they witnessed the use of another aggressive weapon belonging to the men who had first erected that block.

What was it which lashed out, cracked a whip's thong about the skin of the ship? A beam of fire? A bolt of energy? A force which the humans could neither imagine nor name?

Travis only knew that the energy wash of that blow crushed him back into the globe, hurled him into the inner door of the lock with Ross and Ashe thrust tight against him. Their bodies were flattened on the metal wall of the ship until the breath was forced from their lungs and the world went black about them.

Travis was on the floor, fighting for the air his body had to have, pain in bands about his chest. And before his blurred eyes was the open door of the port. In that moment all that mattered was that oblong of emptiness. Beneath the torture of his body, he knew that that space must be shut out for what lay beyond it meant final extinction.

He clawed at the body across his knees, turned over somehow and inched painfully from under its weight, moving in a worm's progress toward the outer port. There was a singing in his ears, filling his head, adding to his daze. Then he was staring out into the glare of sun and sand.

At first he thought he was lightheaded. What he was seeing could not be true. For there was no wind, yet from the hidden floor of the landing space sand was rising in thin, unwavering sheets, walling in the globe. And those curtains of grit arose vertically, unmoved by any breeze! It could not happen—yet before his eyes it did.

He lunged to his knees, thrust against the door, shut out the curtains of sand, the harsh light of the sun, the thing which could not be true. And as his hands fumbled to shoot home the alien bolts, the pain lessened. He could breathe again without the constriction which had held his lungs imprisoned. He turned to the other two.

Alarmed by the congested blueness of their faces, Travis jerked both men up into a sitting position against the wall. Ashe's blue eyes opened.

"What—?" He only got out that one faint word as Travis turned his attention to Ross.

There was a thin thread of blood trickling from the corner of the younger scout's slack mouth. He moaned as Travis shook him gently. Ashe moved and winced, his hands going to his chest.

"What happened?" He was able to get out the whole demand this time.

"The space—marines—landed." Ross's lips shaped the words one at a time. There was a shadow of a grin about them. "—On me, I think."

"Hullloooo down there!" The call was disembodied over the ship's com, but it was imperative. "What's going on?"

Although the hull could cut out sun, sound, and the world without, they could now feel movement through its layers of protection. It was as if the ship were being buffeted by some force. Those walls of sand? Travis hauled himself to the ladder wall and began to climb, seeking the screen by the controls which was now their only link with outside.

He discovered Renfry standing before that link, his disbelieving eyes on thick curdles of sand, sand rising from the ground with steady purpose to engulf the ship. They were on the point of being buried in a sea of grit, and there was no reason to believe that that was not directed, consciously, by active animosity and intelligence.

"Can we get out?" Travis dragged himself to the nearest seat. "Any way to up ship?"

If the tape governed their departure according to the earlier schedule, they were stuck here for another night, another day. By that time the globe could be so deeply buried that there would be no hope of blasting free from the tons of sand. They would be sealed into a living tomb.

Renfry's hands went out to the keyboard of the controls, hesitated there. His lips tightened.

"It's a big risk but I could try."

"It'll probably be a bigger risk to stay." Travis remembered the two he had left at the lock. They must be brought out of danger before the shock of blast-off. "Give me five minutes," he said. "Then blow—if you can!"

He found Ashe on his feet, dragging Ross out into the corridor. Travis hurried to help.

"Renfry is going to try to blast off," he reported. "We're being buried in sand."

They got Ross to a bunk. Ashe flopped into the adjoining one, and Travis barely made it to the next cabin and the waiting cushion there, when the warning shrilled through the com. There was the vibration of laboring engines. But it went on far longer than before. Travis lay tense, willing the wrench of blast-free to come, counting off seconds . . .

The vibration was building up—higher than he had ever known it to go before. And the ship rocked on its base, movement and sound becoming one, a sickening mixture which churned the stomach, deadened thought but not fear.

The break came in an instant of prolonged red agony. Afterward came blackness—nothing at all . . .

Vibration was gone, sound was gone—but sensation remained. And the clean, aromatic scent of the healing jelly which filled the bunks on occasion of need. Travis opened his eyes. Had they pulled free from the desert planet?

He sat up, brushing the jelly from him. It slid easily from his skin, from the suit, leaving the usual well-being of mind and body. The confidence which had been jolted out of him had already flooded back. He got to his feet, went to peer into the neighboring cabin.

Ashe and Ross still lay inert under the quivering mounds of that substance on which the aliens had based their first aid. He climbed to the control cabin.

Renfry was strapped into the pilot's chair, but his head lolled limply on his shoulders, his white face alarming Travis. His questing fingers found a slow pulse. He unfastened the technician and somehow managed, with the aid of weightlessness, to get him to his bunk below. The screen presented only that swirl of dead black which was the sign of hyperspace. They had not only broken loose from the sand trap, they were also embarked on the next leg of the long journey which might or might not take them home.

How long had that portion of the journey lasted before? Nine days by Renfry's watch—nine days between the sand and the fueling port. Nine days until they could be sure that Renfry's blast-off had not thrown the tape off course.

As they recovered from that shock Ashe took command, using the loot they had gathered from the storehouse of records to focus their interest outside themselves. On the plea of hunting another ship's operation manual, he set them to work in shifts at the record reader, processing every tape which could still be run through that machine. More than one promising coil broke, whipped into a tangle they did not dare try to unravel. But even those must be kept for the experts at home to study. For Ashe never admitted after their break from the desert world that they were *not* going to get home. He pointed out that the odds they had already licked totaled a formidable sum and that there was no reason to believe that their luck would not continue to hold.

But even Ashe, Travis thought to himself, *must* have doubts, be as nervous as the rest—though he did not show it—when Renfry's watch marked the ninth day's flight and they had no warning of arrival at the fueling port. They made only a pretense of a midday meal. Travis had calculated rations just that morning. By going on very slim supplies, they would have enough of the food they dared use to see them home—*if* the voyage was not prolonged. He reported that fact to Ashe and received only an absent-minded grunt in reply.

Then—as if to prove all their worst forebodings untrue—the warning came. Travis strapped down, sharing quarters with Ross this time. The other grinned at him.

"The chief's called it right again! Here we go for a shot of gas from the service station—then home!"

Even the discomfort of landing could be forgotten when they did see about them the ruined towers marking off landing spaces, the metallic turquoise sky of their first galactic port. Why, they were almost home!

They clattered down to the space lock and opened it eagerly—to watch for the creeping snake of the fuel line and its attendant robot. But long moments went by and there was no movement in the shadow of the nearest tower. Travis studied the immediate terrain. Had they set down in the same square they had visited before? Might a change in so slight a matter provide the reason for the silence about them?

"Could be due to the time element." As Ashe's voice sounded in his helmet com, the old man might have been reading his thoughts. "We left the second stop well ahead of our former schedule."

They clung to that hope as an hour, and then two, passed and there was no movement from the tower. Pooling their recollections of the place, they were fairly certain that they had landed in the same square. And they avoided putting into words the other dire possibility—that the mechanism of the ancient port had at last been exhausted, perhaps by the very effort put upon it weeks before when the globe had been serviced there.

Renfry spoke at last. "I don't know how much fuel we have on board. I can't even tell you the nature of that fuel. And whether we *can* take off without more is also an open question. But if we can, I don't believe we'll be able to finish the trip. We may be working against time—but we'll have to discover if we can push those machines into one more job. And we'll have to do it quick!"

They swung out of the globe, and Renfry crawled under its arching side, to discover a new catastrophe. If there had been any fuel left in the ship's sealed storage compartments, it was gone now. There was an ominous damp patch spreading from an opening at ground level.

Renfry's voice came hollowly. "That's done it, fellas. She's empty. Unless you can get that pipe line on the job again, we're grounded for keeps."

"What made that open up?" Ross wondered with the bafflement of one to whom machines were still mysterious save for their most obvious functions.

"Might be some mechanism triggered by this." Ashe stamped on the pavement. "Well, let's go and look for the robot and that animated pipe line."

They walked toward the tower. From ground level the structure looked even more pointed and needle-like. There was an opening at the foot, the doorway from which the robot had come. Ashe reached that and stood for a moment peering in.

The chunky robot which had clanked into duty at their first visit was still there, just within the door-way. And beyond, plain to be seen in a rusty, yellowish light, were a corporal's guard of its fellows. All alike, they were backed against the far wall as if awaiting some long-past official inspection.

From a well in the center of the floor, to be glimpsed around the bulk of the robot in the door-way, was a massive piece of metal which Travis rec-ognized as the "head" of the snake pipe line. Ashe reached out almost reluctantly to push the robot. To their surprise the machine, which had appeared so massive and immobile answered to that handling. It did not react the way a shaken alarm clock would. Instead it toppled forward, oddly flaccid. One of the arms clattered loose and spun across the pavement to strike the snake's head.

"It's moving! Look—it's moving!"

Ross was right. In a jerky, sullen manner the heavy end of the mobile pipe line raised, inched forward about a foot while the humans held their breaths in hope—until it fell supinely once more.

"Hit it again," advised Ross.

Ashe edged around the prostrate robot to inspect more closely what they could see of the pipe. This small portion displayed no signs of deterioration. He stooped, took a good grip on the "head" and tugged. Then he hurriedly jumped back while Ross and Travis kicked the robot out of the path of the creeping snake. Two feet—three—out in the open it went—and headed for the ship. Renfry saw them coming and waved, crawling back under the bulge of the globe to make ready for the pipe's arrival.

But they had exulted too soon. Some four feet away from the tower the head sank to earth once more. Ashe tried his former method of revival, without result. They took turns shaking it, together and separately. It was much heavier than the robot and they could not urge it into any further effort.

Renfry came to join in a consultation. He went back to inspect the well from which the pipe emerged, only to return as baffled as before.

"Can we pull it by hand?" Travis wanted to know.

"That's what we'll have to try now." Renfry was grim.

Bringing the light, tough rope from the ship, they fastened lines about the "head," and set to work. At Ashe's command they gave a concentrated jerk. The stubborn pipe gave, started forward, but not under its own power. They gained another four, five feet but the effort required to move that dead weight was exhausting. Now their gains were shorter, and the strain they must exert to produce them grew greater and greater.

Ross tripped, went down, levered himself up, his face set in a snarl. He seized the rope again as if it

were a man he could tangle with—and jerked in con-
cert with the other three. This time there was no
yielding at all, and their feet slipped on the cracked
and age-old stone.

18

Travis sat back on his heels in the immemorial position of the dismounted range rider. The others sprawled beside the tow rope, their faces beet red from their efforts. Renfry squirmed, braced himself on his hands and began to fumble with the latch of his helmet. He threw the bubble back and breathed hard with the immediacy of a drowning man.

"Put on your helmet, you fool!" Ashe raised his head from his arms; his voice in the com was broken by the laboring of his lungs.

But Renfry shook his head, his lips moving in words sealed away by the protection he no longer shared. Travis' fingers went to the fastenings of his own helmet.

"I don't think we need these." He pulled off the bubble and lifted his head to meet the touch of a small, playful breeze. The air was crisp, like that of a Terran autumn. And it filled his lungs in an invigorating way. He reached for the rope, ready to try again.

"There's no use in pulling ourselves blind." Ashe's

voice was no longer rendered metallic by the alien com. "The trouble may lie back in the tower."

Renfry began to crawl on his hands and knees back the length of the pipe, inspecting its surface as he went. At last he staggered to his feet and lurched through the door, the others after him.

They found the technician down by the mouth of the well from which the pipe extended. He was examining the covering there, trying to wriggle the flexible tube back and forth.

"The thing must be caught—below this!" He hammered his fist against the capping.

"Can we get that lid off and see?" Ross wanted to know.

"We can try."

But such an operation required tools of a sort— levers, wedges . . . There was the line of waiting robots—could parts of their bodies be put to more practical purposes? Ross had picked up a loose "arm," shed by the one which had disintegrated, testing the rod's strength with all the force of his own arm and shoulder.

Travis studied the well capping. There was no opening, no vestige of crack into which a wedging tool might be inserted. And now Renfry ran his hands about the ring through which the pipe issued, striving to find by touch what none of them could see. He tapped with the rod, first lightly and then with increasing force, leaving some dents and scratches, but making no other impression on the fitting.

"Does that unscrew?" Ross suggested.

Renfry scowled, spat out a couple of short and forceful words. He transferred his efforts from the pipe to the outer rim of the cover. And there he did make a promising discovery. They worked fast, one at each, to pick the accumulated dust of centuries out of four depressions in which were sunk knobs which might just be the heads of bolts.

Then they turned to the broken robot, dismantled its remains, until they were equipped with pieces of metal to force those heads. It was slow, disheartening work. Once Travis went back to the ship to gather up the containers of the jelly which had poisoned him during the testing of the supplies. They smeared the stuff in and around the stubborn knobs, hoping it would lubricate and loosen, while they pounded and prodded. But their efforts were encouraged when the first bolt yielded, and Renfry used blistered fingers to work it free. And that small success gave a spurt to their labors.

It was nightfall and they were working mainly by touch when Ashe's bolt came free—the second one.

"This is it for now," he told them. "We can't rig any sort of light in here and there's no use in trying to free the rest in the dark. I've hit my fingers more than this blasted thing for the past half hour."

"Time may be running out on the journey tape," Ross answered tightly. He was putting into words one of the two fears which grinned over their shoulders during all those hours of punishing labor.

"Well, we aren't going to lift without fuel." With a sharp exclamation and a hand to his back, Ashe stood up. "And we can't work on in the dark without rest or food. Those things we know—the rest we're just guessing at."

So they stumbled back to the ship, realizing only when they stopped the battle with the stubborn casing how deeply tired they were. Travis knew that Ashe was right. They could not hope to lick the problem by driving their bodies past the point of human endurance.

They ate more than the proper rations for the meal,

wavered to their bunks and collapsed, drunk with
fatigue. And Travis was still stiff in the morning. No
healing jelly had soothed him. He awakened to Ross's
shaking and blinked foggily up at the other's thin face.

"Back to the salt mines, brother!" Ross put the
blackened and torn nail of an abused finger to his
mouth. "I could do with a blowtorch now. Climb out
of your downy bed, but fast, and join the slave gang."

It was midmorning before they worked the fourth
and last bolt out of its bed. And for a long moment
after Renfry threw it from him with emphatic force,
they just sat about the rim of the well, their torn
and blistered hands hanging limply between their
knees.

"All right." Ashe roused. "*Now* let's see if she'll
come up!"

To get levers to raise the cover they had to dismantle two more of the robots. And they carried out
that destruction with savage satisfaction. Somehow,
attacking the unresisting semi-manlike forms gave
them release from some of the frustration and fear.
They got stout bars and went back to attack the well
cover.

They never knew afterward how long it took them
to pry that plug out of its bed. But a last frantic heave
on the part of all, together, suddenly snapped it apart
in two halves, displaying the dark hole from which the
pipe arose.

Though it was day outside, as brilliantly clear a day
as the one before had been, the interior of the tower
was not too well lighted and they had no torch to
explore those depths. Renfry lay down, to thrust both
arms into the well, running his hands along the surface of the pipe as far as he could reach.

"Find anything?" Ashe crouched beside him, peering over one shoulder.

"No . . ." And then he changed that to an excited, "Yes!"

"I can barely touch it—feels as if the scaled coating on the pipe is caught." He wriggled and Travis caught hold of his legs to anchor him.

In the end Renfry did the rest of the tedious job painfully, with frequent halts for rest. He hung head down in that pit, kept from wedging his head and shoulders in too tightly by the others' hold on him. He had to work mainly by touch, since his own body blocked out three-quarters of the already subdued light, and with improvised tools hurriedly culled from the litter about them.

The fourth time they pulled him out for a breather, he rolled over on his back and lay gasping. "I've pried the thing loose as far down as I can reach." His words came one by one as if he could barely summon up the strength to push them out. "And it's still fast farther down."

"Maybe we can work it loose, pulling from up here." Ashe's hands curved about the scaled surface of the pipe where it projected over the side of the well.

"You can try." Renfry rubbed his fists across his forehead as Travis, with a heave he tried to make gentle, moved the technician's dead weight away from the side of the opening, to put his own hands overlapping Ashe's.

Together they strained to move the column of the pipe inside the tube of the well. But it appeared glued to the side where Renfry had fought to free it. Beads of sweat gathered along the line of black hair above Travis' forehead, trickled down to sting across his lips. And in the half-light he saw Ashe's jaw line set—sharp under the thin brown skin—while the cords and muscles of his arms and shoulders stood out to be modeled under the fabric of the blue suit.

Then Ross added his weight to the effort. "You pull," he told Ashe. "Let us push in your direction. If it is ever going to give, that ought to do it."

For a long, long moment it seemed that the pipe was not going to give, that too much damage existed below. Then Ashe flew back, the hose striking him hard in the chest as the obstruction below gave way and Ross and Travis sprawled halfway across the opening.

They scrambled up and Ross hurried to pull Ashe free of the hose. With Renfry trailing, they went back to the outer air of the port. They took up the towrope once again and began the labor of dragging the hose to meet the ship. The scaled pipe moved sluggishly, but they were winning, foot by painful foot.

Then Travis, during one of their all-too-frequent halts, glanced back and cried out. They were three-fourths of the way to their goal, but from under the belly of the hose snake was spreading a stain of moisture which gleamed in the afternoon light. That last rip to free the tube must have weakened its fabric and the unknown fuel was being lost.

Renfry stumbled back, knelt to explore, and jerked one hand away with a cry of pain. "It's corrosive— like acid," he warned. "Don't touch it."

"Now what?" Ross kicked dirt over the stain, watched the soil crumble into slime in the dark smear of fluid.

"We can get the pipe on to the ship—and hope that enough of the fuel comes through," Ashe answered in a colorless voice. "I don't think we can hope to mend the hose."

And because they could see no other way out, they went back to hauling at the towrope, trying not to glance back or think of the fuel seeping out of the pipe line. Renfry nursed his burnt hand against his chest until they at last pushed the end of the hose under the curve of the globe. He got down and crawled under, grunting with pain as he fastened the head of the snake against the opening in the ship.

"Is it feeding through?" Ross asked the all-important question.

Renfry, almost as if he dreaded the answer, put his good hand palm-down on the scaled side of the pipe, holding it there for a long moment while they waited to know the future.

"Yes."

They had no idea how much fuel the ship required— or whether the necessary amount was still available. The moist seepage along the hose continued to spread. But Renfry lay with his hand on the pipe, nodding to them from time to time that the feed of fluid was still in progress.

There came a pop like a small explosion. The head of the pipe dropped from the opening in the ship, the hose now flaccid. Renfry tapped and hammered at the cap which had slid into place, pulling down over it a second protective lock. When that clicked under his efforts he rolled out.

"That's that. We've all we're going to get."

"Is it enough?" Travis wanted to ask—to demand. But he knew that the others were as ignorant as he of the proper answer.

They straggled back to the port ladder, somehow pulled themselves up, and made their way in a blind haze of fatigue to the cabin bunks. What they could do they had done—now their success was back again in the hands of blind fortune.

Travis roused out of a doze. The vibration in the walls— They were bound off-planet again! But were they heading home? Or would that unknown fuel only take them into space, abandon them there to drift forever?

He dreamed—of red cliffs and sage, piñon pine, and the songs of small birds in a canyon. He dreamed of the feel of a desert wind against one's body and the surge of horse muscles between one's legs—of a world before mankind aspired to space. And it was a good dream, so good a one that even when it drifted from him after the way of dreams, Travis lay very still, his eyes closed, trying to will it back again.

But the sterile smell of the ship was in his nostrils, the feel of the ship was under his hands, closing around his body. And his old claustrophobic dislike of the globe was reborn with an intensity he had almost forgotten. He opened his eyes with a forced effort.

"We're still on the beam." Ross sat on the bunk opposite, his face hollow with strain under the blue light. He held up his hands. Both normal and scarred fingers were crossed, and he laughed as he so displayed them. "Soup's on," he added.

They counted the ration tins again that day. The contents of those few containers must be stretched to the limit now. Ashe measured out the portions which must serve for nourishment each waking period.

"We will just have enough if the time element remains the same. Stay in your bunks as much as possible—the less energy you burn the better."

But a man could sleep just so much. And however earnestly they pursued that escape, there came a time when sleep fled and one could only lie, staring up, or with closed eyes, while lone minutes of waiting stretched into hours, always darkened by fears.

"I was thinking," Ross spoke suddenly into the silence of the cabin he shared with Travis, "when we come in we should show up on the radar screens before we land. It'll be just like some bright boy to loose off a missile, just for practice. We can't possibly signal that we're only space travelers coming home."

"We're armed." But Travis wondered what defenses the globe *did* have. He knew little about missiles. Their government—other governments—could have any number of unpleasant surprises waiting to greet air-borne craft which could not adequately identify themselves.

"Dream on." Ross sounded scornful. "I don't see *us* knocking down everything shot at us with those cannon. We don't even know how to aim the things!"

They broke out of hyperspace, that period of discomfort heightened by their weakened condition. But in spite of that weakness, they dragged themselves to the control cabin to watch that cloudy blue ball grow on the vision screen. Travis discovered he was shaking, feeling almost as ill as he had during the food-testing session. Was that blue ball—home? Dared they believe so—or was it a mirage they were all sharing now because they wanted it so badly? Just as the picture device of the aliens could reproduce any man's home site to lighten his loneliness?

But now the familiar lines of the continents sharpened. Ross's head went down, his face hidden in his hands. And Ashe spoke slowly certain measured words Travis knew, though they were no part of his own heritage. Renfry's hands ran back and forth along the edge of the control board, caressingly.

"She did it! She's brought us home!"

"We aren't down yet!" Ross didn't lift his head and his words were sharp, as if perhaps he could insure their eventual safe landing by his very doubt of it.

"She brought us this far," Renfry crooned. "She'll take us the rest of the way. Won't you, old girl?"

They met the jolt of the break into Terran atmos-phere, accepted it, half numbed, still unbelieving. Ross released his hold on the chair, made for the well of the ladder.

"I'm going down." He averted his eyes from the screen as if unable to watch any longer.

And suddenly Travis shared the other's distrust of that window on space. He followed Ross, swinging down the ladder to their cabin, throwing himself prone in the bunk to await their landing—*if* there would be a safe landing.

The thin vibration of a take-off motor was nothing to the pressure of air against the globe skin now. It raised a hum which sang in their ears, through every atom of their tense bodies. All the waiting they had man-aged to put behind them was nothing compared to this last stretch they could not measure by any clock. The feeling that something might—would happen—to negate all their hard-won safety gnawed deep.

Travis heard Ross mutter on the other side of the cabin but could distinguish no words. What were they doing now? Racing night or day around the surface of their world, trying to home on the spot from which the alien journey tape had lifted them weeks ago?

Seconds crawled—minutes—hours ... One could measure this only by uneven breaths drawn with dif-ficulty as the weight of gravity pulled once more. Were they now registering on radar screens, hostile and friendly alike, summoning a net of missiles to fence them off from the firmness of solid earth? Travis could almost picture the rise of such a rocket, trailing a spear tail of fire—coming in—

He cringed as he lay in the bunk, the soft padding rising about his gaunt body.

"Coming down."

Had those words sounded through the ship's com? Or were they only an echo of his own imagination?

He felt the pressure against the padding, the squeeze of chest and lungs, harder to bear because of his weakness. But he did not black out.

There was a jar, the ship rolled, settled slightly aslant. Travis' hands moved to the straps about him. There was complete silence. He was loathe to break it, hardly daring to move—somehow unable even now to believe that they *were* down, that under them must rest the brown soil of his own earth.

Ross sat up jerkily. Freeing himself from the protective harness of the bunk, he made for the door. He walked like a sick man, driven by some overwhelming force outside himself.

His voice came as a whisper. "Got—to—see . . ."

And then Travis knew that he must see also. He could not accept any evidence except that of his own eyes. He followed Ross along the corridor—to the inner lock. And when the other fumbled at the closing, he added his own strength to open it.

They went through the air lock, grabbed at the outer port almost together. Ross was shaking, his head hunched between his shoulders, his face gray and wet.

It was Travis who opened the door. They were facing east and the time must be early dawn, for there was a belt of shadow beneath the curve of the ship while on the horizon light banners spread pale gold. He dropped down, his eyes on that band.

"Company coming." Ross swept out an arm. There was a soaring rumble of sound. A quartet of planes in formation cut across the light patch of sky.

There were spotlights flashing on around the ship— flooding away the shadows. Now Travis could pick out a buckled framework, signs of a disaster. And among the wreckage men were moving, drawing in to the star ship. But beyond them the sun was rising. His sun—rising to light his world! They had made it against all the stacked odds. Travis' hand smoothed the skin of the globe beyond the frame of the open port, as he might have smoothed the arched neck of the pinto that had brought him through a grueling day's ride on the range.

The sun was yellow on the distant hills. And they were the good brown earth of home!

Andre Norton

"The sky's no limit to Andre Norton's imagination...a superb storyteller." —*The New York Times*

Time Traders   0-671-31952-3 ★ $24.00 HC
                                     0-671-31829-2 ★ $6.99 PB

"This is nothing less than class swashbuckling adventure—the very definition of space opera." —*Starlog*

Time Traders II   0-671-31968-X ★ $19.00

Previously published in parts as *The Defiant Agents* and *Key Out of Time*.

Warlock   0-7434-7151-2 ★ $7.99

Three novels featuring one of the most memorable worlds in SF.

Janus   0-7434-3553-2 ★ $15.00 Trade PB
                                     0-7434-7180-6 ★ $6.99 PB

Two novels. On the jungle world of Janus, one man seeks to find his alien heritage and joins a battle against aliens despoiling his world.

Darkness & Dawn   0-7434-3595-8 ★ $15.00 Trade PB
                                     0-7434-8831-8 ★ $7.99 PB

Two novels: *Daybreak: 2250* and *No Night Without Stars*.

Gods & Androids   0-7434-8817-2 ★ $24.00 HC
                                     0-7434-9911-5 ★ $6.99 PB

Two novels: *Androids at Arms* and *Wraiths of Time*.

Dark Companion   0-7434-9898-4 ★ $26.00 HC

Two complete novels of very different heroes fighting to protect the helpless in worlds wondrous, terrifying, and utterly alien.

Masks of the Outcasts   1-4165-0901-1 ★ $24.00 HC

Two novels: *Catseye* and *Night of Masks*.
